MW01097046

Sweet Hope

An Appalachian Ghost Story

Michael Easterling

VALLEY OAK PUBLICATIONS

To those who have been made to feel they do not belong

PROLOGUE

The first time I heard the band Twisted Creek was in 1965 when they brought their hard-driving style of bluegrass music to the Ash Grove, a bohemian coffee house in west LA. At the time, I hated bluegrass. No, that's not exactly true. I hated the banjo. Still do. Playing the banjo should be a felony, same as child molestation. As for banjos, drop them from airplanes—thirty thousand feet should about do it. In fact, that's my plan for winning the war in Vietnam: forget the bombs, drop banjos on the Viet Cong. Better yet, wire the jungle for sound and play "Foggy Mountain Breakdown" twenty-four hours a day. In no time, the bush would empty of V.C with each soldier begging to exchange his AK-47 for ear protectors.

But back to Twisted Creek. On stage, they looked like escapees from a '50s rockabilly band: red blazers, skinny ties, enough grease on their hair to open a chain of lube shops. The guitar player was shorter than the other band members and tried to make up for it with a whipped-up pompadour. Despite dark complexion, heavy eye brows, and a determination not to smile, he looked all of sixteen years of age, though I found out later he was actually twenty-two.

Sitting up next to the stage, I had to cover my mouth to hide my smirk. You see, I was feeling pretty smug about my own guitar playing, having several folksy pick patterns under my nimble fingers along with a recognizable rendition of "Freight Train." What could baby face possibly show me that I didn't know already? Then baby face lifted his big Martin D-45 up to the mic and lit into "Black Mountain Rag." That was the first time I heard Adam Manly Singer, and I knew right then I knew piddly about playing the guitar.

Adam Manly Singer. I thank God for him, despite my continued confusion regarding His existence, not that I'm one of those smug scientists who pooh-poohs God as being the opiate of self-deluded ignoramuses. In fact, I'm the daughter of a man whose belief in God bordered on zealotry. Yet despite years of regular, albeit reluctant, church attendance, there was never an instance when the word of God spoke to me, not that I wasn't listening; it just seemed that, in terms of communication, the line between God and me was down. The closest I've ever come to hearing His voice was in the guitar playing of Adam Manly Singer. Many a time Adam's music has brought me back from free-falling despair to a piece of solid ground.

I used to think J.C. had me pegged: *He that is of God heareth God's words: ye therefore hear them not, because ye are not of God.* Then I learned that communication is as much about seeing as hearing, which perhaps explains my father's faith, for his vision was acute, as evidenced by his ability as an avid bird watcher to see details on birds even without the aid of binoculars. Me, I've always been a bit nearsighted. It took a ghost landing on my head to open my eyes.

The Teacher of Hoagland Holler School

She was ol' Bickum's daughter and her name it was Roseanne,
And such was her beauty, men fought for her hand;
They promised gold and silver, they promised fancy jewels,
But her heart belonged to the teacher of Hoagland Holler school.

But greedy ol' Bickum, he had other plans
To marry off his daughter to increase his lands;
"I'll give you two thousand acres," the gray-haired banker said,
"Come the day your lovely daughter and I are to be wed."

Roseanne and the teacher they planned their wedding day.
They'd have but each other or else run away;
But her hardhearted father got wind of their game,
And with his sons beside him, an ambush he laid.

> *Oh, don't you know when the icy north wind moans,*
> *There's a ghostly horse and rider out upon the road;*
> *Oh, can't you hear, hoof beats loud and clear,*
> *She's come to warn the teacher, the one she loved so dear.*

High above the barren tree tops, Roseanne she saw the flames,
She knew 'twas the schoolhouse her lover had made;
With a man's coat about her to keep away the chill,
She set out upon a pony o'er the frozen hills.

As she entered the clearing, the rifles did sound,
A bullet struck her body, it threw her to the ground;
When her kinfolk gathered 'round, and o'er the body stood,
'Twas Roseanne's pale face that met them with these dying words.

"Oh, you've killed me, my kinsmen, and you've killed my love so true,
And now with my last breath this curse I give to you;
You'll nar see your own son, a handsome boy so fine,
For no male who's a Bickum will e'er live past his time!"

Oh, don't you know when the icy north wind moans,
There's a ghostly horse and rider out upon the road;
Oh, can't you hear, hoof beats loud and clear,
She's come to warn the teacher, the one she loved so dear.

Words and music by Adam Manly Singer and Junie Bickum Gorn

Part One

Santa Barbara, 1970

CHAPTER 1

I'd only thought to rest my eyes, but fell asleep, head on desk, and dreamed. It was a dream I'd had so often, I was thinking of giving it a name. Unfortunately, *The Bride of Frankenstein* was already taken. In this dream, I'm strapped to a gurney while above me a strobe flashes a light so intense it burns into my brain even with eyes closed. Little wonder I woke up feeling what a nice person might have called "cranky." I'd have said "venomous." To make matters worse, the floor began to shake.

"Damn! Damn! Damn!" I muttered "Not again!" I stumbled over to my office door to make sure it was locked, then leaned against a stack of boxes as the first wave of student protesters passed down the hallway outside.

"Stop the war! Stop the war!" they shouted, somewhat in unison. Door and windows rattled in response to stomping feet. Polly, my buffalo head mounted on the wall, shook with delirium tremens. I was tempted to open the door and gawk, but was afraid one of my students might try pulling me into the revolution. It wasn't that I was unsympathetic to the cause, it's just I'm just not the demonstrative type. I once told my old shrink, that Teutonic fart, Dr. Herschbach, that I was possessed of a borderline personality. It was my way of sticking it to him for his obsessive labeling of my every mental twitch. Understand, I wasn't suggesting that I start filleting my fore shanks every time I get a little down in the mouth. By borderline personality, I mean I prefer to ride the fence, safe from the pressures of human intimacy on one side and the vacuum of monk-like seclusion on the other. Okay, so no one's going to vote me Miss Congeniality, but what the hell.

The chanting of "Stop the war!" somehow transmogrified into "Peace! Peace! Peace!"

"I'll take two with a side order of good will," I muttered. I knew the futility of trying to work during one of these demonstrations. To pass the time, I mentally reviewed the bones of the orbit of the eye. By the time I got to "zygomatic," the students had taken the revolution somewhere else. I returned to my desk and opened a box of shell fishhooks and picked up one labeled "P" for Putiidhem, the largest village of the Acjachemen, an Indian tribe located in present day Orange County. On a large California map, I placed a mark at that location then dug out another fishhook. It was damned dull work, but necessary for my dissertation. To counter the tedium, I slipped a tape into my cassette player, a recording I'd made at a party given by the members of the bluegrass band Twisted Creek. The first cut was "Buffalo Gals," and urged on by the partygoers, who were mostly drunk, the band played it faster and faster.

There was a knock at my door. I find interruptions about as welcome as the clap– not that I know. I threw down my pen, stomped over to the door and yanked it open. Standing there was Elaine, one of our more promising anthropology students who also worked part-time as a department secretary.

"I'm sorry, Professor Euphrates," she said. "I know you don't like to be disturbed, but Dr. Webb said it was important I give you this."

I took the proffered pages back to my desk, Elaine following. As the only other chair was piled high with books, she was forced to stand as I looked over what Webb sent, an outline for fall quarter's senior seminar.

"I like your music," Elaine said.

I looked up. "You like bluegrass?"

"Some. Mostly I listen to rock."

"Well, listen to this." I turned up the volume on the cassette player. "The incredible guitar player your hearing is Adam Manly Singer. Every time I try to play along, my right hand goes spastic."

"You play guitar?"

"I pick a bit," I said. "Now, listen to this coming up." Adam finished his break with a series of rapid-fire triplets, each note as crisp as a potato chip.

I turned off the cassette player and picked up the beat-up Yamaha I kept for times when I needed a break from working on my dissertation. "To play those triplets, you've got to do a hammer-on followed by a pull-off." I illustrated: *ba-ba-da, ba-ba-da, ba-ba-da, ba-ba-da, bum!*

"Far out!" Elaine squealed.

"Yeah, well." I set down the guitar. "I'm still working on getting it up to speed."

Elaine nodded, pushed her blond hair back behind one ear, then switched her weight from one long leg to the other. She was annoyingly pretty. I wanted her to leave. I hoped she'd stay.

"Are you planning to take the senior seminar?" I said.

"I'd like to, but I've got a pretty heavy load next quarter."

"Well, I hope you can squeeze it in. You'd be a good addition to our class."

She curled a strand of hair around a finger. "Professor, there's something I've been wanting to ask you. Some of us girls are going horseback riding out at Devereux beach on Friday. Would you like to come?"

I closed my eyes and mentally recalled part of a Bible verse: *but will with the temptation also make a way to escape, that ye may be able to bear it.*

I opened my eyes and pointed to my box of shell fishhooks. "I'm afraid work on my dissertation comes first."

Elaine nodded. "Well, maybe some other time."

I followed Elaine's tan legs out the door, making sure she closed it, then spun back around to my desk and turned the cassette player back on. As the applause of the party-goers faded, Adam launched into a guitar introduction to "The West Virginia Waltz." I'd just got back into the rhythm of sorting out shell fishhooks when there was another knock at my door.

"Damn! Damn! Damn! And Damn!"

I cranked up the volume on the cassette player, hoping the intruder would take the hint and go away–maybe fall down the stairwell while he was at it. But I'd failed to lock the door after Elaine left. The sound of the door knob turning was followed by tentative footsteps on the linoleum.

"If you're not Adam Manly Singer," I yelled above the music, "Then I suggest you get the hell out of here!"

On the tape, Adam sang in his slightly nasal tenor.

And that night beside the stream, how it felt just like a dream,
As the band played the Old West Virginia Waltz.

My head shot up. When the hell did my cheap casette player start playing in stereo? I dropped my pen and spun around in my chair. Standing there, looking like a shorter version of Elvis Presley, was Adam Manly Singer.

CHAPTER 2

I nearly tackled Adam in my rush to hug him. I guess it was the rare instance when I considered fence straying permissible.

"Adam!" I exclaimed, stepping back. "My God, I can't believe it's you."

When Adam grinned, he looked even younger, like a boy telling a joke but already starting to laugh at the punch line. "Best believe it, Miss Parry."

A student stood in the doorway, ogling us. I went around Adam and slammed the door, then motioned for Adam to sit at my desk. After making two piles of books on the floor, I sat in the other chair.

"Just look at you," I said. "You finally made it to the '60s." Gone was the grease. Loose hair covered his ears and shirt collar. He also sported sideburns and a wispy Fu Manchu. "You're only a year too late."

Adam used both hands to brush back his hair. "You know, it still sorrows me that I had to give up my old hairstyle, but it was just getting too hard to find a reliable source of Bardol."

"I don't suppose you ever tried an auto store?"

"Now why didn't I think of that? Back in West Virginia, you want Bardol, you just go to the barber's. But now you got me educated, I may go back to my old ways."

"Don't you dare. Jesus, Adam, how long has it been?"

"Pert near two years, I reckon. Ever since I left Twisted Creek."

"To play rock 'n' roll, you traitor."

Adam hung his head. "I know it, Miss Parry, but much as I do love bluegrass, I sure can't eat it."

It was the old dilemma. Like many art forms, bluegrass is an acquired taste. The problem with acquired tastes is that too few are willing to acquire them. Consequently, there's never been enough bluegrass fans to properly support the musicians.

Adam pointed to the cassette player. "What're we listening to?"

"That's the tape I made of you guys playing at Bobby Ray's apartment." We both listened as Bobby Ray Black, the fiddler in Twisted Creek, bowed a soulful rendition of "Faded Love."

"Bobby Ray always played better drunk than sober," Adam said. He motioned for me to turn the cassette off. When I turned back around, Adam was holding out the Yamaha. "Pick a bit, Miss Parry."

"All right, but I'm not exactly warmed up." I strummed the guitar with a flat pick, checking that it was in tune, then played "Sally Goodin." I didn't play it very fast, but I didn't make many mistakes either.

"Shucks," Adam said. " 'fore long, I'll be taking lessons from you. I like that little hammer-on you throwed in the B part."

"You ought to. You taught it to me."

Adam held his hands out for the guitar. I handed it to him along with the pick. Then with flawless ease, he picked the familiar introduction to "The Teacher of Hoagland Holler School," which was recorded on *Bluegrass with a Twist*, the one and only LP cut by Twisted Creek.

I'd never cared much for the old murder ballads such as "The Banks of the Ohio" or "Little Sadie," but "The Teacher of Hoagland Holler School" is different. For one thing, Adam, with help from his friend Junie Gorn, wrote the song based on an actual incident. For another, the song has the special Adam Manly Singer romantic touch. By "romantic," I don't mean Mantovani romantic, but romantic like *Arabian Nights,* only instead of sandalwood, ivory, scimitars, and veiled maidens, I picture patchwork quilts, a gut-bucket bass, corn pone baking in a Dutch oven, and a whiskered hillbilly with a demijohn slung over his shoulder. When I listen to Adam, I see myself up some lonesome holler; or "in the pines, in the pines, where the sun never shines"; or better yet, at a hoe-down and spinning across the barn floor, my head back, laughing, dizzy with the promise of love, and nary a pesky cloud to darken my delusion. Now, if that ain't romantic, I'm Henry Kissinger.

I joined in, singing the final chorus.

> *Oh, don't you know when the icy north wind moans,*
> *There's a ghostly horse and rider out upon the road;*
> *Oh, can't you hear, hoof beats loud and clear,*
> *She's come to warn the teacher, the one she loved so dear.*

When Adam finished, he leaned the guitar against the desk.

"That chorus still gives me goose bumps every time I hear it," I said. "But the line, 'For no male who's a Bickum will e'er live past his time!' always had me confused. I mean, none of us is going to live past his time."

Adam smiled. "That's just an old hillbilly expression. When somebody says, 'it's my time, now,' it means that it's his time to do what he was put on this earth to do. But I guess we shoulda wrote something like, 'will die in his prime.'"

"No, not necessarily. Your way is more poetic. But did the curse really work? The song doesn't say."

"That's 'cause our record producer thought the song too long already, so we never got to record the last verse." Adam picked up the guitar again.

> *On a hill above the river, in a grave there lies Roseanne,*
> *Been a year since her sweet voice was heard in this land;*
> *Her spirit is restless, her soul not satisfied.*
> *Though the bodies of her kinfolk are buried by her side.*

"Hell," I said, "your producer was nuts to leave that out. It ties everything together."

"Yeah, but you gotta understand record producers, Miss Parry. Artistic considerations take a back seat to what'll sell."

"So how did Roseanne's father and brothers die?"

"Well, shortly after Roseanne was killed, ol' Bickum up and had himself a heart attack. It's not certain what 'come of the brothers. Most folks me and my friend Junie talked to when we were researching this song said they were killed in a mining accident."

"What did the coroner's report say?"

"Coroner's report?"

"Come on, Adam, this happened... when?"

"Well, Roseanne was killed in 1907, so I reckon the brothers must have died shortly thereafter."

"Then there must have been a coroner's report–on the mining accident and the two murders. We're talking the twentieth century here, not the dark ages."

Adam shook his head. "Believe me, Miss Parry, Pamunkey County in 1907 was the dark ages. Heck, I can show you places right now where folks live like they've done for hundreds of years. No electricity. No plumbing. Only difference is maybe now they got some ol' beat-up tractor 'stead of a horse and plow. But they still raise all their own food, make moonshine, go to school as little as they can get away with, and play the same music as was brung over from the old country."

"But Roseanne and the teacher were murdered. Someone would have wanted the perpetrators brought to justice."

"Sure, iff'n that somebody had a personal stake in it. But by all accounts, the teacher was a stranger, and even today strangers are looked on with suspicion. As for Roseanne, the newspaper we come across reported her death as an accident, and who was to say different? No one but the Bickums saw Roseanne get shot. Of course, folks must've had their suspicions, but they'd have to have mor'n suspicions to go after the Bickums, especially knowing they'd be facing at least three loaded rifles."

"I don't suppose there's anyone alive who remembers the incident."

"Well, my granny, Estelline Singer, does, but she won't talk about it."

"Why not?"

"I reckon she still finds it a mite painful to speak of. You see, she and Roseanne were friends."

I sat bolt upright. "Your granny knew Roseanne? Adam, you've got to get her to talk; she's a primary source of information."

Adam shook his head. "You don't know Granny. Torture can't make her do what she don't want."

I sat back. "You know, I've always had this fantasy about Roseanne being this pretty little mountain wildflower, but the image doesn't really fit. Here's a woman who races to save her lover, gets shot off her horse, and still has the strength to damn her murderers. She must have been one helluva woman. I'd give my eyeteeth to know what she really looked like."

Adam questioned me with raised eyebrows.

"What?" I said.

"Miss Parry, you've already done seen her. Twisted Creek used a picture of Roseanne and the teacher on the cover of our record album."

I shot out of my chair. "Get up and help me with Polly, my buffalo head."

Looking a bit mystified, Adam nevertheless obeyed.

"Lift him by his chin, only not too far, or he'll come down on our heads."

As Adam tilted Polly's head, I reached over a pile of boxes, attempting to get into the recess behind Polly's neck.

"Miss Parry, this buff'lar's only got one eye."

"I know," I said, straining to get over the boxes. "I rescued him from a junk shop in Pomona. The owner had a string of Christmas tree lights strung around his head with one flashing red bulb stuck in his empty eye socket. I mean, it was bad enough that someone shot this noble creature, whacked his head off and stuffed it, but then the junk dealer had to add to the sacrilege by turning him into Rudolph the Red-

Eyed Buffalo." I shoved a few boxes out of my way. "Lift a little higher, Adam." From the recess, I slid out a copy of *Bluegrass with a Twist.*

Adam laughed. "I always knew you were a mite peculiar, but keeping a record album inside a buff'lar head?"

"Oh, shut up! You know as well as I do these records are irreplaceable. How many were pressed? Only a thousand! And who knows where those copies are now? I own three. One, as you see, I keep inside Polly just in case the one in my apartment is stolen or destroyed in a fire."

"And where 'bouts is your third copy?"

"You'd have to torture me to find out. And I carry cyanide tablets just for that eventuality."

"I sure wish everyone felt like you 'bout bluegrass, Miss Parry. Then I wouldn't be having to play electric guitar for a living."

We both sat down. I held the album cover by its edges so as not to smudge it with fingerprints. The photograph on the front was of a man and a woman standing in front of an old barn. The man stared into the camera lens, while the woman gazed lovingly at the man.

"When was this photo taken?" I said.

"I reckon sometime just before Roseanne was killed."

"In most of those old photos, the people look like they've just come from their own funerals." The teacher had his black hair slicked back with hair oil. His sloping shoulders dropped off to knuckle-walker arms, too long for his white, long sleeve shirt. In baggy pants, he looked the typical country hick, save for his having an intelligent-looking face.

But it was the face of Roseanne that never failed to mesmerize me. Forget the fact that she was the most gorgeous creature that ever evolved, or that her hair was the reason the gene for touch had been selected, or that her smile made me feel I'd never known happiness. It was her look of devotion that most captivated me.

"What's you cogitating on, Miss Parry?"

I pointed to the man on the album cover. "Look at the teacher.

He's not that handsome, not in the same league as Roseanne. But tell that to her. Look at her face, Adam. Have you ever seen such loving devotion? God, I hope someday, someone will look at me that way."

"You mean like this?" Adam stared at me cross-eyed, his lips sucked in so he looked toothless. I kicked at him, but missed.

The back of the album cover was a photo of the members of Twisted Creek, each holding his musical instrument. Rather than their names being printed out, each member was identified by his signature. The only printed words were the song titles and the name of the producer.

"You sure didn't include much information. No wonder I didn't know who the couple on the cover were. Instead of *Bluegrass with a Twist,* the album should have been called *The Teacher of Hoagland Holler School,* after the song."

Adam nodded. "But the producer wanted something catchier, and he was the one forking out the money." Adam reached out for the album.

"Hold it by the edges."

Adam studied the album cover, squinting a little. Despite his new facial hair, Adam still looked like a kid. Except for tiny crow's feet around his eyes, his skin was as smooth as a cover girl's.

"Adam, why are you here?"

The question seemed to take him by surprise. He set the album on his lap and sat up tall. "Miss Parry, I've come to ask after your services as a professional archaeologist."

"Whatever for?"

"I want you to help me excavate a grave."

"Really? Whose?"

Adam held up *Bluegrass with a Twist* and pointed to the teacher on the cover.

CHAPTER 3

What I liked about Twisted Creek, back when they were still playing together, was that they not only played great bluegrass, but they put on a good show, Bobby Ray Black being a gifted comedian. The running gag was for Bobby Ray to say something so funny, he'd finally get the somber, "vertically handicapped" guitar player to laugh.

Of course, Adam has that boyish grin of his, but on stage–and I can attest to this, having seen Twisted Creek in concert over fifty times–not once did Bobby Ray get Adam to so much as crack a smile.

He wasn't smiling now.

"Jesus, you're serious."

He nodded.

"But why?"

"So's to know what 'came of the teacher," he said.

"But you know what happened. The Bickums shot and killed him."

"How do you know that?"

"Because that's why Roseanne put the curse on her father and brothers, for murdering her true love."

"But where 'bouts in the song does it say she actually saw him murdered?"

I mentally ran through the lyrics. " 'The rifles did sound.' "

"That's right. But how did Roseanne know iff'n any of them shots hit the teacher? You see, Miss Parry, most folks we talked to back in Pamunkey County reckoned like you, that the Bickums killed the teacher, but there was a few old-timers who swore that the teacher got away and lit out for parts unknown."

"So, what difference does it make?"

Adam set *Bluegrass with a Twist* on my desk. "Look, Miss Parry. I grew up in Pamunkey County where stories about feuds, murders, and ghosts were like mountain music–just part of the air. But I never heard a story that affected me the way the legend of Roseanne and the teacher done. I can't explain it, but something 'bout that story just seemed to burrow right inside me. So, I figured if I ever got the chance to know the truth of it, I'd grab it."

"And you think digging up the teacher's grave will reveal the truth?"

Adam leaned forward. "Iff'n I could resurrect his body and get someone like yourself who knows all about dead people to look him over and tell me whether he was murdered or not, then a great mystery would be solved, and maybe the teacher might rest more peaceable, knowing that someone cared enough to find out really what happened to him." Adam sat back. "But if he wasn't murdered, then that's good to know, too, and my friend Junie would sleep a mite easier."

"Look, Adam, I can tell you feel strongly about this. But you can't just go into a graveyard and start digging. You have to have a reason, a legal reason. Also, you have to get permission from the deceased's relatives."

Adam held up an index finger. "One, the teacher isn't buried in a graveyard, but on property I now own. Two, I got me a legal reason. I want to prove that the teacher was murdered, just like Roseanne. Three, the teacher had no kin. Now, I may not be college educated like you, Miss Parry, but I got sense enough not to go digging up a grave without permission. I asked 'round and discovered the teacher's name was Canara Rivers. Now, there aren't a lot folks name of Rivers in Pamunkey County, but the few there are, I've talked to, and nary a one cares whether I dig this grave up or not, 'cause none of them ever had any kinfolk name of Canara."

"Oh, Adam, I wasn't meaning to insult you. I just didn't know how much you've looked into this."

"Trust me, Miss Parry, I've given this a-heap o' thought. And that's why I know I can't do all this by my lonesomes. I've got to have somebody who knows what to look for in a dead body." Adam pulled on his mustache. "And hopefully that same somebody can also play guitar and wouldn't mind spending her evenings sitting around a campfire, picking mountain music and sipping moonshine. And maybe she could even tolerate looking up at the stars and seeing how they were meant to be, without all them city lights competing with them. So, I guess the question is, do you know where I might find such a person?"

Did I really want to go off on an adventure instead of staying here, barricaded behind my door as I sorted shell fishhooks? Did Neil Armstrong really want to walk on the moon?

"Before I agree to anything, there's something you need to know. I'm probably not the best person for the job. I'm your run-of-the-mill archaeologist. What you need is a forensic anthropologist, and I'm sure you could find one who lives a lot closer to Pamunkey County than I do."

"What's the difference between all these 'ologists?'"

"A forensic anthropologist is someone who examines remains with an eye toward possible foul play. In my work, I'm more concerned with artifacts than human remains."

"But didn't you go somewhere one summer to help dig up some old graves?"

"Yes, and thank you so much for reminding me. I went to Israel, only I got such an intractable case of enteritis, they had to send me home."

"Enteritis?"

"Diarrhea, dammit! I think it was the potato salad I ate in Tel Aviv."

Adam grinned. "So I take it you had a pretty shitty time."

This time my kick connected.

Adam scooted his chair back. "But you've taken classes in this forensic anthropology, right?"

"I took one."

Adam was clearly disappointed. "So, what is it you do, Miss Parry?"

"Most of my research involves middens which are basically the trash dumps of native Americans. The most famous one in California is up north at Drake's Bay because Sir Francis Drake actually observed and wrote about the Miwoks who inhabited that area. But there are middens all up and down the coast, anywhere a tribe inhabited an area for any length of time. Here, look at this."

"It looks like a fat fishhook," he said.

"That's exactly what it is. It was carved from a mollusk shell. Now look at my map. You can see that these shell hooks were used extensively by natives living all along the coast from Baja California to Santa Barbara. But that's not the case north of Santa Barbara where other types of fishing implements were preferred. I'm trying to figure out why. Why this shift away from the use of shell fishhooks by tribes of the central coast?"

Adam looked at the fishhook, then at the map, then back to the fishhook. "So you're a professor of fishhooks?"

"Don't you make fun of my work, Adam Manly Singer. It may not be glamorous, like playing in a rock 'n' roll band, but it's important. Sure, I'm studying just one small piece of a great puzzle, but if you get a thousand people, each studying a puzzle piece, then eventually the pieces get put together, and the picture becomes clear. And I've done more than just study fishhooks. You'd be interested to know that I've dug up bones, mostly animal bones, but some human, and by studying those bones, I've been able to add to our knowledge concerning diseases common to native populations."

"So you *have* worked with dead people."

"Yes, some."

"If we dug up the teacher, you think you could tell iff'n he'd been murdered or not?"

"I know I can do a first-rate job on the excavation. And if the teacher was shot or died in a fire, then I could probably verify the cause of death, providing I have enough material to work with."

"What you mean, 'nough material?"

"Adam, all this happened sixty-three years ago. With the amount of rain the east receives, it's likely the remains of the teacher have already decomposed."

"You mean, I've got my hopes up for nothing?"

"Not necessarily. I'll have a better idea once I've examined the site and looked at the soil composition and the drainage patterns."

"Am I hearing you right? You're thinking of accepting my offer?"

I smiled. "Well, if you can be satisfied with a lowly fishhook professor. But I'll take the job only on the condition that I do the work for free."

Adam shook his head. "Now, Miss Parry, I didn't come here hat in hand. I've got money to pay you proper. You'd be surprised how much these rock 'n' roll fans will pay to have their ears blasted."

"Adam, I'm a novice in the field of forensic anthropology. Think of this as just a good training exercise for me."

But Adam wouldn't hear of me working for free, so we haggled until it was agreed that Adam would pay my travel expenses and provide me with room and board while I worked. Also, I would get five guitar lessons.

"But I won't be able to start until the current quarter ends," I said, "which is another two weeks."

"That's fine, Miss Parry. I reckon Canara Rivers has waited this long, two more weeks won't make much difference."

"One more question. Your friend Junie, why will she sleep better knowing what happened to the teacher?"

Adam shook his head. "Junie's not a she. Junie's short for Junius. If we find out that Canara Rivers weren't murdered, that just might take the power off Roseanne's curse."

"Why's that so important?"

Adam leaned forward. " 'Cause Junie's the last living male in the Bickum line."

CHAPTER 4

After Adam left, I went and caught the downtown bus for home. Excited about the prospects of digging up hillbillies, I felt as happy as the time Arnie Kostorsky, my avowed enemy in third grade, tripped and knocked out two of his front teeth on a sprinkler head. I didn't even mind the bus missing my stop.

Of course, in my experience, feelings of happiness have the same half-life as Polonium-216–about 0.14 seconds. No surprise then that my joy was short lived, for when I mounted the stairs of the frumpy Victorian I shared with my landlady, Mrs. Esau, I chanced to look through the screen door into her apartment. Mrs. E was curled up on her couch, clutching her sides. I didn't bother to knock.

"It's just one of my spells," she said, struggling to sit up. "I'm all right."

"Yeah, and I'm Tricia Nixon." I'd seen Mrs. E's spells before, little pains that sometimes left her a bit breathless. But now her face and arms were all blotchy. I placed my hand on her forehead. It was hot. "I'm taking you to the doctor's."

"Oh, pooh! My father used to get this same thing, and doctors never did *him* any good."

I used the voice I reserved for students in my physical anthropology lab who liked to drum on the table tops using tibias. "I said, I'm taking you to the doctor's!"

As I didn't own a car, we used Mrs. E's old Impala station wagon with a steering wheel the size of a clipper ship's. It took all my concentration to keep from scraping barnacles off on parked cars. As it was late, I took her to the emergency room at Cottage Hospital. We had to wait over an hour before a tired-looking doctor could see her. He gave Mrs. E a physical examination, took some blood samples, ran a battery of tests, and eventually came back scratching his head. I drove Mrs. E home and put her to bed with a glass of orange juice and two of the pills the doctor gave her.

"I told you doctors are know-nothings," she said.

For the next two weeks, I was as busy as a bumble bee on Benzedrine. I tried to work at home as much as possible so I could look after Mrs. E. I brought her meals to her bedside, which she picked at except for the desserts. She was more worried about her flowers than her health.

"If I don't fertilize the roses soon, they won't put out a good second bloom."

I'm not a plant person; I can't tell dahlias from Venus flytraps. But following her very specific instructions, I fertilized and watered the roses. I also scratched around in her vegetable patch, hoping I was chopping down weeds and not vegetables.

Dr. Webb, my academic advisor, not only gave consent for me to take time off from writing my dissertation, but was very excited about my first paying job as a field archaeologist. Of course, I didn't mention the form remuneration was to take. He insisted I write up a description of my proposed dig for the alumni newsletter. I included the lyrics from "The Teacher of Hoagland Holler School," and put in a plug for *Bluegrass with a Twist*, not that anyone would likely find a copy.

When I wasn't caring for Mrs. E or teaching my classes, I looked over my undergraduate forensic anthropology text and other meaty tomes dug out of the university library. And at night when I couldn't sleep, which was most nights, I read novels by John Fox Jr. written around the time Roseanne Bickum was murdered. His melodramatic accounts of Appalachian life fueled my imagination. I drifted off, dreaming of hillbillies banging away at each other with Kentucky rifles, of hoe downs that invariably turned into drunken brawls, and of flinty women who watched their men folk die then snatched up their fallen rifles. Needless to say, I had difficulty making time to paint my toenails.

I put off packing until last, since it's something I enjoy about as much as making small talk, or large talk for that matter. Mrs. E, who was nearly back to being her old self, kept me company. She knew better than to say anything as I deliberated over what all to take. She did, however, risk making one suggestion.

"If you're going to be living among hillbillies, Paradigm, you should take along something for protection."

Mrs. E is the only person other than my late father that I let get away with using my entire first name. Everyone else calls me Parry, if he values the current shape of his nose.

"What would you suggest?" I said. "An M-16? Maybe a case of napalm?"

"Mind your sarcasm, Paradigm. You should take along one of my skillets."

It wasn't the first time Mrs. E had offered me the use of her cookware for protection. She actually wanted me to have a skillet out at school. "Just in case you have to wallop one of those commie agitators." Not hard to figure which side of the war debate Mrs. E was on.

"Mrs. E, the feud between the Hatfields and McCoys is over. Besides, I think the airline might frown upon luggage weighed down with cast iron. I'm actually more worried about which guitar to take." I'd heard horror stories of baggage handlers slinging luggage around and of thieves haunting the baggage claim areas. I eventually decided to risk taking my 1950 Martin D-18 because it played like a dream, and I couldn't imagine sitting around a campfire, trying to compete with Adam's booming D-45 with a bunged-up Yamaha.

I finished packing and saw Mrs. E to bed, then stepped out onto the back porch. It was past midnight, and all was quiet save for the distant rumble of the freeway. A few wisps of fog were drifting in off the ocean, but not enough to block out the stars.

As I stood, leaning on the rail, a great horned owl hooted from the nearby park. I closed my eyes and listened for another owl to respond. It seems I can't hear the call of a bird without thinking of my father who, as a boy, longed to be an ornithologist. Sadly, a little thing called the Great Depression got between him and his dream, and he ended up as an electrician. Still, he remained an avid bird watcher all his life, one that members of the local Audubon Society always called upon when they needed an expert's opinion. Though I never came near to matching my father's skills as a birder, the times I shared with him out in the field were some of my best memories.

Despite repeated overtures, the owl was getting no response. For some reason this made me sad, and that's when Mr. D started in with a few warm-up drum rolls. For me, depression is personified by Mr. Potato Head, the toy you get with little plastic facial features you stick in a potato. Only instead of Mr. Potato Head, I call him Mr. D, short for Depression. Snake-eyed, bald as Humpty Dumpty, with eyebrows like Groucho Marx and a frown turned down like Yosemite Sam's mustache, Mr. D resides within my cranium. His amusements are suppressing happy thoughts, crippling self-esteem, and troubling sleep. On good days, he's content to beat tattoos on my occipital bones. On bad days, he uses my frontal lobe like a trampoline, jumping up and down and screaming, "You're shit! You're shit! You're shit!" Over the years, I've learned that writing a letter to my pen pal Teddy often heads off the worst of Mr. D's antics.

I hurried back inside and from my desk drew out a sheet of writing paper.

June 24, 1970

Dear Teddy,

Tomorrow I leave for Hoagland Holler, West Virginia. Mrs. E is almost her old plant-crazed self again, though I think her recovery has little to do with her doctor's ministrations. While straightening her blankets, I discovered the pills he'd prescribed for her (dutifully placed by yours truly on her tray at mealtimes) scattered under her bed.

Speaking of Mrs. E's doctor, I had a dream

about him. It occurred yesterday when I was waiting for Mrs. E at his office. The waiting room was stuffy, and I'd not been getting much sleep. I nodded off, leaning against the magazine rack.

You already know my take on dreams, that they're nothing but the result of synaptic discharges of a brain winding down after a long day's work; their emotional content the product of stimulated neurons within the hypothalamus. Still, I thought this one would give you a giggle.

In the dream, I was in hospital garb, kneeling on the examination room linoleum, looking up at the tired doctor who was back lit by sunlight pouring through a window. I had assumed one of those suffering saint poses seen in old religious art: The Abject Supplicant as painted by Correggio. (With gown open all along the back!)

"Please! Please!" I pleaded. I knew I was asking him to save Mrs. E.

But dreams are playful; things get bounced around. The doctor was now staring out of the dining room window of the house I grew up in. I sensed that I had failed him, only, for the life of me, I couldn't figure out how. I just felt a dreadful heaviness, as if I'd committed a sin for which there was no atonement.

The doctor looked at me with weary eyes. "I'm sorry. I can't cure you. I don't know how."

Then he gave me a bottle of pills.

Part Two

Hoagland Holler

CHAPTER 5

All I saw of our nation's capital was the glow of city lights just before the red-eye special touched down at Dulles. Adam met me at the gate and led me to the baggage claim where my suitcase was already out on the carousel. Adam, ever the gentleman, insisted on carrying both my suitcase and guitar, and I was too tired to make more than a perfunctory claim to being liberated.

"You look a mite peaked, Miss Parry. Maybe I should check you into a motel so's you can get a little shut-eye. I'm afraid it's gonna take us mor'n six hours to get to Hoagland Holler."

"But I thought it was only about one hundred and seventy miles."

"It's not the distance, it's the roads."

"Then how about we look for a place that serves strong coffee?"

We found an all-night diner and Adam and I shared one side of a booth, while my Martin, because I was afraid to leave it unattended in Adam's truck, occupied the other side.

"Any problem with your guitar on the plane?" Adam said.

"No, the pilot was very understanding. He let me stow it with the first-class, carry-on luggage."

"Well, there's not many thieves to worry 'bout in Hoagland Holler, 'ceptin' raccoons, and they're not very musically inclined. Most folks don't even have locks on their doors. I hope that won't bother you none, 'cause the lock on your trailer is busted."

"Trailer?"

"I'm putting you up in a trailer on my property." Adam exhibited dirt-stained hands. "I worked all day, getting it spruced up. I think you'll find it right homey. The roof don't leak, and Granny Estey gave me some blankets, so you'll stay warm."

"I take it there's no heat."

"Not less'n you set fire to your mattress. No plumbing neither 'cept that I connected a hose up to the sink. 'Fraid you'll have to use the outhouse. I apologize, Miss Parry. I'm sorta living camp-style until I get my house built."

"You didn't tell me you were building a house."

With one finger, Adam spun his empty coffee cup. "Actually, I meant to keep that a surprise till I could show you."

"Well, if you need any help, let me know. My father was an electrician, and he taught me how to wire a house."

"No fooling?"

I nodded.

Adam grinned. "Well, I'm gonna need a lot of outlets iff'n I'm gonna be able to plug in all my electric guitars and amps."

I smiled. "In that case, forget I made the offer."

Under the influence of the caffeine, I was starting to perk up. I looked out the window. Nothing was visible beyond the range of the parking lot lights. "I don't like this night travel. Here I am in a part of the country I've never been, and I can't see any of it."

"You've never been to Virginy?"

"The farthest east I've ever been is Ohio. My father grew up in southern Ohio not far from the West Virginia border. You'd be interested to know that his father was a coal miner."

"That explains why you're so quick to learn the ol' mountain tunes. You got Allegheny coal dust in your veins."

I drained my cup of its last swallow and banged it on the table. "Let's hit the road. I'm anxious to see this Hoagland Holler I've heard tell about in song and story."

We squabbled over who should pay for the coffee. I won. Then we were back in the pickup, heading west. After many dark miles on the interstate, Adam turned off onto a secondary road which immediately began to undulate over hilly terrain.

"We're starting into the Shenandoah mountains," Adam said.

I waited until the pickup topped a rise before looking through the back window. There was a long pale streak of light in the east. Soon I could discern the outlines of passing bushes, trees, and the occasional house. Just outside of a burg called Hinton, Adam pulled off the road to jettison his used coffee. When he got back into the truck, he leaned against the steering wheel and looked out through the windshield.

"This is a nice time of day," he said. "Let's just sit a spell."

Slowly, the dawn came on. Off to the right a pond mirrored the brightening sky. To the west, the purple shadow of the earth dissolved, revealing a range of mountains. Because of their nearness, I was reminded of the Santa Ynez range that overshadows Santa Barbara. But as the light increased, I realized the Shenandoah mountains were nothing like the rocky, chaparral-covered Santa Inez Mountains. They were decadently attired in a coat of lush green. Yet it was not just the mountains that were verdant; everywhere I looked, I saw green.

"This is definitely not southern California," I said.

"We could use some of that warm California sunshine this morning," Adam said, rubbing his hands. He started the engine and cranked up the heater before pulling back onto the highway.

I glanced at the side view mirror to see a ball of orange rise above the horizon. Softly illuminated by the sun's slanting rays, the Shenandoahs appeared two-dimensional, like a giant tapestry hung from the sky.

"So many different shades of green," I said, pointing to the mountains.

"You should see them trees come fall," Adam said. "More colors than a rainbow."

We passed an open field where the grass had been mown, leaving a stubble looking dry and brittle. "Now, *that* looks like California," I said.

"Well, it's sure not normal for here. It's on account of the drought. We've had no rain for six weeks, and iff'n we don't get some soon, there's going to be forest fires for sure."

While Adam tapped the steering wheel and hummed "Fire on the Mountain," I leaned my head against the door and closed my eyes. The truck's valves pinged, especially on the upgrade, and I thought to tell Adam he needed to adjust the valve lash, only fell asleep first. I came awake when my head banged hard against the window.

"Jesus!" I yelled.

"Sorry, Miss Parry, I guess I didn't miss that pot hole."

We were off the beaten path and onto one that had been thoroughly mauled. "You know, you really ought to get seat belts."

Adam stopped the truck and turned off the engine. "Think I'll just stretch my legs a bit."

"Aren't you going to pull off the road? Someone could run into you."

"Shucks, Miss Parry, this road sees so little use, I bet could park here a week, and nobody'd give a hoot."

The door on my side was stuck. Adam came around and gave the handle a yank. Then he offered me a hand down, which I refused. We were somewhere deep in the woods. All was quiet save for the ticking of the cooling engine. "Are we in the Shenandoah mountains?"

"You were asleep quite a while. We done crossed the Shenandoahs, and now we're in the Alleghenies. Right over that ways is Spruce Knob, the highest point in West Virginy."

"Is it far to Hoagland Holler?"

"Not the way the crow flies, but the road winds a mite." Adam rested a foot atop a large rock. "Looky there," he said, pointing to a small stream. "Hardly enough water to wet your whistle." In the tree above us, a songbird trilled a melisma. Following my gaze Adam announced, "Redbird."

I nodded. "Cardinals were one of my father's favorite birds. He always lamented the fact that California is outside their range."

From the back of his truck, Adam produced a picnic basket. "I brung along some vittles, thinking you might be hungry, though it seems a mite early in the day for lunch."

"Not if your day started before midnight."

Adam handed me a sandwich wrapped in wax paper. The bread was stale, but I was too hungry to care. Perhaps as an apology for the bread, Adam urged upon me some homemade asparagus pickles. I pulled out a spear out of a jar and bit into it. It was the most delicious pickle I'd ever tasted. I loaded my sandwich with dripping spears. For dessert, Adam had bought a basket of hard and tasteless strawberries that had probably been shipped in from California.

"We should probably sit a spell and let our food settle," Adam said. "From here on, the road's a mite rough. I wouldn't want you to pitch your lunch up over the dashboard."

"I'll have you know, I've never gotten motion sickness."

"Well, in that case," he said, putting things back into the basket, "let's get a move on."

Adam calling the road "a mite rough," was like saying Death Valley in summer is "a mite warm." What with the potholes, the sharp curves, the steep ups and downs, I soon found out how it felt to be tumbled in a clothes dryer.

"Is this the only way into Hoagland Holler?" I had to shout to be heard over the geared down engine.

"Only way from the east." Adam shouted back. "Don't worry, Miss Parry, we'll be down out of this in no time."

"No time" took longer than a Mahler symphony. I was contemplating jumping ship when the obstacle course finally came to an end at an intersection with a maintained road. A bullet-riddled sign hinted that we would find a town should we go right.

"Mascus?" I said.

"Damascus," Adam corrected. "It's the county seat."

Adam turned left, and for about one hundred yards we had the pleasure of driving on asphalt. Fortunately, the road past the pavement was straight and wide, and Adam drove fast enough to take the bumps out of the wash boarding. We were now in farm country, not in keeping with how I had envisioned Appalachia. It looked too modern, too prosperous. Placid black and white cattle grazed behind freshly painted fences. Fields had been tilled with the precision only attained using modern farm equipment. Cute clapboard farmhouses and tidy board-and-batten barns looked as if they stepped out of the pages of

Ideals magazine.

"Is this Hoagland Holler?"

Adam smiled. "This here's Wellsprings. We still got us some twenty miles to go to get to Hoagland Holler."

"Well, it *is* beautiful." But I wanted something else, something primitive like I'd read about in the John Fox Jr. novels. I wanted a glimpse of a buckskin-clad hunter slinking through the woods. I wanted to see a tilting outhouse with a crescent moon cut into the door, or a moonshiner's still kicked over and abandoned.

As if to oblige me, the surrounding hills drew together, closing off the pretty valley. Grinding a gear, Adam downshifted to ascend a cut made in the side of a hill. I leaned forward and looked up. Here the trees had branches like the outstretched arms of old women. Moss hung down like baggy sleeves. Ferns, looking like lacy feather dusters, stuck out of the notches in the tree trunks. Of course, all this was anthropomorphic twaddle, and I found myself wishing I had studied more botany, or any for that matter.

The road suddenly dropped off, and I had to push against the dashboard to keep in my seat. To the left a creek plunged over alternate bands of black and white rock, periodically coming to rest in pools the color of beer complete with a foamy heads. I had the feeling that as we were descending in elevation, we were also dropping back in time, for with the exception of the road–now little more than a wagon track–the land seemed virgin wilderness.

At the bottom of the hill, Adam stopped on a wooden bridge that spanned the creek. I rolled my down window and stuck my head out. The air smelled of rank vegetation and was cooled by the rushing water. Down here, deep within the wooded canyon, the sun was banished, and the dimness was a balm to eyes irritated by the brightness of Wellsprings with its optimistic little farms.

"That there's the famous Twisted Creek," Adam said. "Don't look like much right now, but you should see it after a heavy rain. Twice, this here bridge's been washed out."

"It doesn't look very twisted."

"Not here it don't, but just wait till you see it farther on."

Beyond the bridge were renewed signs of human occupation: little shelves of land dug out and fenced off for gardens.

"That there's the McCoy place," Adams said, pointing to a house sided with what looked like roofing shingles.

"As in the Hatfields and McCoys?"

He shook his head. "No relation. *Them* McCoys is down near the Kentucky line."

We passed a deserted orchard where between the tangled branches I spied a once imposing two-story house, now almost completely shed of its paint.

"That the Muellers' place," Adam said. "As a boy, I used to make ten cents a bushel, picking apples for ol' man Mueller. Worked my tail end off all day for a couple of silver dollars."

"It's rather rundown."

"When ol' man Mueller died, there weren't nobody to run the place, his children having up and moved to Baltimore or D.C. Not much money in apples."

As Adam navigated the ruts in the road, he put more names with the ramshackle houses we passed: Cline, Waller, Floyd.

"That there is Aunt Bessy Messer's place," he said, pointing to a one-room cabin.

"She's your aunt?"

"No relation; ever'body just calls her Aunt Bessy. And that house over yonder belongs to Farmer Ealem. Farmer is his actual first name."

"So that's farmer Farmer's farm?"

"Something like that."

"Maybe he should spell his name with a *Ph*. Less confusing."

"Then everybody would think you was talking about Pharmer Tipton."

I shot Adam a look to see if he's joking.

"I kid you not, Miss Parry. P-h-a-r-m-e-r. Only Pharmer Tipton's not a farmer."

"So, what does not-a-farmer Pharmer do?"

"Oh . . . this and that. Moonshining mostly."

I scouted ahead looking for the next farmhouse. Thick bushes that even I could identify as being blackberries, lined both sides of the road. Occasionally, I spotted a split rail fence in among the canes.

"What happened to the farms?" I said.

"Just wait a spell, and I'll tell you."

A 'spell' took about twenty minutes of pelvis pounding. Except for the wagon track and the split rail fence, the land appeared untouched. Past a stream that ran beneath the road through a culvert, Adam turned onto a road even more primitive than the one we'd been on.

"Almost there, now," he said.

"Thank God!"

He stopped where the road split and pointed up the right fork. "Up that way is where my good friend Junie Gorn lives with Beatty, his ma. Beatty's grandpa was Hiram Bickum. All that rail fence we've been following, that's all their land."

"But Adam, we've been following that fence for miles."

"'Bout four or five, I reckon. The Gorns own 'round five thousand acres."

"Jesus! How can one family own so much land?"

Adam started the truck moving again. "Can't never have too much land, Miss Parry. That's the rule 'round here."

We passed through an open gate clinging to a post by one hinge.

"Now, we're on my land," Adam said.

"And how much land do you own?"

"Forty acres. How much do you think forty acres would cost in Santa Barbara?"

"Oh, about a zillion dollars."

Adam downshifted as the truck started up a steep slope. At the top, he swerved around a huge brush pile then stopped in a level clearing. A wooden picnic table sat in the shade of deciduous trees.

"We're here, Miss Parry." Adam turned the engine off and went around to yank on the passenger door. What with battered bones, jostled organs, and an overdose of asparagus pickles, I was having my first experience of motion sickness, which probably did little to improve my basically irascible nature. When Adam reached out a hand to steady me, I almost punched him. I staggered over to the picnic table, stretched out on the bench, and waited for the waves to subside. When I could bring myself to sit up, there was Adam with one foot on the bench and that boyish grin on his face.

"Well, Miss Parry. What do you think?"

"I think you have the worst roads in the world."

"Shucks, that weren't nothing. You should try driving that stretch come winter."

"I'll put that on my things-to-do list, along with do-it-yourself dentistry." I stood up. "I wouldn't mind lying down on something softer."

"Sure, Miss Parry, I'll drive you down to the trailer."

"God! We have to drive?"

"No, we can walk. I just thought, you being tired 'n' all."

Adam raced to get my luggage, and I let him. "This way," he said, carrying both suitcase and guitar. I stumbled after him and almost tripped over a scrap of wood. Looking up, I saw what I failed to notice before: the frame of a square building with a steep-pitched roof. On the near side of the ridge, a cupola had been framed in.

"Adam, you said you were building a house, not a church."

Adam set down my luggage. "Guess again, Miss Parry."

"Well, it sure looks like a church. You've even got a place to hang the bell." Then it hit me. "My God, you're rebuilding Canara Rivers' schoolhouse!"

Adam beamed. "Yep! Right atop the 'riginal foundation. Course I had to shore it up some."

For some reason, I laughed.

"Laugh all you want, but I always wanted to live in a schoolhouse, least ways, I'd rather live in one than go to school in one. There's an old schoolhouse up to Damascus that they've made up into a real nice house. I'll take you up that ways iff'n we get the time."

"So, you're going to live here?"

"A fella needs to have a place to hang his hat."

"But what about your music?"

"Well, I'm hoping iff'n this rock 'n' roll thing works out, I'll make enough money so's I won't have to be on the road all the time."

Adam picked up my luggage and walked on. Beyond the future schoolhouse, the road angled steeply down through woods so dense, branches blocked out the sun. It felt like we were entering a hole in the ground. Any second I expected to see a giant white rabbit. I sang:

> *In the pines, in the pines, where the sun never shines,*
> *And you shiver when the cold wind blows.*

Adam laughed. "Only these here is mostly oaks and maples."

"And it's too warm to shiver. Actually, I thought it was going to be a lot more humid."

"Usually is, but things is a lot drier 'count of the drought."

"How can there be a drought when everything looks so incredibly green?"

"Things may look green, but they's as dry as tinder. I don't dare fire that brush pile back yonder for fear of setting the woods afire."

We reached the bottom of the hill and picked our way over the rocky bed of a dry creek. "How the hell did you get a trailer down here?"

"I didn't."

I suddenly got one of those funny tummy feelings like I get when my gynecologist says, "This isn't going to hurt."

Adam pointed the guitar case at a tiny shed overhung with branches. "That there's the outhouse." A small piece of wood, painted green, hung on the door. Adam set down the guitar and turned the piece of wood over. It was red on the other side. "Red means 'occupied.'" He turned the wood over again. "Green means 'come on ahead.'" He picked up the guitar, and we started up an incline.

"There it is," he said when we reached the top. "The trailer I told you about. Home, sweet home."

To conceive of a more decrepit trailer would've been beyond the imagination of mere mortals. It appeared to be of the same vintage as a Conestoga wagon. Make that a Roman chariot. A thorough coating of rust eliminated the possibility of determining its original color, but hazarding a guess, I'd have said olive drab. One end of the roof had some spindly, green thing growing out of it. Due to the absence of a hinge, the door hung drunkenly with a gap on top wide enough to stick an arm through. The final selling point was the cracked front window held in place with peeling duct tape.

"It's not the Ponderosa," Adam said.

I snorted.

"But the roof don't leak none, and it's a lot nicer on the inside."

Likely, the devil used the same line at the gates of hell. Yet to my surprise, the interior, though smelling a bit like wet newspapers, appeared relatively clean with not too many cracks in the blistered wood paneling. There was a new oilcloth on the kitchen table, and when Adam opened the tap over the sink, the water ran clear.

"Stove don't work, but meals are up to the house." He opened the cupboard above the stove, revealing a grungy cast iron skillet and a couple of abused pans. "You won't need this stuff."

Across from the stove, a narrow door was open a crack. "This here's a closet," he said, opening the door wider. "I'm afraid I didn't think of hangers, but it'd be a good place to store your Martin out of the way."

I looked past him to the bed. "Adam, that quilt is gorgeous."

Adam smiled. "Granny Estey made it. There's a couple of wool blankets, too, so you'll stay warm."

Suddenly, fatigue swept over me like a cloud of blackbirds. I sat down on the bed. The mattress was firm, the way I liked it.

Adam, looking around, pulled anxiously on his mustache.

"Don't worry, Adam. This is fine. It'll be like the times I used to go camping with my father." I bounced upon the mattress. "Better even."

"Well, I thought to make you a place up near the schoolhouse till

I recollected that time I visited your apartment in LA and you had the windows curtained over like sunlight was poison. So, I figured you staying down here beneath the trees ought to suit you."

"Very thoughtful," I said, trying to keep my eyes open. "I'm sure Conrad Hilton couldn't have planned it better."

"Well, I can see you're plumb tuckered out, so, I'll leave you and come back again 'round supper time."

He pushed open the door. "By the way, Miss Parry. All this land here 'bouts was once owned by an old German feller name of Hoagland, same one the holler's named after. You wouldn't know it now 'cause it's all o'er grown, but once it was a farm, and there's a lot of junk lying 'round you can't see. I say that so's to warn you, case you go wandering. I wouldn't want you stumbling over some rusty ol' harrow."

I made a mental note not to take any flying leaps into the underbrush. Then my head hit the pillow, and I was out.

CHAPTER 6

A sound like that of a creature gnawing on wood woke me.

Oh, joy! There are rats living under my bed!

Groggy from having slept too hard, I slowly sat up then fumbled with the laces on my sneakers. I staggered out to the outhouse and turned the sign to red. Coming back, I heard the ping of Adam's truck engine. He stopped outside the trailer and rolled down the window. "Dinner time. You might want to bring along a sweater. It gets a mite cool at night."

I opened the trailer door.

"And bring your Martin!" he shouted.

I took a sweater from my suitcase then quickly ran a brush through my hair.

"Knock, knock," Adam said, sticking his head in the door. He lifted up the lid of the bench seat under the table and took out a flashlight. "We may need it." He put the flashlight in the pocket of his light jacket. He also grabbed my guitar, which I had left lying under the table.

The truck nearly stalled as we climbed up out of the rabbit hole. Adam parked near the picnic table, and I kicked open the passenger door. "You know, we didn't have to drive. It's not that far."

Adam shut his door. "Why walk when there's a mule to ride? Now, is hot dogs all right with you?"

"They're fine, so long as I don't have to read what they're made of."

He pointed to an ice chest. "Help yourself to drinks."

"Do you have any tea?"

"Reckon I might." He took a coffee pot off a grill fashioned from a metal drum and flung the grounds onto the nearby bushes. "Would you mind filling this pot from the faucet over there?"

As I filled the pot, I looked around. "Where do you sleep?"

Adam pointed with a long-handled fork he used to turn the hot dogs. "Right over there in that tool shed. But as soon as it warms up again, I'll sleep out under the stars."

The hot dogs were hot dogs, but there were asparagus pickles left over from lunch. "These are pure ambrosia," I said, stabbing another spear with my fork.

"Granny Estey made 'em. She used to win blue ribbons ever' year at the county fair."

"She could've won one for that quilt. I'd like to meet her and thank her for letting me use it."

A blue jay, sitting atop the brush pile, complained at our lack of generosity in sharing our dinner. Adam tossed the jay half a hot dog bun. "Something you should know 'bout Granny: her kindnesses are a lot nicer than the actual experience of meeting her."

"I see. And why is that?"

"Well, she's had a hard life, and that's soured her some. Talking to her, she can be a mite… what's the word? Like what you said earlier about our roads being like do-it-yourself dentistry."

"I was being sarcastic."

"That's it! Come to think of it, you and Granny might get along just fine. Hey! I want to show you this new tuning I've been working on." Adam went to the tool shed and returned with his guitar case.

"I call it 'Adam Manly minor.' It sounds like one of the old mountain modes–good for those murder ballads like 'Pretty Polly.'"

Starting with the sixth, he picked slowly across the strings. "It's D, A, D F B F. Gotta make sure you're to pitch, so's you don't bust the first string. Then all you do is fret the second string at D." He strummed a big fat minor chord then began to sing.

> *Pretty Polly, pretty Polly come go 'long with me,*
> *Polly, pretty Polly come go 'long with me,*

'fore we are married, some pleasures to see.

Adam stopped. "Why don't you play along, Miss Parry."

While I got out my guitar, Adam lit a kerosene lantern, for it was getting dark. Then he helped me with the new tuning and showed me the basic chords, which were actually quite easy to form.

"You know this tune?" Adam said.

I nodded. "I have a recording of Jim Rooney singing it."

"That's a mighty fine version, 'specially Billy Keith's banjo part."

"I'm sorry, but the words 'mighty fine' and 'banjo' are not compatible. You wouldn't say 'a mighty fine septic ulcer.'"

Adam, who didn't share my opinion of banjo players and other malefactors, let this one pass. "Reckon you could sing the lead?"

"I reckon," I mimicked, and we sang of poor, pretty Polly, done in by her somewhat-less-than-loving fiancé.

> *He opened her bosom as white as the snow,*
> *He opened her bosom as white as the snow,*
> *He stuck to her heart and her heart's blood did flow.*

I thought we sounded good together, though I knew Adam was holding back so his resonant tenor wouldn't overwhelm my breathy alto.

"Cheery little number, that one," I said when we finished. Something a lot bigger than a moth flew past the lantern.

"Looks like the bats are out," Adam said.

"That reminds me, there are rats living under my bed."

Adam shook his head. "It's a family of possums. We got introduced when I was running the hose up under the trailer. I can run them out of there if you like."

"No, not if it's just possums. They're kind of cute in an ugly sort of way. I've got a few living behind my apartment. Sometimes I see them hanging by their tails from a tree branch when I go out at night to look at the stars."

Stars! I used my hand to block the light. Adam extinguished the lantern and my eyes soon adjusted to the darkness. Framed by the trees, the stars shone like torch lights. Toward the south, the Milky Way poured out of the Teapot.

"You're right, Adam. This is the way stars are meant to be."

Adam answered with his guitar, fingerpicking sweet chords to serenade the night. A shooting star left a glowing tail, bridging the tree line. Adam immediately launched into a lively reel. I used the face of my guitar to tap out a rhythmic accompaniment. There was joy in Adam fingers, there was magic in the sky, and, wonder of wonders, my old pal Mr. D seemed to be taking the night off.

Adam slowed the tempo, changed meter, and went back to fingering chords. I rubbed my neck, stiff from looking up so long. Adam finished with a flourish of harmonics that rang like little bells. As he put his guitar back in its case, I became aware of other sounds: crickets, cicadas, the hoot of a great-horned owl answered at a distance. Adam sat down next to me.

"That was a particularly bright shooting star," I said. "What was that you were playing, 'The Shooting Star Reel?'"

Adam laughed. "I didn't see no shooting star. I was thinking 'bout you saying rats were living under the trailer. That was 'The Rat Catcher's Reel.'"

"Well, I'm going to call it 'The Star Catcher's Reel'," I said, laughing in turn.

"Or 'The Shooting Rat Reel'," Adam countered, and we laughed together.

"Miss Parry, I know it's dark, but would you like to mosey on over to Canara River's gravesite? It's not far."

"Great idea. I can walk off whatever was in those hot dogs."

As I put my guitar back in its case, Adam relit the lantern. It felt odd just leaving our guitars unattended. At home, I always worried about thieves. We walked past the frame of the schoolhouse. The area immediately around it had been cleared of large vegetation and grasses had grown in thickly. I stopped to pull a sticker out of my sock.

"I've been meaning to mow all this down," said Adam, "but I got a mite busy what with you coming 'n' all. Here, let's go this way."

He held up a sagging branch and waited for me to pass under. Downed branches snapped under my shoes; I kicked up last year's leaves.

"How did you find the grave?" I said.

"Well, like I mentioned afore, there's junk lying ever'wheres 'round here. This thing for instance."

On the ground lay what looked like an implement of torture, a rusty metal contraption with row upon row of long, sharp tines. "God, what is it?"

"It's one of them harrows, like I was telling you 'bout. Farmers use 'em to bust up the soil." He held the lantern high, while I safely skirted the harrow. "Anyways, I saw something shiny back here, which is odd 'cause ever'thing made of metal has long gone to rust. Turned out to be nothing but my own trash, a shiny potato chip bag. But then I saw this."

With his free hand, Adam pulled back a low branch to reveal a tombstone sticking up at an angle. I squatted down to get a closer look. The stone had undergone a lot of weathering, but was definitely of human manufacture. Though pieces on both sides had broken off, the top was perfectly round.

"Can you make out the letters?" Adam said.

I shook my head. "Hold the lantern closer."

Adam placed the lantern directly before the tombstone. I moved his hand to one side, thereby shadowing the coarse surface. Two crudely carved letters were revealed: C R. I looked up at Adam. "Canara Rivers?"

It was at that moment that the lantern chose to go out, leaving the smell of burnt wick.

"Tarnation, "Adam said. "Must've run out of kerosene."

The night was as black as my opinion of people who go into the woods unprepared.

"Let's wait a spell till our eyes adjust to the darkness," he said.

"Anyone ever get lost in these woods?"

"Sure, lots of folks, but not tonight. Here, give me your hand. Now, be real careful 'cause here's that harrow."

I took back my hand so I'd have better balance and followed behind, taking tiny steps. But I stumbled over an exposed root and likely would have impaled myself if Adam hadn't caught me.

"You okay?" he said, holding me about the waist longer than I thought necessary. It seemed to me just the type of situation a man loves, a chance to play Dudley Do-Right to poor little Nell. "What the hell happened to the flashlight you took from the trailer?"

"Oh," he said. A rustle of cloth was followed by a beam of light.

"Here, Daniel Boone," I said snatching the flashlight out of Adam's hand, "let me." In no time, we were back, sitting at the picnic table. Adam refilled the lantern and lit it.

"So tell me, Miss Parry, what do you think?"

"Think?"

"'Bout the grave."

I was having difficulty paying attention. The air suddenly felt charged. Goose bumps rose up on my arms, though the night was not all that cold. Then to the east, a distant flash of lightning backlit the trees.

Adam saw it, too. "Reckon we might finally be getting some rain."

I quickly stood up. Then I realized I hadn't answered Adam's question. "I won't be able to say anything conclusive about the gravesite," I said, talking fast. "Not until I've done a careful survey of the ground, and probably not then." I picked up my guitar case. "One thing I can say is that the slope of the ground there suggests good drainage."

There was another flash.

"Meaning maybe the body hasn't decomposed yet?" Adam said.

"Possibly." I grabbed the flashlight. "Thanks for dinner, Adam. I think I'll turn in."

"Here, Miss Parry, let me drive you."

Another flash.

"No, I'll walk."
But it was more like a run.

CHAPTER 7

I've always hated bright lights. I hate the beach unless the sky's overcast. The Mojave Desert terrifies me. I hate Christmas because the best time of the year, when the days are mercifully short, is ruined by blinking lights and the high beams of drivers out gift grubbing and department stores lit up like Nazi rallies.

But most of all, I hate lightning. It's not just the eye-searing incandescence–like flashbulbs popping in my face–but also lightning's unpredictability that wracks my nerves. I compare it to being in the boxing ring with Mohammed Ali, blindfolded, waiting impotently for his next jab.

Walls don't help. I doubt being a mile underground would make a difference, for even when I can't see the lightning, I somehow feel its discharge right down my spine. I blame my astraphobia on my old shrink Herschbach. Yet knowing the cause of my phobia has done damn little to lessen it.

When I got to the trailer, I slid my guitar under the table then yanked open the drawer beside the stove and pulled out matches and a candle. I stuck the lighted candle into a pool of its own wax then perched myself on the edge of the bed with Granny Estey's quilt wrapped around my shoulders and my feet tucked underneath me. My theory was that the mattress would insulate me from the trailer's conductivity. To further reduce my chances of getting electrocuted, I sat equidistant from the walls. Still, when I thought about it–and I tried not to think about it–I couldn't have picked a worse place to be in a thunder and lightning storm: inside a metal can.

Flash!

Within the trailer, the lightning cast a sickly green fluorescence, the color of hospital walls at night. I closed my eyes and counted the seconds until the thunder reached me. *One, one thousand; two, one thousand . . .* Every five seconds was roughly a mile. I got to fifteen before I heard the rumble. The lightning had struck three miles away. Far, but not far enough.

In times of terror, I generally suspend any predilection toward atheism. *Please, God, don't let it get any closer!*

Flash!

One, one thousand; two, one thousand. It was odd how the candle flame was so unwaveringly upright when to me it felt as if all the air in the trailer was being sucked out through the gap above the door. *Eleven, one thousand; twelve, one—*

Rumble! Rumble!

The edge of the storm was fast approaching. So much for my fervent pleas to the Almighty. Shivering, I pulled the quilt tighter about me as I waited like a death row inmate on the electric chair. Hot dogs sure make a lousy last meal.

A gust of wind blew dry leaves against the trailer. I rubbed my arms, my skin tingling as if statically charged. Was I attracting the lightning? If so, I didn't know what I would do about it. I pulled the quilt over my head and waited.

Flash!

The green luminescence passed like x-rays right through the cloth. I put a pillow over my face. I wanted to huddle beneath the blankets, but was afraid to get any closer to the walls. I yearned for a rubber tire to sit on. I counted to sixteen before I heard the thunder. The storm was moving away

Flash!

Somehow I saw the brightness even with the pillow over my eyes. *One, one thousand....* This time I only counted to nine. *Damn! Damn! Damn!*

I pictured the storm advancing like enemy artillery. No, impossible for artillery to make it over the local roads. Make that an enemy bomber—one of those behemoths they used in WWII. I saw it as a movie in black and white, the narrator's excited voice rising to be heard above the sound effects of buffeting winds. *With muscles straining, the crafty German pilot battles gale force winds to keep his Stuka bomber, dangerously overloaded with bombs, from plummeting into the seething North Sea!*

Flash!

The crafty German pilot just dropped one. *One, one thousand....* Maybe the trailer was a homing device, a blip on the enemy's radar screen. The thought was so disturbing, I lost count. Even so, I knew the strikes were getting closer. Oh, why did I ever leave Santa Barbara where the most dramatic meteorological event was fog?

Flash!

I now had the pillow atop my head as puny protection from the lightning's megavolts. Tomorrow, Adam would find my charred body, chicken feathers fused to my brain.

Flash!

One, one thousand; two, one thousand; three, one thousand–

Flash!

Christ! The strikes were starting to come one atop the other.

Kaboom!

No distant rumble that, but a sound like a bomb going off right outside my door.

Flash!

And before I could count–

Kaboom!

The vibration rattled the broken window. But was that the thunder from the last strike or the one previous? Was the storm right on top of me, or did I still have a few seconds to live?

Kaboom!

I couldn't count, my thoughts being like the wind-blown leaves.

Concentrate!

Flash!

One, one thousand; two, one thousand; three one thous–

Kaboom!

Just a half-mile away. Inside this metal lightning magnet, I was a sitting duck, the object of Zeus' sick sense of humor. I had to get to some place safe, but where? Adam's truck? No, that was metal, too. The tool shed with Adam? No, too much intimate human contact.

Flash!

One, one thousand; two, one—

Kaboom!

Knowing the next time could be my last. I jumped off the bed and ran outside, the wind slamming the trailer door behind me.

Flash!

Not green this time, but a wicked white serpent's tongue forking above the branches of the trees. During the split second of illumination, I saw the outhouse. The lovely, wooden, nonconductive outhouse!

Kaboom!

I ran, not seeing where I was going, but guided by the after image of the outhouse burned on my retina. The quilt, dragging on the ground, tripped me up, and I fell onto a padding of leaves.

Flash!

Kaboom!

Flash!

I was up and running from a thousand photographers' flashbulbs going off at once.

Kaboom!

Flash!

Such a garish light! Bloodless! I couldn't tell if the sign on the outhouse was the green or red.

Kaboom!

Not that I cared. I flung open the door, leaped into the darkness, and slammed the door behind me.

Flash

Sizzle!

Kaboom!

I could actually hear the lightning! I sat on the toilet seat, weeping, shaking uncontrollably, my stupid brain going on about the color of the sign. Red? Green? Red? Green?

Flash!

Sizzle!

Kaboom!

Please God! Oh, please, God! Make it stop!

I was living my *Bride of Frankenstein* dream, strapped to the gurney, electrodes attached to my skull.

Flash!

Silver blades pierced every crack in the outhouse wall.

Kaboom!

I saw my father squatting over something on the ground. A red feather.

Flash!

He picked it up and used it to brush away the tears on my face.

Kaboom!

No more, father, please! The treatments aren't working!

He looked so sad. But he nodded his head. *Yes, yes. Enough is enough.*

That's when the lightning stopped, and the rain came on, beating down upon the roof like nails poured from a barrel. But I had never feared the rain, and compared to the thunder and lightning, the rattle was as soothing as a fiddler's waltz. I leaned against one side of the outhouse and listened to the music. Water dripped on my head. I leaned the other way and was dry.

Much later, I stopped shaking, then grew tired. But just before I fell asleep, sitting on the toilet seat, I realized why the rain had sounded so loud.

The outhouse had a metal roof!

CHAPTER 8

There are probably worse places than a shit house to spend the night: the belly of a whale, atop Everest in a blizzard, any Chicago jail. Still your basic outhouse is not designed with sleeping in mind. I pushed my achy bones up off the toilet seat and stumbled out into the predawn light. The ground was wet, but the sky—what I could see of it through the trees—was clear. A cardinal landed on the ground in front of me, danced a half-circle, and sang out a peppy little *cheer, cheer, cheer.* He flew away before I could step on him.

I shut the outhouse door (the sign was turned to green) and walked to the trailer, seeing a lot of deer prints in the soft ground. The trailer's advanced state of decomposition made it impossible to tell if it had sustained further damage from the storm. The inside smelled musty, but I couldn't see where any water had gotten in. I left the door open to air things out and sat at the table, shivering a little despite the heavy quilt still wrapped around me. Rather than distance myself mentally from last night's experience, I closed my eyes and attempted to resurrect my thoughts during my worst moments of abject fear. I thought this courageous. My old shrink Herschbach would have been proud of me. Still, to make sense of what was just a jumble of nightmarish images and sensations, I needed to organize my thoughts in a letter to Teddy, which meant getting up and finding paper and pen, which meant leaving my comfortable seat on the bench. I rested my head upon the table and slept until the sound of Adam's truck woke me.

"So how did you like the light show?" he said, sticking his head through the open door.

My reply came out as a croak. I went to the sink, splashed some water on my face, then drank directly from the tap. Straightening up, I realized I had forgotten to pack a towel. Adam pointed to a drawer next to the closet.

"Are all your storms like that one?" I said, taking a towel from the drawer and dabbing my face. "Because if they are, you can take me back to the airport right now."

"No, that one was a real humdinger, ordered up just special for you."

Humdinger. How quaint. I tried to imagine any of my dope-smoking students using the word. *Professor Euphrates, your lecture today sure was a humdinger!*

I brushed out my hair, grateful for the absence of a mirror. Then Adam drove us up past the schoolhouse, which had a large puddle of water on the subfloor. "I best be getting a roof on soon," he said.

Breakfast was scrambled eggs fried with slices of last night's leftover hot dogs. I didn't have to worry about getting enough to eat: the coffee had an ample amount of grounds. Still, the heavy dose of caffeine was an antidote to the emotional aftershocks of last night's pyrotechnics.

"This morning, I'd like to start by spending some time examining the gravesite by myself," I said.

"Suits me," Adam said. "I'll see iff'n I can get some roof sheathing nailed up."

After consuming my Oscar-Meyer breakfast special, I returned to the trailer to get my small bag of excavation tools and to brush the coffee grounds out of my teeth. My immediate impression on seeing the gravesite by daylight was that it seemed an unlikely place for one. The ground was too sloped, though that might have been the result of subsequent subsidence. The trees that overshadowed the tombstone appeared old. Again, I lamented my ignorance of botany. Without knowing what type of trees they were, or their rate of growth, I couldn't determine their age without chopping one down and counting its rings. I just had to assume that their roots would not have been an impediment to a grave digger back in 1907. What bothered me most was the tombstone itself. Why would anyone place a marker on the grave of someone they murdered? Or had someone else done that?

I started by doing a general survey of the ground around the grave. Not an easy task; in addition to the steepness of the slope, the ground was littered with downed branches, rotting leaves, and not a few good-sized rocks. I got a rake and shovel from Adam's tool shed and used them to expose the surface of the ground. As a result, I found several small pieces that had broken off the tombstone, none with lettering. After taking a few photos, I chose the largest of the nearby trees to be my datum, the point from which all measurements would be made. Then I used nylon string to lay out my first grid. I had just finished when Adam's friend Junie arrived.

My first sight of the co-author of "The Teacher of Hoagland Holler School" was of him standing upon the driver's seat of a moving jeep, shouting "Hee-haw!" like Buck Owens, with an equally insipid grin on his face.

I immediately hated him.

The jeep was still in gear, and as it slowed, the engine began to sputter and the jeep body to jerk. In sync with the jerking, Junie thrust his pelvis forward like he was–forget it. But it must have been a practiced trick, for the jeep safely came to a stop before plowing into the schoolhouse. I returned to my grid, hoping that Junie would get busy helping Adam and introductions would be saved for some time later–Halloween perhaps. No such luck.

"Miss Parry, I'd like you to meet my good friend, Junie Gorn."

Politeness dictated that I extend a hand in friendship. I stuck both of mine in my back pockets. Junie ran his eyes over me while masticating on what I thought was a wad of gum. Silly me. Imagine my surprise when a trickle of greasy brown drool started down his chin. Junie discharged his overflow–splattering my tool bag–and wiped his chin with the back of his hand. Then he jammed his thumbs through his belt loops, pushing down the front of his jeans.

"You wanna fuck?" he said.

"Come on, Junie," Adam said, "act nice."

"Shit, brother, I *am* nice." He did the pelvic thrust thing again.

I looked around for the shovel to hit him with.

But Junie was ahead of me. He jumped into the center of my grid and jammed the shovel into the ground, sending a shower of dirt over my jeans. "Look at me! I'm a fucking archaeologist!"

"Adam!" I yelled.

Adam grabbed the handle of the shovel.

"Fair 'nough," Junie said, "you shovel, I'll use the rake." Junie picked up the rake and used it like a hoe to chop the ground.

"Junie," said Adam.

Junie ignored him.

"Junie!"

Junie just jabbed the ground harder.

Adam stepped into the grid and put a hand on Junie's arm.

Junie flung it off. "Whatsamadder with you, boy? We don't need no goddamn egghead telling us how to dig up a grave!"

"Junie, the professor here knows what she's doing."

"You taking her side ag'in' me?"

"You know better. I just want to see that things get done right."

"Like hell, you ain't!" Junie threw down the rake. "Well, I say, fuck you both!" He stomped off, jumped into his jeep, and peeled away in reverse. We watched the jeep swerve backwards around the brush pile then tear off down the road.

Adam sighed. "I do believe, Miss Parry, that Junie took a fancy to you."

I laughed. "God, has he always been like that?"

"No, Junie was the sweetest boy in the world. But then he done went off to Vietnam and come back a changed person."

I sighed. "A lot of guys have come back like that."

"Yes'm, but this one just happens to be my best friend."

Adam sat down, and disregarding the dampness of the ground, I sat beside him. He looked so sad, I was tempted to put an arm around him.

"You see, Miss Parry, because Junie is kind of short like me, the army used him as a tunnel rat, one of them soldiers that goes down into the Vietcong hide-y-holes. From what I hear, the VC's practically got cities underground. It's dangerous work 'cause the VC set all sorts of booby traps."

"Sounds like it was hell," I said.

"I reckon it was."

We sat in silence for a while, then Adam pointed to the grid. "Mind iff'n I help? I don't feel like working by my lonesomes just now."

"Actually, I was just getting to the point where I could use some help." I explained how I wanted to dig the area within the grid in shallow stages, no deeper than four inches at a time. I waited until Adam had produced a small mound of dirt then used a piece of hardware cloth to sift it into a wheelbarrow. It was hard keeping up with Adam at first, but the farther down he dug, the harder the ground got.

"I never imagined digging up a grave would be such hard going," he said. "I mean, it's already done been dug once."

"That was sixty-three years ago," I said. "Soil can really compact in that amount of time."

Adam wiped the sweat off his forehead with the back of his hand. "Mind iff'n I use a pick?"

"No, so long as you're careful not to pick too deep. This might have been a shallow grave." While Adam went to the tool shed for the pick, I sifted some more dirt. So far, the dig had failed to yield any artifacts, and I had a feeling it wasn't going to; the ground's hardness and its uniform quality suggested it had never been disturbed.

With the first swing of the pick, Adam struck a boulder. The farther down he dug, the bigger the boulder got. It seemed to be attached to the bedrock.

"I'm pretty sure the grave diggers wouldn't have backfilled using a boulder this size," I said. "I suggest we try the opposite side of the tombstone."

By the time I had laid out another grid, it was lunchtime. As an alternative to hot dogs, Adam produced salami sandwiches–not exactly my preferred form of nourishment. I ate half a sandwich then filled up on the last of the asparagus pickles. We rested before going back to work. I sat, leaning against a tree, enjoying the shade, even though it wasn't all that hot. I grew drowsy and dozed off to be awakened by the sound of hammering. To my amazement, Junie had returned to help Adam nail down roof sheathing. Having had enough of Junie to last for one lifetime and several reincarnations, I stole back to the excavation site, glad of my own company.

The second grid proved no more productive than the first, except for the exciting discovery of a rusty tin can lid. After digging down about eighteen inches, I ran into a boulder the size of the one Adam had encountered. Actually, I wasn't certain it wasn't just a continuation of the same rock. By then it was late afternoon, and I was bushed. As I was gathering up my tools, Adam–without Junie, thank God–came to inspect my work.

"Did you find anything?" he said, looking down into the pit I'd dug.

"Not really."

"Well, tarnation! I was hoping you'd have better luck on your own."

"Tomorrow's another day," I said. It wasn't just an expression. More than once an unproductive site had yielded results with a little further excavation. I wiped my sweaty forehead with the back of my hand. "Any chance of a hot shower?"

"No, but I got something better. You bring a swimsuit?"

"It so happens that's one of the things I remembered to pack."

"Then why don't you go on down and get changed, while I put things away."

I had just enough time to change and grab another towel from the drawer before Adam arrived in his truck.

"Is it very far where we're going?" I said, dreading a long ride over the back roads.

"No, just a little ways past the church and post office."

Between Adam's land and the church was a corduroy bridge made of split logs, which spanned Twisted Creek. Even the bridges had bumps.

"It still doesn't look very twisted," I said, looking down from the bridge.

"Just hold on. You'll see."

The road rose steeply on the far side of the creek. A side road, covered in grass except where tires had left deep ruts, ran parallel to the creek.

"Who lives down there?" I said.

"Granny Estey."

"So we're no longer on land owned by the Gorns?"

"Not since we crossed the bridge."

Adam stopped the truck beside a weathered, board and batten shack not much bigger than his tool shed. A faded sign proclaimed it to be the Hoagland Holler Holiness Church.

"If that's a church," I said "I'd hate to see what passes for the post office."

"You're looking at it." Adam said, pointing to a warped plywood box nailed to the side of the church. "You got you a letter to send, you stick it in that box. Whoever's going up to Damascus takes the mail and comes back with the deliveries."

Not far past the church, Adam turned right onto another side road. "Hold on!" he yelled. In order to straddle the yard-deep ruts, he had to drive along the very edge of the road. I looked out my window straight down a steep slope, grateful for the presence of sturdy trees in case we rolled. Thankfully, the road soon ended at the creek.

"Is this your improvement on a hot shower?" I said, pointing to the rotting logs drifting in an eddy

Adam just grinned then pushed open his door and motioned for me to follow. A hundred yards downstream, the creek split around a tall limestone escarpment. We followed along the smaller of the two forks as it wound through a slot canyon no more than fifteen feet wide. Ferns and mosses clung to the canyon's sides. The creek, not more than a foot deep, ran crystal clear over polished marble streaked black and white.

"Adam, this is beautiful."

"Just you wait, Miss Parry, it gets better."

The creek finally lived up to its name as it twisted its way through the narrowing canyon. At one point, where I could almost touch both sides at once, stepping stones had been placed in the water, saving us having to wade through water waist deep. Then as the canyon began to open up again, the sound of falling water could be heard.

"Now, right here, it gets a mite iffy," Adam said. The creek suddenly disappeared as it left the canyon as a waterfall. The alternative exit required a descent along a long, narrow ledge no more than a foot wide. But there were sturdy tree roots for handholds, and soon we were standing on level ground, looking back upstream. Both forks of the creek emerged from separate canyons and plummeted twenty feet or more into a large pool that varied in color from amber to turquoise to royal blue as the water got deeper. Ringing the pool were cliffs banded black and white with ferns growing out of crevices. Trees leaned out over the canyon ridge, reducing the sky to a small oval centered above the pool.

Outings with my father had introduced me to many places of great beauty, Yosemite in particular, yet this small section of Twisted Creek was the equal to any of them.

"Adam, is this Eden?"

"It is, Miss Parry, only we call it Little Marble Canyon. And that there is what we call the Knob." He pointed to a column of rock, round as a bowling ball on top, projecting outward from the opposite cliff face. "C'mon. Let's go for a swim."

He ran down the slope to the pool, discarding clothes as he went. I followed more slowly, savoring the feeling of being Eve on her discovery of the Garden. Birds flitted through the trees, too high up to identify save for a blue grosbeak I knew by its call– a loud *chink*. By the time I shucked my sneakers and the jeans I wore over my swimsuit, Adam was already across the pool, pulling himself out onto a ledge. He ran along the edge of the pool, disappeared into a crevice in the cliff, and reemerged a minute later atop the Knob. It was obvious he was preparing to jump.

"You're crazy!" I yelled.

He waved in response, and instead of jumping, he dove. Like all of Adam's movements, the dive was graceful. He held his arms straight out from his side until the last instant when he brought them together over his head and pierced the water as cleanly as a needle through a taut piece of cloth.

"God! I can't believe you did that," I said, after he had resurfaced. "That must be fifty feet high."

Adam pushed his wet hair out of his face. "Actually, it's only 'bout thirty-five. You should try it, Miss Parry."

"Ha! Not likely. The highest I've ever dived was the high board at the city pool, and only because this creep named Arnie Kostorsky had called me chicken."

"I confess it took me a while to work up the courage to dive. But you can start by jumping. Can't hurt yourself just jumping."

"Famous last words," I said. Yet I was intrigued. What was the point being on an adventure if I wasn't open to new experiences? "All right, I'll do it." I swam across the pool and made my way up the steep trail. But when I reached the top and looked down, I quickly had second, third, and fourth thoughts, and none of them argued for jumping.

"Jesus!" I yelled. "It's twice as far down as it is up."

"Just think like you're like stepping off a curb," Adam yelled back.

That image didn't work for me because I visualized cars the size of skyscrapers. I backed away from the edge to give myself my own mental pep talk. *You think too much. Don't think, just jump.* Turning, I gauged the distance from where I stood to the edge–about five steps. I took my first step forward at the speed of a charging turtle. Then I heard in my head Arnie Kostorsky's sneering taunt: *Chicken shit!* Anger increased my pace to that of a geriatric wearing lead boots.

Then something small and red flitted at the edge of my vision, and I turned to see a bright red male cardinal land just to my right. *I'm pretty,*

pretty, pretty, he bragged, and I had to agree that he was.

But I should have been watching my feet instead of the damned bird. I stumbled over a nub of rock, and would have fallen flat on my face if there had been anything to fall on. Instead, I came off the Knob neither jumping nor diving, but perfectly positioned to do a belly flop. Yet I was lucky, for if I hadn't tripped, I'm sure the bullet would have struck me smack dab in the center of my forehead.

CHAPTER 9

Once during school recess, Arnie Kostorsky slapped me for stealing a pop-up from him during a game of three-flies-up. At age nine, the fat Pole already had hands the size of a catcher's mitt. Needless to say, it hurt. My belly flop was like that slap, only magnified by a factor of ten–like King Kong letting fly with a backhand. In addition, the impact knocked the air out of me, which is a different kind of discomfort–not as painful as getting "Konged," but more terrifying. When it happens all the little alarm bells in the cerebral cortex go ring-a-ding: WARNING! RESUPPLY AIR TO LUNGS, PRONTO! Good advice, but not when you're four feet underwater.

Then I was being dragged out of the pool by Adam. Doing a credible imitation of a suction pump, I lay upon the bank, sucking in the good air and spewing out the bad. As if nearly drowning wasn't enough, there was also the not too insignificant problem of someone shooting at me.

"Adam!" I managed to sputter.

"Shhh. Don't talk, Miss Parry. Wait till you get your wind back."

I gasped. I retched. I also pounded Adam's leg with my fist. "Bullet," I wheezed. I pushed up a little and flung one arm in the direction of that odious Knob. "Someone tried to kill me!"

"Hush, you're all right."

Adam just wasn't getting it. Maybe he hadn't heard the gunshot.

I took in air, retched, struggled to breathe, tried again. "You're not listening!" I said. "Someone tried to kill me!"

"Naw, Miss Parry, if Dewey Bone had wanted to kill you, you'd be dead."

I flopped back down upon the sand. Who the hell was Dewey

Bone, and why was Adam taking my being shot at so lightly? It wasn't Adam who heard the whirr of the bullet, felt it practically part my hair. Now that the pain of the belly flop was teetering down from agony to general misery, the reaction of nearly being shot was tottering up from shock to terror. I started to cry, which only made me feel worse.

Adam rubbed my shoulder. "There, there, Miss Parry, you're all right, now."

His assurance only made me cry harder. Then he began to sing.

> *Hush, little baby, don't say a word,*
> *Papa's gonna buy you a mockingbird.*
> *And if that mockingbird don't sing,*
> *Papa's gonna buy you a diamond ring.*

I couldn't help but be soothed by Adam's voice–doubtless his intent. Adam has the most agile voice I've ever heard, and I've heard a lot of opera singers. He gave "bird" a slight trill. What was it about birds and this place, especially cardinals?

> *If that diamond ring turns to brass,*
> *Papa's gonna buy you a looking glass.*

"Papa can keep his damned looking glass," I said, pushing up onto my elbows. "God, I must look a fright."

"You look just fine to me, Miss Parry."

My towel was within reach, and I used it to wipe my face and blow my nose. Then I sat up, angry at myself for losing control, but even angrier at Dewey Bone. "How dare that son of a bitch shoot at me!"

Adam nodded. "I know just how you feel. Dewey's been shooting at me ever since I was knee high to a skink. Nearly ever' time I go swimming here."

"For God's sake, why?"

"Reckon 'cause this here swimming hole's on his land."

"Then why the hell doesn't he fence it off. Put up a no trespassing sign?"

Adam grinned. "'Cause shooting at folks is a lot more fun."

"Jesus! I can't believe it. He ought to be in prison."

"What for? He's never hit anybody; leastways, not yet." Adam picked up a pebble and threw it into the water. "Not to change the subject, but I sure do admire your style of jumping off rocks, though I don't know as I'd care to try it myself."

I picked up a handful of sand and hurled it at him. But the movement reminded me of my recent attempt to part the waters using my abdomen. I lay on my side, resting my head on my towel.

Adam pushed the hair off my face. "Miss Parry, may I ask you a question?"

"This better not be about my jumping technique."

"This one's a mite more personal. Do you like me a'tall?"

I brushed some sand off my lips. "Adam, right at this moment I can honestly say I hate everybody."

Stung by my words, Adam started to push himself up. I grabbed his wrist and pulled him back down. "Please, I'm still hurting. Just give me a moment to think."

I released him and closed my eyes to consider his question and its implications. I wasn't completely obtuse. Adam wasn't just asking me if I basically liked him, but whether I liked him the way a woman likes a man. The one time I'd dated in high school had been a disaster. Driving home from a movie, my date tried to put the move on me, and I rabbit punched him. The poor guy drove over a curb and threw his front-end out of alignment. For my part, the reaction had just been a reflex, which made me think I lacked the affection gene. What then of my dreams of love?

Frustrated, I sat up and crossed my legs. "Adam, I'm not exactly what you'd call a warmhearted person. That said, I like you better than any man I've ever met with the exception of my father."

"Well, that doesn't exactly say a whole lot since you hate ever'body."

"Stop it! I loved my father more than you can imagine."

Adam stretched his legs out, making grooves in the sand with his heels. "I'm sorry, Miss Parry. I didn't mean any disrespect toward your daddy. I'm just kind of wondering what your plans are for the future."

I found his question irritating. My father was always asking the same thing. "At this point in my life, I'm just trying to finish my dissertation so I can go out and find a teaching or research job."

"I see."

For a long time, Adam stared at the pool, squinting a little. I found myself doing the same. The variations in color were in distinct bands. A fish suddenly lunged halfway out of the water.

"Miss Parry, would you have sex with me?"

I wasn't all that surprised by his request, and I liked the way he phrased it. He didn't ask if I wanted to make love. To make love was definitely a stretch away from my fence, implying a lot of intimate human contact. But for him to say "have sex" seemed to take the intimacy out of it. Sex, the naturally occurring urge by which mammals are driven to procreate, was a process about which I, as a scientist, was greatly curious.

"Miss Parry?"

"I'm thinking!"

And there was something else: I always pictured sex as my gateway to normalcy, and I am certain my father saw it that way too, only he would have couched it in terms of "getting married," and "settling down and having kids." On a physical level, I figure couldn't be all that bad, since it was supposed to be pleasurable. But even it wasn't, it wouldn't be the first time I'd had to endure some bit of unpleasantness in the service of science.

"Okay, let's do it."

Adam laughed. "Just like that? I guess when you decide to do something you–Jesus!"

Adam's rare use of profanity was prompted by me having peeled off my swimsuit and tossed it aside. I straightened my towel under me then looked for him to make the next move. He sat, looking me over, his breath coming quickly. Slowly, he stood up and dusted the sand off his legs. He had gone swimming in boxers patterned in mercifully out-of-style paisley swirls. He quickly stepped out of them.

It was my first experience of male engorgement. Oh joy! Oh rapture!

He sat down beside me and preceded to plant small kisses on my neck then my shoulders. I suffered this until he inched his way down to my breasts and started to gum my nipples.

Gently, I lifted his head so I could look into his face. "Can we just do the sex part now?"

He smiled then used the weight of his chest to force me back onto my towel. The pain when he entered was not nearly as bad as I hypothesized; certainly nothing like a belly-flop from thirty feet up.

I can do this.

I tried to remain an impassive observer, but found it increasingly difficult. As Adam's thrusts became more forceful, I gripped the sand.

I can do this. It's not so bad. I can do this.

CHAPTER 10

In Adam's ice chest, bloated hot dogs bobbed in murky water.

"Don't exactly look appetizing, do they?" Adam said.

My response was cut off by the roar of Junie's jeep. Funny how the thought of Junie was more injurious to the appetite than the sight of decomposing weenies. But it wasn't Junie. A tall, horse-faced woman, decked out in denim, kicked open the jeep door. "What in Sam Hill you doing standing 'round here with your hands in your pockets?" she yelled as she strode toward us. "Dinner's getting cold."

"Junie didn't say nothing about us being invited to dinner," Adam said.

The woman grabbed Adam in a headlock and rubbed his scalp. "Since when do you need an invitation." She planted a big kiss on the top of his head before stepping forward to take one of my hands in both of hers. "You must be that pretty professor I've been hearing so much about. I'm Beatty Bickum Gorn, Junius' ma, and I hope I'm in time to save you from Adam's cooking. Has he fed you anything 'sides hot dogs?"

Smiling in turn, I said. "He favored us with salami sandwiches for lunch."

"Well, he must be branching out. But what am I yammering on 'bout? Let's get on up to the house."

I was given the honor of sitting up front in the jeep. I was grateful the jeep hadn't a roof to bang my head against, for Beatty was a fearless driver. She didn't slow to make the turn at the fork, and the back wheels slid sideways. Neither did she slacken her speed to accommodate the bumps, and I feared decapitation by overhanging branches. At one point, I thought I saw a small stream running alongside the road that might warrant further inspection sometime when I wasn't fighting for my life. Then Beatty skidded to a stop in front of a log house the size of the Cartwrights' Ponderosa.

"I thought they filmed Bonanza in California," I said.

Beatty hadn't heard me, for she was already out of the jeep, running toward the house. "Junie!" she yelled.

Adam and I followed more slowly. Lining the walkway were tall bushes with faded lavender blossoms. Lilacs was my guess. Junie stood in the doorway, holding the door open for us. He didn't say anything, only nodded at Adam and ignored me completely. The inside of the house was as big as a barn. I craned my neck to look up at the ceiling, which had to be at least three stories high. A heavy oak table had been set for four. Beatty rushed in, using hot mitts to carry a sizzling skillet.

"Just take a chair, any chair," she commanded.

As soon as I was seated, Beatty slid a trout onto the blue china plate set before me.

"These come fresh from our pond," she said. "Just help yourself to the rest of the vittles."

Both Adam and Junie reached for the same covered bowl. Beatty slapped both their hands with the spatula.

"Company first!"

Junie reluctantly placed the bowl in front of me. I lifted the lid and was greeted by the steamy aroma of potatoes and mushrooms.

"I like to season my potatoes with morels and just a few chopped ramps," Beatty said. "I hope you're not one of them folks who hates ramps."

"I don't believe I've ever had them," I said. I took a helping then exchanged the potatoes for a dish of vegetable greens.

"Them greens is fresh picked," Beatty said, as she went around, filling our wine glasses. "There's poke, dandelion greens, lamb's quarters, and sour dock, with a little fat back and vinegar thrown in. They go real good with cornbread, which is in that basket there by your elbow." She sat down. "Junie, will you say grace?"

Junie mumbled some shopworn blessing, then guzzled down his

wine. I reached to pass him the carafe, but a sharp look from Beatty stopped me.

"So, Professor Euphrates," Beatty said "how do you find our little valley?"

"By turning left at the highway," Adam answered.

"Now you shush, Adam Manly Singer, I'm trying to carry on an intelligent conversation with the professor."

"Please, call me Parry," I said.

"Parry? Is that short for anything?"

I hate it when people asked about my name. "It's short for Paradigm."

Junie snorted, and I imagined the pleasure of sticking my fork into his hand.

"I was named after my grandmother. Her mother was named Paris and her father, Dima, a form of Vladimir. They were both rather proud, or so the story goes, so they chose a name for their daughter that combined both of theirs. At least, that's what my father always told me. I actually think he named me after a company called Paradigm, which makes circuit breakers. My father was an electrician."

"Well, I guess that when they was gluing together names, Paradigm beats Dim-Ass," Junie said.

"Junie!" Beatty yelled, pointing with a butter knife.

Junie scowled then reached over me for the wine carafe and filled his glass.

"I think Paradigm is a right pretty name," Beatty said, "and a whole lot nicer than some of the names folks go by 'round here. Adam, you tell her about Farmer Ealem?"

Adam, his mouth full, nodded

"Tell her 'bout O. B. Hill," Beatty said.

Adam swallowed. "O. B. stands for 'Our Boy,' "

"Can you believe that, Parry?" Beatty said. "Naming your son, 'Our Boy'? I swear, some folks got mashed turnips for brains. But 'Euphrates,' isn't that from the Bible?

I nodded. "Book of Genesis: 'And a river went out of Eden to water the garden; and from thence it was parted, and became into four heads… and the fourth river is Euphrates.'"

Junie drained his wine glass and set it down hard on the table. "Vladimir, ain't that Russian?"

I nodded.

"So your great granddaddy was a damn commie?"

"Junius," said Beatty, threatening again with her butter knife, "how 'bout you go check the temperature on the you-know-what."

I just saved my wine glass as Junie jarred the table getting up. For a while, we ate in silence, the food tasting better for Junie's absence. I buttered another piece of corn bread. "I could live off these."

"You should try hot dogs dipped in corn meal batter then fried in grease," Adam said.

Beatty laughed. "Boy, you're gonna turn into a hot dog iff'n you don't watch out." She refilled my wine glass. "Parry, pray forgive my boy's manners. He's not been hisself since coming home from Vietnam. I fear war brings out the worst in a man. God made man to bring forth the fruits of the earth and not to go 'bout killing and destroying things. I think it says something like that in the Bible."

I quoted, " 'And God said, be fruitful, and multiply, and replenish the earth and subdue it: and have dominion over the fish of the sea, and over the fowl of the air, and over every living thing that moveth upon the earth.' "

"How is it you know so much of the Bible?" Beatty said.

I smiled. "My father was a regular churchgoer, so I attended my share of Bible study classes. I'm also cursed with a photographic memory. How's this? 'Crest has been shown to be an effective decay-preventive dentifrice that can be of significant value when used in a conscientiously applied program of oral hygiene and regular professional care.' "

Adam laughed, but Beatty just shook her head, not getting it.

"That's what it says on a tube of Crest toothpaste," Adam explained.

"Well, I brush with baking soda, myself," Beatty said. "But what

I'm trying to say is, a man just ain't a man less'n he's got some land to work." She patted Adam's hand. "That's why I done gave Adam them forty acres he's building on."

Adam smiled his appreciation.

" 'Tweren't nothing really, considering that I own nearly five thousand." She laughed. "A person's gotta be downright loony to own that much land. Why, just trying to keep up with taxes is like to kill you. Still, working the land is just the kind of thing Junie needs right now to settle him down. Then someday, God willing not too far off, Junie's gonna have a family of his own, and there will be enough land for his children, and his children's children. And of course, we'll always have the water."

"Water?" I said.

Beatty looked at Adam. "Didn't you tell her nothing?"

Adam shook his head.

"Well, for pity's sake!" She slapped down her napkin, started to stand, then sat back down. "Have you gotten 'nough to eat, Parry?"

I brought one hand to eye level. "I can barely see out."

"Then let me show you something 'fore it gets dark."

Leaving Adam to enjoy the remainder of the "vittles," we went outside where, from an open window, we were suddenly assaulted by Jim Morrison imploring us to 'break on through to the other side.'

"Turn it down," yelled Beatty, banging her fist on the window frame. The music got momentarily louder before decreasing in volume.

"That boy!" she muttered.

I felt sorry for Beatty. I guess it's an understatement to say I'm slow to warm to people, but I took a liking to Beatty right off. She reminded me of Mrs. E, sort of feisty and affectionate at the same time.

We crossed a footbridge that arched over a rushing creek. I stopped to lean on the handrail. Crystal clear water rippled over amber-colored pebbles, reminding me of Yosemite, looking down from Sentinel bridge at the rocks beneath the Merced river. Lavender plants like those in the front of the house lined the creek banks. Beatty backtracked to join me.

"This is lovely," I said.

"It's been a while since I've had the company of someone who 'preciates beauty," Beatty said, patting my hand. "Only time my late husband took much notice of nature was when he was trying to shoot it. It might surprise you, but Junie's a lot more tender than he shows. He used to sit right here and draw pictures."

How nice, I thought *a psychopath with artistic tendencies.* "What are those plants with the lavender flowers?"

"Rhododendrons. Wish you could've seen 'em 'bout three weeks ago. But let's mosey on 'cause the light's failing."

We walked uphill along a path that followed the creek. The leaves of the trees shimmered golden in the sun's slanting rays. Ahead a log building of a more recent vintage than the main house straddled the creek. Beatty bounded up roughhewn steps, and I ran after her onto a landing and through an open door. It was noisy inside, for the room echoed the sound of the creek, which could be glimpsed though the gaps in the plank flooring. Set against the back wall were large stainless steel tanks with pipes running in and out of them. Beatty tapped on a temperature gauge on a smaller tank, which from my experience of umpteen chemistry classes looked like a still.

"What do you think?" she said, returning to stand beside me.

Before I could answer, a pump came on, cranking up the noise level. Beatty motioned me to follow, and we went through a side door into a warehouse with a concrete floor. Hundreds of bottles lined the walls. They varied from soda pop size to five gallon carboys. Beatty opened one of the soda-sized bottles and poured the clear liquid into a Dixie cup.

"Here, try this," she said.

I thought I was about to get my first taste of moonshine. I sniffed the liquid. It was odorless. I took a sip and braced myself for the kick. Nothing happened. I took a swallow. "This is just water," I said.

"Just water!" Beatty exclaimed. "Why that's the purest, clearest, most health-filled water you're ever like to drink. Come right out of Skillet Mountain after being filtered through miles and miles of limestone."

I took another swallow. I was no connoisseur of water. To me, Skillet Mountain spring water tasted like the stuff that came out of the tap. But of course, I didn't tell that to my hostess. "It's delicious," I said.

Beatty picked up the opened bottle along with another Dixie cup. "Let's us go out onto the verandah," she said. We exited the building through another side door. The verandah had a glossy pine soffit from which a kerosene lantern hung. I made myself comfortable in a bent wood rocker while Beatty lit the lantern.

"Could've had electric lights out here," she said, "but I've always preferred the softer glow of a kerosene lamp."

"I know what you mean. There's something romantic about lantern light. I imagine nights on the Oregon trail, the covered wagons glowing like Chinese lanterns."

"That's a pretty picture you paint there, Parry." Beatty filled both cups before sitting in another rocker. "So what do you think of our new little business?"

"I'm not sure exactly what your new business is. You're bottling water?"

"I'm bottling the purest drinking water on earth. Why, it's liquid gold. Think of them folks in the cities with nothing but polluted rivers to drink from. What wouldn't they give for a glass of pure mountain spring water? How does this sound: 'Skillet Mountain Spring Water, Nature's Purest'?"

"I think there might be a problem with the 'skillet' part. I guess I'm thinking of the skillet Adam used this morning to fry eggs."

Beatty laughed. "I've seen that skillet, myself. So, what would you call my spring water?"

I recalled the name of a town Adam and I passed through as we started into the Shenandoahs. "How about 'Brandywine Spring Water'?"

Beatty tapped her chin. "Might do. Kinda has a nice ring to it. 'Brandywine Spring Water, Sweeter than Wine.' You should go into the naming business, Parry." She took a sip from her cup. Jim Morrison's whiney baritone drifted up to us from the house, making an odd accompaniment to the twittering of the birds settling in for the night. "So, you're digging up the dirt on my family's sordid past, are you?"

For a second, I thought she was angry, but then she laughed. "Did Adam tell you about the curse?"

"He did. He said Junie was the last male in the Bickum family line."

"Which means he's a goner, for sure." She laughed again. "Well, I suppose if Junie can survive Vietnam, he's pretty much safe from curses."

"May I ask you a question about your family?"

"Ask anything you want."

"Well, you said earlier you owned five thousand acres. So—"

"So how comes I own all this land when Aunt Roseanne up and got murdered before she could be swapped for land by that no-account, pardon my French, son-of-a bitch granddaddy of mine?"

I nodded.

"Well, Roseanne weren't the only Bickum daughter. There was my momma Sarah Bickum. My granddaddy up and swapped her instead."

"God! You're kidding."

"Best thing that ever happened to her. No sooner did she and that banker tie the knot then he up and died, leaving her ever'thing he owned. And soon after that, my granddaddy and uncles cashed in their chips, so there was my momma free to marry whosoever she pleased, and she married her childhood sweetheart, my daddy, the kindest man this world's ever known. He's the one that built that fine house I'm living in."

The music from the house suddenly cut off.

"Ma!"

Beatty pushed up out of her chair. "What in tarnation has that boy gone and done now?"

We hurried along the path back to the house. Inside, Junie stood behind Adam who sat slumped forward in his chair.

"Oh, my God!" I yelled, starting to go around Beatty.

She blocked me with a strong arm. "Stay put. We know what to do."

Adam groaned.

"What's the matter with him?" I said.

"His trouble is he's a damn fool, lifting all them heavy sheets of plywood onto that crazy house of his. Now his muscles have done gone and locked up on him. Junie, help me get him into bed."

With uncharacteristic gentleness, Junie lifted Adam out of his chair. Then with Junie under one arm and Beatty under the other, they walked Adam toward the hall at the end of the living room. I stepped back to let them pass. Adam's eyes were glazed.

"I think he should see a doctor," I said.

It was Adam who answered. "No, I just need to lie down a spell."

The three disappeared down the hallway. While I waited, I made myself useful by cleaning up. I was comforted by the thought that Beatty seemed familiar with Adam's ailment. When I was done washing the dishes, I poured myself a half glass of wine and sat at the table to await Beatty. It was Junie who returned first. He shot me a murderous look.

"What?" I said.

Junie grabbed the carafe, drank directly from it, then wiped his chin with his sleeve. "Ma said I was to take you on back."

Being alone in the jeep with Junie seemed on a par with sharing a phone booth with a rattlesnake. Yet it was dark, I had no flashlight and wasn't exactly sure of the way back.

"How's Adam?"

Junie didn't answer, which pissed me off.

"Junie!"

He turned away from me. "He's fine. Now, let's go."

Not only did Junie drive like his mother, but the whole time, I felt as if I had so much as cleared my throat, Junie would have erupted like Vesuvius. He slammed on the brakes outside the trailer. I had no sooner put my feet on the ground than Junie floored the gas pedal, spun the jeep around and tore back up the slope. As I waited for my eyes to adjust to the darkness, I listened as the engine's roar gradually gave way to the music of the night. Crickets were fiddlers playing *pizzicato* while cicadas strummed upon tiny washboards. A whip-poor-will, an eastern bird I knew only from its distinctive call, whistled from the woods.

The sounds were soothing, but even after listening for a while, I remained too wound up to sleep. I decided to unwind by writing a letter to Teddy.

June 28, 1970

Dear Teddy,

Guess what? Today in Hoagland Holler, West Virginia, I, Parry Euphrates, finally lost my virginity. Ya hoo! Sound the trumpets! Beat the drums! I'd send out announcements, but I don't think I could stomach writing "loss of virginity," because I've always hated the phrase. Loss implies injury or damage or mishap, which makes my first experience of sex sound like a bad car wreck, when it was actually more like a vaccination: a little pain and then it was over.

And what's the opposite of loss? Gain? Profit? Of course, you can't gain back your virginity once you've lost it, which gets into all that muck about a woman's maidenhead being the guardian of the goddamn holy grail. Frankly, I'm glad to be rid of my virginity, or to use one of Adam's words, to have "shucked" it.

That said, I'm really not feeling all that celebratory. (I can tell Mr. D is having a good belly laugh.) Outside of being a little sore, I really don't feel any different now than when I was pre-shucked.

I know this sounds crazy, especially in light of my religious upbringing and the church's views on premarital sex, but outside of a desire to satisfy my curiosity, I had sex with Adam to prove to myself that I'm a good person, or maybe I should say a normal person, for isn't free love the norm nowadays? Yet whether I'm good or just normal, I still don't feel any different.

Lesson: the wages of virtue are about the same as those of sin.

CHAPTER 11

I was in one my usual snits the next morning, dreading having to talk to anyone, even to the extent of inquiring of Beatty after Adam. Maybe she wouldn't mind if I used hand signals. As for communicating with Junie, I would rather have spent the day cleaning the trailer with my tongue.

But when I climbed up out of the rabbit hole, on my way to the Gorns', I found Adam at his grill, whistling "Red-Haired Boy," as he stood over a smoking griddle.

"Flapjacks," he said, hailing me with a spatula.

The smell of the burning grease made my stomach turn. It must have shown in my face.

"A mite too soon for morning sickness, isn't it?" Adam said.

I wanted to bite him. I did something worse. "I was hoping you'd still be sick." Needless to say, Adam stopped whistling.

I sat down at the table, and Adam slammed down a plate of pancakes in front of me. Ah! the blissful lovers' first post-coital breakfast.

I poured some syrup on my pancakes and took a bite; they were actually pretty good. Adam with his own plate of cakes sat down opposite me. As he reached for the syrup. I placed a hand on his.

"I'm sorry, Adam. I don't know why I said that. I'm just in a foul mood this morning. But I am surprised you're up and about. Last night, you didn't exactly look like the picture of health."

Adam, still miffed, pulled his hand away. "Sorry to say, I feel fine and dandy this morning."

I bit back an angry retort and had another bite of pancake before speaking. "What exactly was the matter with you?"

"I just had a case of what my momma used to call my growing pains."

"You're a little too old to be growing."

Adam took a big bite of pancake and chewed on it for a while. I sensed his reluctance to talk about this. "It's just that every once in a while, I just get these pains. Not bad like they used to be; nothing like when I was a boy."

"What kind of pains?"

Adam cut another chunk of pancake, using the side of his fork. "Achy bones, sometimes muscles, too. Granny said my daddy used to have the same thing."

"Ever see a doctor?"

Adam shook his head.

"Christ! What is it with people and doctors? You're just like my landlady Mrs. Esau."

Adam swallowed his bite of pancake. "Miss Parry, I was brung up by two nurses. I reckon that was doctoring enough."

"I didn't know your mother was a nurse."

Adam shrugged his shoulders in a way that said, *you never asked.*

"Who else was a nurse?"

"Well, Granny Estey is kind of a nurse. And my daddy was a doctor. Had a big practice up in Baltimore where I was born."

I dropped my fork. "You? Born in the city? Adam Manly Singer, the quintessential country boy?"

"Be that as it may, I started out a city slicker."

"So how did you end up in Hoagland Holler?"

"I told you Granny was raised here. When my daddy disappeared, she—"

"Disappeared?"

"He might've run off, though my momma swears he did no such thing. Like to broke her heart."

"I'm sorry, Adam."

"Can't say his leaving meant all that much to me, 'cause at the time,

I was still in my momma's belly." Adam pointed a fork at my now empty plate. "More flapjacks?"

I shook my head. "So, how did you come to live here?"

"Once my daddy left, Granny decided to go on back home, leaving momma with nobody for company exceptin' me. After a couple of years of that, she followed Granny here to Hoagland Holler. I don't think Granny liked that none."

"Why's that?"

He smiled. "I think she was afraid I'd grow up to be the ignorant hillbilly I am."

There was one pancake left, and Adam sailed it like a Frisbee toward the burn pile. A blue jay was on it as soon as it hit the ground. He tried to carry off the whole pancake, but it was too heavy. Two other jays moved in and there was a squabble. A cardinal flew in to see what the fuss was about.

"Blue jays are so beautiful. I wish we had them in California," I said.

"California don't have blue jays?"

"We have scrub jays and Steller's jays and pinyon jays and even gray jays, but no blue jays."

Adam stood up and took my plate and his, and since they were both of paper, flung them at the burn pile, too. "Are you wanting to work alone again this morning?"

I studied his face, looking for any sign of censure. "I'd like to. I'm going to measure out two more grids, this time to each side of the tombstone."

"Well, if you don't need me, I'm gonna nail on some more roof sheathing." He pointed to the overcast sky. "Like to get that roof covered 'fore it rains some more."

"What about your achy bones?"

"Junie's coming to lend a hand."

Hearing Junie's name was all the motivation I needed to get to work. I grabbed my bag of tools from the shed and headed to the gravesite. I'd been thinking about the chances of my finding any human remains, and was pretty sure I wasn't going to dig up anything but decomposed limestone and not-so-decomposed limestone, but I owed it to Adam to keep trying.

The ground within the third grid was just as hard as the ground in the first two, and I was grateful for the cloud covering as I worked up a sweat, digging and sifting. By lunchtime, I hadn't found so much as a tin can lid, just rocks and more rocks. This was when a back hoe would have come in handy. Then again, what would have been the point? Nobody backfills a grave with rocks as big as the national debt.

I joined Adam and Junie for lunch. Beatty spared us a repeat of salami by sending fish salad sandwiches with Junie. For dessert, there were more of the corn muffins we'd had the night before along with honey to spread over them. Mercifully, Junie didn't talk as we ate. He sat on the far side of the table and quietly stewed. After lunch, a crew arrived from the power company. How they got their truck and trailer over the roads was a tribute to perseverance and high clearance vehicles. Adam had been anxious to get electricity as he'd been doing all his cutting by hand.

The crew had to set poles before they could run the power line to the main electric panel attached to the side of the schoolhouse. With some satisfaction, I watched the frustrated two-man crew relocate the power auger half a dozen times before finding a piece of ground relatively free of rocks. Returning to my own digging problem, I lamented not having power tools to make the work easier. Picks and shovels were the most intrusive tools I ever used. More often it was dental probes and toothbrushes.

Toward late afternoon, it began to drizzle. It felt good on my sweaty skin. As I worked in my fourth pit, using the point of the pick to scrape around still another rock, someone's shadow passed over me.

"Well, young lady, have you found China yet?"

I looked up into the smiling face of an old man. He wore heavy, black frame glasses and had his thin hair slicked straight back over his scalp. Black suspenders hoisted up his gray pants as high as waders.

"I'm Brother Lillard." He bent down to offer his hand.

I wiped my dirty hands on my jeans. "I'm Parry," I said, giving his hand a couple of shakes.

"Don't tell me them two strapping boys let a little lady like yourself do all this digging."

"Adam helped me with the first grid, but I actually prefer to work alone. That way I can prevent any discoveries from being damaged."

"And have you made any discoveries?"

"I've discovered that this ground is mighty rocky."

Brother Lillard laughed. "Mind if I have a go?" he said, pointing to my pick.

Why not? At this point, I was fairly certain he couldn't do any harm. Due to his age, I was more concerned I might have to lug his body out of the pit after his heart attack. I leaned the pick handle his direction, and he stepped down into the pit as I stepped out. Before he took hold of the handle, he spit into his hands then rubbed them together. I made a mental note to disinfect the handle before using it again.

Rather than bringing the pick up high over his head, he brought up just a little above his right shoulder.

Whump!

There must have been considerable muscle hidden beneath his long shirtsleeves, for the ground vibrated with the impact of the pick.

Whump!

Brother Lillard worked with the regularity of a machine.

Whump! Whump! Whump!

When he came to a rock, he pried it loose with the point of the pick, hoisted it out of the pit, and went back to picking.

Whump!

I watched, fascinated, as he went on nonstop, never appearing to tire.

After about twenty minutes, he stopped to dab his moist forehead with a handkerchief. "Feels just like old times, back working in the coal mines."

"You were a coal miner?"

A rattling cough was his answer. When he got it under control, he hawked and spat a dark gob into the pit. Nice.

"Been mor'n twenty-five years since I quit them mines," he tapped his chest, "and I'm still coughing up dust."

"There's no need to dig any more. I'm just about done here."

"Just a little longer, that is, if you don't mind."

I motioned for him to go ahead and sat on the edge of the pit and watched. After five more minutes, Brother Lillard set down the pick and sat beside me.

"My, but that sure brings back a lot of memories," he said. "Times was bad back then, but folks was good. Nowadays, it seems the other way 'round. Most folks got it pretty good, only they don't act none too good."

I kept my mouth shut, hoping not to encourage a lecture on present day morality. In my experience when people made comparisons of past and present, they only dredged up what they chose to remember.

Thankfully Brother Lillard didn't push it. "Have you found anything of Canara Rivers?" he said.

I reached out to where I'd set the tin can lid and handed it to him. "Only if Mr. Rivers was fond of pork and beans, or maybe the lid is from a soup can."

Smiling, Brother Lillard handed the lid back to me. "If I remember right, Canara was mostly fond of cornbread dribbled with a little bacon grease."

"You knew Canara Rivers?"

"Not like some folks. Not like my sister Estelline. I never had much time for book learning, so I never went to his school. I know the Bible though, and that's all I need."

"Is that the same Estelline as Adam's grandmother?"

Brother Lillard nodded then pushed himself onto one knee. "And if you have questions about Canara, you best ask her." He stood up, swaying a little, and for a moment, I was afraid he was going to pitch head first into the pit. Then he smiled down at me. "I just stopped by to let you know that we mean to have church come Tuesday night, and you'd be mighty welcome to come join us."

"Thank you," I said. I'd lost track of what day it was, but I made a mental note that come Tuesday night to be busy doing something else. It wasn't that I disliked Brother Lillard. I had known men like him in my father's church. They were always called brother this or brother that. They were usually old, often palsied, smelled like strong soap, got weepy at prayer meetings, and would've gladly given you the shirts off their backs. No, I wasn't going to accept Brother Lillard's invitation because I'd served enough hard time parked on wooden pews.

"I hear you play the guitar," he said. "Bring it along. The Lord loves music."

I resisted suggesting he take up a collection to buy Him a record player.

Brother Lillard went off to talk with Adam and Junie. I was chilly from having sat so long in the damp. Still, I took a moment to study my work of the past two days. The combined grids made a shape like the trademark symbol for Chevrolet except that right in the center was a column of dirt that supported the tombstone. I stepped down and rubbed my hand over the surface of the stone. All the digging must have loosened it, for it fell over into the pit–thankfully, without breaking. But with it upended, I noticed a pointed indentation on the bottom, too perfectly square to be anything but man made. I hauled the Tombstone up out of the pit, planning once I'd written my report and backfilled the grids to put it back in its original location.

I lugged my tools back to the trailer, as I didn't think I would be using them again. I changed out of my damp clothes then sat down to write Adam a report on my findings. This took a while, for I wanted to be exacting, to give Adam his guitar lessons' worth. The hardest part was writing my conclusion. I had to be truthful, yet diplomatic, for Adam had had his heart set on finding the remains of Canara Rivers. It wouldn't do to write that this had all been a big fat waste of time.

CHAPTER 12

I was just finishing up my report when Adam drove up.

"We're eating with the Gorns again," he said. "Grab your guitar, 'cause we're gonna do some picking afterwards."

I pulled my guitar case from the closet, and put it in the truck alongside Adam's. As Adam put the truck in gear, I placed several sheets of paper on the dashboard. "That's a hand-written report on the excavation of the gravesite. I'll send you a typed copy as soon as I get back to Santa Barbara."

He lifted the pages and handed them back to me. "I don't need no copy. Just tell me what it says."

I turned past the cover page.

"Your own words would be fine."

"Well, basically it states that the area excavated doesn't appear to be a gravesite. I've described the condition of the soil and the abundance of rocks. I've also included this hand-drawn diagram showing the locations of several small pieces of the tombstone that I found on the surface." I looked up from the diagram. "Adam, I'm not sure it *is* a tombstone. I'm beginning to think that what we've been calling a tombstone is actually a piece off something bigger." I told him about the pointed notch in the bottom of the stone.

"Tarnation!" he said, hitting the steering wheel. "Sounds to me like it's a piece off a grinding stone. They got square holes in the center to put the axle through. But iff'n it's a grinding stone, how come the letters 'C R'?"

"Maybe Canara Rivers carved the letters to mark the grinding stone as being his."

Adam looked at me. "Now, why on earth would he do that? I mean, who's gonna steal a grinding stone?" He shook his head. "I'm sorry, Miss Parry. It seems I done brought you all this way out here for nothing."

"Don't be sorry. I'm glad I came. I mean, look at this place! It's fantastic! It's wooded and wild, dark and mysterious. It's seems like the loneliest place on earth until you realize just how much wildlife there is." As if to illustrate my point, a wood thrush fled before us, stopped to bob up and down on a rock before flowing off into the thicket. "Hoagland Holler is everything I imagine when I hear the word 'holler.'"

Adam began to sing "Dark Hollow," its lonesome lyrics in tune with the feel of the land. As I sang along, I half expected my well-developing warning system to start clanging. After all, I was having fun, which in my experience was a sure sign that I was about to be hit with a truckload of banjos. I studied Adam's face. I knew singing was as natural to him as breathing. Probably being happy was, too. So, didn't I have the right to be happy? Silly question. Adam was normal, I wasn't.

Dinner that night at the Gorns' was possum stew only I didn't know it was possum until well into my second helping. My reaction, when duly informed, was the cause of much hee-hawing and knee slapping among my fellow diners.

"But... but... it doesn't taste..."

"Something like a possum looks?" Adam offered.

"It doesn't taste... gamey," I said, in lieu of "rat-like" or something worse.

"That comes from the way I cook it," Beatty said. "First off, after I've skinned and gutted it, I let it soak overnight in salt water. Then 'fore I cut it up, I first rub it all over good with salt and pepper. 'Nother thing that keeps it from tasting gamey, as you say, is the spices I use: lots of onions and a few hot peppers to help draw out that wild taste. Then I simmer the meat till tender 'fore adding the vegetables."

I retrieved my spoon out of the stew where I dropped it. "I told

Adam there are possums living out behind my apartment in Santa Barbara. I wonder what my landlady Mrs. Esau would think if some night I invited her over for possum stew?"

"Well, iff'n you like, I'll send my recipe on home with you." Beatty frowned, seeing her son loading his plate with biscuits. "Junie, quit being a hog and pass them biscuits to Parry."

I took two and passed the plate to Beatty.

"So how goes the digging," she said, slathering a biscuit with butter.

Adam answered for me. "I'm afraid I done got the professor out here on a wild goose chase."

Beatty chuckled. "I had me a hunch that'd be the case. But iff'n you had found bones or anything, how would you know they was Canara Rivers'?"

"Well, the assumption was that the letters 'C R' on the tombstone stood for Canara Rivers," I said.

"But say there weren't no tombstone. Could you have still told iff'n it were Canara Rivers you was digging up?"

"Not unless I had medical records identifying specific physical features. People who work in the field of forensic science often use dental records when they're trying to identify a body. Without such information, about the best an examiner can do is to determine the person's sex, age, and race."

"You can tell all that just by looking at somebody's bones?" Junie said.

"Determining race is difficult, though I had a professor who was incredibly good at it. Sex and age are not all that hard, providing you have the right bones to work with. A woman's pelvic girdle is in the shape of a butterfly with wings extended, whereas a man's is like a butterfly with the wings partially folded. And a man has larger muscles, so the areas of attachment tend to be more built up. For instance..." I poked the upper part of my cheek, "...the area where the jaw muscles attach to the zygomatic arch is a more pronounced in men."

Everyone felt the side of his or her face.

"I thought it was the women folk who did all the jawing," Adam said.

"You better watch what you say," Beatty said, reaching out to probe Adam's cheek with her finger. "Parry might just be one of them liberated females."

"You probably won't be able to feel the difference because of all the skin and muscle tissue in the way," I said, "but if I had a woman's skull and a man's side-by-side, you'd be able to see it."

"But iff'n Canara Rivers had been shot," Junie said, "then you could tell it was him 'cause of the bullet hole."

I marveled that Junie was showing an interest, that he was actually being civil. "Without corroborative evidence a bullet hole by itself wouldn't identify the person. To positively identify someone, you need to know of some feature particular to him."

"You mean, something like this," Adam said. He took my hand and guided it along the ridge of his skull. "You feel 'em?"

"Tiny bumps?"

"That's peculiar to the Singers. My momma told me my daddy had the same thing."

"Well, iff'n we find a skull rolling 'round with them bumps on it," Beatty said, "we'll know who to return it to."

Everybody laughed except Junie who went back to being surly. "Hell, why're we wasting time on this? I thought we was gonna play some music."

While I helped Beatty clear the table, Adam got out our guitars. The rain had held off, so Adam and Junie went out onto the deck off the cavernous living room, leaving the double doors wide open. As Beatty and I washed and dried dishes, we were serenaded by Adam on guitar and Junie on harmonica. As much as it galled me to admit it, Junie was good. No, more than good; he was phenomenal. His notes were pure and precise even when matching the speed of Adam's guitar. And God, how that boy could bend a note! Like a blues player only with a tone quality of a violin. They played "Lee Highway Blues" then fairly peeled the paint off walls with a blistering "Devil's Dream."

"Junie's incredible," I told Beatty, as I stood drying a plate. "He should be on the Glen Campbell Show."

Beatty gave me the proud mother's smile. Then she took my dish towel and gave me a shove in the direction of the musicians. There was no way I could play lead at the speed they were playing, but I provided rhythm accompaniment, freeing Adam to play duets with Junie. Their harmony on "Eighth of January" gave my goose bumps goose bumps.

Beatty appeared with a gut-bucket bass. "It's a genuine Washburn," she said, pointing to the faded emblem on the side of the galvanized tub.

I've heard people deride the gut-bucket bass, but if the player can keep the pitch, it sounds almost as good as an acoustic bass, and to my ears, better than an electric one. With Beatty filling out the sound, we were suddenly a band, and thanks to Adam and Junie, a damn good one. Adam sang "Don't Let Your Deal Go Down." I waited until the chorus to come in with harmony:

Don't let your deal go down…

Junie swooped in and out to fill in between the first and second lines.

Don't let you deal go down…

Boom-chugga, boom-chugga, boom went Beatty's gut-bucket bass.

Don't let your deal go down,
Till you last gold dollar is gone.

Then we slowed it down and played "Keep on the Sunny Side" with Beatty and me doing our best to imitate Maybelle and June Carter. This was followed by Adam singing lead on "Nine Pound Hammer" before we upped the tempo once more on a bouncy "Roll In My Sweet Baby's Arms." Then Junie played the instrumental "Billy in the Low

Ground," again bending notes as if they were made of latex.

I was in heaven. No, I was in heaven's heaven, heedless that my state of euphoria inevitably would have to be paid for with days spent the prisoner of Mr. D.

Yet, I wasn't the only one feeling chipper: Adam's grin was working overtime; Beatty beamed; Junie managed not to glower. Even the local wildlife got caught up in the fun: cardinals, jays, and a Baltimore oriole danced around on nearby branches, while a squirrel clambered up onto the far end of the deck railing and sat with paws at the ready, as if he was going to clap along. Any second, I expected the appearance of Bambi and Thumper.

The setting sun managed to peek in under the heavy clouds, illuminating the craggy top of Skillet Mountain. " 'Rocky Top'!" I yelled, and damn if we didn't tear it up, put it back together, and tear it up again!

"Whew!" Adam said, wiping his hands on his jeans when we finished.

"Would you get a look at that!" Beatty said. Both her index and middle fingers had blisters on them. "I reckon I best quit whilst I still got some flesh left."

The three of us played "How Mountain Girls Can Love" and "Soldier's Joy," but it wasn't the same without Beatty. Then suddenly the sky opened and the rain came down in buckets. We rushed back into the house, shielding our instruments with our bodies. Adam declared the downpour the perfect opportunity to burn his brush pile, so we said our good-byes and left. With both guitar cases between my legs, I peered out the windshield as the wipers swung in rhythm to the music still going on in my head. To my great relief, the storm system didn't appear to be generating any lightning.

"That Junie can sure blow the harp, can't he?" Adam said.

"He really ought to be playing professionally."

Adam shook his head. "Junie's not ambitious that way. You may not believe it, but 'round most folks, he's actually kinda shy. His harp playing's the best way he knows to be sociable." He stopped his truck next to the brush pile. The rain had stopped as suddenly as it started. "You want to help me fire this thing?"

"Ordinarily, I would, but I'm pretty whupped. I'm not sure which tired me more, digging all day, or trying to keep up with you and Junie on guitar." Adam drove on. "You know, Adam, it was worth coming here just to play music like we did tonight." I was still drifting on a cloud, feeling as elated as the time Arnie Kostorsky accidentally swallowed paint thinner. I probably should have been shaking in my sneakers, for in my experience, the higher I climbed, the farther I fell.

Maybe this time it will be different. Maybe somebody up there has finally decided to cut me some slack.

Mentally, I put my words to the rhythm of the wipers. *May–be-some–one–up–there–likes–me.*

Stu-pid, stu-pid, stu-pid me.

CHAPTER 13

It seemed I had just fallen asleep when I woke with the need to visit the outhouse. Searching with my feet for my sneakers, I cursed myself for having had that extra glass of wine at dinner. I put on a sweater over my nightgown then opened the trailer door. All was strangely still: no thrumming cicadas, no crickets, no whip-poor-wills. There was something disquieting in this quiet. I stood a while listening, until my bladder reminded me of why I'd left my warm bed. I turned on the flashlight Adam had returned to me and stepped out upon the damp ground. The sound of my footsteps seemed intrusive, which might not have been such a bad thing, for I remembered reading somewhere it was always good to "announce your presence" when walking in the woods. It hadn't been a philosophy shared by my late father. One morning while camping in Yosemite, I came out of the campground restroom and ran smack into a black bear. Unperturbed, the bear detoured around me and went on his waddling way. I ran to tell my father, hoping to trigger some satisfying display of parental concern. All I got was a nod and an inquiry into how many slices of bacon I wanted with my eggs. It wasn't that my father was encouraging me to go bumping into bears, but the one fact he drummed into me time and time again was that the critters you really had to watch out for all walked on two legs.

Which was why I suddenly thought of Dewey Bone. If Dewey thought shooting at people in broad daylight was a kick, how much more so in the dead of night?

Then I told myself I was just being a sissy. " 'The valiant never taste of death but once!' " I proclaimed. No sleepless bird offered to dispute me; no cricket chirred in agreement; I didn't get so much as a rustle out of a leaf. Nevertheless, I found the Bard's words encouraging and repeated them like a mantra as I plodded on toward the outhouse.

Yet despite brave words, I was reluctant to leave the outhouse once finished, for I sensed something had scared the denizens of the woods into silence. I cracked open the door and swept the area with my flashlight. The light revealed nothing but wisps of ground fog. I stepped out of the outhouse, and just like in the horror flicks, my flashlight went out. I banged on it with my fist, and the light came back on, but ever so faintly. Then I realized I didn't need the flashlight; the rabbit hole had a light at the end of it, a fluttering false dawn made by Adam's bonfire. I almost laughed, for this explained the silence: the denizens of the woods, the screechers and chirpers and chatterers, had been made wary by something out of the ordinary: a fire.

Yet my relief was short lived, for the fire glowed menacingly, and I feared it had gotten out of control. I ran up the slope as fast the rain-soaked ground would let me. Alas, all my efforts earned me was the discovery that the ground fog's reflectivity had made the fire appear larger than it was. I stood watching as the wavering light backlit the schoolhouse, causing the upright studs to cast shadows like writhing serpents.

A sudden gust of cold wind made me wish for bed. But as I started back down the road, I thought I heard a sound.

I stopped. Listened. Nothing.

By this time, I was feeling thoroughly disgusted with myself. Obviously, the Bard hadn't been talking about me.

But then I heard it again: a sound like fingers drumming on the face of a guitar. I tried to remain calm, reasoning that it was likely a woodpecker, which was pretty sloppy reasoning as woodpeckers aren't nocturnal.

Ba-ba-ba-dum, ba-ba-ba-dum, ba-ba-ba-dum.

It was a clopping sound I recognized from movie Westerns. I immediately thought of Dewey Bone astride a dark stallion. My mental construct of Mr. Bone hadn't room for him being very literate, but the idea of a headless horseman riding out to strike terror into the hearts of all the Ichabod Cranes of Hoagland Holler likely would have appealed to his wicked sense of fun.

Ba-ba-ba-dum, ba-ba-ba-dum, ba-ba-ba-dum.

Perhaps it was a hunter. Adam told me a lot of men hunted these woods, even at night–especially at night. I saw myself fleeing before a pack of snarling bluetick hounds. I leapt off the road and hid behind a tree.

Ba-ba-ba-dum, ba-ba-ba-dum, ba-ba-ba-dum.

The sound was getting closer. Splashing water told me that, whatever it was, it had waded through the creek bed, which since the rains, had started to flow again. Any second, it would be rounding the curve at the bottom of the slope. I was afraid to look out from my hiding place. I was afraid not to. I risked a peek, a quick out and back with my head. Enough light from the bonfire made it down the rabbit hole to reveal a black horse carrying a rider whose loose cloak whipped about him. I had to hand it to Dewey Bone, the cloak was a truly gothic touch, causing me to taste a goodly many deaths.

Ba-ba-ba-dum! Ba-ba-ba-dum! Ba-ba-ba-dum!

In addition to the hoof beats, I could now hear the horse's labored breathing, a sound like steam escaping a boiler. Yet remembering my father's warning, it wasn't the horse, but the rider I feared.

Ba-ba-ba-dum! ba-ba-ba-dum! ba-ba-ba-dum!

I stood as still as a statue, albeit one with sweating pores and racing heart. Struggling to keep my wits, I willed horse and rider to some place far away. *Nebraska! Nebraska! Nebraska!*

There was a sudden break in the horse's stride, then the sound of hooves skidding to a stop. Could the rider have possibly seen me cowering behind the tree?

Please, God, make them disappear!

Of course, God already had a lousy track record when it came to granting my emergency requests. The horse began to move again, only not along the road, but slowly in my direction. I was debating whether to make a run for it, when I heard a woman's voice.

"Help me!" she cried. "Help me, please!"

I still didn't believe I'd been seen. But if not me, who was she talking to? Maybe Adam had come along to find out what all the ruckus was about.

"Help me, please!"

Help be damned! I was determined not to leave my place of relative safety. Yet my body had a will of its own, and I found myself inching out from behind the tree until I could see horse and rider not ten feet away. The horse was a tall black beast that I almost could have walked under, if I were crazy enough to go near it. As for the woman, she looked like the avenging angel, cloaked as she was all in black with a hood shadowing her face. In contrast was the small hand of pale white which she held out before her. As I moved toward that hand, the horse snorted and shook his head. I didn't need to be warned twice. I jumped back.

"Please," she cried, "you must save him!"

I wanted to tell her I was the last person to save anyone, but my mouth was as dry as a mummy's tomb; it was all I could do to croak, "Save who?"

Perhaps the woman hadn't seen me after all, for she turned quickly at the sound of my voice, and in turning, her cloak parted, revealing a white sackcloth dress.

I gasped.

Two things: one, the woman was obviously pregnant; two, she was bleeding. Even as I stood, watching, a crimson rose grew upon her chest. Then she swayed in the saddle. Choking back my fear, I moved to keep her from falling.

But the woman–perhaps as frightened of me as I of her–tugged on the reins, forcing the horse to step back.

"Please, save him!" she cried again.

I tried to put into my voice a calmness I didn't feel. "Don't be afraid. I want to help." I cautiously moved to close the distance between us, but she again pulled the horse back.

"Please, save him!"

Screw him! I wanted to tell her, but instead took a more mannered approach. "Look, lady, you're hurt. Now, I have a friend, and he's–"

The woman shook her head so violently, the hood of the cloak fell back, revealing her face.

Once again, I gasped, but this time because I recognized her face. It was a face I knew almost as well as my own, for hadn't it kept me company in the sleepless hours of the night? How many times had I studied that face, trying to will those loving eyes away from a gangly school teacher and upon me?

"Roseanne Bickum," I whispered.

She smiled ever so sweetly. "Save *him!*" she whispered back.

Then she fell forward onto the horse's neck. I rushed to catch her, but the damned horse spun about to keep his head between Roseanne and me. Somehow Roseanne managed stay in the saddle. I started around to the horse's other flank, but moved too quickly over the wet ground, and both of my feet shot out from under me. Time slowed. Rather than falling, I was floating in space with Roseanne Bickum hovering above me, a wounded angel with black wings. Then my head struck something hard, and everything went black.

CHAPTER 14

An old woman sat in a rocking chair, knitting. I wanted to ask her who she was and why I was lying in a strange bed in a strange room. But how to phrase both questions using the fewest words, for Mr. D threatened to kick the holy hell out of my occipital bone if I so much as licked my lips? I finally managed an ineloquent, "Aaarrruh!"

The woman set her knitting aside and hobbled out of the room. I closed my eyes, dozed, then woke to her trying to lift my head to drink from a china cup, a movement that set Mr. D to kicking with both feet.

"Aaarrruh!" I cried again, this time varying the inflection to indicate pain.

She released me, and I heard the sound of a chair being dragged across a wooden floor. Sitting beside me, she used a teaspoon to ladle hot liquid from the cup into my mouth. The liquid's grassy taste was partially masked with honey.

"What's–" She took advantage of my open mouth to ladle in another teaspoon. I gagged. Worse pain. As she dabbed my wet chin with a napkin, I grabbed her wrist. "What's this you're giving me?"

With no little strength, she pulled her hand away. Then she came at me with another spoonful. "Oh, just a little something to help you sleep: morphine, codeine, heroin and a pinch of cocaine the vet gives the horses."

I shoved the spoon away, spilling the liquid on the nightgown I wore.

"Child," she said, "it's just a tea made with a few good herbs– skullcap, valerian, and the like."

The herbs sounded on a par with raw opium. But whatever was in the tea was helping to pacify Mr. D, and when the woman offered another spoonful, I swallowed it. "Where am I?"

She gave me a look of mock surprise. "Why, in bed, of course."

Cute, a hillbilly comedienne.

"And where might this bed be?"

She fed me another spoonful. "Where else? In a house."

I shut up and let her spoon feed me. When the tea was gone, she dabbed my chin again with the napkin. "You're in my cabin," she said. "I'm Adam's grandma, Estelline Singer."

"What am I doing here?"

"Well, best as I can tell, you're lying down."

If it weren't for Mr. D and his antics, I would have strangled her. I felt like the city slicker in the song "The Arkansas Traveler." To each of the city slicker's questions, the hillbilly always played the smart aleck.

> *Hey there, hillbilly, can I take this road to Little Rock?*
> *Mister, Little Rock has its own road. You leave this one right here.*

The tea was having its intended effect. I couldn't keep my eyes open. "Where's Adam?" I muttered.

"He'll be back. Now, you hush and go onto sleep. You had a right bad concussion."

"I did?"

She stood and drew the blankets up over me. "Don't you remember?"

I shook my head. Bad move.

"Well, I reckon you'll remember soon enough. It's not something you're likely to forget."

I heard her moving off. "What isn't?"

"Seeing a ghost."

I chuckled. "Seeing a ghost, that's a good one." Adam's grandmother was a real card. I pictured a little shack, and Granny Estey sitting on a wooden barrel smoking a corncob pipe. *Hey there, hillbilly. I don't believe there's much between you and a fool.*

I didn't realize I'd spoken this last aloud.

"Just this cup I'm carrying," Granny Estey replied.

It was the same old nightmare, only this time I could see the usually faceless nurse. It was Adam's grandmother, and instead of electrodes, she was placing a shiny metal helmet over my head, like something out of a Sci-Fi flick.

"Skullcap," I muttered, nearly under from an anesthetic.

"No," she said, "it's valerian. Don't you remember?"

A different scene, my childhood bedroom. I was crying into my father's chest as he held me. "I don't remember anything!"

"Shhh," he said, wiping my tears with a calloused finger, "it'll come back. Everything will be all right."

"No, it won't. Nothing will ever be right again. Why did you make me?"

Then I was in my father's church, third pew from the front where we always sat. The congregation had their heads in the hymnals–all except me. I was studying Mrs. Cadwallader, the minister's wife. Behind her back, I always called her Mrs. Caterwauler for the way she sounded when she sang, like a cat being dragged by its tail, only not so mellifluous. This time, for some reason, I couldn't hear her, though her lips moved, mouthing different words than those being sung. I leaned forward, trying to lip read. Then she spun her head around toward me and with a rictus grin mouthed, "Abomination! ABOMINATION!"

Whenever I'm treated to a recurrence of my dream, I invariably wake up feeling lost–doubly so this time, since, for the life of me, I couldn't remember how I came to be lying here.

Braving Mr. D's umbrage, I sat up with a pillow tucked behind my back. From this position, I could see the rest of the room. A termite would have been in heaven, for not only was the furniture of wood, but the floor, walls, and ceiling. The ligneous effect was softened by weavings on the walls along with embroidered cloths draped over the furniture and a quilt on the bed patterned in a great star radiating outward in triangles of color. A large willow basket filled with balls of colored yarn sat on the floor next to the now empty rocking chair. From another room came the sound of someone plunking out the "Old One Hundred" on a piano. I was glad of the music, for it helped ground me. In my head, I sang the words

> *All people that on earth do dwell,*
> *Sing to the Lord with cheerful voice;*
> *Serve Him with joy, His praises tell,*
> *Come ye before Him and rejoice!*

The only part of any church service that I ever felt merited rejoicing was the hymn singing, providing you could get past the lyrics, which must have been written by lovelorn Methodist spinsters addicted to archaic verbiage. But the melodies themselves were often stirring. I wondered at my pleasure in hymns when I found all other aspects of church services so repugnant. I remember once talking to a violinist, a music student at the university who liked to slum around and play old-timey fiddle tunes. I remember him complaining about the relentless analyzing of great music by his professors. Asked why he put up with it, he replied that no amount of pedantry ever touched the music itself. All he had to do was hear a Mozart symphony, and all the intellectualizing broke away like shattered glass entombing a sleeping princess. Likewise, no moral drivel spewed from the pulpit could ever blemish those sacred melodies for me.

"I thought you might be awake."

I started at the sound of Mrs. Singer's voice. Rapt in thought, I hadn't noticed the music had stopped. She laid an embroidered cloth across my lap (blue flowers climbing on a vine) and atop this a sandwich served on a delicate plate of bone china.

"I should get up," I said, not really wanting to.

"You best stay put. Rest is the best thing for a crack on the noggin.

Besides, never refuse a chance to be waited on."

She sat in her rocking chair and took up her knitting. The sandwich was chicken along with things unfamiliar to my palate. I peeled back the bread to see what all was underneath.

"'Fraid I might be poisoning you again?" Mrs. Singer said.

"No, I was just wondering what was in this."

"Well, the greens are watercress and lamb's quarter, both picked fresh this morning."

"And the little black specks?"

"Black specks? Mercy me, must've forgot to wash the black flies off them greens."

My head shot up.

"Or maybe it's just a bit of ground pepper. Don't rightly remember. Comes from getting old, I reckon. Why, sometimes I find myself doing funny things like talking to my bedpost. Must say, for a bedpost, it's right smarter than most folks I know."

Just for that, I refused to tell her how delicious the sandwich was. I just hoped she'd pull her tongue out of her cheek long enough to explain how I came to be here. Then again, maybe she wasn't planning to. I remember Adam saying that torture couldn't make his grandmother do what she didn't want to do. What Mrs. Singer didn't know was that I had access to the ultimate weapon for loosening tongues, a recording of "Yellow Submarine" played on a banjo.

I finished my sandwich and laid the plate and napkin on the bedside table. Mrs. Singer, rocking slowly back and forth, started to hum somewhat tunelessly. For some reason, I felt a chill and pulled the blankets up over my chest. Then I realized she was humming the melody to "The Teacher of Hoagland Holler School."

"You're starting to remember now, aren't you?" she said.

"Remember what?"

"Who it was you saw on the road."

"All I remember is using a flashlight with nearly dead batteries to visit the outhouse. I guess I must have tripped and hit my head."

"I see." She pulled out a length of yarn out of her basket. "You always in the habit of walking backwards?"

Yes, well, there was that slight deficiency in my explanation; most people when they trip hit the *front* of their heads.

She set her knitting down into the basket. "Mind iff'n a crazy old woman tells you what she thinks happened?"

I signed for her to go ahead.

"Last night, my grandson, sleeping up there in his tool shed, was woken from a sound sleep, which is a wonderment in itself 'cause most times you can't wake that boy using gunpowder. So, he went and lit a lantern to see who was out there doing all the hollering. He found you laid out on the ground within spitting distance of that schoolhouse he's building, which, the way I see it, is a mite out of the way for someone just out to visit the outhouse, unless you're one of them sleepwalkers. Are you?"

I shook my head.

"Well, Adam saw right off you were hurt 'cause there was blood mingled in with the mud you were lying in. Thing is, that wasn't the only thing he saw. Ever'where 'round you was hoof prints, big ones made by a horse like that black gelding name of Atlas that Roseanne Bickum was so fond of."

I raised a hand to stop her. "Roseanne died almost seventy years ago. Are you telling me I was attacked by the world's oldest horse?"

"Just hold on and let me finish. You weren't attacked at all. The way I see it, you saw the ghost of Roseanne Bickum astride Atlas, which is reason 'nough for a body to want to back away quick-like. Problem is, that bit of land up there is mighty rocky, and you fell backward and dinged your head."

I held my up palms up like trays on a scale. "Let's see, either I tripped in the dark and somehow hit the back of my head, or I had the wits scared out of me by a ghost. Hmmm. Which seems more plausible?"

She leaned forward. "Before you go to weighing in on a decision, let me tack on a few more facts. You're not the first one to have seen the ghost of Roseanne Bickum, not by a long shot. That area up there

by the schoolhouse is her old haunts, and when things are just right–
like when something lights up the sky–then she rides out again,
thinking the school's afire and she has to save her true love."

"I see. And I take it you've seen this ghost."

She leaned back. "Can't say I have, and more's the pity 'cause
there's something I've been wanting to ask Roseanne."

"What's that?"

"I want to know what she done with that nice straw hat I loaned
her."

She went back to her knitting, explanation apparently over. I pulled
at a loose thread on the quilt as I thought about what she said. Of
course, I didn't believe a word of it, but damn if it didn't make a good
story, essentially repeating the chorus of "The Teacher of Hoagland
Holler School."

> *Oh, don't you know when the icy north wind moans,*
> *There's a ghostly horse and rider out upon the road;*
> *Oh, can't you hear, hoof beats loud and clear,*
> *She's come to warn the teacher, the one she loved so dear.*

I wish I *had* seen a ghost. It would have been exciting, and, in a
way, far less disturbing than not being able to remember what actually
happened. I realized I was probably experiencing temporary amnesia
brought on by my head injury, but any memory loss was troubling
because of what my shrink Herschbach had put me through.

"Have you *ever* seen a ghost?" I said.

"Child, I see ghosts all'r time." She looked up from her knitting.
"Fact is, there's two in this room right now, one to each side of you."

Involuntarily, I glanced left-right.

"Course one isn't a ghost exactly, but your guardian angel. He
always stands on your right side." She set her knitting in her lap and
studied the area off to my left. "Now the other one is a man in his
middling years, not too tall–kind of wiry. He's got a kind face and eyes
'bout the color of periwinkle blossoms, and there's a little red scar up

there 'long side his nose. Looks like he must have got that nose busted sometime or other. He's wearing a large belt 'round his waist for tools: pliers, screwdrivers, and such. And he's got a white hat on like ball players wear, only this one has the name of some company on it." She squinted. "Hard to see from here, something about electric–"

"Stop it! Stop it!" I cried, covering my face to hide the rush of tears. She had described my father right down to the scar he got when he'd run into the sharp end of a broken branch while out birding. How was that possible? How could she have known what my father looked like when the only person I ever talked to about him was my pen pal Teddy? I gripped the quilt, wanting to rip it apart.

"How come you can see him and I can't?" I cried. "What makes you so goddamn–" Another flood of tears. God, I missed my father. There was so much I wanted to tell him, so much I needed to hear him say. His death had been so unfair! One morning he was helping me pack my lunch, and a few hours later a police officer come to escort me home from school.

Mrs. Singer, clicking her knitting needles, didn't bother to offer me something for my runny nose. Out of sheer resentment, I used the fancy lap cloth.

"Do you really see my father?" I said.

Silence.

"Goddamn it! I have a right to know."

" 'Tain't a matter of rights," she said. "It's a matter of seeing. Everybody's got a guardian angel, and most folks got dead kin looking out for 'em sometime or other."

"You *are* crazy, you know that?"

She pulled up a length of yarn. "Crazy least by your educated standards. A person has got to be a bit crazy to see ghosts. A person has got to stop looking at the world with a book-learning mind, got to learn to see with the heart."

"Well, I guess not all of us are blessed with eyeballs on our aortas."

Silence.

I dabbed my nose again, suddenly feeling very tired and very, very lost. "Sorry. Adam may have told you I tend to use sarcasm a lot."

"Use it myself. It's a good defense against fools."

"Am I a fool?"

She shook her head. "You're just not crazy 'nough to see ghosts."

"I think I'm crazy enough by most standards."

"A body has got to be made crazy by grief, got to have her eyes opened by pain. Then she'll see ghosts."

"Listen! I miss my father every day of my life. I hate myself for being what I am. Isn't that pain enough?"

She set her knitting in her lap. "Tell me, what in this room speaks to you of your daddy?"

There was little that reminded me of him; it was a woman's room, full of feminine things. I pointed to an electrical outlet. "My father, as you may have gathered, was an electrician."

"Is that all you see?"

"Well…" I pointed to the Bible on the stand beside her rocker. "…my father was very religious. He truly believed that the Bible was the word of God."

She nodded. "What else?"

It was kind of like a game of "I spy." I ran my hand across the flowers stitched into the hem of the top sheet. "My father loved nature, especially birds. Next to going to church, he loved to be out bird watching." I leaned forward and placed my hand in the center of the quilt. "He loved to study the stars. He would sometimes get me up in the middle of the night to show me the constellations, especially when we were out camping. He liked his work. It pleased him to do a job well. And he liked to work on his truck, which had all those tool compartments on the sides." I smiled. "He loved hamburgers. There was a place not far from our house that made the greatest burgers–cooked on a grill–and the world's thickest milk shakes. We used to go there every payday."

"You're seeing hamburgers in this room?" she said.

"Well, no. It's just you got me talking about my father."

"What 'bout his children?"

"What do you mean?"

"What did he love 'bout his children?"

"I was his only child."

"Well, then, what did he love 'bout you?"

I rubbed my forehead with both hands. "I don't know. I guess he liked that I was smart and did well in school. I know he liked to take me camping." I had a sudden image of him sitting in his recliner, reading the newspaper as I plunked away on the guitar. "He said he liked to listen to me practice guitar, but I think he was just trying to be encouraging."

"Did your daddy love you?"

"Of course, he–"

"Did he love the way you smiled? Did he love the little tricks you used to play on him as a child, hiding his things? Did he love to tuck you into bed, or carry you from the car asleep in his arms? Did he love the way you would hold out your baby arms, wanting to be hugged?"

I blinked back tears. "Yes, I suppose he did, but he never spoke about such things."

"A child doesn't know her parent. A parent hardly knows himself. But all the things you see that remind you of your daddy are more than just memories; they're where you should be looking for your daddy to contact you from the hereafter."

I bit my cheeks to keep from laughing.

She sighed. "Ever have a time when you was afraid, or something important was 'bout to happen, even if you didn't know it at the time, and out of the blue there was something that reminded you of your daddy?"

"No! And I'm certain I would have–" Then I remembered the other day, seeing the cardinal just before I stumbled off the Knob, just before Dewey Bone shot at me.

"Spit it out, child. You're cogitating on something."

So, I told her what had happened, playing down the cardinal's significance.

She nodded her head. "That redbird was your daddy. He made you to stumble and saved you from being kilt."

"That's nonsense. I wouldn't have been killed anyway. Dewey Bone was just trying to scare me."

"Now, let me tell you something you don't know. Last Saturday they brought Dewey right into this very room 'cause the boiler on his still done blew apart and scalded the poor man something bad. It's gonna be a long time 'fore he'll be doing any shooting with his hands bandaged the way they are."

"But if it wasn't Dewey shooting at me, who was it?"

"Most likely some hunter's shot gone astray. But the point is, it was your daddy, through that there redbird, that done saved you." She picked up her knitting. "You know, when you said your daddy liked to watch birds, I just got this twitchy feeling. Now after what you just told me, I'm sure as eggs in April that your daddy's been using birds to try and reach you."

"Wait a minute. You're telling me that if I see some bird, it's my father trying to communicate with me?"

"If that bird got no call to be there, like that time atop the Knob, then that's exactly what I'm telling you."

"But there are a hundred possible explanations for that cardinal to have been there. I was standing nearly still and–"

"That's your book-learning mind talking. I'm telling you to stop looking with your mind and see with your heart. Your mind can always find a thousand reasons for something, but there's only one reason when you see with your heart."

"But that still doesn't make sense. If my father was truly trying to communicate, why wouldn't he just appear to me like–"

"Like the way Roseanne did?"

"Like the way he appears to you right now."

"Let me tell you first off that your seeing Roseanne is a horse of a different color. That was a matter of being at the right place at the right time. A terrible thing happened that night ol' Bickum laid his ambush. Two of God's favored children were kilt, and when something terrible like that happens, it leaves a streak across time. It's like a scratch on a record, and ever'time when things are just right, that record skips and plays over again. That's what happened when you saw Roseanne. And that record will to go on skipping until such time as things is set to rights.

"As for seeing your daddy, you don't have the sight. There's two ways a body gets the sight. A few folks are just born with it. I suspect that Canara Rivers was one of them. The rest of us get it through pain, through wanting it bad enough. Just hope you never have pain so bad you gotta have it. What you should be doing is trying to see your daddy in the little things, for that's mostly the way the dead talk to us. And remember this: your daddy isn't gonna try forever to reach you. He's got other things he needs to be doing."

"But what could my father be trying to tell me?"

"Child, that's not for me to say. That's for you to pay attention and find out."

CHAPTER 15

Following our little discussion, Mrs. Singer gave me another infusion of tea, and I slept. I don't know when I'd slept so much, when I allowed myself to slip down into Oblivion's waters and forget the world and all its cares. I decided I should get concussions more often.

When I awoke, it was night. A candle burned on the table next to the rocking chair where Adam now sat. He was finger picking "Windy and Warm," an aptly named tune if there ever was one. I closed my eyes and pretended to be still asleep, for I wanted nothing more than to float upon the notes flowing out of his guitar.

For years, I'd lived on a what I called a scary-go-round, strapped to a wooden horse, sometimes going up, most times going down, but always stuck going in circles. Adam's guitar playing gave me hope of getting unstuck. Under his spell, I felt a different person, someone released from fear and self-loathing. Instead of clinging to my fence, I knew what it was to be the person I longed to be: confident, happy, glad to be alive. Nothing else in the world, not a discovery on a dig, nor an academic achievement, and certainly nothing gotten while sitting on a hard pew, ever made me feel that way. In my life, Adam's music was all the joy I had.

The bed sagged under Adam's weight.

"Hey there, Miss Parry."

I opened my eyes and found them blurred by tears.

"You all right?"

I wasn't all right. I doubted I'd ever be all right. I didn't know how to be all right. Herschbach always said the first step was to talk openly about things, but if that were true, how come I didn't get better back when I was talking to him? Maybe because talking to Herschbach was like talking to a door, and who gives a damn what you say to a door?

But it really mattered what I said to Adam, because I didn't want to say anything that would make him not like me. But who was this "me" I wanted him to like? Certainly not the person he'd had sex with. But was it better to let him think me that person, or risk losing his friendship by revealing who I truly was? Yet such a revelation seemed unfair to me because I'd struggled for years not to be that person.

Scary-go-round.

Then again, who said I had to tell him everything? Perhaps I could take a few steps away from my scary-go-round, then hop right back on if things got too hairy.

I slid over on the bed so he'd have a little more room to sit. "Did your grandmother tell you she thought I saw the ghost of Roseanne Bickum?"

He grinned. "I admit to being a mite jealous."

"You want to see a ghost?"

"Well, not just any ghost, but for sure Roseanne Bickum. After all, it was me who gone and wrote a song 'bout her."

"Did your grandmother also tell you I can't remember what happened?"

He nodded.

"Adam, can I tell you something? It really scares me not to be able to remember."

"Don't worry, Miss Parry, you will. Granny says in a couple of days, when you're feeling better, it will all come back to you."

"That's not exactly what I mean." I tried to sit up, but Adam had me pinned under the covers. He immediately stood up. When I got comfortably repositioned, I motioned for him to sit back down. "Only a couple of people know this, but back when I was sixteen, I lost the memory of everything that happened during the previous six months."

"What happen? Did you hit your head?"

"You might say it was something like that. I can't tell you exactly."

Adam pulled on his mustache. "I see. Well, did your memory ever come back?"

I looked at the candle. Curlicues of black smoke rose from the flame. *It'll come back, Paradigm. Everything will be all right.*

"No," I said, "it never did. Those six months are still just a big blank."

"That sounds a mite scary."

A mite? What did I as a girl of sixteen have going for me? What did I have that made me feel good about myself? My social skills? My athleticism? The only thing I could claim was an above average intelligence. Then they took an eraser and wiped out part of my brain. And for what?

Those were the blackest days of my life, days when I cried, screamed, raged, broke furniture, threw my mineral collection through a window. I refused to go to school, refused to eat or leave my bedroom. I made life hell for my father, for Herschbach, for anyone within earshot.

But wrecking my father's house didn't change the fact that there was nothing I, nor anyone else, could do to retrieve my lost memory. Six months of my life had been vaporized, and I had to choose between slitting my throat–an option seriously considered–or going on and working around the blank spot in my brain. Six months of memory loss meant six months of classes that had to be repeated. My father, no doubt feeling guilty, hired a tutor for me. First thing I did was bombard him with questions concerning the arrangement of atoms in organic compounds and had his lazy ass running out the back door in less than ten minutes.

Yet making up classes was far easier than living every day with a patch of gray fog in my head. In the years since, I've tried my best to shunt that grayness off onto a sidetrack, but it's still there, though thankfully shrinking in size as new memories have crowded in around it.

Adam gave my hand a squeeze. "I'm sorry 'bout you losing your memory that time, but now you gotta believe Granny when she says you'll get your memory back. She may not be college trained, but there's no better person in all Pamunkey County for doctoring somebody up."

I didn't know as I believed him, but I gave his hand a squeeze in return. "Thank you for letting me open up to you."

"Anytime, Miss Parry. It just grieves me to think your coming here has caused you so much pain."

"Please, don't feel bad. I'm still glad I came. Where else but Hoagland Holler can a person get shot at and scared by a ghost, both inside of forty-eight hours? I'm just sorry the dig turned out to be a bust."

Adam shrugged. "I figure what's meant to be is what's meant to be. I reckon as soon as you're back on your feet, you'll be wanting to head on back to Santa Barbara."

"Actually, if you don't mind, I'd like to stay a while longer. I could still make myself useful by doing the electrical wiring on the schoolhouse."

"Shucks, Miss Parry, you don't need to do that. It'd be good to have you stay on just for the pleasure of your company." Adam stood up. "Well, Granny told me not to tire you over long."

I was grateful to Granny, because I was once again feeling the need of Oblivion's water.

"By the way," Adam said, turning at the doorway. "I stuck your letter in the mailbox 'long side the church."

"Letter?"

"You know, to your friend Teddy."

"Oh, right. Thanks." I didn't remember giving Adam a letter to mail. More memory loss, I guess. Right now, I was too tired to care.

CHAPTER 16

Two days later, I felt well enough to move back into the trailer. Adam wasn't around to transport me in his truck, but it wasn't far to walk. It was just my kind of morning for a stroll: overcast, not a sky in the cloud. The trailer, when I arrived, smelled of wet possum, or how I imagined wet possum smelled, so I left the door open to air things out and sat outside on a tree stump and worked on a song I'd been thinking about while laid up. I thought I was making progress until I rearranged a few words and short circuited all my rhyme schemes. I tore up what I'd written then returned to the trailer for what I thought would be a short nap, but did not wake until late afternoon. I ran some water over my face, then went up to see how Adam was progressing on the schoolhouse. I found him struggling to raise a wall all by himself. I rushed to his aid and together we got it upright.

"You shouldn't have done that, Miss Parry," said Adam, holding the wall steady with one hand and wiping the sweat off his face with the other. "You're still ailing."

I handed him a two-by-four stud to prop up the wall with. "What happened to Junie? I thought he was helping you."

"I'm afraid me and Junie had a few words. He skedaddled on out of here yesterday, and I've not seen hide nor hair of him since."

I didn't bother to ask what the quarrel was about. With Junie, it could have been anything: the price of a penny stick of gum. I sat on a stack of plywood and watched as Adam framed up another wall until Beatty arrived in the jeep.

"Just come by to see how Parry was doing," she said. "Word has it you was trampled by a herd of ghost horses."

What she said reminded me of the song "Ghost Riders in the Sky."
"Actually, it was a herd of red-eyed cattle."

She got the allusion. "Then you'd best mend your ways, for sure."
We both laughed, then she slipped her arm through mine. "Seriously,
honey, how you feeling?"

"I think I'm on the mend. I just helped Adam lift a wall, and I
didn't feel any pain or dizziness."

"Well, iff'n that's the case," Adam said, "maybe I could get you
two lovely ladies to help me raise another wall."

"Well," Beatty said, giving me a wink, "since you put it that way."

It was a large wall, made to partition the entire width of the
downstairs, but with the three of us lifting, it went up easily. Adam toe
nailed it temporarily in place.

"What's this gonna be?" said Beatty, stepping into the space
created behind the wall.

"The kitchen and pantry," Adam said.

"And what was it in the original schoolhouse?"

"There wasn't any wall here. Granny told me the whole downstairs
was all one big room 'cept for a large coat room near the front door.
I'm gonna make that the downstairs bathroom. The wall right behind
you was where they hung the blackboard, and above that they had a
big picture of General Washington."

"I believe I got me one of them pictures lying 'round somewhere,"
Beatty said. "You're welcome to it, iff'n I can find it." Beatty stepped
back through the partition. "I wanted you two to know dinner is at six,
and don't be late 'cause I'm fixing squirrel pie and I don't want it
getting cold."

"Do we have 'nough time to go for a swim?" Adam said.

"Son, why you want to go bathing in that ol' pond when we got us
a nice shower up to the house?"

"I reckon it's my duty to give Dewey Bone his target practice."

"Well, what about Parry? Maybe she'd like a civilized bath."

"That's all right," I said. "I had a bath this morning at Mrs. Singer's.
I was wondering though if I could use your phone to call my landlady?"

"Course you can. Fact, why don't you ride on up to the house with me now, and we'll let Adam follow after he's done his target duty."

Perhaps out of concern for my recent head injury, Beatty kept her speed under Mach one, allowing to me to take in some of the scenery. The thin cloud covering held in the day's warmth, but it was cool under the trees that bordered the creek.

"How's the bottled water business?" I said.

"Fine. Just fine. Think I might've found me a couple of distributors, one down in Baltimore, and another near to D.C."

When we got to her house, Beatty showed me where the phone was then rushed off to check on her pie. The time in Santa Barbara was past two in the afternoon. Mrs. E answered after the fifth ring.

"Hello?" She sounded a little out of breath.

"Did I pull you away from your roses?"

"Paradigm! It's about time you called. I've been worried."

I held the receiver away from my ear since Mrs. E seemed to think the telephone line inadequate for the distance. "I'm sorry, but when my plane arrived at Dulles, it was two in the morning, and then Adam doesn't have a phone. I'm using his neighbor's. How are you?"

"I'm fine. My doctor hasn't managed to kill me yet. What's it like where you are?"

"Very different than Santa Barbara. Everything's green. And it's humid."

"Sounds like Indiana where I grew up. Have you found what you were looking for?"

"I'm afraid not. Turns out, the gravesite isn't a gravesite."

"Well, I'm sorry to hear that. Does that mean you'll be coming home soon?"

"Actually, that's one of the reasons I called. I'm going to stay on a while and help Adam with the house he's building."

"Well, just don't let him work you too hard. You're always overdoing it. Did you read about the students here setting fire to the Bank of America?"

"No, I didn't. They don't get the newspaper here."

"Well, they did, and it's just disgraceful. Makes me want to go out there and give them what for with my cast iron skillet. Why one of them had the nerve—"

"Mrs. E, I can't talk too long. This is long distance."

"Of course, dear, sorry. You just go along and enjoy yourself and forget about all the nonsense going on here. Oh, but the way, I hope you don't mind, but I read one of your pieces of mail. It was a newsletter from the university, and I happened to see your picture on the front."

Dr. Webb had been busy. "Yes, I wrote an article for the alumni newsletter about what I planned to do here." I wondered where Webb had gotten the picture. Probably from my grad school application.

"Should I send the newsletter to you?"

"No, I'll see it when I get back." I then gave her Beatty's phone number in case of emergency. "I'll call you when I've made arrangements for my flight home."

"Fine, dear. You take good care of yourself, now."

"You do the same. Don't overdo it in the garden."

"There's no rest for the wicked" She laughed. "Or so they say."

I went to the kitchen where Beatty was bent over the oven rack, attacking a bubbling pie with a fork. I placed money on the kitchen counter.

"What's that for?" she said.

"For the phone call."

"Fiddlesticks! You just go on and put that right back in your pocket."

"My father taught me to always pay my debts."

"Well, your daddy taught you right, but you're my guest, and in this house, being a guest means free use of the phone." When I still hesitated, she added, "Iff'n you don't take that money back, I'm a gonna give it to Brother Lillard and his holy rollers, and wouldn't that be a waste?"

I folded the money and pocketed it. "Thank you. You've been very kind to me."

"Must've caught me on a good week." She slid the rack back in the oven. "This needs a bit more time. How 'bout a drink 'fore dinner, that is iff'n it wouldn't be bad for your head."

"A small drink would be nice."

We went into the dining room where a decanter and liquor glasses sat upon a lace doily in the center of the table. I took my accustomed seat while Beatty poured clear liquid into two glasses.

"Here's to health," she said, raising her glass.

We clinked glasses and I took a sip. "Wow! This is definitely not water."

"What you got there is some of Hoagland Holler's finest moonshine."

In my mind, "moonshine" always conjured up a potation as palatable as kerosene, a rot gut guaranteed to make the imbiber snort fire and jerk about with St. Vitus' dance. But Beatty's moonshine had little taste and pleasantly warmed my esophagus as it went down. I was pretty sure she made it herself, but knew enough not to ask.

"Maybe you want me to add a little spring water to it?" Beatty said.

"No, this is fine." I took another sip. "Very smooth," I added, trying to sound like I knew what I was talking about.

"So, how's it feel, seeing a ghost?"

I set my glass down. "I didn't. The ghost story is one of Adam's grandmother's fabrications, and by her own admission, she's a bit crazy."

"Well, I know for a fact that Estelline Singer's got mor'n a few loose screws, but seeing actual ghosts ain't all that uncommon for folks here in Hoagland Holler."

"Have you ever seen one?"

"Yes'm, I did. That was back during the war. I was by myself, not far from here, and saw a man who'd been dead nearly forty years."

"And you knew who he was?"

"Yes'm. He told me. He also had the same look as his daddy who I seen a picture of."

The buzzer on the oven timer went off. " 'Scuse me a moment,

Parry."

I sipped some more moonshine. It was making me mildly euphoric. I wondered if I could sneak some back on the plane with me.

"Pie's done," said Beatty, coming back into the dining room. "That Adam best be getting here soon iff'n he knows what's good for him." She sat down and picked up her glass. "I wished you truly had seen the ghost of my aunt Roseanne. I'd like to know how she looked. My momma told me she was pretty heavy with child that night she went out to warn Canara Rivers."

"She was pregnant? But I thought she was supposed to be marrying the banker."

Beatty laughed. "You gotta understand some folks attitude 'bout children is a mite different here than most places. There's nothing unusual or shameful 'bout a man and woman doing a little early honeymooning. And a baby's a blessing, even if he ain't yours. The important thing is that the child gets loved and provided for."

I pictured Roseanne Bickum made even more beautiful by the flush of pregnancy. "She must have looked like a Madonna," I said, "which doesn't quite jibe with the image of someone in the business of issuing curses."

Beatty set her glass down hard on the table. "Now, let me tell you a little something 'bout that curse. It's just a bunch of hooey dreamed up by a lot of ignorant hillbillies with nothing better to do than to sit 'round on their behinds, spitting tobacco juice into coffee cans and swapping lies. Why, Roseanne Bickum was no more like her daddy than Jesus is like the Devil! She was sweetest and kindest person God ever placed upon this earth, and no more able to curse somebody than I'm able to lift up this here table. And I got that straight from my momma, and who knew better than Roseanne's own sister?"

"But what about her father and brothers all dying within one year of her murder?"

"What about it? Her daddy, damn his soul, died of a heart attack, which was hardly a surprise, considering the man was a glutton and a heavy drinker to boot. And her brothers died in a mining accident. What's so strange about a mining accident? They was as common as door knobs on doors–still are!"

"Who's doing all that hollerin'?" Adam said, coming into the room.

Beatty smiled. "Was I hollerin'? I was just setting the record straight 'bout Roseanne and that silly curse of hers." Beatty leaned across the table and patted my hand. "Sorry, Parry, iff'n I got a bit riled up there, but I've been fighting hillbilly ignorance all my life. That's the real curse 'round here. Makes it mighty hard doing business with city folks. They don't want nothing to do with tobacco snorting hillbillies and their ignorant superstitions."

She stood up. "Boy, you're late. That squirrel pie best not be cold, or you're gonna see me riled up for sure."

CHAPTER 17

Adam had gotten out the blueprints for his schoolhouse, and I studied the wiring diagram as we ate breakfast at the picnic table. "Were you kidding when you said you wanted a lot of electrical outlets for guitars and amps?"

Adam, seated across from me, pointed using his fork with fried egg stuck to it. "If you could just put a few extra right there along the north wall, that'll be plenty."

With a carpenter's pencil, I drew several outlet symbols then looked over the blueprints some more while Adam cleared up the breakfast dishes–throwing them in the direction where the burn pile used to be. The most complex wiring involved a couple of three-way switches. Fortunately, Adam had seen fit to install a large breaker panel, so I wouldn't have to scrimp on the number of circuits I could run. Satisfied, I rolled up the blueprints then went to Adam's tool shed for a hammer and a few other tools. As I nailed in outlet and switch boxes to the framing members, Adam came behind me, drilling holes to run the wires through. It was pleasant work. Junie wasn't around to sow discord, no lightning storms loomed on the horizon, and outside of halfhearted rumblings by Mr. D, all was surprisingly well with Parry Euphrates.

"Do you want me to go ahead and install the switches and outlet receptacles?" I said.

"Might as well. Fact, you can go right on ahead and connect them all up to the main panel. That ways, I won't have to be dragging extension cords 'round ever'where."

"All right, but just be careful you don't nail into a wire and fry yourself."

Once we pulled a few more wires, I connected up a temporary ceiling light, and Adam scrounged up a bulb to test it. "Ta da!" I said, as the light came on. "Now you can work night and day if you want."

By then it was lunch time. Beatty hadn't sent down any of her culinary delicacies, and I had to be content with Adam's edibles, or barely edibles, this time peanut butter and jelly on stale bread.

"I keep forgetting to get ice for the ice chest," Adam said, tapping a stale slice of bread against the edge of the picnic table.

"Where do you get groceries? So far, all I've seen is the church with its sagging post office."

"Nearest place is the Piggly Wiggly up to Damascus, but Beatty lets me store meat and things in her freezer."

"Well, I've experienced Beatty's cuisine, so I can guarantee your hot dogs are safe from any raids from her."

Adam smiled as best he could with a mouth welded shut with peanut butter.

"Beatty has this incredible zest for life," I said. "I wish I could be more like her."

Adam swallowed. "Beatty's something else, all right. She's been like a second momma to me."

"You've never told me much about your mother. Where is she now?"

"Long Beach, California. Eventually, she gave up on my daddy, figuring him dead. And with me already up and growed, she remarried. Floyd, my step daddy, spent some time during the war in southern California and always had a hankering to go back. So, after he and momma got hitched, they up and moved. Floyd got himself a good job working on the docks, and he and momma bought a nice, three-bedroom house. With all that extra room, they invited me to come live with them, and I figured, why not? In California, I found me some other misplaced hillbillies, and we put a band together. I reckon you know the rest of my sad story."

"Young musical genius becomes guitar-playing legend."

"Becomes starving fool, more like."

"Becomes rock 'n' roll star and finds fame and fortune."

"Sounds good to me, 'specially that fortune part. I pert near used up all my savings buying building materials for this here schoolhouse. I just hope I bought 'nough so's I can get ever'thing weather tight 'fore winter comes on."

"Can I ask you another personal question?"

"Yes'm, but it's gonna cost you."

I shot him the same look I used on students who tried to sneak bones out of the anthropology lab to use to make pipes. "Cost me?"

He pointed at the remains of my sandwich. "The rest of that there sandwich, that is iff'n you're not fixing on eating it."

He actually spared me the dilemma of whether to openly pitch my host's food into the bushes or wait until he wasn't looking. Adam took a bite of my sandwich then nodded for me to go ahead with my question.

"Your grandmother and I talked a bit about you. Am I right that she doesn't exactly approve of your career choice?"

"Mor'n right; more like she hates it. Granny's always had this fixation that I shoulda been a doctor like my daddy. Some of it has to do with a bit of mountain lore that says when a man dies leaving an unborn child, then that baby will have the gift of healing. Course that's crazy 'cause I'd make 'bout as good a doctor as Granny would make an astronaut."

"There are different types of healing. I don't know if I'd be here today without your music; it's gotten me through some dark times. You should tell that to your grandmother next time she complains about your chosen profession."

"I thank you for saying that, Miss Parry, but Granny's got a one-track mind. When she says healer, she means doctor."

We went back to work. I continued to wire receptacles while Adam hammered in more outlet boxes. About mid-afternoon, my steam ran out. I could almost hear the whoosh. Too tired to walk down to the trailer, I folded up a piece of canvas tarp and used it for a pillow as I lay on the subfloor. I slept hard, oblivious to the noise of Adam's hammering. When I awoke, the sun was well in the west. All was quiet save for Adam whistling "Sail Away Ladies" somewhere outside the building. I staggered over to the rough door opening, and held onto the frame as I looked out. Adam was picking up pieces of scrap wood and making a neat pile of them.

"God, I really crashed," I said. "I didn't even hear you hammering. Were you?"

"Yes'm," Adam said, kicking a scrap of wood to loosen it from the dirt. "Then I drilled out some more holes. When I came to get you to help me pull some more wire, I found you out like a light."

"Sorry. We can do that now, if you like."

"Naw, it'll keep. I got a feeling you're not quite as mended as you think."

"Well, if appetite is any indication, I am. I wonder what Beatty's cooking for dinner? That squirrel pie last night was delicious."

"Actually, Beatty's gonna join us down here tonight. She's bringing along some steaks I've been saving for a special occasion."

"What's the occasion?"

"Why, haven't you heard? Brother Lillard is fixing to have church tonight."

I'd forgotten all about Brother Lillard and his invitation. "Are you going?"

Adam grinned. "Weren't planning to, but that's no reason why we can't have something special anyhow."

He carried his armful of scraps to the grill, doused them with kerosene and struck a match to them. As I watched the flames leap up, my stomach started growling. I wondered if I would have to resort to stale bread and peanut butter to pacify my hunger. Beatty, God bless her, came to my rescue.

"Here," she said, handing me two covered plastic tubs over the door of her jeep. "Them's potato salad and baked beans. I just hope these here steaks got thawed. I only 'membered to take 'em out of the freezer when I sat down to lunch."

"I read somewheres that eskimos eat their meat frozen," Adam said as he used a stick to level the wood in the grill.

"Well, we ain't no eskimos," Beatty said, handing him a grocery bag, "and neither me nor Parry want our steaks served up burned on the outside and frozen in the middle."

"Don't worry. I'll raise up the grill and cook 'em nice 'n' slow."

Beatty and I sat down at the picnic table. "Boy, do you got something to drink 'sides that muck you call coffee?" Beatty said.

Adam grinned. "I might." He went to the tool shed, which was raised up on piers, and reached underneath.

"Boy, you're gonna get yourself snake bit, reaching under there like that," Beatty said.

"Well, iff'n I do," he said, holding up an earthen demijohn, "I got me the cure right here. Now, let's see iff'n I can scare up another cup."

Adam found a battered measuring cup to add to the two mugs we'd been using for coffee. He handed me the demijohn. "Miss Parry, would you do the honors?"

"Best let me pour," said Beatty, taking the jug from me. "I've seen the way this girl drinks, and I got me a thirst."

She filled the cups to the brim. I took the smaller measuring cup.

"Here's to the Temperance Union," Beatty said. She took a big swig, while I was content with a sip. Beatty wrapped both hands around her mug as if to draw warmth from it. "Either of you seen that no account boy of mine?"

"Last I seen of him was the day 'fore yesterday," said Adam. "He was helping me on the schoolhouse."

"He say where he was going?"

Adam shook his head. "Like I told Miss Parry, I'm afraid Junie and me had a few words."

"What about?—oh, never mind. That gol dern boy would fight you giving him money. Well, he best be back here by tomorrow, that's all I got to say. I got me some distributors 'specting samples of spring water." Beatty took another swig of moonshine.

"Parry's been showing me a thing or two about electric wiring," Adam said, turning the steaks over.

"Have you? Did your daddy teach you that?"

"Yes, he thought it a useful skill for me to have. I suspect he was worried about me making a living in academia, not that anyone is likely to hire a woman electrician."

"Sounds like your daddy were a good man. I wish I could have met 'im. Only thing my husband ever passed on to Junie was how to hunt and how to drink, usually both at the same time."

"Ladies, how do you like your steaks?" Adam said.

"S' long as mine don't go 'moo,' it'll be just fine," Beatty said.

I ordered mine medium rare. Getting up to get plates and plastic ware, I had a moment where I had to hold onto the table. Two sips of moonshine, and my head was reeling. "Would anyone like the rest of my drink? I'm afraid moonshine on an empty stomach is a little too much for me."

"Well, don't waste it," Beatty said, sliding her cup toward me. I poured the remains of my cup into hers, having no fear that my germs would survive the high alcohol content.

The steaks were good, but in terms of flavor, the baked beans got my vote. I asked Beatty her secret.

"It's the molasses," she said. "Feller up the road makes his own. You gotta get the first pour, 'fore it starts getting too strong. Even so, I add just a dab of honey."

Dessert for Adam and Beatty was a refill of moonshine while I had another helping of baked beans. Then Adam got out his guitar and accompanied Beatty and me as we sat side by side, singing "If I Could Only Win Your Love" and the old Carter family favorite, "Wildwood Flower."

"You two ought to sing professional," Adam said. "You sound a lot better than most women singers I hear."

Beatty, made doubly friendly by the moonshine, linked her arm in mine. "That's a good idea. We could go on the road and sell my spring water, just like Flatt and Scruggs used to sell Martha White flour. All we need is a good name for ourselves."

"Well, 'Gorn and Euphrates' doesn't exactly trip off the tongue,"

I said.

"How about 'Doc and Beatty'?" Adam said.

"Or how 'bout 'The Moonshiners'?" Beatty said. "We could do comedy 'long with music."

"*You* could," I said. "I can't tell a joke for the life of me."

"That's all right," Beatty said. "You can tell ghost stories."

We all laughed until Adam told us of a sudden to hush. From across the holler came the sound of men and women joined in song, the words clear on the night air.

> *I want to live a Christian here,*
> *I want to die a shouting;*
> *I want to feel my Savior near,*
> *While soul and body's parting.*

"Hell, my chickens cluck better than that," Beatty said.

For certain, they weren't the Mormon Tabernacle Choir. In fact, one singer had a voice reminiscent of Mrs. Caterwauler. Still, collectively, there was a vitality in their singing that was stirring.

> *I have my bitter and my sweet,*
> *While through this world I travel;*
> *Sometimes I shout, and often weep,*
> *Which makes my foes to marvel.*

I watched Adam. His head would lift as the singers came in under the pitch then swept up to it. This slurring was not a defect in musicianship, but an embellishment done on purpose. When combined with words, so many of which were sung on the same note, it reminded me of a bagpipe or, sad to admit, a fretless banjo, where the banjo player would slide into the pitch, all the while thumbing the fifth string as a drone.

Adam quietly accompanied the singers on his guitar.

But let them think, and think again,
I feel I'm bound for heaven;
I hope I shall with Jesus reign,
I therefore still will praise him.

In all my years of cheerless church attendance, I'd never heard such singing. My father's church was a mainstream denomination; the music sedate, reserved. It wasn't a problem with the hymns, but the way they were sung, as if the notes were holy relics subject to breakage. There was none of the percussive drive, the unbridled exuberance, the rambunctious fervor I was now hearing.

Adam caught my look of interest. "Are you thinking about going on over?" he said.

"It's a temptation."

"How 'bout you, Beatty?" Adam said. "Needing any ol' time religion?"

"No, I reckon I already got me my lifetime supply, thank you."

"Well, iff'n you don't mind, maybe me and Miss Parry will wander on over to the meeting."

"You go right on ahead and get yourself saved."

As I started to clean up the table, Beatty grabbed my arm. "Leave be, girl. I'll take care of things. You two go on, or you'll miss the singing."

"Thank you," I said.

"No need for thanks. Now just you remember, case any of them holy rollers start rolling around on the floor and foaming at the mouth, to watch out none of 'em bites you."

CHAPTER 18

Adam assured me that the church had a "come as you are" dress code, but I insisted on changing out of my dirty T-shirt. While Adam waited outside the trailer, revving his truck engine, I splashed water over my face, ran a brush through my hair, then put on the one nice blouse I'd brought with me. The more I thought about the church meeting, the more my interest was piqued. I was rather hoping someone *would* foam at the mouth.

Adam abandoned me at the door of the church, and, guitar case in hand, slipped inside to sit with the other musicians, an accordion player, and, regrettably, a banjo player. Fortunately, he wasn't one of one of those frenetic Scruggs-style crazies, but a practitioner of the aptly named, though less excruciating, clawhammer style of torment.

Standing alone, blinking back the harsh light of the single bulb suspended from the ceiling, I felt an intruder. It wasn't like my father's church where a shy person could sneak in and find an empty pew in the back. Just getting to the one remaining chair meant running a gauntlet of elbows and knees. I debated whether to barge on in and disrupt the singing, or slink back to the truck and look for something sharp to puncture Adam's tires in retaliation for his deserting me.

I was saved having to make a decision by a rail-thin elder with a weepy mustache who offered me his chair near the open door. Considering how stuffy room the room was, it was a deluxe seat. It also afforded me a quick exit in case of rabid worshipper attack.

Out of the corner of my eye, I studied the woman seated next to me. She sported a considerable mustache herself. Perched upon her gray head was a wide-brimmed straw hat adorned with crushed silk flowers. Her wire rim glasses–currently all the rage among hippies–had probably never gone out of style here. As for her singing, she had a voice that could've pierced sheet metal.

> *How long, dear Savior, O how long shall this bright hour delay?*
> *Fly swift around ye wheels of time, and bring the promised day.*

Neither words nor melody were familiar, and since no one sang from a hymnal, I was forced to mumble along as best as I could. As I mumbled, I tried not to gawk, though there were a few interesting characters, particularly a woman who sang with rapt countenance directed heavenward, all the while using her husband's knee–I assumed it was her husband's–to bang her tambourine on. I recognized Brother Lillard, sitting to the right of the altar, an elegant sideboard which would have done justice to the dining hall of the Sun King, but looked totally out of place in this rustic setting. Brother Lillard leaned forward with elbows on knees, an open Bible in his hands. He appeared to be mouthing a prayer rather than singing.

Also, squeezed into the front was an old water cooler which, juxtaposed to the altar, looked like a rusty water tower erected in St. Peter's Square. Other than the altar, the most striking feature in the room was a large copy of Leonardo's *Last Supper,* hanging slightly crooked on the front wall.

The hymn came to an end. Except for the absence of a mustache, the song leader looked the twin of the man who had relinquished his chair to me.

"What a blessing it is to see all the chairs filled this evening," he said.

This statement was answered with a flurry of "amens" and people turning in their chairs to ogle me. I did my best to return their welcoming smiles.

"Sister?" he said, raising one hand in my direction. "Would you be so kind as to stand on up and introduce yourself?"

In standing, I inadvertently knocked my neighbor's hat off, exposing her thinning hair. She whisked the hat up off the floor before

I could pick it up for her.

"I'm Parry Euphrates," I announced, looking away from the large bald spot on the top of the woman's head.

"Parry Euphrates, what a lovely name. And Sister Euphrates where are you from?"

"From Santa Barbara, California."

This was greeted with excited murmurings–nothing I could make out except for a whispered "professor."

"Is that where your family lives?"

Declining to tell him I didn't have a family, I just nodded my head.

"And are you married?"

Jesus! I was attending church, not applying for a job. I looked to Brother Lillard whose nod and smile seemed to say "you can get through this."

"No, I'm not. Not married."

The song leader turned halfway toward the musicians seated against the wall to his right. "Oh, my. Did you hear that? Not married."

Everyone laughed except the banjo player who turned beet red. I took that moment to sit back down, this time veering toward the door to avoid hitting Baldy's hat.

"Perhaps Sister Euphrates, you could do us the honor of selecting the next hymn for us to sing."

For a terrifying moment, I had thought he was going to ask me to lead them in prayer. "Uh…" I looked around to see if there was a hymnal anywhere. "I…"

A man popped out of his seat and rushed to the wall where a small rack held sheets of paper. I wondered how he was going lift out the paper with both hands bandaged, but somehow he managed, and reaching between the people seated in front of me, he offered me several pages stapled together.

I was too flustered to more than briefly note that Dewey Bone was not the beady-eyed, tobacco-snorting deviate I had pictured. He was actually handsome in a hollow-cheeked, ascetic sort of way.

"Thank you," I said, taking the pages from his off-white paws.

They were faded dittos of lyrics probably kept just for the benefit of visitors. I selected the first title I recognized. "Wondrous Love," I said.

The accordion player sounded a minor chord, the song leader waved his hands, and off we went.

> *What wondrous love is this! Oh, my soul, oh, my soul!*
> *What wondrous love is this! Oh, my soul!*

The key was high for my range. In fact, it seemed high for everyone's. Perhaps this was on purpose, for it forced the singers to really open up and sing out, or in the case of Baldy to open up and shriek. She made me realize why I'd always avoided sticking sharp objects in my ears. Furtively, I dug out a piece of tissue and stuffed it into my right ear. I fear I wasn't sly enough to fool Baldy, and as I sang along, occasionally looking down at the lyric sheet, I felt her eye upon me. I admit, Baldy had a talent for slurring the notes–that rising up to the pitch I had heard earlier. This ability, however, was spoiled by a substantial quiver in her voice. This ululation reminded me of a musical saw, which produces a sound not to be missed, unless you can help it.

"Wondrous Love" ended, then nothing happened for what seemed like several minutes. The song leader stood with head bowed and hands folded like fig leaves over his crotch. Brother Lillard continued to mouth his prayer. Baldy did a wiggle-waggle in her chair like a hen settling in on her nest. A fly buzzed the light bulb then ran smack into a window and fell to the floor to join the other dead flies. Finally, with a snap, Brother Lillard shut his Bible, stood, and set it upon the altar. "Thank you, Brother Norbert," he said, placing a hand on the song leader's shoulder. With hands still folded, Brother Norbert sidestepped into the chair vacated by Brother Lillard.

"Yes'r, it's good to see all these here chairs filled tonight," Brother Lillard said.

"Amen!" chorused the congregation.

"Given my time here upon this troubled earth, I have preached many a sermon, as no doubt some of you old hands can rightly testify to."

"Yes'r!" "Amen!"

"And oh, how wondrous to praise His holy name."

"Hallelujah!" "Praise the Lord!"

"But sometimes it seems like, no matter what I say, folks just don't seem to be listening."

"No, sir!"

"Maybe it's 'cause their minds are troubled. Maybe it's 'cause their hearts are hardened to God's word. Or maybe–and I'd be the first to admit–maybe the fault lies with me."

"No, sir! No, sir!"

"Maybe I've not humbled myself sufficient so that God might speak through me, so that his word might be a lamp to others upon the pathway to righteousness."

"No, sir!"

"On the other hand, you get a heavenly band of God's children joined together in song, and folks sure 'nough listen to that!"

"Hallelujah!" "Praise God's glorious name!"

"And their hearts is opened. And then they know what it's like to be living with Jesus up there in heaven where the singing never ceases and joy is never ending."

A woman sitting next to Dewey Bone jumped out of her seat and started to sing.

And let this feeble body fail, and let it faint or die;

Others stood and joined in.

My soul shall quit this mournful vale, and soar to worlds on high.

Undeterred, Brother Lillard's spoke above the voices of the singers. "Exodus, chapter fifteen, verse one. And Moses said: 'I will SING unto the LORD, for HE hath triumphed GLO-riously.' "

But the congregation wasn't to be out done. Now everyone was on his or her feet, clapping hands, stamping out the beat.

I'll sing hallelujah, and you'll sing hallelujah.

Brother Norbert, having returned to stand beside Brother Lillard, waved his arms like semaphores.

And we'll all sing hallelujah when we arrive on high!

In sheer volume, the congregation, small as it was, would have routed the war protesters back home. Still, Brother Lillard wasn't to be shouted down. His chest swelled like a bellows. " 'The LORD is my strength and SONG, and HE is become my sal-VAAAAA-tion!' "

The congregation answered with another rollicking chorus followed by cries of "Praise the Lord!" "Hallelujah! Hallelujah!" "O, sweet Jesus, how I love you!" and all the while everyone hugging, shaking hands, slapping backs. If I hadn't known better, I'd have thought the town nag had just won the Kentucky Derby. Dewey Bone sought me out to deliver a special hug, an honor only marginally better than being shot at.

During this show of fervor, Brothers Lillard and Norbert went glad-handing through the crowd until, having pressed the flesh with every worshipper, they arrived back near the altar where they stood hugging each other.

"Yes'r! Yes'r!" "Hallelujah!" "Praise the Lord forever and ever! Amen!"

With tears in their eyes, Brothers Lillard and Norbert separated. Then Brother Lillard faced the congregation, and as the commotion subsided, he began to sing another verse of "Wondrous Love." He dawdled over each syllable, varying the pitch so that even the word "to" became a melody in itself.

To God and to the lamb, I will sing. I will sing.

The congregation joined in, making no attempt to match Brother Lillard's inflection, but each person varying the pitch as he or she was so moved. The effect of everyone going their own way was chaotic, yet exhilarating. It sounded both modern and primitive at the same time, like something Stravinsky might have written had he been composing for a hillbilly choir. Then by some understood convention, the congregation pulled back on the vocal throttle so that Brother Lillard didn't have to shout to be heard as he switched from singing to spouting scripture.

" 'It is NOT the voice of them that SHOUT for mastery.' "

The congregation responded by opening the throttle a smidgen.

> *To God and to the Lamb, Who is the great I AM,*

" 'It is not the voice of them that CRY for being overcome,' "
More throttle.

> *While millions join the theme, I will sing, I will sing,*

" 'But the NOISE of them that SING do I hear.' "
And sing they did, or noise they did. Either way, God would have to have been deaf not to have heard it.

> *While millions join the theme, I WILL SING!*

Again, the hymn was followed by the usual whoops, howls and back slapping: "Praise the Lord!" "Sing his praises!" "Yes'r! Yes'r!" "Hallelujah! Forever and ever, amen!"

I was sorely tempted to add, "Go Mets!"

Next to me, Baldy piped, "H'EP me, Jesus! H'EP me! H'EP me!" which seemed out of keeping with the general laudatory theme. Besides, the way she was flailing her arms, I was the one likely to need help.

After a couple of more minutes of this, Brother Lillard raised a hand, and the congregation quieted and sat back down.

"Brothers and sisters," he said. "As I waited upon the Lord this evening, trying to humble my heart so I might receive His divine blessing, I struggled not to listen to the hymns being sung." He lifted a hand toward the three musicians. "I struggled not to hear these fine musicians here. I'm not 'shamed to say, I did not win out in this struggle." Grinning, he faced the musicians. "Y'all just sound too good!"

Everyone laughed.

"Now, we need to let these here boys know just how much we 'preciate 'em."

From the magnitude of the applause, you would have thought the musicians had invented food. Adam and the accordion player acknowledged this outpouring with nods and grins, while the slack-jawed banjo player just sat picking at the wax in his ear. No doubt dementia and banjo playing go hand-in-hand.

Brother Lillard continued. "Then the Lord spoke to me and he said, 'Brother Lillard, you need to speak 'bout a musician tonight. Brother Lillard, you need to speak about… DAVID.' "

"Yes'r!" "Hallelujah!"

"Now most of us know David as being the one who slew Goliath with his tiny slingshot. But David was also a musician. For it says in first Samuel, chapter sixteen, verse twenty-three, 'And it came to pass, when the EVIL SPIRIT from God was upon Saul, that David took a harp, and played with his hand; so, Saul was refreshed, and was well, and the EVIL SPIRIT departed from him.' Now, I don't need to ask if anybody here's ever felt that evil spirit upon 'em."

Up went Baldy's hand.

"Yes, sister, I see your hand. I see your hand, too, brother. And yours… Thankee. And just maybe there's some folks here tonight that are feeling that evil spirit upon 'em right now."

Baldy's hand shot back up.

"Thankee, Sister. Thankee, Brother. Thankee. Don't be shy, now. Don't you be afraid to admit feeling that evil spirit coming on from time to time."

Judging from the show of hands, I was either the only shy person, or the only one not plagued by evil spirits. Yet considering my troubled relationship with Mr. D, I probably should have been waving both arms and legs.

Brother Lillard's speech now began to take on a new inflection, with each phrase rising up like a bubble, only to pop with an audible 'uh.' "But God in his infinite WISDOM, uh, sent us a champion to fight that EVIL SPIRIT, uh. Sent someone whose lap we can lay our weary HEADS on, uh. So, like Saul there in the book of SAMUEL, uh, we can be REFRESHED, uh, and that EVIL SPIRIT will de-PART, uh."

All those little "uh's" made me I think of Lawrence Welk. Uh, wonderful, uh, wonderful.

"Now, some of you here may be thinking that the champion I'm talking 'bout is DAVID, uh. David was anointed by SAMUEL, uh. David was the chosen of GOD, uh. But I'm not talking 'bout DAVID, uh."

"No, sir! No, sir!"

"Some of you may think that MUSIC, uh, is the champion. Music REFRESHES, uh. Music RESTORES, uh. Music makes the EVIL SPIRIT to de-PART, uh. But I'm not talking 'bout MUSIC, uh."

Baldy, wiggling her rear end like a puppy, mimicked Brother Lillard's inflection, "HE'P me Lord, uh! HE'P me Lord, uh!"

" 'Cause music may chase away that evil spirit for an HOUR, uh. May chase it away for a DAY, uh, or a WEEK, uh, a MONTH, uh. But music can never take the evil from our HEARTS, uh. There's only one CHAMPION can do THAT, uh! There's only one man who can walk beSIDE us, uh. Who can be with us every HOUR, uh, of every DAY, uh. Who can lead us out of TEMPTATION, uh. Deliver us from EVIL, uh. So we might walk in RIGHTEOUSNESS, uh. Might walk in the LIGHT, uh. Might be brought before the HOLY THRONE, uh, where our hearts will be washed CLEAN, uh. Where we will live forever FREE of EVIL, uh. And that MAN, uh, is our blessed SAVIOR, uh. That man is JESUS CHRIST!"

That was Baldy's cue. With arms flapping like streamers, she bolted out of her chair. But she wasn't the only one; the whole congregation was as mad as conventioneers who just had their candidate's name tossed in the ring.

I rose up like the rest, and moved a step toward the door to be out of range as Baldy gyrated like an elephantine Elvis. "HE'P me Lord, uh. HE'P, HE'P me Lord, uh."

I couldn't resist. "HE'P me, Rhonda!" I shouted. "HE'P, HE'P me, Rhonda!" What can I say? The evil spirit made me do it.

But truth was, I really didn't think anyone could've heard my little contribution above the general din. Then Baldy's swinging chassis suddenly jerked, as if it had just sideswiped a Buick. I think she had heard me singing after all. To her credit, Baldy tried to get back into the swing, but obviously, her front end was out of alignment. Soon she gave up and stood staring straight ahead like a footsore marcher watching the victory parade leave her behind with the street sweepers. Then she turned her head and fixed me with one jaundiced eye. It was probably the look Lizzie Borden gave her stepmother just before she hacked her up. I took another step toward the door.

During all this jubilating, Brother Lillard had stood stone still with both arms stretching out to heaven, a statue in a roomful of whirligigs. Then the banjo player, as cool as you please, walked over to the water cooler, pulled a Dixie cup out of the cup holder, and poured himself a drink. As he sipped his water, he stood, leaning one arm on the cooler like an office worker on his break. Then–kid you not–he tilted his head back and gargled. No one seemed to mind. Perhaps gargling was an acceptable form of religious expression, like foaming at the mouth.

Brother Lillard slowly lowered his arms, and once again the congregation settled down into their chairs. The banjo player crushed his Dixie cup, opened a cupboard door in the back of the altar, and tossed it inside.

"Oh, how wondrous to praise His holy name," Brother Lillard said. "Amen!"

"To open our mouths, and sing His praises is a mighty fine thing. That's wonderful! That's GLORIOUS! But my brothers and sisters, it is more important that we open our hearts. You see, it's easy to open our mouths…"

"Yes'r."

"But it's a lot harder to open our hearts."

"Amen!"

"It's easy to get up and shout and wave our arms about and have a good time, but it's hard to open our hearts."

"Yes'r!"

"Why is that?"

For once, no one answered. I resisted the temptation to mention certain anatomical features that served to protect the vital organs.

" 'Cause the heart is tender."

"Yes'r."

"Course our mouths is tender, too. Folks talk 'bout tender lips, talk 'bout tender kisses. And ever'one remembers as a child when maybe your daddy or your momma got mad at you, and slapped you hard right on the mouth. And, oh, how that hurt!"

"Yes'r! Yes'r!"

"And maybe later on they was sorry they hit you."

"Yes'r!"

"But them being sorry didn't take away the pain of that slap, did it?"

"No, sir!"

"And you remembered that, and you said, 'That sure did hurt.' You said, 'From now on, I'm gonna keep my big mouth shut, 'cause I don't want nobody to hit me again. Not EVER. 'Cause It HURTS!' "

"Amen!"

"It HURTS!"

"Yes'r!"

"But brothers and sisters, you know just as sure as I'm standing here, the heart's far more tender than the mouth. When you open up your heart to somebody, it's like you're standing NAKED before 'em.

Like you stand with nothing to proTECT you."

"Amen!"

"You're NAKED! uh. They can SEE you, uh. They can see in-SIDE you, uh. They can see your FEELINGS, uh. They can see your LOVE. And you tell 'em, 'I want you to have this love.' You tell 'em, 'I want you to let me LOVE you and be GOOD to you. I want you to open your ARMS and take this LOVE.' "

"Amen!"

"And then they look at you with your heart all open and they say… 'NO!' "

"No, sir!"

" 'NO! I don't WANT your love!' "

"No, sir!"

"They say to you, 'You take that love and give it to somebody else 'cause I don't WANT it!' "

"No, sir!"

"And brothers and sisters, you think that hit on the mouth hurt?"

"Yes'r!"

"You think your daddy or momma slapping you hurt?"

"Yes'r!"

"Well, I tell you right now that slap on the mouth weren't nothing. A HUNDRED hits on the mouth ain't like that one, single 'No!' cried out by your beloved 'cause you've given your heart to someone, and they refused it!"

"Yes'r!"

"They scorned it!"

"Amen!"

"And it hurts!"

"Yes'r!"

"It HURTS! Mor'n a hundred blows! And then you close up that heart, and you put a padlock on it. And you say, 'I ain't NEVER gonna do that again.' You say, 'I learned my LESSON. I ain't NEVER gonna open my heart to NOBODY again. Not EVER!' "

"No, sir!"

Brother Lillard took a handkerchief and wiped his lips. The congregation, now quiet, waited as he slowly folded the handkerchief and returned it to his pocket.

"But I want to tell you something, brothers and sisters." He leaned forward and spoke in a voice just above a whisper, "You'll never know Jesus, iff'n you don't open your heart."

He waited, letting this sink in. "You'll never know the greatest love, the greatest joy you'll ever know, iff'n you don't open your heart to Jesus."

He straightened. "Now, what do we mean by 'open your heart to Jesus'? I ain't gonna tell you what some preachers will tell you, that you gotta make a decision to accept Christ as your savior. 'Cause when you say, 'I've decided to accept Jesus,' that's your mind a-talking. That's like saying, 'I've decided to ask the neighbors over for dinner come Friday,' or 'I've decided to go on up to Damascus next Tuesday and shop at the Piggly Wiggly,' When you say, 'I've decided to accept Jesus as my savior,' that's your mind deciding, just like when you decided to do all those other things. And you can't know salvation just 'cause you DECIDE you're gonna. You can't know JESUS 'cause you got a MIND to. You can't know Jesus with your MIND!"

"No, sir!"

"'Cause the DEVIL lives in the mind!"

"Yes'r!"

"But JESUS…"

"Praise his name!"

"Jesus lives in the heart."

"Amen, Brother!" "Hallelujah!"

"And YOU can't tell Jesus to come into your heart. Who are we to tell Jesus anything?"

"We're sinners, brother!"

"That's right, we're sinners. And sinners can't be going 'round telling Jesus what to do. NOBODY can do that! But, brothers and sisters, you can ask 'im. You can say, 'Jesus, please come into my heart.' You can say, 'Jesus, my heart is wide open, and I'm ready and waiting.

Jesus, I know I closed my heart to you in the past, but now my heart is open, wide open. Jesus, please come into my heart and fill it with your blessed assurance. Fill it with the one love that never fails, the one love that never says, no.'"

"Praise the Lord!"

"How many of you here tonight have opened your hearts to Jesus?"

Arms went up as of one accord.

"I know you have brothers and sisters. I know it 'cause I see God's light shining in your faces this evening."

Brother Lillard began to move through the congregation touching people upon the arm, the shoulder, the head. "Bless you brother, bless you sister. You've done opened your heart to Jesus."

My heart began to race as he approached me, but I was spared being pawed as he passed me over for Baldy, who was sobbing into her handkerchief. I moved out of my chair, and a woman took my place and put one arm around Baldy's quivering shoulders.

Brother Lillard place his hand upon Baldy's straw hat and began to pray. "Lord, we have one of your faithful right here before us."

Rivers of tears flowed down Baldy's wrinkled cheeks.

"Lord, you know she's ever kept her heart open to your son, Jesus Christ. She has attended upon you and received your blessed assurance. Now, Lord, you know how our sister suffers."

"HE'P me, Lord!" Baldy murmured. "HE'P me!"

"You know the pain she feels."

"HE'P me, Lord."

"You know she'll soon be called to join in the heavenly choir where she'll stand before the great throne and meet Jesus and all those who have gone on before."

"HE'P me, Lord!" she cried, stamping her feet.

"We just ask that until that bright and shiny day comes, Lord, that you'll look down upon our sister and ease her suffering."

"HE'P me, Jesus!" she cried, lifting both knees high in the air.

"We ask that Thy face shine down upon her and give her peace."

"HE'P me, Lord." She slammed her feet hard upon the floor.

"For all things is possible through Jesus Christ, our Savior, and we ask it in His name. Amen."

Baldy's head suddenly jerked back, leaving Brother Lillard clasping an empty hat. Then like a python preparing to partake of a fat rodent, Baldy's jaw unhinged, and she let loose with a bloodcurdling screech that rendered my knees to Jell-O. This was followed by a death rattle deep in her throat that set her dentures to clacking. If this wasn't scary enough, Baldy's legs chopped the air like knives on a bread slicing machine. Brother Lillard, having jettisoned the hat, pushed down on Baldy's shoulders, straining to keep her from erupting out of her seat. The woman who'd taken my chair clung to Baldy the way an overmatched bronco buster clings to the pommel of his saddle, too afraid to let go lest he fall and be ground under by the pounding hooves.

Now, while these theatrics were going on, the rest of the congregation had divided themselves into three separate groups. In one, the man who gave me his chair read from the Bible for the benefit of several women, one of whom sat with tears coursing down her cheeks. In another, a woman stood with one hand upon the head of Dewey Bone, praying over him, while a second woman gripped his trembling shoulders. In the last group, four men sat in a small circle, appearing to be doing nothing more than quietly conversing. None of them took notice of the melodrama being enacted in the back of the room. I looked at Adam. He grinned and shrugged his shoulders.

Eventually, Baldy's convulsions subsided. Her head pitched forward, bobbed a while on the sea of her heaving breasts, then flopped over to rest upon the shoulder of the woman still clinging to her. Baldy's complexion, not exactly peaches and cream to begin with, now looked about as rosy as soggy newspaper complete with deep lines of runny ink. I wouldn't have called it the face of Suffering Eased. More like a portrait of Death About to Puke Her Crackers. I shook my head. If this was Baldy's way of alleviating suffering, then I figured she needed to find a different palliative. Euthanasia came to mind.

With a whimper, Baldy repositioned her head, and in doing so, released a trickle of saliva that slowly dribbled onto the woman's dress. It was the drool that did it for me. I signaled Adam that I'd had enough; I needed to return to the world of the sane.

But as I turned toward the door, Brother Lillard stood in my way. He placed one hand upon my shoulder and closed his eyes. "Lord," he said, "here's another among us who suffers this evening."

Annoyed, I decided I'd grit this out rather than make a scene.

"She's has a great pain, Lord."

Obviously, news of my head injury had preceded me. And what with Baldy's histrionics, I certainly could've used a couple of aspirins right then.

But Brother Lillard wasn't talking about any headache.

"Lord, her heart suffers 'cause she misses a dear one."

I didn't like where this was going. I tried to pull away, but Brother Lillard's fingers were steel pincers.

"Lord, you know she misses her daddy and longs to talk to him and tell him of her sorrow. She carries a sweet hope that she will see him once more and receive his assurance. Lord, we ask that if it be thy will, that our sister's prayer–"

With all my strength, I battered his arm, breaking his grip. Then I was through the doorway, running blindly on account of my tears. I'd spent the evening, mentally belittling Brother Lillard's church meeting, thinking of the laughs I'd get when I told my colleagues about it back home.

Now I found the joke was on me.

CHAPTER 19

Adam came running up behind me. "Miss Parry!"

I turned on him. "You shit! Why did you tell that son of a bitch about me and my father?"

"What are you talking about? I've never spoken mor'n a couple of words to Brother Lillard my whole life."

I slammed my fist into his chest. "Liar!" Then I turned and fled down the road. In a little while, Adam, in his truck, came along behind me, his headlights illuminating the corduroy bridge ahead. As the truck drew near, I picked up a rock and hurled it at the windshield.

In a spray of gravel, Adam sped past and stopped on the bridge. Slamming his door, he came at me up the hill. I picked up another rock.

"Don't!" he shouted.

I could see his outline against the taillights. I threw and missed. Damn! Damn! Damn! I picked up another rock.

"Damn it, Miss Parry, just you hold on a minute. How could I have told him 'bout your daddy when you've never ever spoke to me 'bout him?"

He had a point. In fact, there was only one person in Hoagland Holler I'd spoken to of my father, and the road to her house was just to my left. I started down it.

"Where you going?" Adam said.

"To have a few words with your grandmother."

"Well, you can go right on ahead, but I guarantee she's never said a word to Brother Lillard 'bout you."

I kept marching.

"Granny ain't talked to Brother Lillard in years!" Adam said, catching up to me. "Miss Parry, Granny hates Brother Lillard!"

I skidded to a stop. "Damn! Damn! Damn!" I shouted, stamping my feet. Then I dropped to the ground and sat with head in hands. Adam hovered over me. I didn't need to see his face to sense his anger.

"Miss Parry, you got yourself a terrible temper. You gotta do something 'bout that."

"Well, what the hell do you expect?" I said. "That bastard just ripped my heart open, and in front of all those strangers."

"Believe me, Miss Parry, iff'n I'd have known he was gonna say something 'bout your daddy, I'd never have asked if you wanted to 'tend church."

"Christ! I can see why your grandmother hates that bastard. What was it he did to her?"

"I don't rightly know. It happened a long time ago, back when I was just a baby, maybe 'fore that. My family never talked 'bout it. I just know that whatever Brother Lillard done, it was something Granny just can't forgive him for."

"And she's not spoken to him in years?"

"He don't dare show his face at her door."

"Damn!" I said, rubbing my forehead.

Adam crouched down before me. "Miss Parry, is what Brother Lillard said true? Are you missing your daddy and wanting to talk to him?"

I groaned then leaned back against the road cut. Somehow, Brother Lillard had figured out what I wanted more than anything: to see my father again, to hear him say that I was all right just the way I was. It wasn't that I had ever doubted my father's love. But a person can love someone and still not approve of them, and lacking my father's approval, I would always feel a failure, or something worse, which begged the question, what the hell did I have to live for? Brother Lillard had said something about a sweet hope. He might just as well have been talking of voodoo or sorcery, for all my hope rested in the approval of a man ten years dead.

I stood up. "I want to go back to the trailer."

"Okay," Adam said, "I'll drive you."

"No, I'll walk."

"But it's dark. You can't see nothing."

I looked up. Behind the clouds was a moon, and the sky was bright enough for me to see the road.

Adam followed my stare. "You won't be able to see nothing a'tall once you get in under the trees."

I didn't care. I started walking.

Adam pulled on my arm. "Wait." He ran to his truck and returned with a flashlight. "Here," he said, "that'll at least keep you from tripping over some tree root."

I could tell he still didn't want me walking by myself. "Don't worry, Adam. I'm used to being out at night. But if it will make you feel better, I'll stop by the tool shed so you'll know I got back all right."

"Thank you, Miss Parry. I'd sure 'preciate that."

I took my time, doing my best to ignore unwanted thoughts, letting the drone of the cicadas ease the ache in my chest. I ended up using the flashlight only when crossing the bridge. For a long time, I shone the light down on the swift current and watched as the water split itself on river-worn rocks then eddied back in frothy waves. By the time I reached the tool shed, Adam was sawing logs. I guess he couldn't have been too concerned. I stopped at the outhouse. I was so emotionally drained, I nearly fell asleep seating on the toilet seat. As I opened the sagging door of the trailer, I wondered if I even had the energy to change into my nightgown. That's when Junie, stinking drunk, grabbed me by my blouse and yanked me inside.

CHAPTER 20

I screamed as he spun me around and slammed me into the counter. Junie clamped his hand over my mouth. I bit it.

"You bitch!" he hissed.

I tried to knee him in the crotch, but he was leaning in against me, and I couldn't bring my leg up high enough. Junie grabbed me by the throat and bent me back over the sink. I hooked my fists into his sides, but his arms blocked my punches. His strength was terrible. I couldn't breathe. I was sure he was going to break my back.

"Now we can both have us some fun or just me." he said, "It's up to you." He squeezed my throat tighter. Stars whirled before my eyes. I was about to pass out.

"You ain't been nice to me. You been nice to Adam, but not to Junie." He slammed his crotch into me. "Now, you're gonna be nice."

He jammed one hand between my legs and groped me. It was the worst moment in my life. Yet with only one of his hands on my throat, I was able to suck in a little air. Still, I saw stars. I never felt so weak.

"I know you been putting out for Adam. Now, you're gonna put out for me!" He yanked his hand from between my legs and again used both hands to throttle me. "You goddamn whore!"

I knew then that I was going to die. Well, what the hell. Life hadn't been all that jolly, anyway.

But I didn't want to die. Maybe I had more hope than I realized, or maybe I just was pissed that someone else should have the power of life or death over me. I squirmed, tried to speak–impossible with my windpipe choked off. Junie relaxed his grip.

"You wantin' to say somethin'?"

I sucked in air. Two breaths, three. My head started to clear. Junie let me breathe, but kept his hands around my throat. "We'll have some fun," I croaked.

"Good," he said. "Good. Now you're talkin' like a real woman–obeying her man." Then he leaned over and pushed his nose into the top of my blouse.

"Oh!" I cried.

"What now, bitch?"

"My back. You're breaking it."

Junie leaned back, allowing me to straighten up. The relief was so great, I groaned again. Then he was fumbling with the zipper on my jeans. He was sloppy drunk.

"Wait," I whispered. My hands shook, but I managed to pull down the zipper. Then starting at the bottom of my blouse, I undid the buttons, leaving one buttoned at the top. I leaned back with my arms above my head, the movement causing my blouse to open up, exposing the white of my stomach.

"Come on, then," I whispered, wiggling my butt a little.

Junie laughed: a vain, gloating, filthy laugh. Opening wide my blouse, he mouthed my breasts, drooling on my brassiere. I reached up over my head. The cupboard above the sink hinged from the top. I slid my hand under the door. Junie, tired of my breasts, pulled at the elastic of my underpants. The back of my fingers brushed across the smooth surface of steel pots and pans. Junie began to yank on my jeans, trying to get them down over my hips. My hand found the cold, hard handle of the cast iron skillet. With pots bursting from the cupboard, I brought it crashing down on Junie's head. He stumbled back. Gripping the skillet with both hands I swung it sideways, the flat bottom smashing his face. Junie went head over heels backward through the door.

I fell to the floor, sobbing. *Thank you, Mrs. E! Thank you! Thank you! Thank you! Thank you! Thank you!* The need go to pieces was almost overwhelming, but I didn't dare while Junie might still be a threat. Without letting go of the skillet, I used one arm and the edge of the table to get myself onto trembling legs. Then I pushed open the trailer door, which had bounced shut after Junie went through it. He lay on his back, face covered in blood, apparently unconscious.

I hoped to God I'd killed him; I was afraid I had. I collapsed in the doorway, one leg in and one leg out of the trailer. It was terribly uncomfortable, but I didn't have the strength to change positions. I must have sat that way for ten minutes before Junie groaned and slowly sat up. Blood dribbled out of his nose, over his chin and onto his T-shirt. He ran a hand across his mouth and stared at his bloody fingers.

"Why'd you hit me for?"

This was past bearing! "Because, you little son of a bitch, I didn't have a gun to shoot you with!"

Junie took some time to think about this. "Well, I got a gun."

His voice sounded surprisingly calm, considering the pain he must have been in. Perhaps it was shock. Or maybe he was trying to lure me into dropping my guard. I gripped the skillet tighter.

"I got me an M-16," he said.

I could see tears glistening in his one eye not swollen shut.

"I wish to God I had it right now so's you could shoot me with it." He lay back down and covered his face with his hands.

Needless to say, this was not the response I'd expected. Nor could I have imagined what he did next. He curled into a ball and began to cry–great wracking sobs that tore at his throat and caused his whole body to shudder. Streams of snot oozed from his nose, mixing with the blood. I turned so I wouldn't have to look at him. He was disgusting. He was pathetic. He was a mean little excuse for a human who should have got far more than a bop on the head with a skillet.

Yet something inside me actually went out to him, but only because I knew those anguished tears. More than once, I'd cried them myself.

"Please!" he cried, "Please, please kill me!" He lifted his head. "Use the skillet. Bash my skull in."

I twisted around so that both legs were outside the trailer. "Junie, I can't kill you." My voice sounded flat to my ears. "Not now, at any rate."

But he wasn't listening. "Please! Please!" he cried out between gasps for breath. "Kill me!"

He went on like this until a part of me wanted to oblige him just to shut him up. But eventually he quieted down without me having to do him more damage. He sat up and used his handkerchief, but without much effect, for now most of the blood had dried. He looked a fright, but appeared to have gotten himself under control, though there was an urgency to his voice when he spoke. "Please, Professor!" he cried. "Please don't take Adam away from me. You gotta understand, he's all I got. So please, don't take him! I love him so!"

My groggy brain couldn't make sense of this. Then it hit me like a skillet hard on the forehead.

"My God!" I cried, sitting up straight. "You're a homosexual!"

CHAPTER 21

I don't think he heard me. Tears started to flow again, and I was afraid he was going to have another crying jag. I pushed up onto my feet–the effort causing my head to pound–and started toward the tool shed where Adam slept.

"Don't!" cried Junie, reaching out and grabbing one of my ankles. I smashed his hand with the skillet. Junie screamed and sucked on his fingers. I stepped away, but he crawled after me on his knees, gripping his injured hand.

"Please!" he cried, lunging for my ankle again. I sidestepped out of range. "Please, Professor, what are you gonna do?"

"I'm going to get Adam to call the sheriff and have you thrown in jail where you belong."

He held out his bloodstained hands, begging. "Please, I weren't gonna do it. I swear! I was just so…"

I waited for him to complete his sentence. He leaned back on his heels. "You don't know what it's like being me."

It was all I could do to keep from hitting him again. "Look, asshole, I'm sorry if Vietnam screwed you up. But guess what? You're not the only person in this world that's been fucked over. My life hasn't exactly been a bowl of cherries, but that still doesn't give me the right to go around raping people."

His look of hurt mutated into one of rage–all the more sinister for the veneer of dried blood on his face. I lifted up the skillet to be ready.

"What the hell would you know? What would you know 'bout being called fag and queer and homo, and ever' other mean name they can think of? What would you know 'bout having the shit kicked out of you pract'ly ever' fucking day of your life? What would you know 'bout your daddy hating you and telling you, you make him puke, and your momma always yelling at you to be a man?"

"Listen, Jun–"

"No, you listen, Professor. You think I wanted to go to Viet Nam? My momma made me do that. Said it would make a man out of me. Make me wanna get married and have babies. My own momma, sending me off to that hellhole just so's she can get grandkids."

"Junie–"

"Only I weren't no tunnel rat like she's always telling ever'body. You think the army's gonna let some fag be a real soldier? Hell, no! Fags ain't real men. Fags work in the hospital and clean up the shit. 'Hey, faggot, get over here and get this bedpan full of shit. Suck my cock while you're at it, fag.'"

"Junie–"

"No, Professor, you don't know shit! Adam's the only person who's ever treated me kind, treated me like I was a real human being and loved me like a brother, and now he's gonna up and marry some egghead and move–"

"Marry? Junie, what are you talking about? Adam and I aren't getting married."

From his look on his face, you would have thought I'd hit him again. He swallowed. "You ain't?"

"Not that I know of. We're just good friends, that's all."

Junie covered his face and wept into his hands.

Dragging my feet, I went back into the trailer, took a towel out of the drawer, moistened it in the sink, and returned to kneel beside Junie who was still crying.

"Here," I said, pulling one hand away from his face. I began to wash the blood off. I couldn't believe I was doing this. Ten minutes ago, this creep was trying to rape me.

"Ow!" yelled Junie. "Go easy, Professor."

"Listen, you can do this yourself, if you like."

"No, that's all right. Your hand feels good."

I actually made an attempt to be gentle. I must have been thinking about what Junie said. How much kindness had he ever been shown? Had there been a gentle hand to wash his cuts and scrapes, or was he just told to quit blubbering and act like a man? I dabbed at the dried blood above his lip. "How does your nose feel?"

"Like you done broke it. Wouldn't be the first time. Had my nose busted four times when I was in school."

"I guess, you must've learned to be one helluva fighter."

"Yeah, iff'n you like being one helluva fighter."

I lifted the towel away from his face. "I'm sorry, Junie that was callous of me. I'm sorry you had to fight. I'm sorry about all the names they called you."

Junie took the blood-stained towel, folded it, and pressed it against the bump on his forehead. "Seems like I'm the one who should be saying sorry. I swear to God, I wouldn't have actually done... well, you know. But I'm sorry. It were terrible, what I done, and I know it. Only, the thought of you taking Adam away been making me crazy!"

"Junie, you've got to realize, Adam's bound to get married someday. He's not like..." I almost slipped and said "us."

Junie shook the towel in his fist. "He's not a fuckin' fag, like me? Is that what you mean?"

"I wasn't going to say that, at least, not using any of those words. I was just trying to say that someday Adam's going to get married. In the meantime, you can't go around attacking every female friend he has."

"I know it, Professor. I know it. It's just that I can't bear to think of losing him." Junie covered his eyes with the towel. "Jesus! I don't know what I'm gonna do."

I spoke quickly to head off another flood of tears. "You aren't necessarily going to lose him." Junie didn't respond, so I tried another tack. "I'm curious, have you ever told Adam how you feel?"

Junie lowered the towel. "What the hell for? Adam ain't never gonna love me the way I want him to."

"True, but I just thought... I don't know, maybe you'd feel better if you got your feelings out in the open."

Junie didn't respond, and I was too tired to push it. And then it hit me, what Junie had said earlier. I grabbed him by his shirt. "It was you at the swimming hole! You were the one who tried to shoot me!"

Junie actually looked scared. "I ain't never shot at nobody in my life. I hate guns. My daddy was always forcing me to kill things. Said it were part of my man training."

"Then how come you said I was putting out for Adam?"

"I just 'sumed you was, you and Adam being so friendly-like 'n' all."

I let go of his shirt and rubbed my forehead. "Shit! I've got to get some sleep."

Junie was all solicitude. "You just do that, Professor. And don't worry, you got nothin' to fear from me, not now, not ever more."

I studied his face, trying to decide if I should believe him.

"But iff'n it makes you feel better, you take that there skillet to bed with you."

I doubted I had the strength to lift it. I made motions to get up.

"Professor, I think there's things you should know 'bout my momma."

"Junie, I'm exhausted."

"She may act nice, but she's got a devil in her, 'specially when she's desperate."

"What do you mean, 'desperate?'"

"I mean this dumb idea of hers to sell spring water. Have you ever noticed the roads 'round here? There's lotsa places bottling spring water, and they don't have roads like ours they gotta haul things over. I tried to tell her that, but she won't listen none to her fag son. She thinks she's gonna get rich, but truth is, she's gonna lose all that precious land of hers she mortgaged to pay for that damn bottling plant."

"But she told me she's found a couple of distributors. In fact, you're supposed to take samples of water to them tomorrow."

Junie handed me the towel. "Professor, what I'm takin' may be samples, but they sure as hell ain't spring water."

CHAPTER 22

July 1, 1970

Dear Teddy,

It's one a.m., and I can't sleep, though I'm so tired I couldn't lift my pen if it weren't made of plastic. Add to that Mr. D is playing handball against my sub orbital margins, my mouth tastes like rusty tin, and my teeth feel like they've been dipped in glue, even after brushing them three times. As if all this weren't enough, I think the shampoo I'm using is giving me dandruff.

Oh, and earlier tonight, Junie Gorn tried to rape me.

I've a feeling this last has more to do with my insomnia than the gunk on my choppers. I never felt such fear. I thought I was going to die, or worse. It's only because I remembered a cast-iron skillet in the cabinet above the stove that I'm still here. With two swings, I remodeled Junie's face. I'd be a liar if I said it felt good to hit him, though I thoroughly hate him for making me feel so afraid, so helpless. I think we humans survive in this world by kidding ourselves that we're impervious to harm. We're not. And the worst part is, harm can strike without a hint of warning. I mean, I knew Junie wasn't exactly enamored of me, but I more or less chalked that up to his generally odious nature. I never dreamed he had it in for me personally.

So, where is he now? I hope, like me, not

sleeping. But no, he's not in jail, and don't ask me why not. I'll explain some time, but not now. Only one thing about all this makes me glad: Junie's going to have a helluva time explaining his battered puss to his mother.

CHAPTER 23

I was awoken by someone pounding on the trailer door.

"Miss Parry? You in there?" Adam entered, holding a tray made of scrap plywood. He stepped over my jeans and blouse to get to the bed. "I brung you something to eat."

I pulled the blankets up to my neck. Too tired to change into my nightgown, I'd gone to sleep in my underwear. "So, now you're providing room service?"

"Figured I owed you something after what happened last night."

"What about last night?"

Adam's look was a mix of disbelief and concern. "Don't you remember us going to church?"

"Oh, right." My little visit with Junie had rather shoved Brother Lillard and his church meeting to the back of my mental shelf.

"Miss Parry, you don't look too good."

"Well, I had a rather late night."

"How long were you out walking?"

"Not very." I didn't mention my second trip back to the church to stick my letter to Teddy into the mailbox. I pointed to a drawer. "Hand me a T-shirt, will you."

Adam set the tray atop the stove then got me the shirt. As I sat up to put it on, I felt a twinge in my back and mentally cursed Junie. Then Adam set the tray on my lap. It held scrambled eggs, sausage, a large pancake, a glass of orange juice and a glass of milk.

"Junie brought me some ice for the ice chest," he said. "He also brought the milk and orange juice. Said they were for you."

"Did he now? And how is Junie this morning?"

Adam shook his head. "Not good. It seems some tough guys worked him over pretty good."

I stuffed pancake into my mouth to keep from laughing. "Sorry to hear that," I mumbled.

Adam sat at the edge of the bed and watched as I ate. "I'm afraid Junie's never had much luck."

I waited for him to explain, hoping he might say something about Junie being a homosexual, for I dearly wanted to hear how he felt about that. But Adam just watched as I gobbled the still warm sausage, and much as I loathed Junie, I wasn't going to be the first to give away his awful secret.

"So, why did they beat him up?" I said.

Adam shifted position. "I reckon you already figured out that Beatty's been running some moonshine on the side. There's folks 'round here who take a dim view of competition." Adam looked at my nearly empty plate. "You sure ate that fast. I guess I must not be too bad a cook, after all."

"It was delicious, and I was really hungry." I handed him the tray. "So what are we going to do this morning?"

"Morning?"

I looked at my wristwatch. "Jesus! It's almost one."

Adam grinned. "While you've been leading the life of Riley, some of us have been working. I've been cleaning up 'round the schoolhouse and throwing the trash in that there pit you dug, including that rusty ol' harrow."

"If I'd have been doing my job, I would have already backfilled that pit."

"Well, I'm glad you didn't," Adam said, standing up. "You know, Miss Parry, you still look a mite peaked. Why don't you see iff'n you can get some more shuteye?"

I snuggled back down under the covers. "I might just do that."

I heard music. Accompanied by the drone of a bagpipe, voice parts overlapped as if it were a fugue. "Pain in her heart," they sang. "Misses someone." Baldy came in, singing the chorus, "I've got a sweet hope, blessed assurance."

I opened my eyes and the voices faded, but not the drone. Adam was running what sounded like a lawnmower. I sat up, my back complaining, but not as vociferously as before. I looked through the window to get an idea of what the day was like. It might have been overcast, but hard to tell with the window being so dirty.

I picked up my jeans and put them on. My blouse had specks of Junie's blood, so I set it in the sink to soak. Then I got out my Martin and sat at the table, absently strumming the strings. The words of the song I'd heard in my dream still rattled around in my head, but I couldn't recall the melody. I fretted my guitar so only the notes G and D sounded, then as I strummed the strings, I slid into the G's and D's from a half step below, creating an effect that imitated the drone of a bagpipe. To this rhythm, I hummed a low G, which rumbled in my chest. The sensation was pleasant and very relaxing.

But I already had enough relaxation for one day. I put my Martin away and stuck my head out the door. The air was warm, though a light rain was falling. Forgoing a rain coat, I walked up to the schoolhouse, the rain feeling delightfully cool on my skin. I found Adam standing over a lawn mower tipped on its side, oil oozing out like black blood.

"What happened?" I said. "A lawn mower wreck?"

"Just needed to change the oil," he said. With a sweep of his hand, he indicated the area he'd mowed around the schoolhouse. "Look any better?"

"With the exception of the oil slick, it does. Now I won't be getting stickers in my socks."

"You're looking better yourself, Miss Parry. Not so tired."

"I think I've slept more in the last few days than at any time since I started grad school. But right now, I'd like to do some more wiring. Thought I'd start on the upstairs."

"I already drilled out most the holes for the runs. I'll come along and drill out the rest when I'm done here."

The upstairs was to have two bedrooms, the larger with double doors that opened onto a hallway overlooking the stairway. The blueprints showed only one light switch for the bigger bedroom. I walked to the gable end and looked out through the window opening. Adam was raking the cut grass into a big pile.

"Adam, do you want another light switch for the master bedroom? Without it, you'll have to reach around the double doors to turn the lights on from the hallway side."

"Give me a minute here to finish, and I'll come see what you're talking 'bout." He gave his rake a shake to free a tangle of grass from the tines.

"Take your time. I just–holy moly!"

Adam looked up. "What is it, Miss Parry? What do you see?"

"Adam, take six steps to your left."

Adam did as instructed.

"Now, about four steps away from the building. Stop! Back up a little. There, right there! Now, tell me what you see."

Adam looked at the ground around him. "I don't see nothing. Oh, you mean that little scrap of wood there?" He stooped down to pry the wood out of the ground.

"No! Not the wood. Doesn't the ground look different where you're standing?"

Adam scratched his head. "It looks just like plain ol' dirt to me."

"Stay right there. Don't move."

I ran downstairs and out into the yard. I picked up a stick and knelt down. "Look at the dirt here and here," I said, pointing with my stick. "See, the dirt here is darker."

"If you say so, Miss Parry."

I gathered up four rocks and set them at the corners of the darkened area. "There, you see it now, don't you?"

Adam shook his head.

"Go upstairs and look down."

Adam obliged me.

"Now what do you see?" I said, looking up at him.

"I think I see what you're talking 'bout. There's a rectangle of dirt that's darker than the dirt 'round it?"

"What does it make you think of?"

"Like maybe somebody had an old door lying on the ground there."

I needed to make it more obvious. I lay on the ground within the rectangle, legs straight, arms folded over my chest, eyes closed. All I needed were flowers laid over my chest.

"Well, if that don't beat all!" Adam exclaimed. "It's somebody's grave!"

Chapter 24

Adam, having rushed to join me, looked as if he were about to jump out of his integument. "Miss Parry, do you really think it's a grave?"

I held up a hand for silence. Adam's comment about a door had given me second thoughts. I went to the tool shed to get the shovel. I got a pick while I was at it. Abandoning my usual caution, I pushed the shovel as deep as I could into the dark soil then spread the dirt out over the surface. It was uniform in color. I didn't think a rotting door could have stained the dirt to that depth.

"Ground that's been disturbed is often shaded differently than the undisturbed soil around it. It has to do with the various soil types that get mixed up when the hole is backfilled. Often such differences are only noticeable from the vantage point of someplace high up, which is why I didn't notice this patch of dark soil until I looked down from upstairs. Even so, I doubt I would've noticed it if you hadn't mowed and raked the grass."

"But are you saying this here's a grave?"

I leaned on the shovel handle. As an archaeologist, I couldn't claim it a gravesite without further excavation. Still, I had a hunch.

"Yes," I said, smiling, "Yes, I think it is."

Adam grinned. "Well, what're we waiting for? Let's get digging!"

"Wait a minute. We've still got to do this by the book. We don't want to mess everything up in our excitement." I pointed to the stones I had set out. "You know the procedure. Go ahead and lay out a grid while I go get my excavating tools."

By the time I returned from the trailer, Adam had the corners staked out, and run with twine. I pulled a measuring tape out of my tool bag. "We'll let the foundation of the schoolhouse be our datum," I said. We measured straight out from the foundation to the gravesite, then took a second measurement from the tool shed. I recorded both distances in my field book. "Okay, you can go ahead and start digging, but remember, no deeper than three to four inches." I went to get the wheel barrow and the hardware cloth I'd used before as a sifter.

"This ground here is softer," said Adam, as I set the wheel barrow down next to the grid. He waited while I spread the hardware cloth over the wheel barrow before placing a shovelful of dirt on top of it. "I don't even need to use the pick."

"That's another good sign," I said.

I sifted the dirt into the wheelbarrow, not really expecting to find anything so close to the surface. It wasn't until Adam had dug down nearly two feet that we made our first discovery.

"Found something," I said, lifting up a small, misshapen object off the screen.

Adam jumped out of the pit to stare over my shoulder. "Looks like a rock to me."

"No, it's metal, see?" I pointed to circle of rust. "Damn! This thing's really encrusted with dirt. I'll have to soak it in water." But first, I made a note in my field book as to where in the grave the object had been discovered. "You know, it just occurred to me that this might be a shallow grave. Maybe it's time we switched places, and I did the digging."

"Let me do it, Miss Parry," Adam said, stepping back down into the pit. "I got me a feel for the dirt now."

"All right, but be very careful. Use a gentle touch, just like when you're playing the guitar."

"Maybe iff'n I sing to him, Canara Rivers might just slip out of his grave nice and easy."

> *Wake up, wake up Canara Rivers,*
> *What makes you sleep so sound?*

I felt a chill run down my back. Adam must have felt one too. "Kinda spooky," he said, "singing like that 'bout a real person."

Distant thunder rumbled in agreement. I made a face. Bigger raindrops were starting to fall.

"Don't worry, Miss Parry. It's not gonna be a big thunderstorm. I can tell."

"Actually, I was thinking more about water getting into the pit. We may have to quit and cover all this up to protect it from the rain." Yet we continued to work, though the rain didn't slacken. After a while, the dirt began to clump, making it harder to sift.

"Damn!" I yelled. "How does the soil look down there?"

"The rain's soaking into the ground," Adam said, "but it's not really muddy or anything."

"Well, it soon will be. I think we better think about covering things up."

Using the pick, I began to dig a trench to channel the run-off away from the upper side of the pit. "Adam, can we use one of your pieces of plywood to cover the pit with?"

He didn't answer.

"I'll need some help. The plywood's too heavy for me to lift by myself."

Adam didn't seem to be listening.

I turned toward him and raised my voice. "Adam, if we don't get this pit covered, we're going to have a muddy mess!"

"Miss Parry, I think I may have found something."

I dropped the pick and stared down into the pit.

Adam, crouching, rubbed his fingers over a projection. "I think it's a boot."

"Okay, don't do anything." I ran to my tool bag and took out my Instamatic camera. "Lean back a little," I said. I took a picture, using the flash. Trading the camera for a small scraper, I stepped down into the pit. Carefully, I scraped dirt away from the projection. At one time, it might have been a boot; now only the rubber sole remained.

"Get me a dental pick out of my bag," I said.

Adam leaped to obey.

"And a small brush!"

After scraping and brushing for several minutes, I was rewarded with five yellowish nubs.

"What are they?" Adam asked.

"They're the distal ends of the phalanges."

"The what?"

I looked up and smiled. "They're bones, Adam, the ends of the toes."

Adam danced a little jig.

I laughed to see him so excited. But then a gush of wind blew the rain sideways into my face. I shook my fist at the sky. "Why now?"

We worked fast, covering the pit with the plywood. While Adam worked to expand my trench, I placed a canvas tarp over the plywood and weighted it down with rocks. Then I grabbed up my tool bag, and we ran to the schoolhouse. We were both soaked to our skins, but too excited to care.

"Be right back," Adam said. He ran to the tool shed. I saw he was going for the jug of moonshine. I ran to get the coffee mugs off the picnic table. Sheltered beneath the roof sheathing, we toasted our discovery.

"Can you believe it, Miss Parry, we found Canara Rivers' grave!"

"We found someone's grave. It's too early to know if it's Canara's."

"It's Canara's, all right. I just know it." He drained his cup then set it on the floor. "Here, dance with me."

I set down my mug, then Adam spun me across the floor as he sang.

> *Hot corn, cold corn, bring along a demijohn,*
> *Hot corn, cold corn, bring along a demijohn,*

Except for being dripping wet, it was my romantic notion come to life. I was up a lonesome holler, dancing, my head back, laughing. And if I didn't have the promise of love, I had the next best thing: the chance to solve a sixty-three-year-old mystery. I leaned my head back further, water flying off my wet hair, as I sang along:

> *Hot corn, cold corn, bring along a demijohn,*
> *Fare-thee-well, Uncle Bill, I'll see you in the morning,*
> *Yes, sir!*

Adam released me. With my eyes closed, I spun circles on my own just because it felt good. When I opened my eyes, I saw Adam, on the floor, clutching his sides.

"Adam!" I yelled, as I rushed to his side. Red blotches appeared on his face. "It's your growing pains, isn't it?"

He answered with a moan.

"I'm going to get Beatty," I said, starting to get up.

"No," he whispered, "take me to Granny's."

I helped him to his feet. He couldn't straighten up, and even small steps pained him. We stepped out from the protection of the roof, and into the chill of the rain. When we finally got to the truck, I helped Adam slide onto the passenger seat then ran around to the driver's side.

"Dammit!" I cried, looking at the empty ignition switch. "Where're the keys?"

"In my pocket," Adam croaked. He leaned away from the door and struggled with the pain of lifting his arm.

"Here, let me," I said. I reached across his lap and dug deep into his pocket.

"Now you come on to me," he said.

"Oh, shut up!" I found the keys and started the engine. I went as slow as I could without stalling. Even so, Adam cried out at every bump.

"Oh, Adam, I'm so sorry."

"That's all right, Miss Parry. The pain goes away eventually."

I parked as close to Mrs. Singer's cabin as I could. That still left about one hundred feet that we had to cross on foot. "Mrs. Singer!" I yelled, running around to the passenger side to yank on the door. Adam nearly fell out of the cab. I pushed against him to keep him upright. "Put your arm around my neck."

"No, I can walk on my own." But only very slowly and bent over like an arthritic old man. Little bits of hail, mixed in with the rain, bounced off the ground. Ahead of us, the door on the screened porch opened, and Mrs. Singer, motioning with her hand, encouraged us forward.

"Take him into the guest room," she said, when we reached the door. Behind us, she dragged a kitchen chair for Adam to sit on while I helped him out of his wet clothes. His chest and arms were also blotchy.

"Sorry 'bout all this," Adam said.

I knelt to untie his boot laces. "All I got to say is you better not being wearing those ugly paisley boxers."

Adam managed a chuckle.

I pulled off his socks then his jeans. Mrs. Singer handed me a towel then disappeared with Adam's wet clothes.

"Ow! Don't rub so hard," Adam said. I was actually rubbing very gently. I got him as dry as I could and helped him into bed.

Mrs. Singer returned with a cup of something steaming. "Here, drink this."

Adam took a couple of sips then lay down. Mrs. Singer covered him with a blanket then turned to me. "You best getting yourself out of them wet clothes or you're gonna catch a chill."

"I'd need to go back to the trailer to change," I said, not wanting to leave Adam.

"You just go right on ahead. We'll be fine."

The rain hadn't let up, and I was glad for the truck. After changing into dry clothes, I stopped at the schoolhouse to examine our initial discovery, which I'd left soaking in a glass of water. The water had loosened the dirt, and gentle rubbing revealed a rusty belt buckle with a few strands of leather still attached. I wrapped the buckle in a handkerchief and took it with me. I got back to Mrs. Singer's to find

Adam asleep.

"What was in the drink?" I asked her.

"Just my usual. Morphine, codeine, heroin and a pinch of cocaine the vet gives the horses." She motioned for me to follow her into the kitchen. In one corner, an oil stove was cranking out smelly heat, which felt good despite the fact that it wasn't all that cold.

"I made us some tea," she said. We sat at the table and Mrs. Singer poured a pale golden brown liquid into two cups.

"Tincture of opium?" I said, pointing to the tea.

She sighed. " 'Fraid I'm plumb out of opium; we'll just have to make do with chamomile. There's honey there if you like."

I stirred in a teaspoonful.

"Well, I know Adam's a fool," Mrs. Singer said, "but I figured a smart professor like yourself should know enough to come in out of the rain."

"I'm afraid we got caught up in our work. I think we may have discovered the grave of Canara Rivers."

Mrs. Singer set down her cup. "You don't say. And what exactly makes you think that?"

I explained about the toe bones we found before the rain forced us to stop. "Of course, it's too early to say if the grave is actually Canara Rivers', but considering its location and the fact that it's a shallow grave–which suggests a hasty burial–I think it likely. Which reminds me…" I took the handkerchief from my sweater pocket and unfolded it, "…we found this."

Mrs. Singer pushed her glasses higher onto her nose and leaned forward. She took the buckle and held it to the light. "Why, this is Canara Rivers' for sure. He was the only man on earth who ever wore a belt."

I took the buckle back and rewrapped it. "It's just one bit of information. But judging from the buckle's size, I think it's safe to say it came off of a man's belt. That information itself likely eliminates the skeletal remains being female."

Mrs. Singer stood up. "Which means the body can only be one of a maybe a million people." She hobbled out of the room and came back a minute later. "Adam's sleeping like a baby," she said, sitting back down.

"What exactly is the matter with Adam? He said his mother called it his 'growing pains.'"

She smiled. "That's what we used to tell him as a boy. Said it were his bones growing to make him big and strong. Course, we was just trying to make him feel better. Truth is we had no idea what ailed him."

"Didn't you ever take him to a doctor?"

"Course, we did. Had him up to some big monkey-me at Johns Hopkins hospital, but he didn't know what to make of it either. Fortunately, Adam's growing pains got less as he got older, though lately they seem to be acting up again."

"Adam said his father had the same thing."

"Did he, now? Imagine that." She shifted sideways on her chair. "Made a pot of soup. Would you care for some?"

"Yes, thanks. I think all Adam has for us to eat is some peanut butter and stale bread."

"I baked fresh bread this morning." She pointed to a bread box on the counter by the sink. "Why don't you slice us a few pieces to go 'long with the soup."

We ate in silence. I watched the water pour off the eaves, while Mrs. Singer stared into her soup. By the time we finished, it was nearly dark. I got up and rinsed the empty soup bowls in the sink. "If you don't need any help with Adam, I think I'll go back to the trailer before it gets completely dark."

She didn't respond, but sat, moving her mouth around, causing her dentures to clack.

"Mrs. Singer? I thought I would–"

"Heard you the first time. Sit down. I got something I want to show you."

I dutifully sat as she got up and left the room. In a few minutes, she returned carrying a quilt. "Move that salt and pepper out of the way," she ordered. She unfolded the quilt and laid it out on the table.

It was small, more like a throw, and appeared to be very old. "I made this back when I first left the mountains. Made it when I got to feeling homesick."

I fingered the material. Time had faded the colors, but the pattern was still clear. Blocks of solid blue alternated with blocks further subdivided into four squares. Within each of these smaller squares was an equilateral triangle with a vertex pointing in toward a small circle in the center. Though geometric in the design, the divided squares suggested a four-petalled flower, each petal a different color.

"I call this pattern a friendship circle," she said, tracing her finger along the outside edges of the triangles. "'T ain't your usual friendship circle pattern, but one I made up, thinking of my childhood friends." She pointed to a red triangle. "This here represents my Brother Lillard." She moved her finger laterally to a triangle of pale yellow. "And this one's Roseanne Bickum. Course, opposite her is Canara Rivers. The color of his triangle has faded, but it used to be a deep purple, the color of the kings of old. Back then, we used to look up to Canara Rivers 'cause he'd been places while in the navy, like down to the Caribbean and once over to England." She chuckled. "You'd have thought he'd been to the moon the way we sat 'round, drinking in his stories. Course, none of us had ever been further than a day's ride from home on shank's mare.

"But it weren't just his travels that made Canara big in our eyes. They say a king, iff'n he's a good one, wants for the happiness of his people, wants 'em to grow and prosper, just like a mother wants for her child. Canara Rivers made us feel like we was important. He wanted to know what was in our minds, what we dreamed of doing, and eventually we began to hanker after the moon ourselves, 'stead of wanting to stay here in Hoagland Holler like our kinfolk always done.

"I s'pose some folks found that troubling, a teacher urging his students to be different than their kin." She chuckled again, perhaps recalling some particular incident. "No, the well-worn groove sure weren't for Canara Rivers. But there weren't no harm in him, only dream stuff and maybe him being a little full of himself. And there weren't no doubt that he cared 'bout his students and knew a lot of facts, too."

"Was it Canara's influence that lead you to leave Hoagland Holler?"

"That was some of it. Mostly, I was sick at heart at what the Bickums done to Canara and Roseanne, and I wanted to get away from people like that. Course, Roseanne was a queen in her own right, which is why I wanted to make her little triangle gold, only there weren't no scraps of cloth colored gold to be had, so I done my best and dyed some sacking using goldenrod. Roseanne was as beautiful as any queen in a fairy tale, and sweet tempered too with none of the greediness of her daddy."

"Why did you use red for your brother's triangle? Red is equated with passion."

"That's right. Oh, the stories I could tell 'bout Lillard in his younger days and all his tomcatting! Mostly funny stories, 'cause most times he'd end up with a bucket of cold water thrown on his head just like an ol' tomcat caterwauling outside your window at two in the morning. My, oh my, Lillard sure did love the ladies."

"Did your brother's passion ever cause friction between him and Canara Rivers?"

"You mean, did Lillard and Canara fight over Roseanne?"

I nodded.

"Never for a second. Now, don't get me wrong, Lillard would've liked to have wooed Roseanne for himself. But he knew that what Canara and Roseanne had 'tween 'em was true love. Deep down, people like Lillard want more than to just be tomcatting 'round. They yearn for something that's true, something that can't be broken, can't be defiled. Without something true to guide 'em, their red nature just burns 'em up."

She started to fold the quilt back up.

"Wait a minute. You haven't said anything about your triangle, the green one."

"Who said that triangle's me? Besides, it weren't for me to say what my color was. I just threw that green in there to balance out the colors." She handed me the quilt. "Here, I want you to have this."

"What? No, I couldn't. It's a family heirloom. Adam should have it."

"P'shaw! What would Adam want with an old quilt? Besides, I'm not exactly giving it to you; it's more like a trade."

"Trade? For what?"

"I want you to do something for me. Iff'n this here grave you're digging up turns out to be Canara's, then I want you to come and tell me first."

"Why?"

"'Cause I'm asking you to."

I didn't like to be bribed. Then again, I didn't think that if would make any difference if she was the first to hear. "All right."

"Thank you, Professor. Now let me find something to put this quilt in so's it don't get wet." From a cupboard alongside the stove, she brought out a large plastic bag. She handed me the bag then looked out the kitchen window. It was pitch black outside. "Sorry 'bout you not getting back to the trailer 'fore dark."

CHAPTER 25

July 1, 1970

Dear Teddy,
Tonight, a gentle rain is falling, a soothing patter upon the trailer's roof. I've come to like living in a trailer; I can be close to nature and cozy at the same time.

I had dinner with Mrs. Singer: soup and homemade bread. (When was the last time you had homemade bread?) Afterwards, she showed me a quilt she made over half a century ago. She called the quilt's pattern a "friendship circle" with each of three colors representing one of her childhood friends: gold for Roseanne Bickum, purple for Canara Rivers, red for her brother Lillard. There was also green, which I'm sure represented her, though she refused to admit it. Sometimes she smiles like a Cheshire cat with dentures.

So, tell me, what color do you think I am? Please, don't say black. More likely, I'm gray, sort of neutral, neither here nor there.

Now, get this: when she was done displaying the quilt, she folded it up and gave it to me. A sixty-year old, handmade quilt! Yet, I fear a friendship circle quilt is wasted on me. I mean, if I count all the friends I have, I can barely complete a circle, and that's only if I include myself. In the way of friendship, that's little to show for twenty-six years of living.

There's a student in the anthropology department by the name of Elaine who invited me to go horseback riding with some of her friends. I declined her offer, but if she ever asks again, I think I just might accept.

CHAPTER 26

Next morning, it was still raining, normally my kind of weather, only now it prevented me from excavating the grave. I put on my rain jacket and walked up to the schoolhouse, half expecting to see Adam up and about as he was after the last time he got a bout of his "growing pains." Up and about he might have been, just not at the schoolhouse.

While I was there, I inspected the gravesite. Wind had rearranged the tarp, despite the weight of the rocks. Resisting the urge to peek under the plywood and thereby expose the pit to the rain, I straightened the tarp and added more rocks to weigh it down. I was then ready for breakfast, such as it was: dry cereal taken from the tool shed, along with milk from the carton bobbing in the now iceless ice chest. I ate, sitting cross-legged atop a short stack of plywood, staring at puddles on the sub floor made by rain leaking through the joints in the roof sheathing. I finished breakfast and was looking for a broom to sweep away the puddles when Junie arrived on "shank's mare," as Mrs. Singer would say, his face covered in bruises in all the colors of an anemic rainbow. Yet his smile seemed genuine enough.

"Morning," he said, entering the schoolhouse through the space between the studs. "A mite wet, ain't it." He looked around. "Where's Adam?"

Before I could answer, he saw the tarp covering the gravesite.

"What's that?"

I didn't know if I should tell him.

But he guessed. "You found another grave, didn't you?"

"Another? The first one was nothing but rocks."

"Well, what 'bout this one? Is it Canara Rivers?"

I shrugged. "Too early to tell. I just wish it would quit raining so I could get to work on it."

"I want to help you."

"How? You know a dance to stop rain?"

"You know what I'm saying, Professor. I want to help you dig up Canara Rivers."

Distrust must have shown in my face.

"Please, I know you got a right to hate me, but I'm asking you to give me a second chance. I won't fail you, I promise. Besides, you got to remember I got as much interest in finding out about Canara Rivers as anybody, maybe more."

I got up off the plywood. "First off, let's get one thing straight. If you ever try anything like you did the other night, you're going to pay with a lot more than a bruised face. I've written a friend, telling him what happened, and he'll sic the law on you if any harm comes to me.

"Second, if you're going to work with Adam and me, you'll have to promise to follow my instructions to the letter, otherwise you could destroy clues that might tell us whether it's the actual grave of Canara Rivers."

"I'll do whatever you tell me, Professor, cross my heart. If you say, 'be a dog,' I'll bark."

This forced a smile from me. "Well, first off, quit calling me Professor. Parry will do."

He walked forward, hand out. "And I'm Junie Gorn. Pleased to meet you, Parry."

He was asking for a new start. I didn't know if I would ever like Junie, but I was willing to give him another try. I shook his hand.

"So, where's Adam?" he said.

I explained about Adam having another attack of his growing pains. "I was just about to drive over to his grandmother's to see how he's doing."

"Mind iff'n I tag along?"

In the spirit of second chances, I nodded my assent. As it turned out, Junie did more than just behave himself, he entertained me, playing "The Wabash Cannonball" on his harmonica as I drove Adam's truck. I actually drove slowly just to prolong the concert.

We got to Mrs. Singer's cabin just as Brother Lillard came out the back door. "Well, lookee there," Junie said. "What's he doing here?" We both got out of the truck.

"Morning, Professor. Morning, Junie," Brother Lillard said, stepping sprightly, oblivious to the rain.

"Pardon me, Brother Lillard," Junie said, "but since when have you and Granny Estey been getting along?

"Since this morning, Junie. Since my sister asked me to come pray for Adam."

I started toward the cabin. "If Adam's that sick, we need to get him to a hospital immediately."

Brother Lillard barred my way. "Adam's in the hands of the best physician, the good Lord."

I made to go around him, and he threw out an arm. "Hold on there, young lady."

Junie was suddenly at my side, ready to knock Brother Lillard down if necessary.

Brother Lillard looked at both our faces then smiled. "I can see Adam's got himself some good friends, but fact is, Adam's just fine, thanks to God's mercy, though he had a pretty rough night. Right now, Estey don't want nobody disturbing him, 'cause the boy needs his rest."

Junie and I relaxed a little.

"But I'm sure glad you came by, Professor, 'cause there's some things you and me need to talk about. You can stay to listen if you want to, Junie."

"Is them religious things?" Junie said.

"I reckon you could say that."

"Then I think I'll head on home."

"I'll drive you," I said.

He patted the nonexistent fat on his belly. "Naw, I need the exercise. Momma said you're to come to dinner. It's chicken and dumplings tonight."

"What if Adam can't come?"

"Then just bring your lonesomes." He pulled up the collar of his jacket. "And your hunger, 'cause Momma makes mighty good dumplings." Junie nodded to Brother Lillard, then headed up the drive.

"You don't mind talking to me, do you?" Brother Lillard said.

"No. In fact, there are some things I want to say to you."

"Then let's us go on up to the church where we'll be out of this rain." He went around to the passenger side of the truck.

The inside of the church smelled musty. Brother Lillard cracked a window, then pushed one of the chairs toward me and sat in another. "First off," he said, "I want to know iff'n you're all right. I have it in my mind that you took off of a sudden the other night."

"No, first off, I want to know where you get off saying all those things you did about me?"

Brother Lillard looked taken aback. "What things might that be?"

I did my best to imitate his singsong style of preaching. " 'She has a pain in her HEART, Lord, 'cause she misses a LOVED one.' Who told you I missed my father? And who gave you permission to talk about me in front of strangers?"

Brother Lillard shook his head. "I don't rightly remember saying anything like that."

"Don't try to worm your way out of this! Adam was there and can back me up."

Brother Lillard held up a hand, ensuing for peace. "Young lady–"

"The name's Euphrates, Professor Euphrates."

He gave me a sad smile. "Professor Euphrates, I don't doubt for one second I said those things you accuse me of. But, as God is my witness, I do not remember saying 'em."

"How the hell could you–"

Again, he held up a hand. "Iff'n you could forgive the ramblings of an old man, I'll explain. You see, when I'm preaching, I mostly don't know what I'm saying."

"You mean, you don't write out your sermon ahead of time?"

"I never wrote one word of a sermon in all my days of preaching. For one thing, I can't write–can't read much neither. But even if I could write as good as Saint Luke himself, I'd never write out a sermon 'cause that would be my mind wanting to do the preaching. That would be me trying to put my own words in God's mouth. When I preach, I first ask the Holy Spirit to enter into me and speak through me. And usually, thanks to God's goodness, that's just 'bout what happens. Then I'm nothing but a voice box that God uses to speak unto others. All the time, I get folks come up to me after church and say, 'Brother Lillard, thank you for what you said tonight. You spoke straight to my heart, and it was just what I was needing to hear.' I tell 'em it weren't me speaking, but the Holy Spirit, and what's more, I don't rightly remember a single word I said."

"So you're telling me you don't remember what you said about me because it was God, not you, speaking to me."

He nodded.

"You never talked to anyone about me? You never talked to your sister Estelline?"

"One of the burdens I carry is that, until this very morning, I haven't spoken to Estelline in years."

"Why is that?"

" 'Cause I done some things in my younger days I'm not proud of. But that was before I met the Lord." He leaned forward and tapped my knee. "But let's not get sidetracked, here. God spoke to you about the pain in your heart, about you missing your daddy. When God speaks to us, we need to listen, listen with our ears, but respond with our heart. My question is, what're you planning to do now that God's spoken to you?"

I pushed my chair away from him. "You know, you're just like your sister, only instead of hearing things, she sees things–like guardian angels and the ghost of my father looking over my shoulder. You two really ought to go into business together." I swept my hand in an arc, outlining an imaginary banner. " 'Lillard and Estelline. Hear the voice of God! See the dead!' Between the two of you, you could make a fortune."

He ran a hand through his thin hair. "Well, first off, you got it wrong 'bout me and Estelline, leastways in a spiritual sense. By trying to talk to the dead, Estelline's practicing the black arts. That's devil worship, and one day she's gonna meet Jesus and have to answer to that. Second thing is, God's love ain't for sale. It's free to anyone who opens her heart to him. And last, you're still not answering my question about that there pain in your heart."

"Whatever pain I have is none of your or anybody else's business!" My voice sounded harsh even to my ears, but I was pissed. "What do you want me to do, get down on my knees and ask God to forgive me for my sins?" I slipped out of my chair and knelt on the concrete floor. "Oh, Jesus, I'm nothing but a SINNER, uh. Forgive me because I'm trying to live my LIFE, uh, the best I CAN, uh. Trying to play the cards I've been DEALT, uh. Trying to do the best I can with a SHITTY HAND, uh. Forgive me, God, for being what YOU MADE ME, uh! Forgive me for not listening to all the religious CRANKS in this world, uh, for not listening to YOU when you never TALK!"

I had to stop and catch my breath. Brother Lillard stared at me with wide eyes behind the thick lenses of his glasses. Then he threw back his head and roared with laughter. Feeling more than a little silly, I pushed myself back up onto the chair and waited as Brother Lillard took off his glasses, wiped away his tears of laughter with a handkerchief then blew his nose.

"Is that what I sound like when I'm preaching?"

"Well, more or less. I must say that you're the first preacher I've ever heard who worked 'Piggly Wiggly' into his sermon."

"I said, 'Piggly Wiggly?'"

I nodded.

"Hah!" he said, slapping his knee. This time, I had to laugh along with him.

"But Professor Euphrates, you must understand we're not like some of those other churches you may have gone to. We don't try to trick folks, luring them down to the altar with heart-tugging hymns.

What we believe mostly boils down to just one thing: to keep our hearts open to God. Iff'n a body can do that, then God will surely take care of the rest."

I had nothing say to this. I was full up with religion for one morning. Still, I was curious about two things. "Brother Lillard, you said you couldn't write or read. How is it you can quote so many Bible verses?"

"Well, I can read a little–not enough to hurt me any–and I listen real good. It's one of God's gifts that any Bible verse I hear, I remember, including chapter and verse."

"I've another question: the woman who sat beside me in your church, I take it she has a terminal illness."

Brother Lillard smiled. "Sister Edith's been dying for as long as I've known her, which is mor'n fifty years. With Edie, religion is her main form of entertainment, not that I doubt for a moment she's one of God's saints. She used to be what we call a 'runner.' When the spirit would come over her, she'd go running around the room, knocking things over. After she knocked over the water cooler and sorta flooded everything, we came to an agreement. She could go ahead and do whatever it was the spirit moved her to do so long as she stayed put in her chair. This has worked out well for all concerned. But to answer your question, Edie's actually as strong as an ox, and will probably outlive us all."

Brother Lillard stood and I did also. "For my own part, I'm sorry iff'n what I said the other night angered you. Professor Euphrates, I don't dare try to understand all of God's ways, for they are truly mysterious. But I do know that he talks to us through others, which is why it's important that we worship together. I'm saying this 'cause we'll be meeting again come next Tuesday, and we'd be mighty glad to have you join us again."

I planned never again to set foot in his shoe box of a church. Yet I knew that, in his own way, Brother Lillard was a good man, even if he had pissed me off.

"Please, call me Parry," I said.

CHAPTER 27

That night, Beatty's hospitality was primarily bestowed upon her son. She gave him first helpings of everything, often serving him herself.

"Don't he just look a sight," she said, pride obvious in her voice. "And to think he took on them bullies and never let 'em steal one drop of my deliveries." She rubbed Junie's head affectionately. "Yes'r, my boy's quite a man."

Junie, looking sheepish enough to sprout wool, couldn't look me in the eye. For my part, I was glad of the attention he was getting as it took the focus away from the food, for this was one of Beatty's dinners I wasn't looking forward to, having always hated that peculiar brand of white paste people call dumplings. Hated, that is, until I bit into ones made by Beatty.

"God, these are incredible!"

Beatty grinned from her place at the end of the table.

"My father used to make dumplings," I said, "or tried to. How come yours taste so good when his always came out like glue?"

"It's the lard," she said.

"Lard?"

"Don't care what you're making–pies, cakes, bread, dumplings–it won't have any taste less'n you use lard."

"You know, you really should start a cooking school," I said. "People would pay a lot to come to this beautiful place and learn regional cooking."

Beatty looked pleased. "Well, I dare say I might be able to show 'em a thing or two."

Junie waved his fork, "That's not a half-bad idea. Only folks could learn a lot mor'n cooking. They could learn all the ol' crafts, including mountain music." He looked over his shoulder into the cavernous living room. "Hell, this ol' barn would make a great lodge. I bet we could fix things so we could house ten, maybe fifteen people at a time."

Beatty shook her head. "Don't you be getting any highfaluting ideas. We got 'nough on our plates already." She turned to me. "Junie told me you done found the grave of Canara Rivers."

"It's only speculation it's Canara Rivers' grave, but I've a piece of evidence that suggests the remains are those of a male." I set the rusty belt buckle on the table. "Doesn't that look like the style of belt buckle a man would wear?"

"You dug this up?" Beatty said, picking up the buckle.

I nodded.

"I'd say any belt buckle you found would have to be a man's. The ladies of my mother's day didn't wear no belts. They wore dresses made to show off their figures." She pushed her chair back. "I'll be back shortly." She crossed the living room and into the back of the house.

I looked to Junie to explain Beatty's sudden disappearance. He shrugged then took a sip of wine.

"I still think a school where people could come to learn the ol' mountain crafts is a good idea," he said.

"It's a *great* idea, especially the idea of learning music. There are more people interested in bluegrass and old-timey music than ever before. I mean, look at me. I grew up in southern California, which is sunshine, surf, and the Beach Boys–about as far as you can get from moonshine, dark hollers, and Gid Tanner and the Skillet Lickers."

Hearing "skillet," Junie winced.

"But even someone like me would jump at the chance to come here for a week or two to study with the likes of you or Adam."

Junie shook his head. "Won't never happen while Momma's alive. She's too fixated on her bottling plant."

I dished up another helping of chicken and dumplings, making a mental note to ask Beatty for her recipe.

"Found what I was looking for," Beatty said, striding back into the room. "This was one of the fancy dresses my momma wore as a girl." She held it up against her. The dress, all satin and lace, was yellow with age. "Course, momma was considerably smaller than myself, which is why I've never been able to wear any of her dresses. But I dare say this would look good on you, Parry." She motioned for me to stand up.

With more than a little reluctance, I came around the table, and she held the dress up against me.

"Looks to be a perfect fit," she said. "Let's see what you look like in it."

"You want me to put it on?" I hated dresses, especially the frilly type. Last time I wore a dress was at my father's funeral.

Beatty nodded.

"But it's a family heirloom. I'd feel terrible if I were to damage it."

"Fiddlesticks," she said. "You can change in the room the phone's in."

I dutifully took the dress to the den, shut the door, and stripped down to underwear and socks. The dress went on easily enough until I tried to button up the back. Either Beatty's mother had had help getting dressed, or she'd been a contortionist on the level of Houdini. I succeeded in buttoning the two bottom buttons and the one at the top, but the others resisted all my twisting, straining, and cursing. "Screw it." I told a mirror. I hated the way I looked: Little Bo Peep minus bonnet and crook.

"I can't get this buttoned," I said, coming back into the dining room.

Beatty rushed to my aid. "Let your air out," she ordered.

I exhaled and she closed the latch on the iron lung.

"I can't breathe!"

"Ladies weren't supposed to breathe," Beatty said, stepping away. "Now, don't she look a peach?"

Junie stood up and presented me with a mock bow, one leg in front of the other. "Madame Euphrates."

I would have kicked him, but movement in the dress was

impossible. Of course, Adam had to choose that exact moment to enter the room. He stopped dead in his tracks.

"Miss Parry?"

He looked pale, which I attributed to his illness, but also a little dazzled, like he was seeing me in a way he really liked. I didn't want to encourage him. "Baaaa," I said, "have you seen my sheeeeep?"

Adam smiled. "Miss Peep, you look right beautiful."

"I'm going to look like a corpse if I don't get out of this straight jacket." I breathed in, and to my great relief, two buttons became flying projectiles. "Thank God!" I said, as everybody laughed.

Beatty placed a hand on Adam's shoulder. "Boy, you're looking a mite like a corpse yourself."

"I'm actually feeling a lot better."

"Could you eat something?"

Adam shook his head. "I had me a bite at Granny's."

Beatty pulled out a piece of paper out of her pocket and handed it to Adam. "Feller called. Said you was to call back at that number. Sounded like it was real important."

Adam unfolded the slip of paper. "This is my agent's number. I'd better see what he wants." He went to use the phone, thereby depriving me from getting unjacketed.

"Parry," said Beatty, "would you mind setting some dessert plates whilst I get us the cake I baked this afternoon? It fell a little, but I think it still might be edible."

She went to the kitchen, leaving me alone with Junie and his impish grin. "One word about the way I look," I said, "and I'll hit you again."

By its appearance, Beatty's cake looked like three layers of chocolate heaven. Still, the idea of lard in a cake seemed on the order of flavoring ice cream with bacon grease. All doubts were allayed by my first bite. The cake was scrumptious. I was debating whether I could risk seconds when Adam literally came bounding into the room.

"I don't think you're gonna believe this," he said, dropping down into a chair. He shook his head as if he still didn't believe it either.

"How do we know what to believe less'n you tell us?" Beatty said.

"Clarence White has quit the Byrds."

"Well, so what?"

But I leaned forward, resting a hand on Adam's arm. "And?"

"And," said Adam, managing to enlarge his grin, "they're fixing on me taking his place."

Junie and I leaped out of our chairs and pulled Adam out of his. Then the three of us danced a merry circle. "The Byrds!" we screamed like star-struck teenagers.

Beatty had to shout to be heard. "What's so all-fired important about some birdies?"

We broke our circle, but still held onto each other.

"The Byrds," Junie said. "B-y-r-d-s."

" 'Turn, Turn, Turn,' " I said.

" 'Eight Miles High,' " Junie added.

Beatty shook her head, still not getting it.

"They're a pretty well-known rock band," Adam said.

" 'Pretty well-known?' " I said. "Adam, you're going to be rich and famous."

"Well, I don't know 'bout that, Miss Parry, but I'm gonna make a lot more money than I'm making now. My agent's meeting me in D.C. tomorrow to go over the contract with me."

It was out of my mouth before I even thought. "What about the grave?"

It took Adam a moment to refocus. "Oh, yeah. Well, I'm afraid I'm gonna be gone for a couple of days." He patted Junie on the back. "But Junie here can work with you. I hear it's suppose to stop raining tonight."

My happiness for Adam overrode my own disappointment. I wrapped my arms around him and gave him a hard squeeze. "The Byrds!"

Adam leaned his head against mine. "I guess, Miss Parry, it's my time now."

My time now. Roseanne Bickum had used similar words when cursing her kinfolk. Of course, Adam wasn't a Bickum. Besides, I wasn't superstitious.

So why did I feel a sudden ghostly chill?

CHAPTER 28

Iwoke to clear skies. In less than ten minutes, I was dressed and up to the schoolhouse, hoping to catch Adam before he left for D.C., but his truck was already gone. Small wonder. If I'd been asked to join the Byrds, I wouldn't have been able to sleep. As it was, I hadn't slept much because I was thinking about the dig. I forced myself to eat something, knowing that once I started excavating the grave, I'd be too engrossed to stop. The milk had gone sour, so I dumped it on a bush along with the murky water in the ice chest. Then I ate dry Wheaties out of the box. Yum.

While I dined, I watched the gravesite as if it might sneak away. The extra rocks had held the tarp in place. I just hoped I wouldn't find a swimming pool underneath the plywood. I was in the tool shed, trading the cereal box for my excavating tools when Junie surprised me.

"Morning," he said.

I jumped. "Jesus! I didn't hear you drive up."

"Here." He thrust a plastic container into my hands. I opened it and found scrambled eggs, bacon, and two slices of toast. "I hope they ain't cold."

Cold or not, I was glad for the food as two handfuls had been my limit on dry Wheaties. "Your mother's a saint," I said, piling eggs atop a piece of toast.

"Iff'n you say so."

I offered the other piece of toast to Junie. He shook his head. "Anything I need to know 'fore we start digging?"

"Well, I'm pretty sure we're down to the skeletal remains. So, from here on, it's small scrapers and brushes. I think I'll have you working the sifting screen. Don't be surprised if I stop to take a lot of pictures. And I'll be taking notes. Can you deal with a slow pace?"

"Arf! Arf!"

I put the lid on the plastic container and set it aside. "Okay, let's dig up some bones."

We lifted the rocks off the tarp and stacked them well away from the pit. My hands we're actually trembling as we folded back the tarp. "We should pull the dirt away from the edges before we lift the plywood," I said. I started toward the tool shed to get a hoe, but Junie headed me off. He returned carrying the shovel and a mattock.

"Wasn't there a hoe?" I said.

Junie shook his head. "These here are the only digging tools Adams got, excepting a pick."

I let Junie use the heavier mattock, while I scraped with the shovel. Despite all the rain, the soil beneath the surface was fairly dry. But the plywood had glued itself to the ground. I nearly stumbled when, pulling hard, the plywood suddenly came unstuck. We laid the plywood in a sunny spot to dry. I returned to the grave, hoping I wouldn't see a lot of standing water. What I saw was infinitely worse.

"Damn!" I cried. I rubbed my eyes, as if that would change what I was seeing. "Damn! Damn! Damn!" I shot Junie an accusatory look. "Did you do this?"

"Do what?"

"This!" I yelled, pointing down into the pit.

Junie looked down. "What is it I'm supposed to have done?"

"Somebody's already been digging. Look!" Bones were everywhere, some of them sticking halfway out of the mud, some pressed into the mud by someone's boots. "Christ! It's a goddamn mess!"

"And you're thinking it was me that done it?"

"Well, somebody did it!" Of course, I had no evidence of Junie having vandalized the gravesite, but right then I wanted to smash someone, and he was the only person within striking distance.

Junie placed a hand on my shoulder. "Tell me what to do, Parry.

Tell me how it fix it.”

I slapped his hand away. “You can’t fix it! It’s ruined! It’s–” There was an unwelcome lump in my throat. I swallowed it and went for my Instamatic. “Move away from the pit,” I ordered. I took a few pictures from different angles. “I’m going to figure out who did this. And when I do, I’m going to take that son of a bitch and…”

“Bang ’im on the head with a frying pan,” Junie said, smiling.

I was too pissed to see anything funny in this. “A bang on the head will be the least of his worries.”

Junie scratched the side of his swollen nose. “You really think you can figure out who done this?”

I didn’t answer because I didn’t know. Figuring out who had wreaked this havoc meant first figuring out why he would want to. Yet realizing this, I suddenly felt more hopeful.

“Are you still willing to work with me?” I said.

Junie staggered back, feigning a look of shock. “What? You want me, the son of a bitch who done messed all this up, working with you?”

“I didn’t call you a son of a bitch. I–” I closed my eyes, thinking of how I must have sounded. “Junie, sometimes when I’m angry, I just lash out. I’m sorry.”

Junie nudged a small rock with his foot. “Well, now you mention it, I have noticed you are a mite prickly. Course, I never lash out at nobody like that.”

This got the intended smile out of me.

“Well,” he said, hitching up his jeans. “I reckon I can forgive you. And if you’re still wanting a dog, I’m still willing to bark.”

“What I want is for a certain somebody to shut up and drag that piece of plywood over here next to the grave.” As Junie dragged, I unfolded the tarp. “There’s been a change of plans. You’re going to work in the pit.” Junie helped me spread the tarp over the plywood. “I want you to remove bones and anything else you find and set them on the edge of the pit. If a bone’s stuck in the ground, don’t go yanking on it. I’ve got special tools you can use.”

“And what’re you gonna do?”

"I'm going to reconstruct the skeleton right here on top this tarp."

Junie carefully lowered himself into the pit. He soon had a pile of bones gathered, more than I could keep up with. But he also found a few things other things: two rubber soles, a shoelace that miraculously hadn't disintegrated, two very rusty metal buttons, and a folded piece of cloth that might once have been a handkerchief. But nothing to indicate who the person was or when he had died: no wallet, coins, keys–not even a pocket comb, either of rubber or bone.

Over the next hour, Junie's pile of bones decreased as I began to catch up. After requesting my special digging tools, he added a few more bones to the pile. "I think that's 'bout all there is."

I turned from examining a rib bone. "There's got to be more. Keep looking."

"Can I use a shovel?"

I walked to the edge of the pit and surveyed the bottom. Junie was right; there didn't seem to be anything left. I handed him the shovel. "Just be careful. Ease the shovel into the ground." I gathered up the remaining bones. "Everything you dig up, dirt included, put here." I tapped the ground where the bones had been. "We'll sift through it all later."

After several minutes of more bone sorting, I announced that the skeletal remains were that of a male.

"How do you know?" Junie said, leaning on the shovel handle. "'Cause of that thing on the cheek bone?"

"No, I'm looking at the pelvic girdle; it's definitely a male's, and judging by the surface of the pubic symphysis, I'd estimate that he was about thirty years old, give or take five years."

Junie nodded. " 'Bout the same age as Canara Rivers when he died."

"You're still assuming that these remains are those of Canara Rivers." I looked at Junie's pile of dirt. "Have you found anything else?"

Junie shook his head. "And I don't reckon I'm gonna. This ground is getting harder'n cement."

"Damn!" I walked over to the pit. Junie dropped the shovel and it hit the bottom with a sound of metal striking stone. "You're probably down to where the grave digger stopped." I squatted down and took a handful of dirt from the small pile Junie had made. "Did you see any bone fragments?" I sifted the dirt through my fingers. "They might have looked like small stones."

"No, and I was being real careful just like you said. You got some bones missing?"

I dusted off my hands. I couldn't think of a reason not to tell him. "Junie, this skeleton has no skull."

Junie jumped out of the pit to see for himself. I had the bones laid out on the tarp so the skeleton looked like an elaborate stick man. A stick man with no head.

"Whoever got to this grave ahead of us done stole the skull," said Junie. "That's downright spooky."

I shook my head. "You're making another assumption; the skull might not have been placed in the grave in the first place." An idea which seemed to me even spookier.

"Then why'd someone go and mess up this here grave iff'n he wasn't looking to steal something?"

"How do we know what he was looking to steal? Besides, why does anyone do anything? Was does Dewey Bone shoot at people instead of just putting up a no trespassing sign?"

Junie didn't have an answer to that. He nudged a fibula with a finger. "When you was looking over these bones, did you find something that coulda told you how this feller died?"

I shook my head. "I've looked for nicks or cracks–anything that might suggest an injury. To my eyes, the bones all appear normal. Then again, I'm not a forensic anthropologist."

" 'Course iff'n Canara Rivers was shot in the head, then takin' the skull would keep us from proving that."

"Why would anyone care if we prove Canara Rivers was shot in the head? His murderers have all been dead for nearly seventy years."

Junie crossed his arms over his chest. "So, what do we do now,

Parry?"

I didn't know. Something besides the vandalizing of the grave was troubling me; something I had failed to do. But what? "I need to sit and do some thinking."

I sat on the rough steps of the schoolhouse, opened the plastic container with the remains of breakfast, and took out a limp slice of toast. It hit me on the third bite: I had gone about this dig all wrong, and for that reason I was partly responsible for the gravesite having been vandalized. If this had been one of my middens, I never would have just started digging without first doing extensive research. Then I would have made some arrangement for the site to be protected during excavation. But instead of following my usual procedure, I had just jumped right in because I wanted to show off to Adam. As a result, I'd made it easy for someone to wreck the gravesite, and since I knew nothing about Canara Rivers, I hadn't a clue as to why.

"Junie, when you and Adam were writing the song, "The Teacher of Hoagland Holler School," how did you go about gathering information about Canara Rivers?"

While waiting for me, Junie had been pitching rocks at a tree. He stopped half way through his delivery. "By talking to ever'body who ever knew anything 'bout him."

"Did you do anything else?"

"Like what. There ain't exactly a book you can read about him."

"I know that, but did you check out old newspaper articles or go through voting or tax records?"

"Whatever for?"

"Those sources often provide useful information about a person."

Junie completed his pitch then turned toward me. "Digging 'round in records sounds more like something in the professor line of work. As songwriters, we was just wanting to bring all the old stories together."

I stood up. "What day is it? I've lost track."

"It's Friday."

"Good, the county offices will be open."

"What you got in mind?"

"To drive up to Damascus and do some basic research." I slapped my forehead. "Damn! Adam took the truck."

"That's okay. I'll drive you on up to Damascus."

"Won't you be needed to make deliveries?"

"Not for a couple of days." He pointed to the tarp. "What about them there bones?"

"We've got to put them where no one can get to them, preferably someplace with a heavy padlock on it."

"Folks don't have much use for locks 'round here. Fact, the only key I own is the one to the jeep."

"So how can we keep the bones safe?"

"You figure whoever stole the skull is fixing to steal something else?"

I didn't answer because I just thought of a place to secret away the bones. "Junie, do you think you can find me a box about yay-by-yay?" I made rough dimensions with my hands.

"All them bones in a box that tiny?"

"Take away water and tissue and not much remains of the human body, especially one that's missing a skull."

"Well, we got all type of boxes up in the warehouse. I'll go and get us one."

While waiting, I sifted through the dirt pile Junie made. He hadn't lied; he'd been very careful. I found zilch.

Junie must have doubted my estimate, for he returned with a box bigger than I needed. We carefully packed away the bones and put them in the back of the jeep. Then I had him drive me down to the trailer. I gathered a few clothes and toiletries and stuck them in a brown grocery bag along with my notebook.

"I'm bringing a few things just in case I need to stay over," I said as I put the bag in the back of the jeep. I'd have to figure some way to get back here from Damascus.

"I can stay over with you, iff'n you like."

My face must have registered my revulsion.

"I thought we was gonna be friends," he said.

"Sorry."

Junie spun the tires. I wasn't sure if it was because he was angry since that was his usual means of acceleration.

"Iff'n we're gonna spend the night up to Damascus," he shouted over the engine, "I gotta get us some things."

He skidded to a stop just short of a barn near his house. He went in and returned, dragging a large metal army surplus container. I jumped out of the jeep to help him lift it.

"Jesus!" I said, struggling to lift my side up over the rear panel of the jeep. "What's in this thing?"

"Just things me and daddy used to take whenever we went hunting."

"Are we going hunting?"

"Adam told me you liked to camp, and camping's cheaper than motels."

Junie drove the short distance to the house. I got out and waited while he went inside. I saw a flash of red and followed it around the side of the house. A cardinal hopped along the railing of the deck.

"So, should I go camping with Junie, or not?" I said, remembering what Estelline Singer said about looking for my father to communicate to me through birds.

In answer to my question, the cardinal flew away.

"A lot of help you are."

I returned to sit in the jeep and wait. Eventually, Junie returned along with Beatty. He was carrying two sleeping bags and an overnight bag. Beatty, holding a grocery bag, leaned against the driver's door while Junie stowed his gear in the back.

"Junie tells me you two are going up to Damascus," she said.

"I hope you don't mind us taking the jeep. I want to do some research on Canara Rivers at the county offices."

Beatty stepped back to let Junie open the driver's side door. She handed him the bag, which he tossed into my lap.

"Lunch," he said.

I opened the bag and saw among other things two pieces of last night's cake. I made a mental note to get something for Beatty while in Damascus, a nice gift to thank her for all her kindnesses.

"Boy, you take care on the roads. Don't be driving fast and scaring Parry."

"Hell," said Junie, "this old wreck don't know what fast is."

He ground the gears into reverse and swung back around without looking.

Beatty waved. My wave back was cut short as Junie tore out and I grabbed for something to hold onto.

"I need to stop at the church," I shouted.

Junie nodded and shifted into second.

As I expected, the church was empty. I opened the door on the back of the altar. The interior of the altar held a stack of missionary pamphlets, a small trash can with a few Dixie cups, and now the remains of Canara Rivers. Brother Lillard had mentioned that the church was only used on Tuesdays, so I trusted the bones would lie undiscovered at least until then. Outside, Junie was sorting through the mail he had taken from the mailbox.

"Somebody's been writing to a feller name of Teddy Dob... Dobz..."

I grabbed the letter out of his hand. "Dobzhansky!"

Junie grinned. "A boyfriend, I hope."

I didn't reply, but jammed the letter into the bag with my clothes.

CHAPTER 29

In my mind, I'd pictured Damascus as a run-down mill town perched on the disintegrating banks of a polluted river with a once noble courthouse now falling into ruin. What I got was as lovely a town as ever graced a calendar. The houses were white clapboard with long sloping lawns of lush green. The downtown buildings were of brick and stone, some with vines growing up them. Even the Piggly Wiggly with its veneer of ocher-colored bricks, seemed in keeping with the town's timeworn gentility. Trees, some as tall as the tallest buildings, made tunnels of the narrow streets where people ambled in an atmosphere of day long twilight.

My kind of town.

All along Main Street, the Stars and Stripes hung from every lamppost, and red, white and blue banners graced the storefront windows. With so much going on, I'd completely forgotten tomorrow was the Fourth of July.

With a turn that nearly snapped my head off, Junie swung into the parking lot next to the courthouse and snagged the one remaining parking space. He switched off the engine and leaned against the door. "Now what?"

"Now, I pay a visit to the court recorder and check out some old documents. Want to come along?"

"Nah. I think I'll mosey on over to the Piggly Wiggly and pick up a few things. How long you gonna be?"

"I don't know. Probably quite a while. Is there someplace we could meet later?"

Junie tapped one hand on the steering wheel. "Well, there's a tavern down the road called Lickory Holler. When you're done, you'll likely find me there getting lickeried up."

I bit back the urge to remind him about a recent, painful episode when he'd been liquored up and instead got my notebook out of my grocery bag. The courthouse was built of blocks of gray limestone, all polished except for the cornerstones which had been left rough cut. Red, white, and blue bunting drooped from each of the slender double-hung windows on the second floor.

In contrast to this comely exterior, the inside looked as if it had been remodeled back in the '30s by an accountant. Save for the entryway, the ceilings had been lowered, the walls scraped clean of bygone woodwork, and the floor covered with linoleum, now cracked and peeling. I followed the arrows pointing the way to the court recorder's office located at the end of a dingy hallway. The room was unoccupied except for a woman about my age pecking away on a typewriter.

"May I help you?" she said. Her voice had none of the hillbilly twang I'd grown accustomed to.

"I'd like to look at your tax records."

"Any particular year?"

I thought for a moment. Due to matters beyond his control, Canara Rivers had likely skipped his 1907 property tax payment.

"For the year 1906."

"Nineteen-o-six?" From her look, you'd have thought I just asked her to bench press her desk. She got up and pushed open the little gate that separated her space from the public area.

"Is that a problem?" I said.

"I'm new here, and I don't know where records that old are kept. Just a moment." She walked to a door at the far end of the room, her high heels clicking on the linoleum. She rapped on a door, opened it, but held on to the handle. "There's a lady here who wants to look at records from 1906."

I heard the scrape of a chair follow by a man's voice. "O-six?" He made it sound like an accusation. The woman came to stand beside me. The man, now that I could see him, followed her legs with his eyes.

He stopped in the doorway, his bulk filling most of it. He had small black eyes, bloodhound cheeks, and a belly that spilled out over his waist band. I thought him a hillbilly version of Sergeant Garcia from the '50s TV show *Zorro*. He gave me the once over, turning down his puffy lips at what he saw.

"All the old tax records are kept down in the basement, southwest corner. Now, whose records are you looking for, missy?"

I think that was the first time I'd ever been called "missy." The novelty of it kept me from making his lips puffier. "Canara Rivers," I said.

The name meant nothing to him, but he didn't admit it. He waved a paw. "Down there in the southwest corner." He turned away and shut the door behind him.

I turned to the woman. "So how do I get down to the basement?"

"I'll show you." She started toward the door then did an about face and ran clickety-clack back for her sweater on the back of her chair. "I hate it down there. It's freezing."

She led me to an unmarked door halfway down the hallway. Opening it released the smells of earth, mold, and paper. As for freezing, that was an exaggeration; the air coming up out of the basement had to be at least thirty-four degrees. She stepped down one step, flicked a switch, and a bare light bulb illuminated the stairway.

"This place gives me the creeps," she said, clutching her sweater about her neck.

"You don't have to go down," I said. "I can find my way around."

She gave me a grateful look.

"But I'm kind of turned around. Which way is southwest?"

"I'm not sure. I guess I could ask." She bit her lip. Asking probably meant consulting Sergeant Garcia again.

"Don't bother. I'll find it."

The basement was divided into two sections with a locked door closing off one. There was no ceiling, only cobweb-strewn rafters holding up diagonal floorboards which creaked under the weight of footsteps overhead. I flicked a light switch and banks of overhead bulbs came on. There was no other switch; it was all the lights or none. I walked down the center aisle, reading the titles at the end of each row of shelves. Tax records were midway down. I hung a left and started looking for the year 1906. Invariably, what I'm looking for always winds up being on the very bottom shelf. I pulled out a box marked "Pamunkey County, 1906" then sat on the cold concrete floor.

Probably the records had been alphabetically arranged at one time, but over the years the entries had gotten jumbled. I realized I'd have to sort through the whole box. I scooted back so my back rested against the shelf behind me. It took a couple of hours of rummaging to learn that the county had no record of Canara Rivers having made a property tax payment for 1906 or any year prior. Likely such a free spirit as Canara Rivers hadn't been a property holder. Hiram Bickum, on the other hand, had paid his taxes on time. Obviously, Hiram had been an upstanding citizen, if you discounted his proclivity towards murder.

I pushed up off the floor, my joints creaking, and staggered off to find the voting records. It was nearly three o'clock. I had two more hours to gather information, provided I didn't get hypothermia first. The voting records were down near the end of the hallway where it was a little warmer due to a small window which admitted hazy rays of sunlight. Needing to find the voting records for the presidential election prior to 1907, I mentally calculated back from the year Kennedy was elected, then pulled down a thick binder labeled 1904, amazed to find it wasn't on the bottom shelf. Alas, when I opened it, the contents all spilled out onto the floor. Judging from the fact that many of the pages were dirty, it probably wasn't the first time this had happened. I sat once again on the cold floor and began to sort through the scattered pages. Each page held a list of printed names (all male, of course) followed by the voter's party of affiliation (mostly Democrat with a smattering of Populist). Next was age, address, and finally the voter's signature (quite a few X's). Entries under race were uniformly "white," except for a rare "f.c." entry.

I forced myself to stay on task and not to go off on a quest looking for the funniest first name (Barly? Jugger? Hog?) I had gone through about half the pages and had them back in the binder when I heard voices coming down the stairs.

"Who the hell left all these lights on?"

It was Sergeant Garcia. I didn't feel obliged to tell him it was me. I just hoped he wouldn't turn them off when he left. His arrival made me realize how sore I was from sitting. As I stood to stretch, I stepped on a page lying halfway under the bottom shelf and bent down to retrieve it.

And there it was: the name Canara Rivers right at the top of the page. "Hah!" I cried. Under "political affiliation" was written "Socialist." Canara was the first Socialist I'd come across while perusing the records. Under race, there was that mysterious "f.c.," and at the end of the line, Canara's signature. It was silly, but seeing his clear script gave me goose bumps. It gave me a sense of Canara Rivers as a real live person, not just the subject of folklore. Sixty-six years ago, he had stood, perhaps in this very courthouse, to sign his name and exercise his right to vote.

"Oh, it's you. I thought I heard somebody."

I turned to see Sergeant Garcia with a gray-haired lady in tow. Garcia fixed a jaundiced eye on the pages still on the floor.

"They fell out when I opened the binder," I said.

"Well, they wouldn't have if you'd been more careful."

I shoved the page with Canara River's entry under his nose. "What does this mean, 'f.c.'?"

Garcia pulled reading glasses out of the pocket of his shirt. "You talking about this feller here, 'Canara Rivers'?"

I nodded.

"Was he one of your kin?"

"No."

He grinned. "Just checking 'cause your Canara Rivers was a nigger."

The woman spoke up. "Josh, you hush now."

"Canara Rivers couldn't have been Afro-American," I said. "I've seen a photograph of him."

The woman peered over Josh's shoulder. "Appearances can be deceiving," she said. "The letters 'f.c.' meant 'free person of color,' and covered all manner of racial types. What did the man look like? Did he have dark hair and eyes? Perhaps a hooked nose?"

"Yes… well, maybe."

"I'll bet you this Canara Rivers was Melungeon," she said.

Josh snorted. "Like I said, nigger!"

"Joshua, I believe we're done now, thank you. You may go back to doing whatever it is you're supposed to be doing."

Josh handed me back the page. "Make sure every page is put back in alphabetical order. And don't forget to turn the lights off!"

I moved a step closer to the woman. "What's 'Melungeon?'"

The woman rubbed her arms. "Can we go talk where it's warmer?"

I stared at the pages still on the floor.

"I suggest you just stuff them back in the binder," she said. "They're only going to fall out again the next time someone opens it, if anyone ever does."

I did as she suggested. I even switched off the lights as we left. Upstairs we sat on a bench in the hallway.

"There, that's much better," she said. "On really hot days, back before Albert got us an air conditioner, I used to spend afternoons down in that basement. It's always cool down there, no matter what. Now, let me see if I can answer your question. Melungeons were a mysterious people–not Indians, not negroes like Josh claims. They were here in Pamunkey County back before it was Pamunkey County, before white settlers arrived. They've been called the lost race, and there are some who believe they were one of the lost tribes of Israel. Like so many people who weren't white-skinned, they were discriminated against, listed as a free people of color in the official records despite their unknown racial origin. That, of course, gets into some unpleasantness I'd rather not discuss. The person you really need to talk to about Melungeons is Maylord Walters."

I wrote the name in my notebook.

"He's our local historian. I'm sure Maylord would be tickled to tell you far more than you ever wanted to know about the people of Pamunkey County, including Melungeons."

"Do you know where he lives?"

"All the way out to Sand Run, I'm afraid."

"I suppose I can find his name in the phone book?"

"I'm not sure Maylord has a phone, but don't let that stop you from visiting him. Maylord is old, doesn't get around much anymore. I'm certain he'd love to have a visitor, especially a pretty young woman like yourself."

Several people, including the recorder's secretary, walked past, their brisk pace a clear sign the work day was over.

"Well," the woman said. "I guess we best leave before they lock the doors on us."

We stood up and started toward the entrance.

"Are you a student?" she said.

"I'm an archaeologist working on a project for a friend." I held the heavy entry door open for her.

"An archaeologist? I don't think we get many of those. I hope you're not planning to dig up anything too sordid about us hill folk. I'm afraid much of our past is not what it should have been."

"What I'm working on is all old history."

"A lot of families have lived here for generations and generations. What others call "old" doesn't seem very long ago to some of us."

We stopped at the bottom of the steps.

"Well, I must be getting home to Albert. It was nice meeting you Mrs. ..."

"Miss Euphrates. Parry Euphrates."

"And I'm Lula Swett. Good luck with your work."

I stood at the bottom of the steps, thinking. It was five o'clock and the library was likely closed. Even if it wasn't, I felt tired and sore from sitting so long on concrete. I reckoned it was time to join Junie at Lickory Holler. As I strode down the street, I passed the recorder's secretary leaning against a stone wall, sucking on a cigarette with obvious need.

"Did you find what you were looking for?" she said.

"Yes, thanks." I said, slowing my pace.

"That's good." She took another hard pull on her cigarette.

I took a few more steps, then stopped. "Damn!" I muttered. I was about to stray from my fence.

I walked back to the secretary. "Don't let him give you shit," I said.

"Pardon?" Smoke drifted out of her open mouth.

"Your boss, Fatso."

She made a face. "He gives me the creeps."

"Don't let him."

"How?"

I looked down at her footwear. "For one thing, ditch the heels. And wear slacks. Whatever's comfortable."

"I don't know. They have certain attitudes about appearances here. Especially a woman's."

"Maybe they're due for an attitude change. If Fatso doesn't like it, tell him to stuff it."

She smiled. "That'll be the day, me saying that. I'm afraid of him."

"Then make him afraid of you. Trust me. He's all bluff and blubber."

She nodded, but didn't look convinced. Oh, well. I'd done my bit to advance the cause of women's liberation.

Lickory Holler lived up to my expectations. It was dark and dingy and smelled of a century of cigarette smoke. A single bulb hung directly over the pool table where two old men stood using cue sticks to prop themselves up. The only other illumination were two neon beer signs behind the bar, and the glow of the jukebox, out of which the unmistakable voice of Buck Owens was lamenting that it was "crying time again." Junie sat at the bar, softly accompanying Buck on his harmonica, a bottle in front of him. I saw, as I got closer, it was a Pepsi-Cola.

"Buy you a drink?" Junie asked.

"I'll have what you're having."

Junie signaled the bartender who uncapped a Pepsi and set it in front of me. No glass, no ice.

"So, you find what you was after?" Junie said.

"I made a start. Tell me, do you know where Sand Run is?"

"Sure, out where all the hillbillies live."

"I thought you lived where the hillbillies lived."

"Naw, we're real sophisticats by comparison. Why do you ask 'bout Sand Run?"

"A man lives there who's a local historian. I'd like to ask him a few questions."

"What's his name?"

I glanced at my notebook. "Maylord Walters."

Junie grinned. "Ol' Maylord. Talk your ear off and never notice it lying on the ground."

"You know him?"

"Kind of. When I was a kid, he used to come 'round to all the schools and talk 'bout the first settlers and the Indians and all that. Not bad stuff, but, God, he's got one of them dial tone voices that puts you right to sleep."

"Well, would it be possible to go visit him?"

"Sure." He took a sip of his Pepsi and set the bottle back on the counter. "Just not tonight."

"Why? Is it far?"

" 'Bout thirty miles."

"Well, the days are long. We could probably get there and be back before dark."

"It's that 'probably' that troubles me." Junie turned to the bartender. "Hey, Merle. Parry here's thinking 'bout visiting Sand Run after dark."

Merle didn't look up from the newspaper he was reading. "Better take a bear gun," he said. "Better yet, a Sherman tank."

I looked Junie. "That bad, huh?"

"Some mighty tough characters hole up in Sand Run, and they're the nice ones. We'd be better off going tomorrow in the daylight. Least that way we can see who's shooting at us."

"So what do we do now?"

"Head on out to the county campground and fix us a bite to eat. I got us some grub at the Piggly Wiggly."

"Hot dogs?" I said.

In response, Junie played the Oscar-Meyer wiener song.

CHAPTER 30

The campground boasted a lake, but it wasn't visible from our campsite, one of the few not yet taken on that holiday weekend. As we didn't have tents, there wasn't much to set up. The box Junie had brought along held a wide assortment of cooking and eating utensils, including metal plates, but Junie insisted on using the paper ones he'd bought. Having gotten me resigned to hot dogs, Junie produced steaks for dinner. My rating of him was beginning to climb out of negative numbers. We cooked the steaks on the campground grill and ate them with thick slices of tomatoes and a potato salad Junie had gotten from the deli at the Piggly Wiggly.

"I'll probably be ten pounds heavier by the time I return to California," I said.

"I should think that'd please you," Junie said. "You're too skinny."

"That's what my landlady says. Damn! I meant to phone her when we were in town."

Junie pointed. "There's a phone down there by the restrooms."

I looked at my watch. It was nearly seven. "Right now, she's probably working in her garden. I'll call her after I've helped clean things up."

Junie threw our paper plates into the fire pit, drizzled some lighter fluid over them then lit them. "Well, I did the dishes."

I rinsed the utensils in the nearest faucet and returned to sit on the bench beside Junie.

" 'Fraid I didn't bring no wood for a camp fire," he said.

"That's all right. It's too hot for one anyway."

For a while I stared at the fireless fire pit and thought about what I had learned at the courthouse that afternoon, which wasn't much.

Junie didn't force me into conversation, which pushed his rating up another notch. Later, he went for a walk, while I went to make my phone call.

"Hello? Paradigm?"

"Mrs. E, I'm sorry to call collect, but I'm using a pay phone. I'll pay you when I get back."

"Oh, pooh! Don't be silly. How are you?"

"I'm fine." I told her of the discovery of what I thought might be Canara Rivers' grave, omitting the part about the grave being vandalized.

"That's wonderful. I have good news, too. Do you remember that nice doctor, the one I had you take me to see at the hospital? Well, he's discovered what ails me."

"Wonderful! What did he say?"

"You're not going to believe this, but all these years, I've had something called familial Mediterranean fever. My previous doctors misdiagnosed my problem because this particular ailment only occurs in people of Mediterranean descent, and of course I don't look anything like someone from one of those places. But my grandmother on my father's side was a Rhodes, and her people came from Greece… or was it Cypress? I forget. Anyway, that explains why my father had this same ailment, and it seems he passed it along to me. I only wish he'd had a doctor like mine. He suffered so much."

"So, there's a treatment for it?"

"My, yes. The good doctor gave me a medicine called colchicine. I took that and after just a few hours, I felt better than I had in years. Paradigm, I have so much energy, now! Wheee!"

I pulled my ear away from the receiver. I wasn't sure Mrs. E with even more energy was such a good thing. "Mrs. E, I'm so happy for you."

"Thank you. By the way, your Professor Webb called. Paradigm, he sounds like such a nice man, and he thinks so highly of you. Did you know he was originally planning to study horticulture at the…"

As it was her nickel, I let Mrs. E ramble on.

"... and we must have talked for over half an hour. But anyway, the reason he called was that he wanted me to let you know that you might be receiving a visitor. A member of the university alumni read the article you wrote, and I guess got very excited."

I dropped the phone and scrambled to pick it up.

"Paradigm, are you still there?"

"Yes, Mrs. E, I'm still here. I can't say I'm very happy about this news. This happened to me before. Someone who took a couple archaeology courses thirty years ago now wants to vacation at my dig and play like he's Louis Leakey. I'm sorry, but in my experience these amateurs are always a big pain in the neck."

"Well, perhaps he won't visit, after all. Paradigm, I'd better ring off. I'm cooking dinner with fresh herbs from the garden. Oh, wait till you see my roses! Do you know when you're coming home?"

"No, not exactly, but I suspect as soon as sometime next week. I'll call and let you know."

We said our good-byes, and I hung up. I stood a while, watching a friendly game of horseshoes then found a path to the lake and sat, soaking my feet. Orioles chattered in the trees overhead, though I couldn't see them in the glare of the setting sun. The only detractors were the mosquitoes. I eventually tired of providing them with dinner and went back to camp, not that their appetite was less keen there. I got into one of the sleeping bags just to escape them.

Despite the mosquitoes, it felt good to be camping. It also felt good to be doing what I was supposed to be doing: research, piecing together the big picture that was the life of Canara Rivers. I didn't know if talking to Maylord Walters could add pieces to that picture, but it was my experience that one thing often led to another, and often to something of real significance.

I treated Junie to breakfast at a restaurant on the outskirts of Damascus. It was crowded, probably because most other places were closed for the Fourth. While we waited for our pancakes, I tried to phone Maylord Walters and warn him of our coming. He wasn't listed in the directory, and the operator didn't have a number for him. I returned to our table where Junie was looking through the jukebox selections.

"It appears Maylord Walters doesn't have a phone," I said. "How are we going to find his residence once we get to Sand Run?"

"Sand Run ain't exactly New York City. It's a bunch of tarpaper shacks inside what looks like a junkyard. We'll look for names on mailboxes. Iff'n we get desperate, we'll ask somebody."

The day was already warm by the time we finished our breakfast. Fortunately, the dense woodlands we drove through shielded us from the harsh sunlight. A few miles northeast of Damascus, Junie turned onto a secondary road which followed a creek. For miles, the terrain alternated between woodlands and sections of pasture with well-maintained farmhouses. I began to wonder if Junie's comments about Sand Run had been another of his little jests. Then the road ran out of pavement and began to switch back up a steep mountainside. Once again, I was forced to hold onto whatever I could, as Junie's driving made no allowances for pot holes or exposed rocks. Up and up we went until we finally entered a cloud bank, and immediately the air grew chill.

"This place is cursed," Junie shouted. "Always cloudy and cold. Only a moron would live up here."

Because of all the overhanging branches, it was not only cold, but dark. Curtains of moss, beaded with droplets of water, dangled from gnarled limbs. Junie slowed to cross a creek. The jeep bounced over the rocky bottom. By midstream, the water was up to the bottom of the doors. I leaned toward Junie and tucked my feet up under my rump as water began to seep in under my door.

The instant the front tires touched dry land once more, something black leapt out of the bushes. I spun my head, and was face to face with the slavering maw of a dog with bear-sized fangs. It was only because I'd been leaning away from the door that I still had a face. I was too dumbstruck to scream. He lunged again, and only Junie's foot hard upon the gas pedal saved me from getting mauled. With a sound like a baseball bat hitting a pipe, the dog's head struck the jeep's roll bar. That didn't slow him a tick. Again, and again, he lunged, his teeth snapping, his snarl a grinding deep in his throat. Even as we began to pull away, he pressed the charge. Afraid he might jump the rear panel, I picked up a loose tire iron to hit him with. Then as quick as the dog began the attack, he broke it off. It was then I happened to look up the hill where a tumbledown cabin clung to the hillside. A man dressed only in boots and overalls sat on a sagging porch with a shotgun across his lap. His wolfish grin told me that we had just made his morning.

I was about to flip him off when Junie grabbed my hand. "Don't!" he yelled. Still grasping my hand, he drove one-handed for about a quarter of a mile then stopped where the absence of roadside vegetation prevented another sneak attack.

I yanked my hand out of his. "Jesus!" I screamed. "That son of a bitch wanted that dog to kill me!"

Junie grinned. "Welcome to Sand Run."

I was shaking. "Christ! What the hell kind of place is this?"

"Don't worry, Parry, we'll be all right, so long as we follow the rules."

"Rules? What're you talking about, rules? We were minding our own goddamn business. How about a rule against vicious dogs?"

"This ain't Santa Barbara, Parry. You ain't gonna get some nice lady from animal control to come up here and enforce the leash law. Now, the first rule is to act like you got a reason to be here."

"I thought that's what we were doing."

"Second rule is not to provoke nobody, even if they provoked you first. That's just what some of these ol' boys up here would like. Iff'n you'd have flipped off that yokel back there, he'd have given us both barrels with his shotgun."

"It would've been worth it just to get that asshole thrown in prison."

"Prison? What're you talking 'bout? Iff'n he'd have shot us, his kinfolk would've come out of the woodwork, and that'd been the end of it. Cops would never find our bodies. Hell, they wouldn't even bother to look. And this here jeep? It'd end up in the bottom of a lake."

"You make these people sound the mafia."

"Mafia's pussycats by comparison. Now, the third rule is not to look nobody in the eye. Iff'n you happen to look somebody in the eye by mistake, and they happen to nod, then you nod back right smartly and thank your lucky stars. Iff'n they don't nod, you best run like hell and hope they's feeling merciful today."

"Or they're a bad shot."

"Ain't none of 'em a bad shot. And the fourth rule…" He started the jeep forward. "…the fourth rule is never to come up here in the first place."

I didn't know how much of what Junie said was true and how much was hyperbole, but judging by our reception so far, I kept my eyes fixed straight ahead where they wouldn't make contact with anyone unless he happened to be standing in the middle of the road.

Yet curiosity forced me to look out of the corner of my eye, especially when we passed a cabin. Junie hadn't been kidding when he talked about tar paper shacks. Tar paper seemed to be the preferred exterior siding in Sand Run. Covered porches were another standard feature, along with crooked chimney pipes poking through roofs of corrugated metal. Most of the chimneys had smoke coming out of them, for regardless of what the weather was like in the rest of West Virginia, it was bone-chilling cold in Sand Run. I shivered, wishing the jeep had a top, wishing it had armor plating.

Junie rounded a curve and skidded to a stop. A large branch blocked our way.

Ambush! My heart hammered in my chest.

But Junie hopped out, swung the branch off to the side, and we were on our way again without incident.

I yelled to be heard over the engine. "That branch looked like it'd been there a while."

"Probably," Junie shouted back. "Most folks up here don't got cars, leastways none that run. They don't care if there's a tree blocking the road, providing they can walk 'round it."

We topped a rise and immediately plunged down a steep hill. To my right, I caught a glimpse of a creek between the trees.

"We're coming into what you might call Sand Run proper," Junie yelled.

The road widened, and the trees drew back, revealing a piece of bottom land interspersed with shacks. Every yard had a least one rusty auto in it; some looked like junkyards. There were several trailers of a vintage similar to the one I currently slept in. The average person would have thought they were junk, too, until he saw smoke coming out of chimney pipes. There was even an old school bus with a chimney pipe sticking out one of the windows and a porch attached to one side.

As for stores or a school or a public building, I saw none. I wanted to ask Junie what the typical resident of Sand Run did to make a living, but the feel of the place discouraged speech. It was as if the shacks had ears. They definitely had eyes. I could feel them on us.

The road made a loop through town. Junie drove slowly. Except for chimney smoke there was no movement: no children playing, no one working on a car, no neighbors talking, no one hanging clothes on a line. The town looked deserted. Keeping my voice as low as I could, I said, "Where is everybody?"

Junie leaned toward me. "Vampires only come out at night."

Another thing I noticed about Sand Run: there were no mailboxes. So how the hell would we find Maylord Walter's place? Junie must have noticed this too, for he pulled anxiously on his lower lip. Then he pointed straight ahead. There was a long driveway overarched by two lines of trees. At the end of this arboreal tunnel sat a small white farmhouse neatly trimmed in blue. Junie turned into the driveway. The driveway was bounded by split rail fences, and rather than the usual junked cars, there was a large vegetable garden behind one fence and a bit of pasture behind the other. I usually balk at metaphors involving sunlight, but compared to the rest of Sand Run, the farmhouse with its air of industry was like a ray of sunshine seen from bottom of a well.

Junie parked near to the house and turned off the engine. He made no move to get out.

"Now what?" I said.

"Now, we just sit tight till somebody acknowledges us."

"What if they acknowledge us with a shotgun?"

For an answer, Junie set the transmission in reverse.

The front door opened and a bald head poked out.

"That's Maylord," Junie said.

Smiling, Maylord waved for us to come in. He seemed to have been expecting us.

"Welcome," he said, holding the door open. "I am very glad you're here. Please, make yourselves at home."

I stepped past him into a small dining room. The table was covered with books, papers, and photo albums. Maylord walked around us with slow, shuffling steps. "Please excuse the clutter. I'm afraid disorder is the plight of the historian." He slid out one chairs. "Miss Euphrates, if you would sit here, please, and Junie, just there opposite."

"You remember me!" Junie exclaimed. "All those years ago when I was in elementary school."

"Not so many years for some of us. As I recall, my little lectures were your opportunity to take a nap."

Junie grinned. "Yeah, but I learned a lot from those naps."

Maylord sighed. "Osmosis, no doubt. Now, would either of you like something to drink? No? All right, now let me see." He tapped his lips with a forefinger as he studied the piles of materials on the table. "Which one is it?" He pulled one photo album from a stack and opened it. "Being the de facto county historian, I feel it's my duty to note the activities of Pamunkey County's oldest families. I'm particularly interested when a member of one of these families acts commendably."

He slid the album in front of Junie. The page held a newspaper clipping with a photo of Junie in uniform and under it the headline: "High School Graduate Serves Country."

Junie was obviously touched. "You saved this?"

"Yes, son. It's important. You did our county, and our nation proud." He pulled out a chair at the head of the table and sat down.

"Now, if I understand right, Miss Euphrates, you want to know something about Melungeons."

"Before you start, I want you to know that I tried to phone, but couldn't find a number for you. I'm glad Mrs. Swett told you we were coming."

"Actually, Lula called my grandson who contacted me using a citizen's band radio. Phone service up here is spotty due to the pleasure certain locals take in shooting at birds sitting on the phone lines. Occasionally, they shoot out the line too. In my day, they were better shots. I'm just grateful that, so far, they've had the sense to leave the power lines alone. That does bring to mind, however, the Worber brothers who in 1932 stole a long section of the phone line, planning to use it for their still. They had the notion that the line was a hollow copper tube through which the voice of the caller traveled. In Sand Run, the adjective describing someone of limited mental resources is 'worbered'."

Maylord opened a book as thick as a dictionary and began to leaf through it. "What did Lula tell you about Melungeons?"

"That they were a race of people who predated the first white settlers," I said. "A lost race, she called them. Possibly one of the lost tribes of Israel."

" 'Lost' is a word often connected with Melungeons. Ah, here it is." He drew his finger across the page. "Melungeon: from the Turkish words melun, meaning lost or damned, and c-a-n, pronounced djin, meaning, 'soul'." He closed the book. "There you have it, a lost soul. Of course, there are other possible derivations of 'Melungeon.' One is 'melungo,' a word derived from the Portuguese meaning 'shipmate.' When the Melungeons were first encountered by English explorers in what is now western North Carolina, they described themselves as being 'Portyghee' and claimed their ancestors had either been shipwrecked or abandoned off the North Carolina coastline. The Portuguese, of course, were involved in the slave trade very early on; captured Barbary coast pirates, Turks taken prisoner during one of the countless skirmishes with the Ottoman Empire, Moors driven from the Iberian Peninsula. It was also the policy of their neighbors, the Spanish, to send *Conversos*, Jews and Moors who had converted to Catholicism, to colonize areas of the new world. Ships carrying *Conversos* were often crewed and captained by Portuguese sailors— Captain Juan Pardo comes to mind, which brings us back to the word 'Portyghee.' It seems possible that one or more Spanish or Portuguese ships, manned by Portuguese sailors and carrying either *Conversos* or Turkish slaves, wrecked off North Carolina, and the castaways survived, perhaps with the aid of the Indians. The survivors then intermarried with the Indians and later migrated inland, perhaps for reasons of security. Thus, you have the origin of the Melungeons."

"When was it that these English explorers supposedly encountered the Melungeons?" I said.

"Sixteen fifty-four by one account."

"The English already had colonies established by then. Isn't it just as likely that a group of indentured servants ran off, which would mean going inland from the coastal colonies, and intermarried with Native Americans? Years later, when the main body of English settlers started to immigrate west, they encountered this biracial isolate."

"Excellent point! In fact, there is another possible derivation of 'Melungeon,' this from the French word *mélange*, meaning 'mix.' The *mélange* theory for the origin of the Melungeons is similar to the scenario you just described, that isolated groups of whites, Indians, and also negroes intermarried. There are, however, problems with this theory. One is the Melungeons' own account of their origins. I've learned the hard way that it doesn't pay to discount the testimony of the very people you're studying."

"Unless that testimony was incorrectly recorded," I said.

"Miss Euphrates, you have the mind of a true scholar. But there is an even greater problem with the *mélange* theory, one that cannot be discounted by inaccurate records. It is a matter having to do with diseases. Now, there are certain diseases that are associated with people of Mediterranean descent: Machado-Joseph disease, thalassemia, Bechet's Syndrome–"

"Familial Mediterranean fever?"

Maylord blinked. "Yes, that, too. Now, if you were to take a world map and shade those regions where these diseases primarily occur, you would see one shaded area around the Mediterranean Sea—not northern Europe, certainly not England—and another much smaller area in Appalachia, only here the diseases would be restricted to just those people known as Melungeons. Now, if as you suggest, Melungeons are a mix of Indians and English settlers, how do you account for them having such a high incidence of these Mediterranean diseases?"

"I'm not familiar with these diseases. I take it they're not communicable."

"They're only inherited."

"Okay, assuming that all this is correct, that Melungeons are people of Mediterranean descent, tell me about letters 'f.c.' They were entered on Canara Rivers' voting record under 'race.' Mrs. Swett said that 'f.c.' stood for 'free person of color.' Isn't that a term for Afro-Americans who were formerly slaves?"

" 'Free person of color' was a catchall for anyone who was not pure white. It essentially labeled that person as a second-class, or even third-class citizen. Melungeons have historically been treated like negroes and denied the civil and legal rights that whites took for granted. Melungeons were, and still are in some cases, persecuted. They were thrown off their land and forced to resettle elsewhere, likely only to be thrown off their land again. They were not permitted to intermarry with whites, to go to school with whites, to use the same public facilities. The fact that Canara Rivers was allowed to vote at all is unusual and probably reflects other factors that served to elevate his status. I suspect that in his case it was the fact that he was better educated, that he was a school teacher."

"Do you know anything about Canara Rivers?" I said.

"You mean more than what can be learned from the ballad "The Teacher of Hoagland Holler School"?"

"You heard our song?" Junie said.

"Yes, son," Maylord said, "and it's a fine song, and right in most of its particulars, I might add. Historically speaking, Canara Rivers is important as an educator. He established the first school in Hoagland Holler, which, as you know was subsequently burned down, and never rebuilt."

"But I don't get it," Junie said. "I've seen Melungeons, and they ain't like whites or Injuns or negroes. They look more like Arabs, and Canara Rivers, iff'n you've seen his photo, don't look like no Arab."

"History shows us, Junie, the fallacy of making assumptions based on stereotypes," Maylord said. "Despite miscegenation laws, whites and Melungeons have been intermarrying for over three hundred years. Consequently, many of those 'Arab' features, as you call them, have all but disappeared. A person may not even know they have Melungeon blood until they come down with one of these Mediterranean diseases. You might be interested to know that Abraham Lincoln's mother, Nancy Hanks, who was born just north of here, was Melungeon. The actress Eva Gardner is another Melungeon, and that singer all you young people like so much... what's his name?" Maylord snapped his fingers a couple of times. "The one who shakes like he has the palsy."

"You're telling me Elvis is a Melungeon?" Junie said.

"Yes, that's the one."

"I kinda find that hard to believe."

Maylord shrugged his shoulders.

"Well, regardless of Canara Rivers' appearance," I said, "the existence of 'f.c.' on his voting record shows that he was known to be a Melungeon."

"But that still don't make no sense," Junie said. "I know the folks of Hoagland Holler 'cause I've grown up with 'em, and they's not what you might call tolerant. They'd have never let their kids go to no school taught by a Melungeon."

"Maybe the fact that Canara Rivers had a Melungeon ancestry was not widely known," I said.

Junie shook his head. "This here's Pamunkey County. What one person knows, ever'body knows. Ain't that right, Maylord?"

"I'd have to side with Junie on that point, but not with his opinion concerning tolerance." Maylord sighed. "You see, Junie, this is what comes of sleeping through lectures. The study of history allows us to understand the past as it actually was, so that we see not only the bad, which, unfortunately, is mostly what gets written up, but also the good. Today people think of past race relationships as being black and white." He smiled at the aptness of his analogy. "But history shows us that not everyone was as intolerant as you suggest. Canara Rivers is a case in point, for the fact is he *did* teach at the Hoagland Holler school for several years.

"Now, undoubtedly, everyone in Hoagland Holler knew that Canara Rivers was Melungeon, but maybe they also saw and accepted him for what he was, a good teacher and someone who would give their children the education they needed. Or maybe they just liked Canara Rivers as a person, regardless of his bloodlines.

"You see, Junie, when I went around speaking to all those young students, I didn't do it for my health. I've always believed that history, when studied in depth, allows us to see our predecessors as being a lot better than we give them credit for, a lot more tolerant, a lot more Christian in their outlook."

"That said, it's obvious that not everyone in Hoagland Holler liked Canara Rivers," I said. "I don't suppose you have any historical documents that mention him?"

"As a matter of fact, I was able to locate one." Maylord opened another photo album. "I found this while waiting for you to arrive."

He turned the album toward me. Beneath a film of clear plastic was a yellowed newspaper clipping.

"That is an original news article taken from the Damascus *New Era* dated May 6, 1905," Maylord said. "Someone gave this to me back when Junie's song was being played on the local radio station."

The text was headed with a photo of Canara Rivers and several of his students. I recognized Roseanne. She looked a lot younger than the photo of her used for the cover of *Bluegrass with a Twist*.

"That there is Granny Estelline," Junie said, looking over my shoulder.

I looked at the girl he pointed to, but couldn't see the resemblance. Much of the picture was taken up by some mechanical contraption with a big wheel connected to it. I read the article beneath the photo.

School Project Teaches Mechanical Skills

Under the direction of their teacher, Mr. Canara Rivers, the students of Hoagland Hollow school have been learning how a gasoline-powered engine works. The project began when student Sam Perry discovered a discarded engine while cleaning his uncle's barn.

"Uncle Hud had this motorcycle engine sitting around in his barn," explained Sam, "and I asked him if I could have it."

The problem was what to do with the engine once he had obtained permission to take it. Wisely, Sam took his problem to his teacher.

"I told Sam I would help him get the engine running provided he let his classmates share in the rebuilding of it," stated Mr. Rivers. "Our nation is relying more and more upon engines to do our work, and anyone who understands engines is in a good position to have steady employment."

Mr. Rivers is no stranger to machines, having spent six years as a machinist on the battleship USS Texas. But being a good teacher, he kept his coaching to a minimum.

"It wouldn't have done for me to fix the engine for them. I stayed in the background and only came forward when the students were really stumped. I'm proud of the way the students, boys and girls, have applied themselves and got this engine working again."

But with the students' success came another

problem: what to do with the now functioning engine? Enter again the noble Sam.

"I knew I couldn't take the engine back once so many people had worked on it. We put our heads together and came up with a use for it that everyone in Hoagland Holler can share in."

Adding a lot of elbow grease to their brain work, the students affixed the engine to an old foot-peddled grinding stone. Now everyone in Hoagland Hollow can sharpen their knives and axes the modern way.

"Ours is a peaceable community," said Mr. Rivers, "though every once in a while, tempers rise and a fight breaks out." Smiling, he pointed to the students' completed project. "Now, we tell everyone that if they have an ax to grind, they best do it here."

A feeling of sadness came over me. Trust Junie to notice. He placed a hand upon my shoulder.

"That article really brings Canara Rivers to life, don't it?"

I nodded "Every little bit I learn about him makes me like him more."

"History," said Maylord, "it teaches us of the frailty of man, but also of his nobility."

"And his tragedy," I said. I looked closer at the grinding stone. "Mr. Walters, do you have a magnifying glass?"

"I couldn't work without one. Junie, would you hand Miss Euphrates the magnifying glass? I think you can see it there at the end of the table."

I focused the magnifier on the grinding stone. "I think the piece of stone Adam found, the one we thought was a tombstone, may have come from this grinding stone." I slowly circled the magnifier outward.

"What exactly are you looking for?" Junie said.

"I'm looking for Canara Rivers' initials carved into the stone," I couldn't see any initials, but that didn't prove they weren't there as the photo was very faded.

"Can I look?" Junie said.

I slid the photo album toward him along with the magnifying glass. "Would it be possible for me to get a copy of this article?" I said.

"There's a Xerox machine at the Piggly Wiggly we can use when we go to town," Maylord said. "I read that they'll be open today until five o'clock."

Junie looked up. "We?"

"I was hoping you would give me a ride to town in your historic conveyance," Maylord said, smiling. "I've been asked to say a few words at the Fourth of July picnic."

"What time is your speech?" Junie said.

"Now, why do you ask, Junie? Are you wanting to schedule your nap?"

"I was just wanting to know what time we should leave."

"I thought we'd leave now," Maylord said, "unless there is anything else I can help you with, Miss Euphrates."

"I can't think of anything right now. Thank you. You've been very informative."

"It has been my pleasure. Now, just let me find the notes for my speech, and I'll be ready to go."

I waited for Maylord, while Junie went out to start the jeep.

"Do you own a recording of "The Teacher of Hoagland Holler School"?" I said.

Maylord, shifting a stack of books, shook his head. I decided I would send him my third copy of *Bluegrass with a Twist* once I returned to Santa Barbara, which meant sneaking into Mrs. E's apartment and removing it from the bottom of her secretary desk where I taped it.

"Ah, I found my notes. Now my jacket."

He pointed to a wind breaker draped over the back of one of the chairs, and I handed it to him. "You know, Miss Euphrates, you're not the first person to ask me about Canara Rivers."

"Really?"

"Yes, there was a young man, about your age. A very earnest young man as I remember." Maylord picked up a walking stick leaning in the corner next to the door. "This was a long time ago. During the war, I believe."

"I don't suppose you remember his name."

Maylord shook his head. "Too long ago, I'm afraid." He turned from the door and stroked the stubble on his chin. "Though I may have it in my notes."

"That's okay," I said, trying to hurry Maylord along. Junie had been revving the engine.

I let Maylord have the passenger seat while I sat in the back atop a sleeping bag. As we headed up the hill, leaving Sand Run, the sun broke through the clouds. Sunlight did little to improve Sand Run's appearance, and the way the sun flashed in and out of the trees gave me a headache. I opened a Styrofoam ice chest Junie had purchased. Inside were two cans of Pepsi nestled in ice. I popped their tops and handed one to Maylord and the other to Junie. For myself, I held a handful ice against my aching forehead while I thought some more about Canara Rivers. Likely he'd been a good teacher, liked by his students. I wondered if the same could be said of me. I'm afraid my students thought me standoffish or something worse.

Of course, I shouldn't have assumed Canara had been a good teacher based on such little evidence. Assumptions were something I had to guard against, which got me to thinking about the connection between Canara Rivers and Melungeons. I had assumed Canara was Melungeon because of what Lula Swett had said. But the "f.c." after his name could just have well meant that the Canara Rivers had ancestors who were Afro-Americans, or native Americans, or some other racial type that labeled him as nonwhite. I would have to ask Maylord about that when we got to Damascus.

I was so busy with my thoughts, I actually forgot about the dog until Junie slowed to re-cross the creek. Then I saw him streak out of the bushes.

"Not this time, you son of a bitch!" I yelled. As the dog made his leap, I slung contents of the ice chest onto his head. The way he yelped, you'd have thought I had hit him with bricks instead of ice. He ran off with his tail between his legs. "Why, you little chicken shit!" I yelled after him. It was then I noticed Mr. Boots 'n' Overalls running down the slope toward us.

"What the hell d'you do to ma dog!" He raised his shotgun.

"Duck!" I yelled. I hit the deck behind the rear panel while Junie, slamming the gas pedal to the floor, hunkered down in his seat. Maylord didn't twitch, but sat bolt upright.

"Maylord!" I screamed. Then there was a boom and a hailstorm of buckshot that rattled against the metal of the jeep like handfuls of gravel flung by a giant.

Junie didn't stop until he'd put two hills between us and our assailant. "Ever'body alright?" he said.

I was, but I saw a trickle of blood on Maylord's forearm. "Maylord, you've been hit!"

Maylord didn't even glance at the nick. Still sitting ramrod straight, he appeared disdainful of the whole incident. "Rupert is just like his daddy and granddaddy," he said. "He likes to scare folks, but he's always careful to load with rock salt."

CHAPTER 31

Damascus celebrated the Fourth the old-fashioned way with a picnic on the fairgrounds. People spread their blankets in the shade of the trees and feasted on fried chicken, potato salad, dinner rolls, and pie while listening to music and speeches. The music was great; the speeches, sub-optimal. I had to side with Junie concerning Maylord's rhetorical style. When Maylord spoke, sitting across the table, his voice was well-modulated, but in front of a crowd, he sounded like the One Note Samba, every word on the same pitch. I noticed Junie wasn't the only one nodding off.

Following this entertainment, there was little scheduled until the evening's fireworks show. Junie and I watched for a while as kids scrambled to corral terrorized pigs. Then I skipped the sack races to wander about on my own, looking at the craft booths. I bought Beatty a set of hand woven placemats done in a colonial coverlet pattern as I was informed by the weaver, an attractive young woman with hair long enough to sit on. Later, Junie and I met up and pigged out on corn dogs, onion rings, snow cones, and frozen bananas-on-a-stick, all this on top of the deli sandwiches we'd purchased at the Piggly Wiggly when we stopped to Xerox the news clipping of Canara Rivers and his students. Then we catnapped on the grass until it was time to join the flood of people pouring into the grandstand for the fireworks show.

"I think I'll skip this," I told Junie.

"How come?"

"Fireworks just aren't my cup of tea."

He looked back and forth between me and the grandstand, his allegiances obviously torn.

"You go on and enjoy the show," I said. "I think I'll look in on the horses over at the horse barn.”

“You sure?”

I nodded. “Where will you be afterwards?”

“Well, some of us’ll be playing music, so–”

“Great! I’ll keep my ears open for your playing.”

I hurried away. It wasn’t that I just disliked firework shows; I hated them, being too much like a display of thunder and lightning. Earlier, I had scouted out the horse barn as a likely place of shelter during the aerial bombardment. It also had the advantage of being rather cool and lit only by light filtering in through the dirty windows. Most of the stalls were empty. I pushed around a couple of bales of hay until I’d made myself a fairly comfortable recliner.

Bang! Crackle! Sizzle! Boom! The fireworks had begun. I closed my eyes and tried to imagine myself lying beside a tranquil stretch of the Merced River in Yosemite. I had almost succeeded when the bank of overhead lights came on.

“Damn!” I muttered, sitting up. A girl of about high school age led in a horse I’d seen earlier pulling a beer wagon. The horse dwarfed his handler. I watched in awe as she led him past me and stopped at a water trough a little farther on. The extent of my experiences with horses was watching lovely Doñas and dashing Dons parading on horseback during Santa Barbara’s Fiesta Days. Yet the horses they rode were pygmies compared to this one. His legs, though thick as tree trunks, appeared short in proportion to a body the size of a locomotive boiler. Yet even with short legs, it would have taken a step ladder to mount him, and, of course, his sinewy neck arched up even higher.

As the horse drank, the girl untied the ribbons plaited into his white mane, then freed his tail, which had been wound up into a short stub. The horse took a moment to shake out his glossy hair before going back to drinking. From a carrying case, the girl produced a brush and rubbed the horse using a circular motion, creating a dusty haze that hung in the air. The horse’s skin shivered in delight to this grooming. With water dripping from his muzzle, the horse nudged the girl, and she in turn brushed his broad nose. Obviously, the two had a great affection for one another, and watching them made me feel like a voyeur.

"You don't mind me watching, do you?" I said.

The girl looked my way, smiled and shook her head.

"He's so big, yet seems so gentle," I said.

"The Colonel's a real gentleman." She exchanged her brush for one with thicker bristles. "Do you own a horse?"

"The only horse I ever owned had a stick for a body. I don't even have a cat."

"Would you like to brush the Colonel?"

I stood up. "He won't mind?"

She handed me the brush. I lightly swept the brush down the Colonel's ginger-colored flank. He turned and gave me a look that said, "Really now, what was that?"

"Don't use a long stroke," the girl said, "and don't be afraid to put some muscle into it, otherwise you'll never get the dirt off him. Here, I'll show you." She used a brisk, short stroke, flicking her wrist at the end of it. It was harder than it looked. After a couple of minutes, I was sweating. Yet there was something comforting about brushing the Colonel, as comforting as running my fingers through the coarse hair of Polly, the buffalo head mounted on the wall in my office. Outside the fireworks continued to bang, sizzle and boom, but inside, standing in the presence of this gentle giant, I felt surprisingly calm.

While I brushed, the girl used a comb to untangle the Colonel's mane. She worked with an efficiency born of experience. I'd only started brushing the Colonel's other side, when she finished with his tail and packed away her comb. Then she opened the upper half of an outer door and leaned on the lower part, watching the fireworks.

I bit back a curse. Not only had she let in all the bangs and booms, but the flashes and flares as well. I turned my back to the open door, but the Colonel, curious about what all the commotion was, swung around to be facing outward. It was scary to have so much horse moving about so close to me.

"Here, I'll put him in one of the stalls," the girl said, taking up the lead rope. With the agility of an acrobat, she flung herself atop the Colonel. I wasn't sure why she did this instead of just leading him away. Perhaps to show off. But whatever her intention, the Colonel was having none of it. Ignoring the tug on his mane, he strode toward the half-open door with me in his way. The Colonel was so broad, there was nowhere for me to go but backwards. I tripped over the carrying case that held the grooming tools and landed hard on my rump. The girl tried to rein in the Colonel by pulling harder on his mane, but that was about as effective as holding back the sea with a fork. Fortunately, the Colonel was too much the gentleman to just run me over. He turned sideways and declared his annoyance with me by shaking his head and snorting.

"Are you all right?" the girl said, leaning down toward me.

I didn't answer. Couldn't answer. Though still on my rump, my body seemed to be rising up. The walls stretched as if made of rubber; the roof arched to accommodate me. I felt I was being pulled from this time and place to another time and place where there was also a giant horse and a slip of a girl perched upon his back. It was a dizzying, disorienting, disjoining sensation of dèjá vu.

Then the interior of the barn blazed as the firework's grand finale began. It was as if someone had thrown a switch, for in that instant it all came back: the dark road, the tree I'd stood behind, the black horse's scream. I saw Roseanne, pregnant, bleeding. "Save him!" she cried. The whole scene replayed in my brain, complete in every detail. I had no idea how long this took, but when I finally returned to the here and now, I was flat on my back, blinking against the light, the girl standing over me.

"Hey there, you all right?" She looked frightened and more than a little out of her depth.

I slowly sat up. Was I all right? Actually, I felt great. I offered a smile to reassure her.

"I really saw a ghost," I said.

CHAPTER 32

The girl's response to this announcement was to wrinkle her forehead and bite her lower lip. "Maybe I should get some help."

I stood up. "No, I'm fine. Never felt better."

"You sure?"

"Absolutely." Still feeling a little tipsy, I staggered out of the barn.

I saw a ghost!

I had no idea where I was going. Didn't care.

A for real ghost!

I must have been heading toward the grandstand, for I was soon breasting the stream of exiting celebrants. I stood in the roadway and let them stream around me. It made me think of those stories about pioneers crossing the prairies and getting caught in a buffalo stampede, which made me think of Polly, and then the Colonel, then Atlas.

And a ghost horse!

I reached out toward a woman dragging two unruly children. "I saw a ghost!" I informed her. She pulled her loved ones tight to her and gave me a wide berth.

A man who reminded me of my old shrink Herschbach touched me on the arm. "You all right there, Miss?"

I gave him a big smile. "Never felt better." He probably thought me drunk. He wouldn't have been very wrong.

As the crowd began to thin, I spotted an empty bench and sat down.

I saw a ghost!

But the euphoria that initially accompanied this revelation now had a worrisome edge to it, for I was thinking of Herschbach. Maybe I hadn't seen a ghost, after all. Maybe the vision of Roseanne Bickum perched upon Atlas was the product of a psychotic episode.

Everything in me rose up against this. Why couldn't I just leave be? Why was it necessary to twist around what amounted to the closest thing I'd ever had to a religious experience and make it out as a psychosis? Yet I owed it to the experience itself to examine it objectively, and as a scientist I could do no less.

I tried to recall what I'd read about psychoses, but it had been too many years since I took a psychology class. I took another tack, asking myself whether, prior to the night I'd seen Roseanne, I'd ever had a psychotic episode. I racked my brain, but could not come up with a single incidence. Despite years of torment at the hands of Mr. D, I'd never suffered from delusions; I'd never seen little green men, or thought myself Joan of Arc, or considered the Ford Pinto a really neat car.

I sighed and leaned against the back of the bench. No, I had actually seen a ghost, a pregnant one no less, and the feeling was wonderful and liberating. All my life, I wanted to experience something inexplicable, something that couldn't be reasoned away or chalked up to a temporary malfunction of the senses, something that proved there were other levels of existence besides the mundane plane I dwelt upon. Okay, so maybe a seeing ghost wasn't quite in the same league as hearing God speak from a burning bush. But it was something, a start.

"There are more things in heaven and earth, Horatio, than are dreamt of in your philosophy," I quoted for the benefit of a lamppost. I was a Hamlet, but one sure of his convictions. I truly saw a ghost. I rose up off the bench, feeling like a captive bird taking flight.

And that's when I heard what seemed like voices from heaven.

> *Oh, if I had the wings of an angel,*
> *Over these prison walls I would fly.*
> *I would fly to the arms of my darling*
> *And there I'd be willing to die.*

It was the music Junie had mentioned earlier; the grittiest, lonesomest, sweetest sounding music in the whole world: bluegrass. I hurried across a rise and looked down on the grassy area where we'd picnicked earlier. Directly below was a campfire encircled by a dozen musicians all playing "The Prisoner's Song." But they weren't the only group. I counted several other campfires, each ringed with pickers. There were fiddlers, mandolin pickers, guitar players. I saw dobros, harmonicas, jaw harps, washboards–even a clarinet. Together the groups produced a marvelous meld of mountain music with tempos ranging from slow and soulful, to bouncy, to finger-flying fast. Those who didn't play, danced; those too old to dance, clapped, stomped their feet, and hollered to the heavens. The atmosphere was festive, celebratory, almost bacchanalian. Folks laughed and whooped it up and carried on, and all so friendly, they didn't even seem to mind there being banjo players in their midst.

I hurried down the slope. The biggest jam session centered around Junie. Even among so many fine pickers, he stood out. Junie played an "Orange Blossom Special" that practically had people pulling their hair out. I pushed in as close as I could. There was hardly room to move my hands to clap along. Someone offered me a snort from a demijohn. I politely declined. In my state, alcohol was superfluous. Only one thing would have made my happiness complete: to be playing along on my Martin.

The woman standing next to me bumped me with her hip. "Hey there, Lady!"

I recognized the county recorder's secretary, now in jeans and T-shirt. "Hey!" I hollered back.

"Isn't this great?"

"It's fantastic! I just wish I'd brought my guitar."

"You play?"

"I try."

She grabbed my arm and pulled me out of the circle. I wanted to stay and listen to Junie, but she was insistent. She dragged me to where another group was playing "Fox on the Run." The lead singer was a mandolin player with hair that hung over the back of the chair he was sitting in. Still gripping my arm, the secretary waited until the song ended then pulled me forward. It was only then that I noticed the mandolin player was confined to a wheelchair.

"Eddie," she said to him, "this is the lady I told you about. This is…"

"Parry," I said.

"Would it be all right if Parry played your guitar?"

Eddie gave me a lazy smile. "You pick?"

"A bit."

He handed a set of keys to an older man sitting in a lawn chair beside him. "Dad, would you get my guitar out of the trunk?"

A woman I assumed was Eddie's mother sat in another lawn chair, holding a big-eyed baby sucking his thumb. In a few minutes, Eddie's dad was back, carrying a chipboard case

"You need a pick?" Eddie said.

I shook my head. I always kept a flat pick in the coin pocket of my jeans. I moved off a little so I could hear myself tune. The guitar was one of those new Japanese knockoffs. The action was a tad high, but the sound box had a lot of punch.

I moved back to the group just as they started playing "Salty Dog Blues." By song's end, I was fairly warmed up.

"Pick a tune, Parry," Eddie said.

"How about "Blackberry Blossom"?" I rolled out eight bars of introduction at a pace I knew I could sustain. No one faulted me the tempo. We went around in a circle, each picker taking a break on his instrument. When it got back around to me, I added all the flashy syncopated tricks I had learned from Adam.

"My God!" someone shouted. "It's Adam Manly Singer!"

"*Eve* Manly singer!" someone else said, to general laughter. I smiled and kept on playing. At the end of my break, I got some applause.

"That's some fine picking," Eddie told me when we finished. "What else you know?"

"Have you played 'Sally Goodin' yet?"

"Yep, but we weren't properly warmed up." Eddie signed to a fiddler who sported a Santa Claus beard. "Kick it off, Anse."

Anse set a furious pace, but I managed to hold my own. And so it went, playing tunes, trading breaks, and swapping licks for what seemed like minutes, but was really hours. The make-up of the group varied as pickers came and went. I stuck by Eddie since I couldn't very well go wandering off with his guitar. Besides, Eddie's voice, which reminded me of Carter Stanley's, was easy for me to harmonize with.

During one of our infrequent rests, I noticed that Eddie's parents had left, and one of the lawn chairs was now occupied by the secretary, holding the toddler I'd seen earlier.

Eddie nudged my arm to get my attention then handed me a joint. I hesitated. "It's great shit," he said in a tight voice. "Sand Run sinsemilla."

I took a puff to be sociable then passed it along. I was never big on marijuana; it always burned my throat. This stuff was no exception. I had a coughing fit to the general amusement of my fellow musicians. But at least now I knew how the good citizens of Sand Run made a living. Drumming the body of the guitar with my fingers, I watched as the joint made the rounds.

"Junie, my old war buddy!" Eddie cried. "What the hell you do to your face?"

I turned to see Junie and Eddie doing one of those intricate, male-ritual handshakes. Then Junie pulled up a lawn chair, and he and Eddie had a pow-pow while the rest of us played "Red-Haired Boy" for the third time that night. Our music circle had gotten progressively smaller as the hours passed. We were now down to half a dozen pickers and most of those began to pack up their instruments after we finished the tune. I looked at my watch. It was nearly two a.m., so I couldn't blame them for wanting to call it a night. Still, I didn't want the music to end.

"How about one more?" I said to Anse.

He gave me a tired smile. "Sure. What's your pleasure?"

I had noticed that whenever Anse was given the opportunity to select a tune, he invariably chose a waltz. I never minded because it gave me a chance to practice playing in three-four. "How about "The Kentucky Waltz"?"

Anse peppered the waltz with some amazing triple stops, and as a final flourish, used a little vibrato as he held the last note. Then with a nod, he tucked his fiddle up under his arm and disappeared into the night. I put Eddie's guitar back in its case then pulled the remaining lawn chair up and sat beside the secretary.

"You play nice," she said.

"Thanks. I'm just a beginner compared to these other pickers, but I have fun." I angled my lawn chair so I could see her better. "I'm afraid I didn't get your name."

"It's Carol," she said. She patted the toddler on his back "And this here's Billy."

"Hello, Billy," I said, even though he was asleep. I looked over at Eddie, still in conversation with Junie. "I take it Eddie's your husband."

She nodded. "We've been married almost seven years now."

"I really appreciated him letting me use his guitar. I haven't had this much fun since I smashed up a forty-five of "Close to You" by the Carpenters."

Carol laughed. "Well, I'm glad we could pay you back for the advice you gave me about my boss."

I looked away. "I don't know what got into me. I don't usually stick my nose in where it doesn't belong."

"No! What you said was right on. Just after you left, he came waddling out of the courthouse, looking just like he owned the world and everyone in it. Can you believe that son of a bitch stopped right there on the public street and put his arm around me?"

"What did you do?"

She grinned. "Well, he's got this breathing problem–won't let me smoke in the office–so I got up my nerve and blew cigarette smoke right in his face. He had a coughing fit, wheezing and snorting, and every time he tried to get a breath, I blew more smoke."

"Jesus!"

"I know I shouldn't have done it, but I was just so fed up with all his pawing, and the way he leers."

"What happened?"

"Well, he tried to get away, but as you know, he's not exactly Jim Ryun. I followed him, blowing cigarette smoke until I had him begging me to stop. That's when I told him that if he ever touched me again, I'd do a lot worse than blow a little smoke in his face."

"Good for you! Now, what do you think will happen?"

"Nothing. He's a big coward like you said. Doesn't matter anyway. My parents have offered to put me through nursing school. We're just waiting till Eddie's feeling more himself before we move back to Baltimore." She leaned toward me and spoke in a soft voice. "Since Vietnam, Eddie's been needing to be near his folks." In leaning, she woke Billy who began to whimper. Carol turned toward Eddie. "Eddie, we need to go!"

Eddie didn't reply, but continued talking to Junie.

"Great!" Carol muttered. "So much for getting Billy to bed tonight." Billy, now wide awake, reached out for me to take him.

I could count on the toes of one foot the number of times I'd held a baby. Billy put his arms around my neck and laid his head upon my chest. Perhaps he was listening to my heartbeat for it was suddenly doing double-time. I couldn't explain it–I'd rarely given a thought to being a mother–but holding Billy was better than playing music, better than making a new archaeological discovery. I didn't even mind that his hands were sticky. With Billy in my arms, I felt complete, and I knew right then and there that I had to get me one of these.

"You don't know how unusual this is," Carol said. "I mean, Billy's very shy of strangers."

"Can I keep him?"

"Not this one. He's my miracle baby." Carol lowered her voice again. "At first, we didn't know if we could have a baby after Eddie got shot up so bad in Vietnam." She smiled. "But Eddie's all right in *that* department.

"But then I was sick the whole time I was pregnant, and if that wasn't bad enough, Billy was too long coming out. All those months, sicker than a dog, and then nearly losing Billy just as I was giving birth. Fortunately, I had a great doctor. He did a last-minute C-section and saved him." She reached over and ran her hand through Billy's fine hair. "He saved my darling, didn't he?"

Billy opened his arms to be taken back. When Carol lifted him out of my arms, I felt a chunk being taken out of my heart.

"Woman, that child should be in bed," Eddie said, wheeling his chair toward us.

Carol rolled her eyes. "You don't say."

"Nice picking with you," Eddie said, addressing me. "Hope we can do it again sometime."

"I'd like to. And thanks for the use of your guitar. Next time, I'll have my own."

Junie and I helped them load chairs and instruments into the trunk of their car. Then they drove away, leaving us in the parking lot, empty save for Junie's jeep.

"Now what?" I said. "Back to the campground?"

"Naw, we can just throw down our sleeping bags right here on the grounds. Nobody's gonna mind."

We unrolled our sleeping bags on the grass beneath the trees. I was too wired to sleep. I lay in my sleeping bag, looking at the stars peeking through the canopy of leaves, all the while hearing fiddle tunes playing in my head.

Junie, also unable to sleep, turned in his sleeping bag. "You missed one helluva fireworks show. What did you do?"

For a second, I thought to tell about regaining my memory, but held back, unwilling just yet to share my experience of seeing a ghost.

"Oh, nothing much." I closed my eyes and relived the sensation of being pulled into another time and place. "Petted a horse."

CHAPTER 33

July 5, 1970

Dear Teddy,

It's around five in the morning, and I'm writing by streetlight, sitting in Junie's jeep parked at the fairgrounds in Damascus. Needless to say, I can't sleep. It's all because I had a bad dream, and I guess I'm frightened, which is all the more disturbing since I've always considered dreams to be nothing more than harmless synaptic discharges in the resting brain. That makes more sense than dreams being the expression of suppressed thoughts and feelings, or whatever crap it was Freud used to preach. Granted, it is likely that the brain never actually rests, which makes me think that dreams are the offshoot of the brain using the body's downtime to process information. Dreams are like the doodles a person scribbles when he's thinking. But contrary to pretenses of shrinks out to fleece poor dupes with head problems, these doodles aren't the forlorn cries of repressed emotions. At least, mine aren't.

Why did I get into all that?

Anyway, in my dream I was hospitalized with a distended stomach. I was either pregnant, or bloated from pigging out on all the junk food I ate today. Whatever the cause, my bladder was screaming under the pressure of my enormous belly. I called for a nurse and in walked Junie, wearing the uniform of an orderly.

Holding a cast iron skillet, he explained that cuts in funding necessitated the use of skillets as bedpans.

Then, for some reason, I was running down the hall. A doctor, the same one that I had taken Mrs. E to see, was chasing me with a knife.

"Save me! Save me!" I screamed. Patients and visitors scurried to get out of my way. Two male orderlies, dressed in combat fatigues, grabbed me, hauled me into a room, and slung me onto an operating table. The doctor, smiling, shut the door behind him. "It's all right," he said, "I'll save him." The doctor looked so friendly, so kind, the sort of doctor you'd be willing to entrust your life to. Then he turned on the overhead operating lights. You know how much I hate bright lights, and it's particularly alarming when they are reflecting off a carving knife. I struggled to get free, but the orderlies' hands were Vise Grips.

Then my dream took another turn, and I was on Adam's property, and there was Carol, a woman I met today, astride a horse, even though she was obviously pregnant (Carol, not the horse). "He saved him," she said, patting her stomach. At that moment, the pain in my bladder suddenly vanished. (No, I didn't wet my pants.) But quickly overriding my sense of relief, was a feeling of having lost something precious that I knew I'd never get back.

End of dream.

Weird, huh? Unfortunately, I can't seem to shake this one off, and writing to you about it has only increased my anxiety. The closest I can come to describing what I'm feeling is a sense of foreboding. But what am I supposed to be afraid of?

I think the lesson of this dream is to stay away from corn dogs.

CHAPTER 34

J unie stopped the jeep so we could watch the black thunderheads building above the ridge line to the east. "Looks like we're in for a helluva storm," he said.

The jeep, of course, lacked a roof. "What'll we do if it arrives before we get back to Hoagland Holler?" I said.

Junie, grinning, started the jeep forward again. "Get wet, I guess."

Damn! Damn! Damn! Not only was I in no mood for getting wet, I certainly didn't relish another display of lightning like the one that had welcomed me to Hoagland Holler. I already had enough to deal with; I was simultaneously operating on too little sleep and suffering the consequences of my Fourth of July pig-out. All I had been able to stomach for breakfast was a cup a coffee. Now it felt as if a critter were trying to auger its way out of my stomach.

Breakfast was when Junie and I decided we'd return to Hoagland Holler. With both the library and the local newspaper office closed on Sunday, there was little I could do in the way of gathering information on Canara Rivers. Besides, Junie had deliveries to make for Beatty that afternoon. I was actually glad we were going back, for I wanted the quiet of the trailer to sit and think about what I'd learned so far, hoping that when Adam returned, I could offer him a theory as to who was buried in the grave we discovered.

When we reached the section of road that passed through the Bickum's land, I imagined myself the owner of it all, and discovered I liked the idea. "It must be great to have so much land," I yelled above the engine noise.

Junie responded by taking his hands off the steering wheel and giving the finger to both sides of the road. I felt like hitting him. If he had grown up like I had, in a shoe box of a house on a postage stamp of land, he wouldn't have been so contemptuous of his good fortune. If I'd been in his shoes, I'd be doing everything possible to help Beatty make a go of her bottling plant.

A couple of raindrops hit on the windshield. "Looks like we're going to beat the storm," I yelled.

"The longer it holds off," Junie shouted, "the worse it'll be."

"Are you still planning to make deliveries?"

"Momma ain't gonna let me off just 'cause of a little rain."

As Junie slowed for the turnoff to Adam's property, I waved him on. "Drop me off at the church." I wanted to check that no one had disturbed the box of bones.

"How you gonna get back to the trailer?"

"I'll walk."

Junie dropped off me along with my bag of stuff then hurried away. The box of bones was as I left it. I set it atop the altar then sat on one of the folding chairs and for the next hour or so thought long and hard about the box's contents, occasionally jotting down a few notes. I repeatedly went over the bits of information I had gathered, trying to find something that would allow me to conclude that the bones were definitely those of Canara Rivers. Too bad Maylord Walters hadn't told me that Canara Rivers had possessed a unique physical feature: a severed limb, a clubbed foot. If only he'd been a hunchback.

All that I knew for certain, or near to certain, was that Canara Rivers was either a Melungeon, or was descended from some racial minority. But race was difficult to determine, and I doubted whether the world's most skilled anthropologist could have looked at Canara Rivers' skull and said it was someone whose ancestors came from the Mediterranean region.

But, of course, I didn't have his skull. Someone had taken it. But who, and why? I had no answers, so didn't waste time in speculation. I laid the bones out upon the altar to reexamine them. An hour or so of effort yielded nothing: no evidence of deformities or signs of injuries. At the bottom of the box were the few items of apparel we'd found: the belt buckle, the shoe lace, the buttons. Carefully, I unfolded the half-rotted handkerchief.

Clunk.

Something hit the floor. I sprang like a cat after a mouse and caught it just as it was about to roll under the altar. It was a small coin, but so encrusted with dirt, I couldn't tell if it was a dime, nickel, or penny. Tingling with excitement, I filled a Dixie cup with water from the water cooler then placed the coin in it. I willed myself to wait and let the water do its gentle work of loosening the dirt. While waiting, I tried not to get my hopes up. The coin had been a long time in the ground; most likely corrosion had done its worst. Yet any marking might provide a clue to the coin's age and consequently give me some idea when the body had been buried. I wondered who I could call who knew anything about coins.

The sound of an engine interrupted my thoughts. I looked out the window to see Junie's jeep skid to a stop, glass carboys in the back tilting forward then settling back again. I hurried to intercept him at the doorway. "I thought you were supposed to be making deliveries."

"I'm just going now. I stopped so's to take you on up to the house 'fore it starts raining in earnest." He looked over my shoulder. "How come you're sitting 'round in the dark? Don't the light work?"

"I just lost track of time. Besides, darkness is relative."

A sharp gust of wind brought with it hard drops of rain. "You coming or not?" Junie said.

"I want to stay here a little longer." I wanted Junie to disappear so I could get back to seeing if the coin could yield any information.

Junie discerned my anxiousness. "You've found something, haven't you?"

I gritted my teeth. "It may be nothing—"

He pushed his way past. I flicked on the light switch by the door before following.

"So what'd you find?"

I picked up the Dixie cup. "Remember the handkerchief we found? There was a coin nestled in one of the creases. It was encrusted with dirt, so I set it to soak."

With Junie looking over my shoulder, I reached into the Dixie cup and began to gently rub the coin between my fingers.

"It's a nickel!" he yelled.

Hand shaking, I lifted the nickel out of the cup and held it up toward the light. One side had a buffalo. I turned it over. Beneath the profile of an Indian was a date, clearly discernible: 1938.

"Damn! Damn! Damn!" I yelled. I dropped the nickel. It bounced upon the altar then landed among the pile of bones.

Junie dug out the coin and examined it. "Nineteen thirty-eight? That can't be. Canara Rivers was killed in 1907."

"You're always making these stupid assumptions," I snapped. I waved my hand in the direction of the bones. "Whoever he is, he's sure as hell not Canara Rivers. He died in 1938 or sometime thereafter."

"Well, iff'n he ain't Canara Rivers, who is he?"

"How the hell should I know? Probably some drunk they didn't bother to give a decent burial."

Junie carefully laid the nickel on the altar. He looked sad. In fact, he looked like a boy who'd just been told his dog was dead.

"I'm sorry, Junie. I know you wanted him to be Canara Rivers."

He looked away. "That's all right. Maybe some things is best not to know." He pushed the nickel with his finger. "I guess that means you'll being going on home now, don't it?"

"Unless you've got another grave to dig up. I'm not looking forward to telling Adam I struck out again."

"He called, by the way. Said he'd be coming on home tonight." He took a step toward the door. "I think I should tell momma 'bout all this. She's been curious to know what all we been up to. You want to ride along? She baked up some corn pone, special."

"That's awfully nice of her, but I'm afraid my stomach's still upset. I think I'll just sit here a little while longer. Tell Beatty thanks for me, and that I'll see her tomorrow."

After Junie drove off, I turned off the light and sat in the gloom. Distant thunder rumbled, but I was too dulled by fatigue, disappointment, and a stomach ache to react with more than minimal trepidation. After a while, I got up and put the bones back in the box. Through the west window, a streak of indigo blue showed between the dark ridge line and the darker clouds. I'd never seen such a dramatic sky, simultaneously sublime and ominous. I had told Junie I was going to return to the trailer, but now I decided to wait out the storm here. After all, the church wasn't made out of metal.

Turning from the window, I was arrested by the reflection of the sky in the glass carboy atop the water cooler. The curvature of the glass intensified the streak of indigo, bending it to look like a jeweled scimitar. I sat down, closed my eyes, and recalled my dream of last night—the doctor standing over me, knife in hand, smiling, "I'll save him." Salvation seemed a recurring theme of late. There was my dream in which I was running down the hall in a hospital gown, pleading to be saved. There was Carol, both in my dream and at the fairgrounds when she told of how a doctor had saved her son Billy. And, of course, there was the ghost of Roseanne Bickum, astride Atlas, asking me to save Canara Rivers.

Then it hit me, as hard as a belly flop from thirty feet up.

Parry Euphrates, you damned idiot!

I was always scolding Junie for making assumptions, yet all along I'd been making the stupidest assumption of all.

A flash of lightning announced the arrival of the storm. I continued to see a red after image, even with my eyes closed. Then I saw Roseanne as she was that dark night upon the road—her cloak open, the bloody rosette upon her breast. I held my hands upward toward her.

"Roseanne, I'm so sorry! I thought it was Canara Rivers you wanted saved."

CHAPTER 35

I pushed three chairs together and lay across them, using the shopping bag with my overnight clothes as a pillow. Thunder echoed down the holler, and I started to cry. Of course, thunderstorms always reduced me to emotional jelly, yet the sadness I felt seemed little connected to the discharge of electrons going on outside.

I remembered once when a silver-tongued preacher had been invited to speak at my father's church. For once, I actually listened, for this man seemed privy to my every wicked deed, a diviner of my dark soul. Deeper and deeper I sank down into the pew as my feelings of guilt increased exponentially to the number of words he spoke. It wasn't long before I was feeling shame to the nth degree. Thus, I was emotionally primed for his eventual pitch to come forward and be absolved of my sins by accepting Jesus as my personal savior. Though reason pleaded with me to stay put, I found myself, along with a number of other emotionally punch-drunk dupes, down at the altar, blubbering away.

The problem was, Jesus didn't happen to be hanging around the altar that night, taking in the general weeping and gnashing of teeth, and dishing out redemption as a panacea. I can't say I blamed him. Bonanza was on at about the same time, and who in his right mind would've passed up the Cartwrights for pathos? And my tears, despite being well-intentioned, or so I thought at the time, were, in truth, nothing but the product of guilt and self-pity. The whole experience left me feeling dirty, manipulated, misused.

So, why the hell was I thinking of all this now? Because just like that night in my father's church, I felt I was being called to do something against my better judgment, something that would take me so far from my fence, I would never, ever find my way back.

But what?

I didn't want to think about it. I couldn't stop thinking about it. And the fact that Roseanne Bickum's entreaties had not been in behalf of Canara Rivers opened up whole new freeways of thought. I now saw various bits of information in a different light: Mrs. Singer leaving Hoagland Holler; the disappearance of Adam's father; Beatty seeing a ghost; Melungeons; familial Mediterranean fever; Adam and his unaccounted-for sickness. Taken together, these told a story as macabre as any conjured up by the fevered brain of Poe.

A sound broke in upon my thoughts. I sat up to better listen. A tree limb, pushed by the wind, was rubbing against the eaves, making a sound like a bow drawn across the strings of a bass fiddle. In my mind, I heard Adam, backed by Twisted Creek, singing "The Teacher of Hoagland Holler School."

> *But greedy ol' Bickum, he had other plans,*
> *To marry off his daughter to increase his lands...*

I recalled the first time I sat at Beatty's table and listened as she told me that a man is not a man unless he has land. Now I saw that statement for what it was: self-serving hokum served up to justify greed. Hiram Bickum had probably thought something similar when he shot Canara Rivers. And likely this same justification had been used by whoever killed the man whose bones lay in the box.

I used both hands to wipe the sweat off my forehead. Now I understood the feeling of foreboding that had haunted me since my dream last night. I had to get to Adam. I had to tell him all I'd learned and warn him. Junie said he was returning tonight. Maybe he was back already, wondering where I was.

So why didn't I get up off my chair? Wasn't I good at finding my way in the dark? Hadn't I walked the road from the church to the schoolhouse a least half a dozen times?

Don't do it, Parry! I warned myself. *It's just like that time at your father's church. It's bound to turn out bad. Besides, Adam will be safe as long as no one knows what you've figured out.*

Despite my inner warning, I found myself on my feet. I felt my way to the door, opened it and was immediately greeted by a flash of lightning.

Damn! Damn! Damn!

I shifted from one foot to the other. Another flash ripped across the sky, and for an instant all was black and white and overexposed. Then with my better judgment clinging to my hand, begging and screaming for me to stay put, I walked out into the storm.

CHAPTER 36

Ididn't bother to count the seconds between the flash and the thunder's boom, for I truly didn't want to know how close that last strike had been. The lightning had but one useful purpose: for a split second, I could see where I was going. Without it, I might as well have been blind. I actually found I could walk better with my eyes closed, following the image of the road burned upon my retinas. Navigation by sound was another option, listening in which direction the creek lay. I soon developed a third means of finding my way: every time I strayed, either a thorny blackberry bush, or whap on the head by tree limb redirected me back onto the road.

Another flash of lightning. Involuntarily my eyes opened as it seemed some of the errant electrons passed down my spine.

Ignore it, dammit! Focus on the goddamn the road!

I hurried forward until the image of the road again faded. I was near the corduroy bridge spanning Twisted Creek. My fear, besides being electrocuted, was to miss the bridge and fall headlong into the water. I went forward sideways like a crab until my front foot touched the first log of the bridge. I squatted down and ran my hands in each direction, trying to determine how far I was from either side. This precaution earned me a splinter in the base of one hand. As I dug at the splinter with my teeth, the sky opened up. It was like someone up there had cranked open all the valves. Forgetting the splinter, I began to inch my way over the logs. The pounding of the rain masked the sound of the creek, and the darkness played havoc with my sense of balance. In daylight, I could have crossed the bridge turning cartwheels. Now, the logs seemed to move under my feet, my legs wobbling like the one and only time I tried to ice skate.

Another flash of lightning revealed that I was too near the downstream side of the bridge. As I stepped toward the center, thunder slammed against my chest, and I flailed my arms to keep from falling. If I had had any sense, I would have gotten down on all fours and crawled. But that feeling of foreboding urged haste, that and another line from "The Teacher of Hoagland Holler School" that kept playing over and over in my head.

No male of the Bickums will live past his time.

The feel of the logs gave no indication as to whether I was going in a straight line or angling toward one side of the bridge. Deciding it would do Adam no good if I fell off the bridge and drowned, I stood as still as my quivering quadriceps permitted and waited for another bolt of lightning to reveal my position. It was a long time coming. In my head, I ran over the words to *Don't Let Your Deal Go Down*. I got through all verses and still no lightning. My toes, gripping the log, began to cramp. I ground my molars in frustration. The one and only time when I actually wanted Zeus to exercise his pitching arm, and he suddenly decided to join the players' strike. In frustration, I held my hands upward toward the heavens. *I'm waiting.*

Of course, it's a fool who tempts the gods. Lightning and thunder arrived atop each other. I screamed, stumbled forward. To avoid a fall and a face full of splinters, I stepped wide to the right where there was naught but air to land upon. My second scream was cut off when I hit the chill waters of Twisted Creek. I came to the surface sputtering and coughing, blood throbbing in my ears. I had sense enough to get my feet downstream before me. My left foot smacked something solid, possibly a bridge support. I tried to grab onto it, but it was slick with algae. Then I was under the bridge. I knew this because I could hear the rushing water echoing off the logs above me. I thrust out both arms, trying to grab onto anything, but was soon out from under the bridge and bobbing along toward a bumpy ride over the waterfalls of Little Marble Canyon. My head crashed through a wave just as I was taking in a breath. Spewing back the water, I felt my body drop into a trough. When I rose up again, I kept my mouth shut then struck out crosswise to the current. My efforts succeeded in getting me into another channel that carried me away even faster. I stoked harder, smashed against a boulder, was swept around it into an eddy where I was laundered through a whole spin cycle before a little voice told me to try standing up. I stood and found myself in water barely to my waist. As I stumbled toward what I perceived was the far shore, a rock turned beneath my feet, and I fell face first into the water. Rather than try to stand again, I did the breaststroke until my chest scraped against the creek bottom. Then I dragged my body out of the water. I was battered, bruised, shaking, and generally in no mood for turning cartwheels.

A flash of lightning revealed that I had been washed down about two hundred feet below the bridge. A stretch of rocky shore now lay between me and it. I decided to chance more bruises rather than fight my way up the bank and risk getting lost in the woods. With no help from Zeus, I somehow managed not to trip on the rocks. When I finally pulled myself back onto the road, I was too exhausted even to curse. But that feeling of foreboding still wouldn't let me rest.

No male of the Bickums will live past his time.

I was starting to hate that song. I pushed up onto my feet and staggered forward. At least, I was across the bridge. Wind drove stinging rain into my face. It was a blessing for it helped to revive me, and felt warmer than my sodden clothes. Twice I veered from the road to be prodded back by the point of a branch. Once I fell, tearing a hole in my jeans. Zeus took pity and illuminated the junction where the Adam's driveway split off from the main road. Then as I drew near the schoolhouse, I was aided by light spilling down the slope. Adam had returned and switched on the light I had wired. I struggled up the slope, no doubt looking like Quasimodo hobbling up the stairs of Notre Dame, only not so graceful.

I passed the cooking grill, barked my shin on the corner of the picnic table. "Adam!" I cried, my voice filled with pain. "Adam!"

Shadows moved inside the schoolhouse. I went up the roughed-in stairs, my soaked sneakers making squishy sounds on the steps. "Adam?"

It wasn't Adam's movements causing the shadows. A cardinal, gone crazy, was beating its wings against the light bulb.

"You'll kill yourself!" Tired as I was, I rushed to switch off the offending light. With the return of darkness, the cardinal halted his attack on the light bulb, and calling "kew, kew, kew," flew off into the night. Then as I stood facing in the direction of the gravesite that I had excavated with Junie's help, lightning, my arch enemy, struck somewhere behind me. Then there was another flash, this time from the direction of the grave, and simultaneously with it, the thunder's percussion thumping against my chest. Not surprisingly, I was suddenly overwhelmed by fatigue. I slumped to the floor and leaned back against a stud. I attributed the pain in my chest to one of my many encounters with sharp branches. Another flash of lightning, and this time I counted the seconds.

One thousand and one, one thousand and two... I stopped counting when I reached ten. The storm was moving off, and the rain, judging by the sound, was also slackening. So, where the hell was Adam? I needed to turn the light back on so he would know I was here. I gave myself another minute to rest up. One minute became two. My fatigue troubled me. My father and I used to think nothing of ten-mile hikes along the steep trails of the Sierras. I vowed to get back into hiking once I returned to Santa Barbara.

Then came another distant flash, and I happened to look down. I hadn't remembered running into a branch hard enough to cut myself, but I must have, for I saw upon my shirt the unmistakable image of a blood-red rose.

CHAPTER 37

I never did turn on the light. Instead, I fell asleep, chin upon my bloodstained shirt. Pain brought me awake, fingers probing my chest. I moaned.

"Hush," said a voice, not unkind. "I'm just checking to see where you was hit."

A hand slid down my back, fingers exploring. I screamed. The hand quickly withdrew.

"Bullet done passed clean on through. You was smart to turn that light off, Professor. 'Nother second, and I'd have shot you clean through the heart." A chuckle. "Still it was pretty good shooting, considering all I had to see by was a bit of lightning."

I squinted against the brightness of a kerosene lantern.

"Is my light bothering you?" The lantern was set down on the subfloor and the flame adjusted downward. "Adam told me, you don't care none for bright lights."

"Beatty?"

She didn't answer.

"Beatty, am I going to die?"

Silence.

"Please, I don't want to die."

"P'shaw! Death ain't so bad. My daddy once told me it was like walking into another room, only this one has got all your loved ones waiting there to greet you. Then you can look 'em square in the eye and tell 'em, 'I done fought the good fight. I upheld the family honor.'"

"I don't have a family, Beatty."

"Well, more's the pity. Me, I got plenty of kin. My people have lived in Hoagland Holler for nearly two hundred years, and when the time comes for me to meet 'em face-to-face, I gotta be able to say I held onto what they fought so hard for."

I ran my tongue across my lips. My mouth was fearfully dry. "This is all about the land, isn't it?"

Beatty sighed. "I reckoned you'd figure it out, Professor. I 'mire your smarts, but you had no right sticking your nose in where it don't belong."

"It's not 'Professor.' It's Parry! God, I can't believe I admired you. You were my…" I stifled a sob.

"Your what?" She slapped my leg. "What was you gonna say? 'Friend'?" She spat on the floor. "I took a dislike first time I laid eyes on you. I knew right then you was one of them she-men. And if that ain't bad enough, you had the nerve to go acting like you was better than me. What's the matter with name of my spring water, Professor? Ain't 'Skillet Mountain' good 'nough for you? I wanted to kill you right then. Hell, you was lucky that day atop the Knob."

"That was you?"

Without answering, she stood up.

"Beatty!"

"I done wasted enough time jabbering. Now, I gotta try and make this look like an accident."

I saw that she had already been at work. Adam's power saw lay on the floor next to a severed extension cord, the exposed wires gleaming like snake eyes. My stomach lurched, pushing bitter bile into my throat. As she dragged the cord toward me, I tried to crawl away, but could barely move my legs.

"What's the matter, Professor? You ain't 'fraid of a little ol' power cord, are you?" She dangled the gleaming copper wires inches from my face.

"Take it away, please!"

She grinned. "What iff'n I was to tell you that I'd electrocute you less'n you stood up?"

"Please, Beatty, I can't s–"

"Zzzzzzzzzzz!" she hissed, jabbing the cord at me, stopping just short of my nose. "Get up!

"I'm trying to tell you, I can't!"

She held the end of the cord an inch from my right eye.

"Please!" I begged, sobbing. "Please, don't!"

Beatty swung the cord from one eye to the other. "Eeney, Meeney Miney, Moe, catch a nigger by his toe…"

Terror drove me to try harder to stand. I got one foot under me, but when I tried to grab onto a stud with a hand, red hot pain shot through my chest. "Jesus!" I cried.

Beatty grinned. "The Lord helps them that helps themselves."

She taunted me with more hissing sounds. I closed my eyes, but still saw her, only now I imagined her holding two electrodes, one in each hand, and leaning forward to attach them to my head.

"You mean to tell me you can't even stand to save your own life?"

"Beatty! Stop it, please!" I made one more attempt, but my body was lost to my will. I went slack, weeping tears of fear and rage. "I can't! It's impossible!"

"Good! That's just what I've been waiting to hear." She touched the exposed wires to the palm of her hand. "'Tweren't plugged in… not yet, anyways." She dropped the cord on the floor and moved off beyond the range of lantern light. When she returned, she was carrying a large demijohn. I recognized it as being the one Adam kept under the tool shed. Squatting next to me, she yanked out the cork. "Drink?"

I managed a small shake of my head.

"You oughta drink all you can," she said with a sly grin. "Moonshine's a good painkiller. Might do you good."

When I didn't respond, she took a long pull from the jug then tamped the cork back in. "You gotta understand, Professor, I ain't no cruel woman. I was actually fixing to knock you 'long side the head, only I got me to thinking 'bout all you said 'bout bones. Then I figured hitting you might leave some mark there for some busybody to find. So, I reckon you only got yourself to blame iff'n what's gonna happen now hurts a mite."

Beatty stood and lobbed the demijohn high up through the air. It shattered on the plywood floor, the liquid running in every direction. She snatched up the lantern. "A body shouldn't drink and use power tools at the same time. My husband told me that."

"You'll never get away with this," I said.

She shrugged. "I might. I did before. This here's Hoagland Holler, after all. Then again, I might not. Either way, you'll be dead, taking all you know with you to the grave." She squatted and took my chin roughly in her hand, forcing me to look down the black tunnels of her eyes. "All that matters is that Junie, and only Junie, will have the land." She stood up. "Good-bye, Professor. Say hello to your daddy for me. I sure would've liked to have met him."

She strode away taking the light with her. I listened to her footsteps. They suddenly stopped. An arc of light fell just short of me. The lantern shattered upon the floor. There was a whoosh, and the floor was awash in blue flame

CHAPTER 38

I wish I could say that I looked upon my end philosophically, sitting calmly, thinking lofty thoughts about death and its meaning. Then again, there wasn't much on my mental index card under "death" to draw meaning from. The only moribund thoughts I'd ever entertained concerned suicide, and suicide isn't so much about death as stopping the pain of living. Yet never had life been sufficiently unbearable to prompt me to swallow a bottle of sleeping pills or nod off with my head in the oven.

Now, as the flames grew higher, all I could think about was wanting to live, and so I struggled against the grim reaper, if it can be said to struggle when you can't budge your limbs. Yet if my body was unresponsive to my mental pleadings, it wasn't insensitive to pain. The smoke made me cough, and each cough was like a knife in my chest. But the direction of the wind was in my favor, blowing most of the smoke away and slowing the march of the fire in my direction. On the down side, the wind acted like bellows, stoking the flames. A canvas tarp ignited with almost an explosive intensity. Burning fragments drifted on the air. I wagged my head to dodge them, but one ember lodged in my hair and smoldered. Beyond the leaping, red tongues of fire, I caught a glimpse of a dark sky—even a bright star near to the horizon. But soon the flames, like dancing devils, joined hands and formed a solid wall of fire.

> *Devil's in the cornfield, sitting with a gun,*
> *Fire on the mountain. Run, boy, run.*

Of course, I couldn't run. I could only watch as the flames crept toward my legs. The heat at first was like that of the sun on a hot summer's day; then a sun lamp placed too close; then… well, then I began to scream.

My mind seemed everywhere at once, or rather, I seemed of many minds. One mind was the watcher. It watched as the untied lace of one shoe became a slow-burning fuse, watched as the soles of my shoes sizzled and smoked, as my pant cuff caught fire.

Another mind was in charge of my voice, only this mind seemed to be working somewhere off on its own, my screams coming back to my ears as if someone was crying out from another room.

But the third and last mind was fixed upon a large mural whose theme was time: my time. It was heavily brushed with the past. I saw my father's face in countless expressions; Mrs. E, holding out a bouquet of fresh-picked roses; even the details of my forgotten mother's face. But most of the mural depicted a future that would never be: a teaching job; archaeological discoveries; finally getting *Black Mountain Rag* up to speed. I saw my own true love, and a child running toward me with outstretched arms. I wanted to stay and watch the child, but my first mind, the watcher mind, forced my eyes back to the fire. I saw one of the dancing devils separate himself from the others and spring toward me. He was waving a flag of some kind, which he tossed over my head, shutting out the light. Then I was being lifted up, screaming with the agony of it, and carried through the wall of fire, which smelled of roasting flesh.

Then there was coolness, and sweet air, and the wet ground delicious as I lay upon my back. The flag had fallen away, and I saw that the sky had cleared, and there were stars shimmering in the hot air as sparks drifting by like summer fireflies. Stars and fireflies disappeared as a face I could only identify by the heavy eyeglass frames, hovered over me. Blistered lips outlined an open mouth through which air was sucked with a rasp like a rusty pump handle.

"Brother Lillard?" I said.

He pressed a large handkerchief against my wound then covered me with the flag, which I now saw was not a flag, but a large denim jacket. I was grateful, for I felt chill despite the heat from the fire. I closed my eyes, yearning to sleep, but could not for my distress in hearing Brother Lillard's tortured breathing.

Because the ground sloped, I manage to roll on to one side. Brother Lillard sat hunched over, one leg beneath him, the other pointing straight toward me. His clothes were pocked with burn holes, exposing cooked flesh.

"Brother Lillard?"

He looked up and smiled, white dentures against blistered skin.

"You saved me," I said.

He blinked twice in response.

"Why?"

He didn't answer. I suspected the fire had finished the job on his lungs begun by the coal dust. Yet not quite finished. Words came eventually, but unnaturally high and thin, almost like a whistle. "Child, how could I let you burn?"

Indeed, how could he, for wasn't Brother Lillard one of the good elders? Not only would he willingly have given the shirt off his back, or in this case, the jacket, he would never have let someone suffer if it was in his power to stop it.

"Thank you," I said. "I…" What words could I offer for my deliverance?

"Ephesians 5:20," he said. " 'Give thanks–' " He broke off, coughing, fluids burbling up in his throat.

I quoted the verse for him. " 'Give thanks always for all things unto the Father in the name of our Lord, Jesus Christ.' "

He looked pleased, even as he gulped air like someone who'd been too long under water. Between each inhalation he got out a few syllables, each one sounding like a hack saw cutting through bone. "I carved them letters."

"What letters? The ones on the grinding stone?"

He nodded before going into another coughing fit. Then his struggle to breathe lessened, and when he spoke, he was back to the whistle-voice. "Old man Bickum busted it up. Smashed the engine, too. He had a mighty hatred of Canara Rivers." He licked lips ringed with oily beads of perspiration. "I sneaked back… took the biggest piece. Carved on it. Hid it."

"But why?"

"For Canara Rivers. So's he'd have a gravestone. You know, they never found his body in the ashes."

Seeing the schoolhouse, now completely engulfed in flames, I could understand why. I shuddered, knowing how close I'd come to being a shovelful of gray powder.

Brother Lillard moaned. I thought it was the heat of the fire, considerable even across the distance he had carried me. "Can you move farther from the fire? There's an open grave just behind me. It'll have cool water in it."

He shook his head. "It's my conscience that burns. I am a wicked man."

"How can you say that? You are truly a good man."

"You don't understand. I was the Bickum's curse. I brought that mountain down on them poor Bickum boys, and God in his anger took Estelline's son as punishment."

The second floor of the schoolhouse suddenly collapsed, sending up fountains of sparks. He waited until the fire quieted down. "'Vengeance is mine. I will repay, saith the Lord.'" Out of long habit, he added, "Romans 12:19."

Another section of wall toppled down. I watched as it broke into a thousand burning pieces. When I looked back, Brother Lillard sat with eyes closed, his chest heaving. Then came an ominous gurgle from deep within his chest.

"Brother Lillard!"

His voice was barely audible above the crackle of the fire. "Estelline never forgave me for it. Please, tell her…"

Foam appeared around his mouth, and he started to gag.

"Brother Lillard!"

He threw out an arm. That got him leaning forward, and fluid poured from his mouth like water from a backed-up drain. Yet he couldn't clear his throat and was drowning in his own fluids.

I was helpless to aid him. I could only watch as his body trembled. Then he was still. He'd stopped fighting. Almost casually, he wiped away the sputum from his mouth. He lifted his head and smiled a benediction. Then his eyes were looking beyond me, and for a moment they brightened as if in wonder, yet that may have been a reflection of the fire flaring up, for the next instant, the light was gone from his eyes, and his head dropped to his chest. Then his body seemed to fall in upon itself until he lay sprawled, face down, on the ground.

A large knot lodged itself in my throat, making me feel as if I, too, was going to choke. It was a while before I could recite the words I hoped he would hear, words which, as always, appeared in my mind as if printed upon a page. " 'Remember not the sins of my youth, nor my transgressions, according to thy mercy remember thou me for thy goodness' sake.'" My photographic memory failed to recall the verse number. I concentrated, wanting to remember it for the sake of Brother Lillard and his goodness.

I looked heavenward for help from the wavering stars. "Psalms 25:7," a voice whispered.

CHAPTER 39

I think no more than fifteen minutes had elapsed between Beatty's starting the fire and Brother Lillard's death, yet it seemed like fifteen lifetimes. Despite Brother Lillard's ministrations, I had lost a lot of blood–was still losing it–and was now too weak to roll onto my back, even though the point of a rock dug into my ribs. Yet if my body was failing, my will to live only strengthened. My reasons were hardly noble. I wasn't thinking of Brother Lillard's sacrifice, though I'm certain I should have been. No, I was thinking about my future as it was portrayed in the mural, and I wanted to stick around to see if reality jived with depiction. Less worthy was my desire to see Beatty pay for what she did.

Where was the dear lady? Obviously, she hadn't lingered near the scene of her crime, otherwise Brother Lillard would have joined me in her improvised crematorium. Likely, she had returned home so that Adam, when he came looking for me, would find her whistling as she whipped up another chocolate cake.

I closed my eyes so I wouldn't have to look at poor Brother Lillard while I considered the possibilities for my immediate future. If I didn't bleed to death, and if Adam found me before Beatty did, then I might live–provided Beatty didn't wind up killing us both. But if Beatty was first to discover that my heart still beat, however feebly, then I'd have the privilege of being killed a third time. Then again, if–

Too many "ifs." I opted to rest my cerebrum and concentrate upon staying conscious, and since my brain was shutting down all but the most necessary functions, this was no mean task. I first tried naming of the bones of the orbit of the eye, but that required too much energy for a brain operating on emergency power. I had better success with music. I sang the words to "The Old West Virginia Waltz" because the words were embedded in my brain cells. But it was too much like a lullaby, so I switched to something peppier: "Bile Them Cabbage Down."

> *Bile them cabbage down, down,*
> *Bake that hoecake brown,*
> *Only song that I can sing is "Bile Them Cabbage Down."*

Those lines were all I could remember, which was all right since I never liked the song, anyway. But as I was repeating the chorus for the umpteenth time, I realized I was about to go under; not only was I forgetting words, I couldn't recall the reason for trying to remember them. Then I got a jolt of auxiliary power, for I heard the familiar ping of a truck engine in need of a valve adjustment. I opened my eyes, realizing the next few minutes would decide my fate. My hope lay in Adam driving directly to the schoolhouse rather than going to Beatty's first. In this, the fire was my ally, for surely Adam would see the fire's bright glow.

The engine's RPMs suddenly jumped, along with my heartbeat. But then they fell off just as quickly. Had Adam stopped? What was he doing? Waiting was a nightmare as I fought to stay conscious.

> *Bile them cabbage down, down,*
> *Bake that hoecake brown—*

Again, the engine roared, and this time it was accompanied by skidding tires and the screech of metal as the truck frame protested the bumps in the road. The arc of headlights swept across the trees, and was followed by tires skidding to a stop.

"Adam!" My voice was a kitten's mew. I breathed in as deeply as I could, and was about to try again when I heard a familiar woman's voice shouting to be heard above the fire.

"I looked out my kitchen window, and that's when I come running and met you on the road."

A second later, Beatty came around the corner of the schoolhouse, using both hands to shield her face from the heat. Adam followed, walking like a man who'd just seen his own death.

"I'm sure sorry, Adam," Beatty said, "but it looks like we're a mite too late for water buckets."

Adam stood, head in hands, his back toward me. I didn't know what to do. Play dead? Try to warn him? Where had Beatty put her gun?

Before I could make a decision, Beatty turned. Her eyes went wide as she took in Brother Lillard then myself. Then she was running toward me. She knelt by my head so Adam couldn't see her putting a hand over my mouth. "It's Parry, and she's bleeding bad!"

I bit her palm. She yanked her hand away, but just as quickly replaced it with the other, this time cupping her palm. She looked over her shoulder. "I saw some rags in the truck. Run and fetch 'em quick!"

Adam must have hesitated, for Beatty had to repeat her command. "Run!"

I heard Adam's retreating steps, then Beatty's mouth was next to my ear.

"I just can't kill you, can I?"

She dug her thumbs into my neck, probing for my windpipe, but I had already anticipated her and managed to burrow my chin into my chest.

"Damn you!" she cried, banging her fist on my head. But striking me gave her an idea. She sprang to her feet, and cast about for a large rock. Thank God, Adam had done a good job clearing the site.

"Hah!" Beatty yelled. She ran to where the road to the trailer began its descent down the slope. Using both hands, she lifted up a good-sized skull crusher.

I clamped my eyes shut. *Hurry, Adam! Please, hurry!*

I'd heard it said that when you're about to die, time stretches out before you. I don't know about that, but it seemed more time elapsed than was needed for Beatty to complete her dark deed. I opened one eye. Beatty was still standing where she had picked up the rock, her head cocked in an attitude of listening. Some noise along the road had gotten her attention.

Ba-ba-ba-dum.

A welcome chill galloped down my spine

Ba-ba-ba-dum, ba-ba-ba-dum.

Beatty, still holding the rock, took two steps forward and peered down the road.

Ba-ba-ba-dum, ba-ba-ba-dum, ba-ba-ba-dum.

Then Beatty, dropping the rock, cried out, "Jesus, save me!"

Ba-ba-ba-dum! Ba-ba-ba-dum! Ba-ba-ba-dum!

Beatty began to back pedal. She stumbled and fell hard on her ass just as the ghost of Roseanne Bickum, astride Atlas, topped the slope. Roseanne reined in Atlas, just saving Beatty from being trampled. Angry at having his bit yanked, Atlas reared, and Beatty threw up an arm to shield herself from his slashing hooves.

"No!" she cried, rolling away.

Atlas returned to earth, but stamped restlessly. Roseanne, still pregnant, still bleeding, leaned from her saddle and looked down on Beatty. "Save him," she said. "Please, save him."

Roseanne's record was still stuck in the same old groove. This time, however, I had an answer for her. I don't know how, but I managed to sit up.

"Roseanne!" I cried, leaning on one arm.

Slowly, Roseanne turned her head toward me. "Save him," she said.

"Roseanne, your son *was* saved."

She blinked a few times in response, but she was still stuck singing her old song. "Please, save him."

"Listen to me!" I yelled. "Your son was saved! I don't know how, but he grew to be a young man. A fine young man, only she…" I pointed to Beatty, "…she killed him when he was in the prime of his life!"

"No!" Beatty cried. "Don't listen to her, Roseanne." Beatty tried to scramble to her feet, but Atlas stepped forward and knocked her back down. Beatty slithered backwards, frantic to get her legs out from underneath the horse's. "She an outsider. She—"

"And she's a Bickum," I yelled. "It was her grandfather that killed Canara Rivers. He did it for the same reason she killed your son. For the land!"

Beatty reached up and yanked Atlas's bridle to get Roseanne's attention back to her. "Don't listen—"

But it seemed Atlas had already decided against Beatty. He swung his head, knocking Beatty sideways into the dirt, then lashed out with his hooves, barely missing Beatty's head.

"She's a murderer!" I cried

"No!" screamed Beatty, dodging the hooves. "It weren't like that. I had my own to look after. What was I to supposed to think with your boy asking all 'round 'bout Canara Rivers?"

Roseanne had been moving her head back and forth as she followed the verbal volley between Beatty and myself. But this last from Beatty was tantamount to a confession. Roseanne fixed eyes of fiery coals on Beatty, then she let loose with a shriek like a factory whistle announcing doom. Beatty clamped her hands over her ears and curled into a ball.

I waited, shivering, until Roseanne exhausted her supply of steam. "She's a liar," I said. "The only reason she killed your son is because she's greedy! And now, if you don't stop her, she's going to kill your grandson who's standing right there!"

Roseanne's head shot up. Adam, his mouth agape, stood halfway between Roseanne and the burning schoolhouse. Urged by a pull upon his reins, Atlas moved around Beatty and came to a stop before Adam. For a while, Roseanne just stared down at her grandson, who had the sense to close his mouth. Then she smiled and Adam smiled back. I blinked back tears. How many times had I studied the cover of *Bluegrass with a Twist*, never noticing how Roseanne's smile matched Adam's boyish grin? Roseanne reached down to touch her grandson's face. And that's when Beatty tried to make her escape.

"Roseanne!" I shouted.

Roseanne wheeled Atlas, cutting Beatty off as she streaked toward Adam's truck. Beatty spun on her heels, and sprinted back toward the road to the trailer. She grabbed up the rock she had planned to bash my brains out with and hurled it at Roseanne's head.

But Beatty had forgotten; Roseanne may have looked solidly alive, but she wasn't. The rock passed through Roseanne's skull and kept right on going. Until you've actually seen such a thing, you can't imagine how disturbing it is. Beatty blinked a few times, obviously surprised, but then she grinned. She had deduced the same thing I had: if Roseanne was not of substance how could she be of danger?

Yet the physical laws of the afterlife evidently work according to different principles. When Beatty grabbed up another rock and came at me, Atlas reared up and struck her on the shoulder, and she went backwards, top over teakettle, landing face down in a pile of grass cuttings. Slowly, she got back to her feet, clutching an injured shoulder. Roseanne kicked Atlas in the ribs to close the gap between her and Beatty.

Beatty looked down the steep slope toward the trailer, then leaped in that direction. Roseanne swung Atlas to cut off that retreat, which may have been just what Beatty had planned, for the instant the horse broke, she again ran in the direction of Adam's truck. It took but a flick of the reins, and Roseanne had Atlas alongside Beatty, forcing her toward the woods where I'd made my first, failed excavation. It was not a direction that appealed to Beatty. Twisting and turning like a cornered fox, she tried to get around Atlas, but he was always right there to herd her back toward the line of trees. It wasn't long before Beatty and Roseanne were swallowed up by the darkness beyond the fire's light.

For a while, I tried to follow the sound of the chase, but what little life remaining in me was draining away like the last drops of moonshine from a broken demijohn. The arm that supported me gave way and my head crashed to the ground.

P'shaw! Death ain't so bad... like walking into another room, only this one has got all your loved ones waiting there to greet you.

I wish I could report that the last thing I saw was my father, binoculars in hand, waiting to introduce me to the rich bird life of paradise. But the fact is these were the last three things I was aware of: a distant scream; a hand gentle upon my head; and finally, as the last breath left my body, a downward plunge.

Part Three

Afterlife

CHAPTER 40

Dear Teddy,

I'm writing to you from the afterlife. I use the word "afterlife" because, whatever this is, it sure ain't heaven. I'm afraid I got sent to the other place. I can't say I'm not disappointed. I realize I was never a paragon of virtue, but the idea of a merciful God condemning someone to an eternity of punishment always seemed inconceivable. Well, shows you what I knew.

So, what's it like, this afterlife? Well, it's pretty chaotic; it moves around a lot. Think of a boat in a storm, the waves crashing over the deck, then imagine you're upside down or sideways (there's really no up or down here). I think that's the worst part. I mean, it's bad enough feeling seasick all the time–dizzy, achy, pukey (weren't they three of the seven dwarves?)–but it's downright terrifying having nothing to ground me– no up or down, no sky or land, just gray waves and vomit going every which way.

I take it back. The worst part is that there's banjo orchestra here, playing "Foggy Mountain Breakdown" over and over again.

So, you may ask, how is it that I'm able to write to you? The truth is, I don't have a goddamn clue. (At this point, it seems inconsequential whether I use the word "goddamn" or not.) I seem to be writing in my head, but I see the words appearing as print on typing paper, and believe me it's no mean feat to be typing in the midst of a typhoon. I guess it's my desperate attempt to bring order out of chaos. Writing to you has always been my ground.

When I'm not typing or puking, I try to think what I might have done differently, so that I wouldn't have ended up here. It's funny, but even now, I don't regret sinning. Fact is, I was never brave enough to be a really good sinner. No, in the end–or after the end– my regrets have less to do with what I did, than what I didn't do. I regret not taking time to hike more. I regret not going horseback riding with Elaine and her friends. I regret, as a kid, on a rainy, indoor day, not making out with Susie Blankenship when she wanted me to. I regret not substituting a full life for a life full of shame. I regret that I never loved myself just as I was.

Oh, yes, and I regret not buying that mint condition, prewar Martin D-28 from Billy Ray Black because I was afraid I wouldn't have enough money for college text books. For that alone, I deserved damnation.

I'm going to close now. Things seem to be changing, the gray appears to be lifting. Probably some new form of torment. I hope you get this letter. Somehow I doubt it.

CHAPTER 41

Death should have brought some consolations, foremost a deliverance from bright lights. No such luck. I opened my eyes to be greeted by shafts of dust-flecked sunlight entering obliquely through a window. I blinked several times then followed the frustrations of a fly, bashing itself against the window pane. It made me think of a mad man beating his head against a wall, which made me realize something else hadn't changed either: Mr. D, my rambunctious old buddy, still hung out in my cranium. Thanks to him, my head felt like the mad man's.

Out of the corner of my eye, I spied Estelline Singer sitting in her rocking chair, knitting. This vision produced no small amount of consternation. Had my storm-tossed boat finally been cast upon shore, and now my punishment would be an eternity in the company of Estelline Singer and her droll wit? Or had I somehow washed back onto the shores of the living? I pinched myself, hoping the age-old litmus test for determining states of consciousness would apply in this case. The result favored the latter scenario; it seemed I was once again alive. My response was somewhat less than gracious.

"I think I'm going to puke."

Setting aside her knitting, Mrs. Singer pushed up out of her chair. "Don't! You've little enough in you as is." She held a white enamel pan under my chin. Try as I did to keep things down, a little came up.

"Is that it?" she said.

I nodded.

She took the pan away and returned with a cup of what looked like boiled blood. "Here, drink."

I took a sip and came wide awake. "Jesus! What the hell is this, transmission fluid?"

"You hush, now! It's just a little something to help you get better: morphine, codeine, heroin, and–"

"I know, I know, a pinch of cocaine the vet gives the horses." I took another sip. I think it *was* blood, blood mixed with ground asphalt. "What'll happen if I don't drink this?"

"Oh, nothing much. Death, rigor mortis. Course we'll bury you 'fore you start to bloat."

Under the circumstances, my choice was obvious. Still, I held back.

"Don't tell me you'd rather die than drink a little bit of medicine."

"No, it's just that… I thought I *was* dead."

" 'Twere a near thing, and you're not out of the woods yet." She went to the window and drew the curtains over it. "Now drink 'cause I want you to sleep some more."

I drank everything, including the little fuzzy things floating around in the bottom of the cup. Whatever was in the elixir soon had me in lullaby land. This time I stayed on dry land. In fact, I dreamt I was at a bluegrass festival, and there was Bill Monroe, backed by the Blue Grass Boys, singing "Blue Moon of Kentucky." After playing a long set, they surrendered the stage to The Country Gentleman, my favorite bluegrass band after Twisted Creek. Thus, I was suitably miffed when, halfway through their set, I woke up. I'm not sure what woke me, for all was quiet save for the creak of Mrs. Singer's rocker as she knitted by candlelight. It was a scene from a Currier and Ives print and should have brought me peace. Instead, I fixed upon the flame of the candle.

"Where's Beatty?" I said.

Mrs. Singer looked up. "You always come out of a sleep that way? No, 'Hello,' or 'My, what a nice evening it is.' Just 'Where's Beatty?' " She pulled out a length of yarn. "Well, I guess 'Where's Beatty?' is a mite better than 'I think I'm gonna puke.' "

"Please, I've got to know. Where is she?"

Mrs. Singer knitted several more stitches before answering. "I hear tell they buried her yesterday."

I sat up quickly–too quickly; my head spun. "She's dead?"

"I hope so. I just hate it when they bury folks alive."

"But... how?"

"Well, according to what I heard, the sheriff deemed her death an accident. Seems she fell into that pit–the one you dug when you were first looking for Canara Rivers–and sort of skewered herself on the tines of that rusty ol' harrow Adam had tossed in there. Guess it don't pay to go wandering 'round at night when you can't see where you're going."

"And what about Brother Lillard?"

Mrs. Singer sighed. "We buried my brother this morning."

"This morning? How long have I been... out of it?"

"Ever since Adam dragged you in here."

I gritted my teeth. "I figured that much. What day is it, now?"

"It's today, same day you finally woke up."

I leaned back against the headboard. "You're hopeless."

Mrs. Singer chuckled. "It's Tuesday evening, July 7th, 1970. At least, I think it is. Iff'n you like, I'll go consult my bedpost."

"No, I'll take your word for it." I closed my eyes, trying to remember what day it was when I died. For a second, I panicked, afraid I'd lost my memory again. Then I recalled being with Junie in Damascus on the Fourth of July–a Saturday. It was Sunday night when Beatty shot me. Like Christ, I'd risen from the dead on the third day. I dare say, any other similarities between Him and me ended there. "I wish I could have attended Brother Lillard's funeral. Were there many people?"

"A sight mor'n showed up to see Beatty laid to rest."

"He saved my life, you know. When I tried to thank him, he quoted scripture."

Mrs. Singer smiled. "That sounds 'bout like Lillard. Did he say anything else?"

"Yes, he said that he was responsible for the deaths of Hiram Bickum's sons, and he seemed to think that God took Roseanne's son as punishment."

She set her knitting down on her lap and stared into a dark corner.

"He also said that you never forgave him." I waited for a response, but she continued to study the shadows. "After that he only was able to speak a few words, but I'm fairly certain he wanted me to tell you he was sorry."

Mrs. Singer choked off a sob. She stood, her knitting falling to the floor, and hobbled out of the room. I was sorry to see her go; there was much I still needed to ask her. Yet I had owed it to Brother Lillard to say what I did.

Left alone, I recalled the scene at the schoolhouse just before I lost consciousness. I remembered hearing a scream. Had I known at the time what had befallen Beatty, I likely would have risen up like Lazarus and done hand springs. Now, I felt nothing. No gladness or sadness at Beatty's death. I didn't even have any feelings about not having feelings. Of course, I wasn't fully resurrected yet, as evidenced by how quickly I fell back to sleep. When I woke, it was morning, and Adam now sat in the rocking chair, looking out through the glass in the double doors. I studied his dark, handsome face. I saw there were other features besides his smile that he shared with Roseanne Bickum.

Adam must've felt my eyes upon him, for he suddenly turned, and seeing me awake, smiled. I moved over on the bed and motioned for him to sit beside me. When he was comfortably settled, I leaned forward and, with no little amount of pain, grabbed him roughly by the front of his shirt.

"So tell me! How long does it take to find some goddamn rags?"

Adam swallowed. "That's just it, Miss Parry, I didn't remember there even being any rags in my truck. But Beatty seemed so for-certain sure. I swear, I must've tore that truck apart, looking for 'em."

I released him and leaned back against the head board.

"Sorry," he said.

"That's all right. Your grandmother came to the rescue."

He frowned.

"What's the matter?"

"What you just said: 'your grandmother.' All this time I've been somebody different than who I thought I was." He began to tick off points on his fingers. "My granddaddy was Canara Rivers, not somebody named Singer like I'd always been told. And that means I'm part Melungeon–"

"How did you know that?"

"Junie told me what you two learned up in Damascus."

"How does that make you feel?"

"Miss Parry, can I ask you to hold off on your questions and let me finish? Where was I? Oh, yeah–Melungeon. On top of that, I've just learned that the woman I've always thought of as a second mother murdered my daddy."

"I'm so sorry, Adam. That must–"

"Hush! Let's see, what else? Oh, my granny's not really my granny. My real granny's a ghost 'bout ten years younger than me. And finally, as if all that ain't enough, Junie tells me I now own thousands of acres of land, which is fine, only there's a mountain of bills set against them. So, to answer your question, I feel like someone whose insides have been stolen and replaced with those of a stranger."

"You're wrong. You're still Adam Manly Singer."

He looked at me, uncertainty in his eyes. "Am I?"

"Yes, and Adam Manly Singer is a mighty fine man."

Adam squeezed my hand.

"Now, I have something to tell you. Last Sunday night, when Beatty shot me, I died."

Adam quickly pulled his hand away.

"I'm not a ghost, you fool. I'm talking symbolically, here. The point is, being dead gave me a whole new perspective on life. It made me think of all the ways I should have lived my life differently. I've always been ashamed of myself, and that's made every day a living hell. Well, I don't care if I *am* abnormal. Hell, I don't even care if I'm an abomination. I won't live like that anymore."

Judging by Adam's expression, I had him totally baffled.

"Look, you just said that you feel like you're someone different. Well, I really *am* different, only I've known it for a lot longer than a couple of days. Hell, I can't remember when I *didn't* know it."

"Know what, Miss Parry?"

I took in a deep breath and held it. Did I really want to go through with this? Odd that I felt so little emotion. "Adam, I'm a homosexual."

No reaction.

"Adam, did you hear what I said? I said I'm—"

"I heard you, Miss Parry." He was smiling now.

"You find that funny?"

"No, I find me funny. All this time, I was thinking you must not like me very much."

I rubbed my forehead. "You've lost me. What does that have to do with me being a homosexual?"

"Remember that time at the swimming hole when we… well, you know?"

I blinked a few times before it hit me. Then I buried my head in my arms. "Christ! Was I that bad?"

Adam gently pulled my arms back down. "No, you were just fine. You just didn't seem to be very into it, is all. But I thought it was because, maybe deep down, you really didn't like me."

"Adam, I love you. I just can't love you the way a woman loves a man. I mean—"

"I know what you mean, Miss Parry," Adam said, grinning. "But listen, what's between you and me don't have to be like that."

"So, it doesn't bother you, me being a homosexual?"

Adam took his time before answering. "I guess it'd be a liar to say I'm not disappointed. But that don't change my feelings none. I like you, Miss Parry. Fact, I like you just the way you are."

I gripped Adam's hand and struggled to swallow the softball in my throat.

"You all right, Miss Parry?"

I nodded. "It just that… Adam, you're the first person who's ever told me that."

"Told you what?" said Junie appearing in the doorway, a fancy hatbox tucked up under one arm.

Adam grinned. "That she plays a mean version of "Sally Goodin."

"That reminds me," I said. "You owe me five guitar lessons."

Adam scratched behind one ear. "Well, I don't know as you rightly deserve 'em, seeing all the trouble you've caused 'round here."

I aimed a right hook toward his chin, but only got half the distance before pain had me gulping air like a landed fish.

"Miss Parry!"

"I'm all right." I laid a hand over my bandaged shoulder. "It's just that for a second there, I forgot I'd been shot."

With a thud, Junie dropped the box onto the table next to the bed. "And for that, you got my momma to blame." He stood ramrod straight, as if preparing for a volley from the firing squad. Only the tears in his eyes belied his bravado. He cleared his throat. "Adam, I got me some things I need to talk to Parry 'bout alone."

I wasn't sure I wanted to be alone with Junie. After all, his mother *did* try to kill me. About that, he offered no apologies, but got straight to the point.

"You should have a look at what's in that box there."

I really had only one arm that I could use. Junie watched my awkward attempts to lift the box off the table, before grabbing it and dropping it in my lap.

"I found it whilst going through momma's closet, looking for a dress to have her buried in. I don't rightly know what to do with it."

I lifted the lid off the box and peered inside "Oh, damn!" I tilted the box over and a human skull rolled out onto the bed.

"I guess it don't take no archaeologist to figure out why momma done stole it."

I ran the tip of my finger around a smooth, bullet-sized hole made in the occipital bone.

"I remember what Adam said 'bout him having them little bumps on his head," Junie said. "I noticed this one's got the same thing."

He was right. I traced a line of small protrusions near the sagittal suture. "Where are the bones I left in the church?"

"I got 'em in the box up to the house."

I rolled the skull back into the box. "Please, put this with them.

I'm sure Mrs. Singer will want to give Adam's father a proper burial."

Junie nodded, but made no move to retrieve the box.

"What are you going to do now?" I said.

"Right now, I'm trying to rescue some of Adam's inheritance from them buzzards that call themselves bankers."

"Half that inheritance is yours."

He shook his head. "I hate Hoagland Holler. Once I get things sorted out, I'm going somewheres else."

"Where?"

"I don't rightly know. Every place just seems like the same ol' hell."

I didn't know what to tell him, though I knew exactly how he felt. In my experience, there seemed little hope unless you were somehow reborn. Even then, rebirth wasn't all it was cracked up to be. My confession to Adam meant I would no longer have to hide my homosexuality from him, but that still didn't change the fact that I was what I was.

Having nothing more to say, Junie picked up the box and left. I dozed for a while to be awoken by the delicious aromas emanating from Mrs. Singer's kitchen. When she brought me fresh baked bread and a bowl of soup, I consumed them with all the delicacy of an industrial vacuum cleaner.

"That was quite a disappearing act," Mrs. Singer said, watching from her rocker. "You must be feeling better."

"I am, thanks to you. I guess you must have treated bullet wounds before."

"Oh, a time or two, though if that bullet had struck you a mite lower, you'd have been needing the undertaker 'stead of me. 'Tweren't like Beatty to miss a heart shot. She must have ate something that threw her aim off."

"It wasn't indigestion," I said. I told her about the cardinal, how its frantic behavior had forced me to turn off the light.

"A redbird, out at night like that? I reckon I don't have to tell who that was."

I placed a hand over my bandaged shoulder. "If that was my father, why couldn't he have just prevented Beatty from shooting at me in the first place?"

"He did all he could, and 'twere 'nough." She stood and took down a large leather-bound book from a corner cabinet then exchanged it for my empty plate. "Here, I've marked some pages. Take a gander whilst I go get started making some more soup."

The book was a photo album. I ignored the markers and started at the beginning. I didn't know most of the people, but there were a lot of photos of Adam as a boy with a woman who must have been his mother. It wasn't until I was farther along that I realized it wasn't Adam at all, but Adam's father, and the woman was Estelline Singer when she was young. There was a particularly fine, eight-by-ten of Adam's father in a graduation robe. The faded lettering at the bottom read: Canara Rivers Singer, MD. Class of 1935.

" 'Twere a mistake to give him that name."

I started, not having heard Mrs. Singer come back into the room. She swapped me the album for another cup of her vile tea. She stood staring at the photo, while I debated my chances of getting away with pouring the sanguineous ooze into a nearby potted plant.

"Drink!" she commanded, not taking her eyes from the photo.

I took a sip. "Yum."

"You're not supposed to like it. You're supposed to drink it and get well."

She closed the photo album and took it with her to the rocking chair.

"Why was it a mistake to give him that name?"

She didn't answer, but absently stared at the album cover. I figured it wouldn't do any good to push her, so I sipped the bog water and tried to think of something more pleasant, like a quartet of banjo players each picking "Foggy Mountain Breakdown" in a different key.

"What would happen if I only drank half of this?"

"Then you'd only get half well, though I'm not sure which half. If I rightly recollect, it's the legs that rot and fall off."

I mentally cursed then drank.

She set the album on the side table. "Course there never was a Mr. Singer. I chose that name 'cause a 'singer' is what the Indians used to call a medicine man. You see, Candy–that's what I called Canara Jr.– he was destined to be a healer. I tried never to lie to the boy. I told 'im his daddy was a teacher and that he was killed in a school fire. But no matter how many times he begged me, I refused to tell him the actual circumstances of his daddy's death or where the school was. You see, I didn't want him coming back here, not ever." She sighed. "Then a few years after he started his doctoring, he told me and Ginny–that's Adam's momma–that he was going away for a few days to do some fishing. 'Tweren't anything odd 'bout that; he was always going off fishing, only this time he never came back. Course, we contacted the police, but they never found hide nor hair of him. I reckon they just figured he'd skipped out on Ginny, but we both knew better. I suspected Candy found out something 'bout his daddy, maybe from one of his patients who recognized the name Canara Rivers on his medical diploma hanging on his office wall. After the police came up empty handed, I came back here, hoping to find a clue to Candy's disappearance. But it was all hush 'n' shush, and I had to use other means to find out what happened."

"You contacted the dead, didn't you?"

She nodded.

"Did Candy tell you he was murdered by Beatty?"

"You've got to understand things is never too clear when you're talking with the dead. But I figured something like that had happened. If not Beatty, then maybe one of her kin."

"Then why didn't you do something?"

She leaned forward. "Like what?"

"I don't know. Talk to the sheriff. Tell him your suspicions. Get him to launch an investigation so that your son's murderer, I mean Roseanne's–"

"He *was* my son! Roseanne may have had the birth of him, but I raised him like he was my own flesh and blood. I loved that boy, body and soul!"

"All the more reason to see his murderer brought to justice."

"Tell me, Professor, what's justice? Lillard killing the Bickum boys 'cause they shot Roseanne and Canara Rivers? Beatty killing my son 'cause Lillard killed the Bickums? Me seeing Beatty hanged 'cause she killed my boy? One of Beatty's kin shooting Adam to avenge Beatty?" She shook her head. "I already lost me one boy, and it liked to kill me. I say, best leave justice to God."

I closed my eyes and thought about my role in all of this. Mrs. Singer's decision not to avenge her son's murder had broken the string of vendettas and had allowed Adam to grow up in peace. Now I'd gone and stirred up things. What if one of Beatty's relatives should decide her death wasn't an accident? "I guess it would have been better for all concerned if I'd never come here."

"Fiddlesticks! Who's to say what's for the best? Now don't you want to hear how I rescued Roseanne's baby?"

I leaned forward, all ears.

"I was at Roseanne's house that day her daddy laid the ambush for Canara Rivers, the day he set fire to the schoolhouse. Both Roseanne and me knew he was up to no good. I argued with her not to go, but it was like arguing 'gainst the sun rising. Roseanne had a terrible love for Canara Rivers.

"I stuck 'round the Bickum place, frightened, but needing to know what would happen. I never imagined them blackguards would bring Roseanne back, wrapped in a horse blanket. They laid her in her own bed and ordered me to fix her up proper for burying. For the life of me, I didn't know why they just didn't throw her into a hole in the ground. Maybe they had a little conscience, after all.

"I locked the door on 'em, not that it mattered; the cowards took themselves off to the barn to get drunk. But when I went to remove Roseanne's bloody dress, I found she still had a spark of life left in her. She moved her hand over the bulge in her belly and spoke to me in a whisper. 'Save him,' she said.

"Now at the time, I had some reputation as an herb woman, young as I was, and I'd helped my own momma deliver many a baby. But the thought of what I'd have to do to get that baby out made my blood run cold. But then I looked at Roseanne and saw her begging me with her eyes. 'Please, save him,' is what those eyes said.

"Well, I knew I didn't have much time iff'n I was gonna do it. I once seen my momma take pups from a prized bitch that'd been kicked bad by a horse. I ran to the kitchen to get what was needed. Afterwards, I dressed Roseanne in her best silk and stuffed a pillow up under her clothes. Then I wrapped up the baby in that horse blanket and took him away, vowing he'd never grow up to be a Bickum."

Mrs. Singer laid a gnarled hand alongside her forehead, her rheumy eyes brimming with tears. " 'Twas the thought of Roseanne's love for that baby that kept my hand steady, for Roseanne Bickum was a mighty loving woman. She loved Canara Rivers mor'n she loved her own life, and it was her love for Canara's son that kept her from making a sound, even though her heart was still beating when I cut that baby out of her belly."

CHAPTER 42

It took a week before I was ambulatory, a week of foul-tasting potions and worse smelling poultices to "draw out any poisons." When I could stand without getting dizzy, I walked out onto the back porch and leaned against a post. A light rain was falling. I listened to the patter of raindrops on leaves and compared this discourse to the chatter of nearby Twisted Creek. A flock of blackbirds joined in on the conversation. It was another perfect moment in Hoagland Holler and should have given me some cheer, but I was still feeling numb. I tried not to read too much into this. I recalled a documentary film about the Serengeti which showed the animals' reactions to the rains that brought an end to the dry season. Initially, they appeared indifferent. It took a few days to soak in the fact that the long drought was over. Then they went berserk, frolicking and cavorting in celebration of having survived. Perhaps this time next week I would be doing back flips. Somehow, I doubted it.

When I could bear to travel, I had Adam drive me to the nearest pay phone, a journey of fifteen miles. I preferred the discomfort of the local roads to setting foot again in Beatty's house. Fortunately, the phone booth was well away from what looked like a remodeled hen house that served as both a market and a bar.

"Hello?"

"Mrs. E?"

"Paradigm? For land's sake, I was beginning to think you'd dropped off the face of the earth. Why didn't you call? There's nothing the matter, is there?"

I wasn't going to lie; she would find out sooner or later. "Mrs. E, someone shot me. Fortunately, the bullet went high, and passed cleanly through the upper part of my shoulder."

Silence.

"Mrs. E, are you still there?"

"I'm coming back there on the next flight. My God! What kind of people would shoot an innocent, young woman like you? They must be animals! Oh, my goodness! What kind of doctors do those hillbillies have? You just hang on, and I'll get you to a good physician."

"Mrs. E, calm down. There's no need for you to come back here. I'm fine. The person who treated me is an expert with bullet wounds. Mine is clean with very little muscle damage. I just lost a lot of blood and sometimes get a bit woozy is all."

"Then you'll need someone to look after you, to carry your luggage."

"I have someone to look after me, and Adam will help with my luggage. I didn't call to upset you, only to let you know that I'll be here a little longer and to ask you to call Dr. Webb and let him know."

"Oh, Paradigm, are you sure you don't need my help? Sometimes we don't make very good decisions when we're sick or injured."

"Mrs. E, trust me on this one. I appreciate your concern, but I'm fine, honest."

"You young women, so independent!"

I looked through the dirty glass of the booth to see if there were any eavesdroppers. Adam had gone inside the hen house. That left just a few actual chickens scratching about in the dirt.

"Mrs. E, I have something else I need to tell you."

"Not more bad news!"

"I don't think of it as bad, exactly. I just think it's time you should know." I took a big breath. "Mrs. E, I'm a homosexual."

Again, silence.

"Mrs. E?"

"Paradigm, dear, that's not really news. I've known it for quite some time now."

"Really? But... how?"

"It just seemed obvious to me."

"And it never bothered you?"

She laughed. "Land's sakes, no. You make it sound as if you've been hiding a criminal record. My Herbert had a few quirks in the sexual line. Remind me to tell you about them sometime. It will have you racing to a nunnery, a real one, not the Shakespeare kind."

I closed my eyes and rubbed my hand across my chest where I felt a spasm of pain. Good pain. "Mrs. E?"

"Yes, dear?"

"You've always been so kind to me. Thank you. And thank you for being so understanding."

"Promise me you'll let me pick you up at the airport. I don't care what time you get in. You know, some of those men get jobs as cab drivers because they're not fit for anything else."

The next day, we re-interred the remains of Canara Rivers Singer, "we" being Adam, Mrs. Singer, and myself. Adam's mother had wanted to come, but her current husband had been injured on the docks. I didn't know where Junie was.

I'd arranged the bones within the shallow grave in more or less anatomical order, adding the bits of clothing we'd also discovered. Over this, Adam draped one of Mrs. Singer's quilts. Then we all held hands and sang "Will the Circle Be Unbroken," followed by Adam singing "Softly and Tenderly" with such sweetness, he had Mrs. Singer weeping into her handkerchief and me swallowing softballs again. I said a silent prayer–something I had not done in years–for Roseanne, Canara, and their son, asking that they be allowed to finally rest in peace. As Adam backfilled the grave, Mrs. Singer read from the book of Psalms:

" 'He sent from above, he took me, he drew me out of many waters. He delivered me from strong enemies, and from them which hated me… He brought me forth also into a large place; he delivered me because he delighted in me.' "

It was while Adam was tamping the dirt with the backside of a shovel that Junie showed up. He was dressed in a dark suit that filled out his scrawny frame and made him appear quite handsome. He whispered a few words to Adam, and together they went to back to his jeep and returned bearing a tombstone, which they set upright in the loose soil.

"I had it made up in Damascus," Junie said. "I hope you find what it says agreeable."

Canara Rivers Singer

1907-1942?

Husband–Father–Son–Physician

The words were few, but to those of us who knew the story of Roseanne's son, they spoke volumes. Beatty had been right when she said that Junie possessed more tenderness than he showed.

Then while Adam was tamping the soil around the tombstone, Junie tried to slip away. With surprising speed, Mrs. Singer grabbed his hand and drew him close.

"You're a good boy," she told him, patting him on the arm.

Junie, looking unconvinced, hung his head.

"Well, come on," Mrs. Singer said, addressing us all. "I fixed us some vittles. Candy wouldn't have wanted us to stand 'round moping."

But when we got to where the truck and jeep were parked, a station wagon came bounding up in a cloud of dust. It was the dirtiest car I'd ever seen. I could barely make out that it had California license plates.

"Oh, shit!"

"What?" Adam said.

"My thesis advisor warned me about this. It's some alumni jerk come to check out my digs."

A woman emerged from the car, her face hidden by dark hair as she spoke to a passenger concealed behind the dusty windshield. Then she turned toward us. "Excuse me, but I'm looking for Professor Euphra–"

What happened at that moment was like a scene from one of those old, gushy movies where two strangers, each dressed to the nines, enter a crowded ballroom from different directions. As they survey the crowd of celebrants, their eyes suddenly latch onto each other, and their orbs go off like flashbulbs. 'Tis but a moment before the fated lovers are tripping the light fantastic several inches above the ballroom floor. It's typical Hollywood schmaltz, guaranteed for a giggle, and wasn't really descriptive of what passed between the woman and myself the instant our eyes met.

We didn't dance until later.

God knows how long we would have gone on ogling each other, if Mrs. Singer hadn't suddenly groaned and gone slack against Adam. He eased her down to a sitting position on the ground. The cause of this reaction appeared to be the passenger who had emerged from the station wagon and stood, resting one hand atop the car door. He was old, a relic. Silvery wisps of hair swept up over his bald, liver-spotted pate. He was as thin as a willow, but age had bent the trunk. A smile, both apologetic and wistful, hung on his face.

"Hello Estey," he said in a voice that belied his antiquity. Then he stepped from behind the car door, and I saw his knuckle-walker arms made longer by stooped shoulders.

"Jesus!" I cried.

"What's going on?" Adam said, using his legs as a backrest for Mrs. Singer.

Before I could reply the woman made introductions. "My name is Helena Rivers," she said, "and this is my grandfather, Canara."

Needless to say, we didn't lack for something to talk about as we sat around Mrs. Singer's kitchen table, not that we all fit. I claimed a seat next to Helena, leaving Adam and Junie to lean against the kitchen counter. As Helena pressed her leg against mine, I felt a rush of heat. It's a wonder my jeans didn't ignite.

Of course, none of us faulted Canara for being alive. But a perfectly good legend, not to mention a great song, had been built around his death. So, we felt entitled to a tale of daring-do sufficient to make up for the legend's demise. Perhaps Canara felt that the pressure was on, for he swallowed three times before confessing that on the day the Bickums were dousing the schoolhouse with kerosene, he was happily off somewheres, playing with a new fishing rod.

So much for a well-planned ambush. Tack on stupidity to the list of Bickum defects.

Of interest, however, was the "twitchy feeling" Canara had had that some skullduggery was in the works. Perhaps he possessed a bit of "the sight" as Mrs. Singer suspected. That said, he hadn't an inkling that Roseanne had been murdered and didn't learn of it until several days after the fact. Then he became "a mite unhinged," to use his words, and he wandered for weeks in the woods, living off dried blackberries, hickory nuts, and the occasional scrap of bacon pilfered from somebody's smokehouse. When his unbalanced mind eventually tipped back toward the side of reason, Canara decided to quit the mountains rather than fight the Bickums. Legally, he had no recourse, for it was only his word against Hiram Bickum's that the burning of the schoolhouse and Roseanne's murder were not accidents; the word of a nearly friendless Melungeon against that of a solid Scots-Irish, taxpaying citizen with oodles of gun-toting kin to back him up. As for avenging Roseanne's murder by other means: "I just never had it in me to be a killer."

So, Canara wandered off to California where he landed a job as a machinist and eventually found someone else to love. That union lasted just long enough to produce a son whose daughter, Helena, ended up going to college in Santa Barbara, majoring in journalism. She now worked part time for a farming magazine published in Fresno, and part time growing specialty herbs on a small plot of land near highway 41, the gateway to Yosemite. And it was there that she received the alumni journal with my article on the front.

"We tried to call you," Helena said, "but your number's unlisted, and the school wouldn't give it out. They claim there's been threats made against teachers by radicals."

"So, we up and come back to Hoagland Holler," Canara said. "I decided it was high time to put a few ghosts to rest."

Adam and I looked at each other. With any luck, the ghost was already resting.

Then Mrs. Singer recounted how she had saved Roseanne's son. The news that he had another son rattled Canara, and when he learned of the manner of his first son's death and how we had just minutes ago reinterred his remains, he slumped over in his chair, and Helena had to run and fetch her grandfather's pills. I pitied Canara; it was bad enough to have never shared in his son's life, but doubly cruel that the son should perish in the same violent manner as his mother.

Later, when Canara was up to it, we all walked back to the grave site. It was an evening of bright greens and soft blues, not too muggy, not too many mosquitoes. Orioles chattered in the trees while a blue grosbeak flitted around the edge of the clearing and serenaded us with roller coaster glissandos. For a long time, Canara stood over his son's grave, a hand upon the tombstone, his head bowed. Mrs. Singer stood beside him, her hand atop his. In the shade of the toolshed, Adam and Helena quietly discussed their newly discovered kinship. That left me in the company of Junie, who had ditched his coat and tie and stood with sleeves rolled up and hands in pockets.

"I never imagined writing a dinky ol' country song would wind up turning my world upside down," he said. He kicked a clod of dirt.

"I don't think that's entirely a bad thing," I said. "If it's any consolation, my world's been made topsy-turvy, too."

Junie's scowl assured me it wasn't.

"Here," he said, yanking a letter from his hip pocket. "I picked this up at the post office while I was up in Damascus."

"For me? But how–" My heart skipped a beat when I saw the name on the return address.

"Now don't tell me you hate getting letters too," Junie said.

Drawn by my look of distress, Adam came over. "Adam," I said, "how can this be? No one had an address for me here."

"Well, there weren't no return address on that letter you gave me to mail your friend Teddy. I figured you must've forgot, so wrote your name 'long with my box number and mailed it off. I didn't do nothing wrong, did I, Miss Parry?"

"No," I lied, stuffing the letter in my back pocket. "No, it's all right." But it was far from all right.

We finally had those vittles Mrs. Singer had fixed. While the food was being set out, I snuck back to the bedroom where I'd been convalescing and hid the letter in my field notebook. When I returned to the kitchen, Adam and Junie were adding a leaf to the kitchen table so we could all sit around it. I again sat next to Helena and tried to uphold my end of the conversation as I picked at my food. I wanted to talk to her. I *yearned* to talk to her. But my mind was on that letter in my notebook.

In contrast, Adam and his grandfather only stopped talking just long enough to swallow their food. When the vittles were consumed and the table cleared, Adam brought out the blueprints for the schoolhouse, and he and Canara pored over them while Junie stared over their shoulders. That left the chore of washing dishes to the women. I helped a while then made an excuse of feeling lightheaded and retired to the bedroom where I picked up my notebook and slipped out through the double doors. It was nearly sundown. I walked until hidden from the house by the woods then found a suitable tree that provided a backrest as I sat beneath it. I tore open the envelope and held the letter before a shaft of sunlight.

3 July 1970

Dear Miss Euphrates,

I am delighted that my mysterious correspondent has finally chosen to reveal herself, though I confess to having had suspicions as to her identity. Through the years, your letters have shown your determination to remain psychologically engaged, bringing ever increasing insights to the issues with which you have so long contended.

I wonder though, in light of recent thinking, or I should say, rethinking, whether, for the most part, you struggle needlessly? Likely you are aware of the great debate taking place, both within and without the American Psychiatric Association, to remove homosexuality as a mental disorder from the DSM-II. I, myself, have been active, in a small way, in the formal discussions related to this issue. I believe, as an insider, I can assure you that the time will soon come when such a removal will be made. Though much research still needs to be done not only in the area of homosexuality, but all human sexual behavior, I have come to believe that, with a few exceptions, homosexuality it is not an abnormal psychological condition, but one of any number of natural variations in human sexual expression. In this, as in many things, it shows that though the Creator never made us equal (a great American misconception), he certainly made each of us divinely unique.

My telling you this is an indirect confession. For years, I treated you for a problem which was not a problem at all. Forgive me. I am particularly remorseful when I recall how, in my determination to effect a cure, I consented to the use of electro-convulsive therapy. You may remember I had my reservations, but your father was adamant we should try it. I'm not trying to place the blame onto your poor father's shoulders. Your father loved you, and like me, he only wanted what was best for you. But electro-convulsive therapy is questionable even in cases where the conditions appear to merit it. It is also an exacting procedure and upon occasion, as you well discovered, insufficient doses of tranquilizing drugs are administered. I will say no more of that other than again, please forgive me.

I hope I have interpreted correctly that your willingness to include a name and return address on your letters is a sign you are now open to a two-way correspondence. I will always be happy to receive your letters and will respond, or not respond, as you direct. Perhaps if you are ever again in the Los Angeles area, you might stop by my office–not for therapy, of course, but so that I might have the pleasure of seeing you and hearing what I am sure are your many accomplishments since last we met. I remember you fondly as a remarkable young woman, and I wish you all the best.

I am respectively yours,
Augustus V. Herschbach, MD

P.S. I once had the privilege of hearing Theodore Dobzhansky speak. He was a brilliant synthesist in the field of anthropology, and I am honored that you should associate me with him.

I leaned my head back against the tree and closed my eyes. A nuthatch's incessant *nyak, nyak* provided a slower counter rhythm to the throbbing going on in my head. I wasn't sure which bothered me more, the fact that after all the years spent thinking I was an abomination, Herschbach finally saw fit to tell me there was nothing really the matter with me, or whether my loss of anonymity had effectively killed Teddy, for I wouldn't dream of writing to Herschbach now that he'd discovered who his secret pen pal was.

Yet neither Herschbach's belated apology, nor the demise of Teddy seemed to affect me as I would have expected. I still felt numb. Then again, I was still in the Serengeti, just now seeing the first drops of cool rain in a very, very, long time.

Opening my notebook to replace the letter, I saw the lyrics to the song I'd started writing before I got shot and had continued working on while recovering.

Sweet Hope

Each time there's a knock at my door,
I try not to run 'cross the floor;
I'm learning to find patience with time,
What's good is worth waiting for.

Seems a long time since you went away,
And I miss you more and more each day;
But faith keeps me strong, it helps me push on,
Taming this heart to obey.

'Cause I've a sweet hope of a promised land,
A sweet, sweet hope for when we'll walk hand in hand;
'Tis a blessed assurance of glory divine,
When you'll come back to this poor heart of mine.

So much time spent scribbling for two lousy verses and a chorus. I hastily wrote the words for a bridge.

There are sweet, sweet faces, and sweet, sweet lips,
Sweet, tender kisses that I have missed;
And sweet tears of laughter with no one to share
Those brief tender moments,
When I almost hear,
Those sweet words that tell me you care.

As I stared at the paper the words began to blur. Then my tears fell upon the page, causing the ink to run. I dropped my notebook, cradled my face in my hands, and the rainy season began in earnest. It wasn't just the kisses I had missed, or never having anyone to share my laughter and sorrow, but knowing that the one person I loved most would never hear Herschbach's verdict on homosexuality. To my father I would always be a disappointment.

I ripped "Sweet Hope" from my notebook, tore it to pieces and flung the fragments into the air. One came floating down onto my lap. It read: *a sweet hope of.* I closed my eyes and thought about what Brother Lillard had said about sweet hope, that it was a willingness to keep the heart open.

a sweet hope of…

Of what? To Brother Lillard, it was a hope of God's love and assurance. I again recalled that night in my father's church when I went down to the altar. Yes, I'd been feeling guilty. And yes, there was an element of self-pity. But wasn't there courage as well? Courage to go before my fellow sinners and confess to a need. Wasn't that really what Brother Lillard meant by "sweet hope," having the courage to open the heart and admit of need?

And what did I get for my courage that night? God's eternal silence, and a strong dose of shame.

I picked up the scrap of paper off my lap. *A sweet hope of…*

Of love? I hadn't any hope of love at all until today when I looked into the eyes of Helena Rivers. Yet what hope was there for us when I would always feel my father's disapproval of the relationship I wished to have with her?

a sweet hope of…

I thought of how Mrs. Singer said my father was trying to talk to me through birds. It wasn't that I doubted her, exactly, for Roseanne's ghost convinced me of the dead's ability to communicate with the living. But how could I hope to communicate with someone whose vocabulary was limited to *cheer, cheer, cheer* and *purty, purty*?

a sweet hope of…

A hand touched my shoulder and I started.

"Sorry," Helena said, "I didn't mean to startle you, but Junie saw you leaving the cabin, and I thought, if you don't mind, I'd like to join you."

I wiped away the tears with the back of my hand. "I don't know if

I'd be very good company right now."

She sat down beside me, anyway. "Here," she said, handing me a feather. "A little bird told me to give this to you."

"A little bird?"

She nodded.

"Christ!" I yelled, "Not you, too!

Helena, perplexed, canted her perfect head.

"You're another Estelline Singer," I said. "Now I suppose you're going to tell me the feather is a message from my dead father."

Helena's knit brow relaxed, then she laughed. "I think you have me confused with my granddad; he's the one with clairvoyance. I just found this lovely feather outside the cabin and thought to give it to you."

I took the feather and held it by the base of the quill. The vanes were a dark, blue-green iridescence. A barn swallow's was my guess, which made me recall a time when my father took me bird watching at Mission La Purisima, north of Santa Barbara. Barn swallows were swooping in and out of the long covered walkways where they were building their mud nests in under the eaves. Through binoculars, we spied two males copulating on the tile roof, or trying to. I told my father that the birds were proof that homosexuality was common in nature and shouldn't be condemned in humans. He countered that infanticide was not uncommon in nature, but that didn't mean humans should practice it.

So, was this feather a message from my father? And if so, what was he trying to tell me? Was the feather supposed to remind me of what he said that day at the mission, or was it a token of peace, his way of saying he now agreed with my argument?

"Damn! Damn! Damn!" I muttered.

"What is it?" Helena said.

"How do you ever know what to believe?"

Helena sat a while studying me before speaking with a voice of quiet assurance. "I think you know what to believe." She leaned forward and placed a hand over my heart. "You know here…" She brushed the back of her hand across my temple. "… and here. Trust your experience, Parry, trust yourself."

But I was too much the scientist to accept that. "There are many truths outside my experience."

"True. But I sense from what you said about Mrs. Singer that you're confused by other people's beliefs. I think you must weigh their beliefs against what you know for yourself to be true. For myself, I cannot live someone else's beliefs, no matter how much I'd like to."

I smiled. "You know, when I was a kid on one of our camping trips to Yosemite, my father woke me in the middle of the night and carried me piggyback out into the meadow across from Curry Village. He wanted me to see the stars. I wish you could have been there. It was a moonless night and above the cliffs, which were actually blacker than the sky, the Milky Way was this brilliant bridge of light arching from Sentinel Rock to Yosemite Point. I had such a feeling of wonder, such a feeling of connectedness. I think that despite my scientific bent, I have a spiritual component to me. But never in my father's church did I ever feel anything like what I felt that night in Yosemite. If, as you say, I should trust my experience, then I'd have to say that Nature is my God. But if I had said something like that to my father, it would have been as if I had spoken blasphemy."

Helena nodded. "I think I know what you mean. Christianity with all its trappings and weight of history claims authority in matters spiritual, and that's hard to go against. But you've got to if you want to claim the spirituality that's rightfully yours."

I remembered something else about that night in Yosemite: just before nodding off, still sitting in my father's lap, I heard him say "I love you, Paradigm." Despite my father's frustration with my indifference to his religion, despite his disapproval of my homosexuality, I knew that deep down my father loved me. That, at least, was something. A great something. About the rest… well, I'd just have to find my own way to acceptance.

"And stop listening to birds!" I said.

"What's that?" Helena said.

I shook my head. "Nothing."

Helena smiled then turned to look toward the creek. "God, it's so beautiful here, so green. When we left Fresno, it was a hundred and eight degrees, and all the hillsides were baked brown."

I laughed. "My father refused to admit to them being brown. He always said those summer grasses were colored 'California gold.'"

"Granddad's has been talking to Adam about staying here and helping him rebuild the schoolhouse. I was wondering whether you'd like to drive back to California with me. Maybe we could do some camping on the way. I know this incredible place in Colorado."

"God, yes!"

Helena laughed at my enthusiasm. "Well, that's settled. Now, in the meantime…" She stretched out upon the ground and lay with her head upon my lap. I lightly combed her nut-brown hair with my fingers, feeling happier than I'd felt in a long time. As darkness came on, the night critters warmed up their voices. Each had its own register: the bats squeaked as they circled above our heads, the cicadas filled the mid-range with their washboard rasp, while down by Twisted Creek the bull frogs brought up the bass. Then from Mrs. Singer's cabin came the sound of Adam's guitar, rolling out the intro to "Sally Goodin." Junie joined in on harmonica, then a third instrument.

"Jesus!" I yelled. "What the hell is that?"

Helena sat up. I couldn't make out her face in the dark, but I could hear the smile in her voice. "That's granddad playing the banjo. Isn't he good?"

I bit back a sharp retort. Once again a Bible verse came to mind. *By him were all things created.* It was hard to imagine a benevolent God creating a banjo, but I was no one to judge. I tried as best as I could to put my own smile into my response.

"He sounds great!"

Made in the USA
San Bernardino, CA
22 July 2019